The Best
AMERICAN
SHORT
STORIES
2006

GUEST EDITORS OF THE BEST AMERICAN SHORT STORIES

1978 TED SOLOTAROFF
1979 JOYCE CAROL OATES
1980 STANLEY ELKIN
1981 HORTENSE CALISHER
1982 JOHN GARDNER
1983 ANNE TYLER
1984 JOHN UPDIKE
1985 GAIL GODWIN
1986 RAYMOND CARVER
1987 ANN BEATTIE
1988 MARK HELPRIN
1989 MARGARET ATWOOD
1990 RICHARD FORD
1991 ALICE ADAMS
1992 ROBERT STONE
1993 LOUISE ERDRICH
1994 TOBIAS WOLFF
1995 JANE SMILEY
1996 JOHN EDGAR WIDEMAN
1997 E. ANNIE PROULX
1998 GARRISON KEILLOR
1999 AMY TAN
2000 E. L. DOCTOROW
2001 BARBARA KINGSOLVER
2002 SUE MILLER
2003 WALTER MOSLEY
2004 LORRIE MOORE
2005 MICHAEL CHABON
2006 ANN PATCHETT

The Best
AMERICAN
SHORT
STORIES® 2006

Selected from
U.S. and Canadian Magazines
by ANN PATCHETT
with KATRINA KENISON

With an Introduction by Ann Patchett

HOUGHTON MIFFLIN COMPANY
BOSTON • NEW YORK 2006

Copyright © 2006 by Houghton Mifflin Company
Introduction copyright © 2006 by Ann Patchett

The Best American Series and *The Best American Short Stories*® are registered trademarks of Houghton Mifflin Company.

All rights reserved

No part of this work may be reproduced or transmitted in any form or by any means, electronic or mechanical, including photocopying and recording, or by any information storage or retrieval system without the prior written permission of the copyright owner unless such copying is expressly permitted by federal copyright law. With the exception of nonprofit transcription in Braille, Houghton Mifflin is not authorized to grant permission for further uses of copyrighted selections reprinted in this book without the permission of their owners. Permission must be obtained from the individual copyright owners as identified herein. Address requests for permission to make copies of Houghton Mifflin material to Permissions, Houghton Mifflin Company, 215 Park Avenue South, New York, New York 10003.

Visit our Web site: www.houghtonmifflinbooks.com.

ISSN 0067-6233
ISBN-13: 978-0-618-54351-9   ISBN-10: 0-618-54351-1
ISBN-13: 978-0-618-54352-6 (pbk.)   ISBN-10: 0-618-54352-X (pbk.)

Printed in the United States of America

MP 10 9 8 7 6 5 4 3 2 1

"Once the Shore" by Paul Yoon. First published in *One Story*, No. 58, June 20, 2005. Copyright © 2005 by Paul Yoon. Reprinted by permission of the author.

"Awaiting Orders" by Tobias Wolff. First published in *The New Yorker*, July 25, 2005. Copyright © 2005 by Tobias Wolff. Reprinted by permission of International Creative Management.

"The Ambush" by Donna Tartt. First published in *Tin House*, Vol. 7, No. 2, Winter 2005/2006. Copyright © 2005 by Donna Tartt. Reprinted by permission of International Creative Management.

"Secret" by Maxine Swann. First published in *Ploughshares*, Vol. 31, No. 4, Winter 2005/2006. Copyright © 2005 by Maxine Swann. Reprinted by permission of The Wylie Agency, Inc.

"Dominion" by Mark Slouka. First published in *TriQuarterly*, No. 121, July 2005. Copyright © 2005 by Mark Slouka. Reprinted by permission of the author.

"So Much for Artemis" from *Send Me* by Patrick Ryan. First published in *One Story*, No. 53, March 10, 2005. Copyright © 2005 by Patrick Ryan. Reprinted by permission of The Dial Press/Dell Publishing, a division of Random House, Inc.

"Refresh, Refresh" by Benjamin Percy. First published in *The Paris Review*, No. 175, Fall/Winter 2005. Copyright © 2005 by Benjamin Percy. Reprinted by permission of the author and Curtis Brown, Ltd.

"Self-Reliance" by Edith Pearlman. First published in *Lake Effect*, Vol. 9, Spring 2005. Copyright © 2005 by Edith Pearlman. Reprinted by permission of the author.

"The View from Castle Rock" from *The View from Castle Rock* by Alice Munro. First published in *The New Yorker*, August 29, 2005. Copyright © 2005 by Alice Munro. Reprinted by permission of Alfred A. Knopf, a division of Random House Inc. Reprinted by permission of McClelland & Stewart Ltd.

"Tattooizm" from *Permanent Visitors* by Kevin Moffett. First published in *Tin House*, Vol. 7, No. 2, 2005. Copyright © 2006 by University of Iowa Press. Reprinted by permission of University of Iowa Press.

"Cowboy" from *Gallatin Canyon* by Thomas McGuane. First published in *The New Yorker*, September 19, 2005. Copyright © 2006 by Thomas McGuane. Reprinted by permission of Alfred A. Knopf, a division of Random House, Inc.

"The Dog" by Jack Livings. First published in *The Paris Review*, No. 173, Spring 2005. Copyright © 2005 by Jack Livings. Reprinted by permission of the author.

"After a Life" from *A Thousand Years of Good Prayers* by Yiyun Li. First published in *Zoetrope*, Vol. 9, No. 2, Summer 2005. Copyright © 2005 by Yiyun Li. Reprinted by permission of Random House, Inc.

"The Conductor" by Aleksandar Hemon. First published in *The New Yorker*, February 28, 2005. Copyright © 2005 by Aleksandar Hemon. Reprinted by permission of Aragi Inc.

"Today I'm Yours" by Mary Gaitskill. First published in *Zoetrope*, Vol. 9, No. 4, Winter 2005. Copyright © 2005 by Mary Gaitskill. Reprinted by permission of the author.

"How We Avenged the Blums" by Nathan Englander. First published in *The Atlantic Monthly*, June 2005. Copyright © 2005 by Nathan Englander. Reprinted by permission of Aragi Inc.

"Grandmother's Nose" by Robert Coover. First published in *Daedalus*, Summer 2005. Copyright © 2005 by Robert Coover. Reprinted by permission of Georges Borchardt, Inc.

"A New Gravestone for an Old Grave" by David Bezmozgis. First published in *Zoetrope*, Vol. 9, No. 2, Summer 2005. Copyright © 2005 by Nada Films Inc. Reprinted by permission of Nada Films Inc.

"The Casual Carpool" by Katherine Bell. First published in *Ploughshares*, Vol. 31, Nos. 2 and 3, Fall 2005. Copyright © 2005 by Katherine Bell. Reprinted by permission of the author.

"Mr. Nobody at All" by Ann Beattie. First published in *McSweeney's*, No. 16, March 2005. Copyright © 2005 by Irony + Pity Inc. Reprinted by permission of the author.

Contents

Foreword ix
Introduction by Ann Patchett xv

PAUL YOON. *Once the Shore* 1
from *One Story*

TOBIAS WOLFF. *Awaiting Orders* 20
from *The New Yorker*

DONNA TARTT. *The Ambush* 30
from *Tin House*

MAXINE SWANN. *Secret* 43
from *Ploughshares*

MARK SLOUKA. *Dominion* 60
from *TriQuarterly*

PATRICK RYAN. *So Much for Artemis* 70
from *One Story*

BENJAMIN PERCY. *Refresh, Refresh* 91
from *The Paris Review*

EDITH PEARLMAN. *Self-Reliance* 105
from *Lake Effect*

ALICE MUNRO. *The View from Castle Rock* 112
from *The New Yorker*

KEVIN MOFFETT. *Tattooizm* 143
from *Tin House*

THOMAS MCGUANE. *Cowboy* 163
from *The New Yorker*

JACK LIVINGS. *The Dog* 173
from *The Paris Review*

YIYUN LI. *After a Life* 191
from *Zoetrope*

ALEKSANDAR HEMON. *The Conductor* 204
from *The New Yorker*

MARY GAITSKILL. *Today I'm Yours* 221
from *Zoetrope*

NATHAN ENGLANDER. *How We Avenged the Blums* 237
from *The Atlantic Monthly*

ROBERT COOVER. *Grandmother's Nose* 252
from *Daedalus*

DAVID BEZMOZGIS. *A New Gravestone for an Old Grave* 259
from *Zoetrope*

KATHERINE BELL. *The Casual Car Pool* 291
from *Ploughshares*

ANN BEATTIE WITH HARRY MATHEWS. *Mr. Nobody at All* 310
from *McSweeney's*

Contributors' Notes 359
100 Other Distinguished Stories of 2005 370
Editorial Addresses of American and Canadian Magazines
Publishing Short Stories 374

Foreword

WE LIVED LAST SUMMER, my husband, two sons, and I, in a two-hundred-year-old summer cottage on a hilltop in rural New Hampshire. Although the house showed the wear and tear of its recent history, as temporary housing for actors from the summer stock theater up the road, it had clearly been much loved in the past, the cherished retreat of an unmarried schoolteacher and her bachelor brother. We bought the house — impulsively some would say — "as is," seduced by the mountain view, the rolling fields, the stillness. Only when it became ours did we discover just what we had — a bat colony in the barn, a leaky roof, odd bits of furniture, a box of 1950s Christmas ornaments . . . Laying claim to the place, we cleaned furiously and made countless trips to the dump, ridding our new home of its assorted ashtrays, stained dishtowels, questionable pillows, and moldering throw rugs.

Much of what we inherited, however, we kept. The dented but serviceable pots and pans, the pliant decks of cards and satiny wooden chessmen, the childlike oil sketch of Mount Monadnock, the faded beach towels, worn as soft and thin as bed sheets, and — the books. The books! The titles on the shelves bespoke a simpler, more innocent era of longer attention spans and discursive narratives, fewer distractions and less technology, a time when people, perhaps, really did do less and read more. I could imagine Miss Whyte and her brother settling in on the screened porch on sultry August afternoons, tall glasses of iced tea in hand, he engrossed in *A Countryman's Year,* while she persevered through Van Wyck Brooks's *The Flowering of New England.* Upstairs, Thornton Wilder resided alongside Henry James, Louis L'Amour, the Ediths (Hamilton and Wharton), Babar, and a clutch of local naturalists, poets, and historians. *The Field Guide to Ferns* was much thumbed; the broken-spined Peterson's guide, its pages folded down and marked in pen, had clearly lived for generations on the porch table, alongside the chunky black binoculars. It would have been sacrilege to move them. The books told their own silent story, the literary history of this small house, the tastes and predilections of the readers who had turned pages here before us.

It didn't take long for us to fall under the spell of cottage life. Even my six-foot-two husband soon stopped complaining about showering with knees bent and head tucked in the old claw-foot tub next to the kitchen. The sky overhead was vast, dawn and dusk magnificent. We paid heed to the moon's nightly journey across the sky, observed birds by day and were entertained by fireflies at night. Lying in bed, windows open, we listened to the wild, insistent call of owls, the echoing yips of coyotes singing in the field below, resuming the hunt.

Our own lives in this place did slow down. After fifteen years of reading short stories, I knew I'd finally found the perfect office for the job: the screened porch, with its wicker chaise longue, its expansive view of the Monadnocks, its long, discernible history as a sanctuary for readers. When I stretched out in the chaise, it was easy to get down to the business at hand — reading the short stories of 2005 in paradise. As the weeks went by, the magazines accumulated on the porch, my pile of short stories for Ann Patchett grew higher, and other family members, their own books under their arms, demanded time in the choice corner seat. No problem. There was always the porch glider, the Adirondack chair by the fire pit, the hammock under the maple tree, the picnic table — fine reading spots all. We grew quiet, content, so gratified by the pleasures of stories that before long we were reading out loud to one another. Inviting friends for dinner, I'd suggest, "Bring something to read afterward."

One evening a writer friend arrived with Hemingway under her arm, and after the dishes were cleared she put her glasses on and turned to "Big Two-Hearted River." "The river was there," she read, and we leaned in closer around the table. Five or six minutes later our friend paused and looked up, checking in with the two restless adolescents in her audience. "It's a long story," she said a bit apologetically. "Should I go on?"

"Yes," I insisted, ignoring the teenagers.

"He felt he had left everything behind," she continued, and then, suddenly, almost magically, the story opened up and drew us in. Half an hour later, the final words hanging in the air, we knew that we'd just experienced something lovely and profound — the power of stories to lift us up and out of our everyday lives and deposit us on distant shores, and then to return us, startled, enriched, and changed somehow, to our own familiar surroundings.

When I became the annual editor of *The Best American Short Stories* in 1990, I was the mother of a three-month-old baby, hoping I could somehow keep a toe in the publishing world while raising small children at the same time. I promised Houghton Mifflin five years, and began to read. Sixteen years and thousands of stories later, that baby boy is driving and shaving, and the time has come for me to pass stewardship of this venerable series into the capable hands of Heidi Pitlor, who has for a number of years worked in-house at Houghton Mifflin, overseeing all the details of the publication of *BASS*, in addition to editing much fine literary fiction and writing a novel of her own.

When I assumed the role of annual editor, my predecessor, Shannon Ravenel, had these words of advice: "Read everything." Most years, that means some three thousand short stories, from well over three hundred publications both large and small. Reading Alice Munro's latest masterwork in the pages of *The New Yorker* is always a treat, but not exactly heavy lifting. The real work, and, too, the reward of reading everything, of course, is coming upon wonderful stories in less-traveled territory: a gifted writer's experimental new work, a promising voice finally ripening into magnificent maturity, the astonishingly assured first story by a brand-new writer, appearing unheralded in a small magazine after some astute editor has plucked it from a pile of unsolicited manuscripts. The joy of discovery never does grow old, and it goes a long way toward explaining why all four of the editors of this ninety-one-year-old anthology have ended up doing lengthy tours of duty — we became captivated by the thrill of the hunt.

But there is a deeper satisfaction beyond the adrenaline rush of seeking and finding, and my quiet summer on the porch, capped by a tryst with Hemingway, reminded me of just why I chose to spend so many years of my life as a hired reader of stories. Because they can be consumed in a sitting, we tend to think of short stories as the equivalent of literary bonbons, small bites to satisfy a small craving or to fill a little space in the day. Short they may be, and yet the work of digesting a good story is anything but quick. Did my story-sated self and my grudgingly acquiescent spouse and children really want to bear witness to Nick Adams setting up camp in the wilds of Michigan, watch him make coffee, prepare to fish, contemplate the river and the trauma of his past? In fact, I'm not sure, in the moment, that we did. And yet, a friend appeared with a story to share, and one summer night "Big Two-Hearted River" was heard at our table and demanded something of us, its audience. To my surprise, we not only gave it, but found ourselves grateful for the opportunity. In the same way, the best stories I've read over these years have seemed to require nearly as much of me, the reader, as of the writer, a kind of passionate engagement that challenges not only my intellect but my humanity. Reading, reading actively, strengthens the soul.

It would be tempting now, having taken Shannon's advice to "read everything" for sixteen years, to conclude my own term as editor by opining about trends and changes in the landscape of the American short story, or to try to answer, if only to my own satisfaction, the question: What is the secret of a good short story?

And yet, I think I will resist. In my first foreword, to the 1991 volume edited by Alice Adams, I wrote, "I am beginning to suspect that it is the question itself that will keep me reading through the years ahead, for each good short story offers a unique answer, not a formula that can be handily lifted and applied to some other piece of fiction. A good story has a way of announcing itself . . . When you're done reading, you don't have to ask yourself whether it worked or not." Today, looking back, I would have to say, "Exactly." The best stories were often hard to find, but they were always easy to spot. Since 1915 it has been the task of the annual editor simply to make sure that the stories published in any given year, whether in the most visible magazines with the largest circulations, or in the tiny campus journals or shoestring ventures put out on kitchen tables, get read by a committed and discerning eye, considered on their own terms, and then, if warranted, given the opportunity in these pages to reach a wider audience of readers. It has been my great honor, and my great pleasure, to do this work. I am thankful to the hundreds of editors who have provided me with subscriptions to their excellent publications, to the writers who have participated in these annual celebrations of the short story by permitting us to publish their work, to the guest editors who have so willingly set aside their own projects in order to read and judge stories, and to the many readers who have taken the time to write letters both critiquing and appreciating these collections.

I suppose that anyone who has spent most of her adulthood reading for a living pauses at times to wonder, Does what I'm doing really matter? The answer to that question came to me a couple of months ago, in a letter from an inmate in a Texas prison. "It is true I did wrong in the past," he wrote, "and must serve out my time, but to help me pass that time I love reading great short stories." He had read, and reread many times, the 1993 edition of *BASS*, edited by Louise Erdrich, and his letter included wise, deeply felt reflections on each of the twenty stories in the book, responses that were both spot-on literary analysis and also, clearly, an attempt to help him make sense of his own circumstances. He concluded, at the bottom of a painstakingly handwritten page, "I just wanted to present a little evidence showing the effect these stories had on me and will continue to have upon me — that I did grow in understanding of myself and the world — a prerequisite to rehabilitation. And so I thank you and the publisher and the authors for laying the highways and the byways and providing the transportation to understanding."

So there it is. A soul growing stronger, thanks to stories, tangible proof that stories do matter — old stories read aloud around a dinner table, new stories in the latest issues of our glossy magazines and varied literary journals, and, of course, the stunning stories that, each year, a distinguished guest editor chooses to recognize by placing them between the covers of these books.

To say that Ann Patchett and I had fun working on *The Best American Short Stories 2006* would be an understatement. From the first hasty e-mails to the hours-long telephone conversations at the end, she brought unprecedented enthusiasm and judiciousness to this process. She is, surely, every story writer's ideal reader, eager to love, slow to fault, exquisitely attentive to the text and all that lies beneath it. The twenty stories that appear in this book were not chosen lightly; the ones that don't were, most assuredly, read with great care. Edie Clark joined me in the homestretch to ensure that no 2005 story went unread, and I was grateful for her good judgment.

The stories chosen for this year's anthology were originally published in magazines issued between January 2005 and January 2006. The qualifications for selection are: (1) original publication in nationally distributed American or Canadian periodicals; (2) publication in English by writers who are American or Canadian, or who have made the United States or Canada their home; and (3) publication as short stories (novel excerpts are not knowingly considered). A list of the magazines consulted for this volume appears at the back of the book.

With the 2007 volume, Heidi Pitlor becomes the fifth annual editor of *The Best American Short Stories*. Publications that want to make sure that their contributors will be considered each year should include the series editor on their subscription list: Heidi Pitlor, The Best American Short Stories, Houghton Mifflin Company, 222 Berkeley Street, Boston, MA 02116.

K.K.

Introduction

THE SHORT STORY is in need of a scandal.
   The short story should proclaim itself to be based on actual events and then, after a series of fiery public denials, it should hold a press conference in Cannes and make a brave but faltering confession: None of it actually happened. It was fiction all along. Yes, despite what's been said, it has always been fiction and it is *proud* to be fiction. The short story should consider staging its own kidnapping and then show up three weeks later in *The New Yorker* claiming that some things happened that cannot be discussed. Or perhaps the short story could seek out the celebrity endorsement of someone we never expected, maybe Tiger Woods, who could claim that he couldn't imagine going out to the ninth hole without a story in his back pocket. They are just the right size for reading between rounds of golf. It doesn't really matter what the short story chooses to do, but it needs to do something. The story needs hype. It needs a publicist. Fast.
   I can speak to the matter with great authority because I've been reading a lot of short stories lately, and the very large majority of them have been shockingly good. They are better than the novels I've been reading. They are more daring, more artful, and more original. Yet while I know plenty of people with whom I can discuss novels, there are only two people I know with whom I can swoon over short stories: Katrina Kenison (more on her later) and my friend Kevin Wilson, a young writer who reads literary magazines the way other people read pulpy spy novels, the kind of friend you can call in the middle of the night and ask, "Have you read the

latest issue of *Tin House?*" As valuable as these friendships have been to me, I am sorry to say they are not enough. Since I have recently given my life over to short stories I need to find a larger audience than two. I have the zeal of a religious convert. I want to stand in the airport passing out copies of *One Story* and *The Agni Review*. I want to talk to total strangers about plot and character and language, about what makes that Maxine Swann story so moving and the David Bezmozgis so surprising. How did that Kevin Moffett story manage to lull me into such a trance? I'm more than willing to take the message to the people, but the short story is going to have to work with me here. It needs to be a little less demure.

The first thing the short story needs to think about is casting off the role of The Novel's Little Sidekick, the practice run, the warm-up act. I was extolling the virtues of a particularly dazzling short story to an editor friend recently when she cut me off in mid-sentence, said she didn't want to hear it. "I'll only fall in love," she said bitterly, "and then I won't be able to buy the book, and if I do buy the book I won't be able to sell it." Short stories, it seems, are a dead-end romance in publishing. In the rare instance when a house finally does break down and buy a collection, the usual stipulation is that it must be followed by a novel, a.k.a. something that might sell. But must one think so far down the road as to how things will end? Love the short story for what it is, a handful of pages in a magazine. The short story isn't asking to be a collection, and it certainly isn't trying to pass itself off as a potential novel. Who's to say the short story writer has a novel in him? Is a sprinter accepted to the team on the condition that she will also run a marathon? Certainly many people do both, and some people do both well, but it always seems clear to me when a novelist has turned out a short story or a short story writer has stretched a piece into a novel. There are a handful of people who to my mind are equal in their talents, John Updike leading the list, but then John Updike could probably win a hundred-meter race as handily as he could run cross-country.

It was a genuine challenge to pick a mere twenty stories out of the more than one hundred twenty I received. I would have been happier turning in thirty or even forty, so many of them were excellent, and yet I know I couldn't put my hands on the twenty Best American Novels for 2006. So what accounts for so many successful

Introduction xvii

stories? (Remembering, of course, that this is not actually a volume of the best short stories in America. These are just the stories that I like best, and I am full of prejudice and strong opinions. The genius of this series, and certainly the reason for its longevity, is that it relies on guest editors who arrive every year with all their own baggage about what constitutes a wonderful story, and as soon as they feel comfortable in their role as the arbiter of Best they are replaced by another writer who is equally sure of his or her own taste. That's one thing you can say for writers — we know what we like when it comes to writing.) It could be that stories are easier to write than novels, but having taken a crack at both myself I am doubtful of this. I think it is more the case that short stories are expendable. Because they are smaller, the writer is simply more willing to learn from her mistakes and throw the bad ones and the only pretty good ones away. Knowing that something can be thrown away encourages more risk taking, which in turn usually leads to better writing. It's a sad thing to toss out a bad short story, but in the end it always comes as a relief. On the other hand, it takes a real nobility to dump the bad novel. The novel represents so much time that the writer often struggles valiantly to publish it even when it would be in everyone's best interest to chalk it up to education and walk away. I know a lot of people who published the first novel they ever wrote. I can think of no one who published his first short story.

So why, if what I'm telling you is true, and let's assume for the sake of this introduction that it is, aren't more people running out to buy their copy of *Harper's* and turning directly from the index to the short story? Short stories are less expensive, often better written, and make fewer demands on our time. Why haven't we made a deeper commitment to them? I am afraid it has something to do with the story's inability to cause a stir. As a novelist I would say I read well over the average number of novels (whatever that is) per year. It doesn't take much to get me to read something new. I'll pick up a novel based on a compelling review, the recommendation of a friend, even a particularly eye-catching cover. I troll the summer reading tables in bookstores to fill in the holes in my education. I am forever picking up something I've always meant to read (*Zeno's Conscience* is on the bedside table now waiting for me to finish writing this, and there is still so much Dickens). But everything I mean to read, and nearly everything I have read no matter how obscure, has had some means of catching my attention. The uncollected short story in its magazine or literary journal has nothing but the author's name and possibly a catchy title to flag you down. Only in its largest venues does a short story manage to score an illustration. It does not go out and get you. It waits for you. It waits and waits and waits.

Unless of course you have the brilliant good fortune to be chosen as the editor of *The Best American Short Stories* one year. Because while a single short story may have a difficult time raising enough noise on its own to be heard over the din of civilization, short stories in bulk can have the effect of swarming bees, blocking out sound and sun and becoming the only thing you can think about. So even though it goes against my nature to point out the ways in which I am luckier than you, I must say that in this case I am, unless you too have short stories mailed to your home. And even if you *did* have stories mailed to your home, you probably didn't get them from Katrina Kenison, and that's where my real advantage comes in. These aren't just any short stories I've been getting, the normal cross section of good and bad. These stories have been intelligently and lovingly culled from the vast sea of those that are published. Katrina does the part of this project that is work, hacking her way through all that is boring and poorly written in order to send me the gems. She reads everything so that I can read what is good, and I read everything that is good in order to put together everything that I think is best. Stories have been showing up on my doorstep in padded envelopes, a steady stream of fiction that I piled in strategic locations near bedsides and bathtubs and back doors. When you get enough short stories spread around the house, they gather a force of momentum. The more stories I read, the more I wanted to read stories, the more I recommended stories, the more the stories created their own hype simply by being so vast and varied and good. The stories offered me their companionship, each one a complete experience in a limited amount of time. No matter where I went, I did not mind waiting, seeing as how I was rich in stories. I went ahead and pulled into the endlessly long line at the touchless car wash on Sunday morning, took a story out of the glove compartment, and started reading. I was able to put other work aside in order to read because for this period of time short stories were my job. I did not have the smallest twinge of guilt about lying on the sofa for days at a time reading. Could there be anything better than that? I felt as if I had spent the year in one of those total-immersion language camps, and in the end I emerged fluent in the language of short fiction.

Of course I was no beginner. While I can trace the short story back to my earliest days as a reader, my true connection came when I was twelve years old, the year I read Eudora Welty's "A Visit of Charity." There had been other stories before this, stories I liked, "The Necklace" and "The Gift of the Magi," the stock assignments that were the backbone of every junior high English class, but "A Visit of Charity," even though it was a story about a girl, seemed infinitely more grown-up to me. It didn't reward the reader with a plot twist at the end or present a clear moral imperative. Even more startling was the fact that this author, whose photograph and biographical paragraph preceded the text, had only one date after her name, 1909, and then a dash, and then nothing. Again and again I returned to that photograph to look at the long, gentle face of the author. She was both alive and in a textbook, a coupling I had never seen before. As sure as I was by the age of twelve that I wanted to be a writer, I was not at all sure that it was the sort of thing the living did. The short fiction market was cornered by dead people, and this Eudora Welty was, as far as I could tell, the first one to have broken the trend. I decided at the start of seventh grade to cast my lot with the living and chose Eudora Welty as my favorite writer, a decision that has served me well ever since. Four years later I was sixteen when Miss Welty came to Vanderbilt to give a reading, and I got there early and sat in the front row holding my big, hardback *Collected Short Stories of Eudora Welty*, which my mother had bought me for my birthday that year. It was the first reading I had ever been to, and when it was over I had her sign my book. I held it open to the wrong page, and she looked at me, and said, "No, no, dear. You always want to sign on the title page." And she took the book from me and did it right. For the sheer force of its heart-stopping, life-changing wonder, I will put this experience up against that of anyone who ever saw the Beatles.

The short story has made some progress since the dark ages of the middle seventies, and I do believe that the living are now taking up their fair number of pages beside Hemingway and Faulkner. With Alice Munro leading the way, a case could be made that we are living in the golden age of the short story this very minute. A golden age there for the taking.

The impressions we pick up as children, when our minds are still open to influence and as soft as damp sponges, are likely to stay with us the longest. Ever since I saw that picture of Eudora Welty alive and well in my seventh-grade reader, I haven't been able to shake the notion that short story writers are famous people and that short stories are life-altering things. I believe it is human nature to try and persuade others that our most passionately held beliefs are true so that they too can know the joy of our deepest convictions. I was standing in my kitchen fixing breakfast the morning I heard on the radio that Eudora Welty had died. It was July 2001, and I remember that the room was full of light. I called my good friend Barry Moser, the illustrator who had worked with Miss Welty on that most memorable edition of *The Robber Bridegroom*, and told him I was going to the funeral. He said he would meet me there.

I spent that night in Meridian, Mississippi, with my mother-in-law, and in the morning I made the short trip to Jackson. There was a rainstorm on the way that made the last leg a harrowing drive, but just as I got to town the weather cleared and cooled. I picked up Barry and his wife, Emily, and the three of us went to the church together a full two hours before the service was scheduled to begin. We went that early because we were certain it was the only way we would ever get a seat. I expected people to be waiting in the streets. I was ready to stand in the street myself, but we were the first ones to arrive. And while the church was full, in the end there were still a few empty seats around the edges. The coffin seemed tiny to me, but then Miss Welty had been growing shorter over the years. There were plenty of stories about her being barely able to see over the steering wheel of her car.

If you have ever been to Mississippi in July, you will know there is no reprieve from the heat, and yet on this particular day the rain, which under normal circumstances only makes the situation worse, had somehow made it better. When we went to the graveside it was no more than seventy-five degrees, and thus the closest thing to divine intervention I have ever experienced. When the hero of my life was buried, I had a discreet cry among friends standing in the cemetery. A woman approached me and introduced herself as Mary Alice Welty White. I knew her, of course. My beloved col-

Introduction xxi

lected stories was dedicated to her and her sister, Elizabeth Welty Thompson. I had seen her name every time I opened the book. Mary Alice Welty White asked me my name. She asked me if I was a friend of her aunt's, and I said I was not. I told her I was a great admirer and had come to pay my respects. Then she asked me where I was from.

She took my arm. "There's someone I want you to meet."

We took small steps. The ground was soft, and we were both wearing heels. She led me to the line of cars that had driven over to the cemetery and to a group of teenaged boys who were leaning up against those cars. Their ties were loose, and their jackets were off. They were ready to get out of there.

She introduced me to one of the young men. He didn't seem as if he would have been especially interested to meet anyone. "This is Ann Patchett," Mary Alice Welty White told him. "She drove all the way from Nashville to come to your aunt Dodo's funeral. She didn't even know her, and she drove all this way. That's how important your aunt Dodo was."

The boy and I exchanged an awkward how-do-you-do and shook hands. Mary Alice thanked me for coming.

Even at the funeral of the greatest short story writer of our time, a member of her own family needed to be reminded of her standing. The short story never was one for calling a lot of attention to itself, but in the face of so much brilliance I think it's time we started paying our respects.

The Best American Short Stories is the short story Olympics. It is the short story's moment in the sun. I am grateful to Houghton Mifflin and to Katrina Kenison for making sure that at least once a year we put them front and center where they belong. As for their arrangement in this volume, I am partial to the democratization of the alphabet. It seems to me the fairest way to line things up. However, this year the alphabet put Ann Beattie at the front of the line, and while she certainly deserves to be there as a writer, her story, which is not exactly a story but maybe some sort of novella, performance piece, massive example of creativity and nonconforming genius, seemed like the weight the book needed at the back end. By reversing the alphabet, Paul Yoon's beautiful story "Once the Shore," which is the first story he published and the first story I picked for this collection, floated effortlessly up to the front. When I was a girl in Catholic school, the nuns were forever doing that to us, getting everyone in a line and then making us reverse our places so that the first should be last and the last should be first. It seems like a good lesson for the short story. Enough with the humility. Move to the front of the line.

ANN PATCHETT

The Best
AMERICAN
SHORT
STORIES
2006

PAUL YOON

Once the Shore

FROM ONE STORY

ON THIS PARTICULAR EVENING the woman told the waiter about her husband's hair: parted always on his right and combed finely so that each strand shone like amber from the shower he took prior to meeting her for their evening walks. "There was a time," the woman said, "when he bathed for me and me alone." She knew his hair — its length, smell, and color — long before she knew the rest of him. Before he left for the Pacific. Before his return and their marriage and their years together. When she opened the door it was what she noticed first. And in the heat of the remaining sun, she swore you could see a curtain of mist rising from the peak of his thin head.

At this, she laughed quietly and almost at once grew silent and looked out toward the distant hills and the coast where, long after sunset, the East China Sea lay undulant, its surface of silver reflections folding over one another like the linking of fingers.

She was in her sixties, an American from upstate New York, who was a guest at the Shilla Resort on the southern side of Cheju Island. She had arrived several days ago, and no one was sure how long her visit would last. She was a generous tipper. And preferred loose linen outfits that hid the shape of her body. In her possession was a single piece of luggage, the perfect size, the hotel staff joked, for a head.

Her own hair she let fall in the most graceful of ways, all the way down past her shoulders. It clung to the backs of chairs or the cushioned elevator walls or, as the maid noticed, it stubbornly refused to sink into the depths of the shower drain, clenched in a gray-white fist.

Her husband used to maintain navigation equipment on an aircraft carrier not too far from here, she mentioned. He was dead now, a few months having passed since his heart stopped just as he awoke and attempted to flip the duvet away from his body.

On that morning she bathed him with a wet cloth. Lifted his limbs and wiped his brow. His comb she dipped into the water bowl beside her and then proceeded to brush his hair, gray now, parting it on the right as he had always done since the first day they met in front of her parents' home in a small town where, in winter, the snow was ceaseless.

The other waiters called him Jim. Short for Jiminy because a group of them had watched the Disney animated classic *Pinocchio* one night in a conference room of the resort. The youngest of the waiters, they decided, resembled the cartoon cricket: thin limbs and a round head with big, wide, dark eyes. A smile as magnificent as a quarter-moon. And so they — all of them in their thirties, having worked here for much longer than the boy and used to teasing him — began saying the name out loud, calling him Jiminy, over and over again, seated in velvet plush chairs and rolling their tongues and smoking hashish they had obtained from a Spanish backpacker in exchange for leftover food. They had difficulty pronouncing the name. The boy corrected them, using three distinct syllables. "Easier to say 'Jim,'" he told them, and they nodded with a drug-induced acquiescence.

He was twenty-six and originally from the mainland, fifty kilometers north, where his parents and brother still remained. After attending the university in Seoul, he went on to military duty.

It was during training exercises at sea that he first saw the coasts of Cheju Island. By boat he and the other soldiers his age circled it, marveling at the bright foliage and Halla Mountain at its center, once a volcano, which rose nearly two thousand meters. Cars the size of pebbles moved along the highway, it seemed, without effort, without anywhere really to go. There, they were told by an officer, the distance from one destination to another never took longer than an hour by car, from the waterfalls, hiking trails, caves, to the beaches and the mountain's peak. This fact stayed with him. Long after his duty, long after he saw the island again through an airplane window as he arrived to look for work. And it was, a year later, what he told his diners.

His brother, a fisherman, often teased him about working at a resort. But he couldn't imagine working anywhere else. The snug white jacket they were required to wear like a second layer of skin; the sound of uncorking a bottle of wine in front of his tables; the warmth of dinner plates. Here he met guests from all parts of this world. And almost always the food was served outdoors on a long porch that faced two hills and the East China Sea. He was, every night, witness to the setting sun. And in all of these patterns he was assured of an ineffable logic that at once bound him to the resort property and at the same time provided him with a sense of openness and possibility.

Until last night, as he stood behind the seated American widow. Though it wasn't her exactly. It wasn't the way the woman related the story of her husband's hair, to which he tried very hard to listen. Or the fire-red sun, which seemed to set a little later that night, bobbing on the crest of a hill, as though rather than going down it had decided to pitch and roll along the slope.

It wasn't any one of these things.

It was, in fact, the manager of the resort — a man who was very fond of Jim — who led him into his office in the middle of dinner and told him that his brother, while catching tuna, as he had been doing for the past few years for their uncle's company, was killed when a United States submarine divided the Pacific Ocean for a moment as it surfaced, causing a crater of cloudy water to bloom, the nose of this great creature gasping for air while its body collided against what could have easily been a buoy or some type of detritus.

But what keeled and snapped upon impact was a fishing boat. And within it a crew of fishermen. Their bodies, once broken, sunk into a dark depth, their limbs positioned, without effort, in the most graceful forms known to any dancer.

It was morning, and she sat at her usual table closest to the stone ledge, occupied by the distant strokes of a swimmer in the outdoor pool. Beside her, at another table, a Canadian man was reading aloud portions of the news to his companion. It was the incident with the U.S. submarine that caused the American widow to shift her attention. The bodies had not yet been recovered. An admiral gave a press conference and formally apologized for this tragedy, unable to give further information at this time.

Her husband used to clip articles out of the newspaper. Anything having to do with the Pacific. It was a type of hobby, she assumed, like collecting butterflies. He tucked them inside photo albums. He never showed them to her. She knew about it only because, cleaning out his study, she had opened one, thinking they contained pictures. Years' and years' worth of collecting. She immediately shut the books. It was as though she had opened her husband's diary and it felt wrong to do so, even if he was no longer present. "It just isn't right," she muttered to herself and then returned the album to its spot on the shelf.

The waiter called Jim approached the diners with a tray of orange juice in highball glasses, and when he placed two on the table for the Canadians, he lifted his hand very slowly, as though attempting to slow time. He furrowed his brows and rubbed his eyes, and the woman stiffened her back as he passed and quickly took the order of another table without meeting their gaze. He had forgotten to slick his hair, she noticed, so it seemed dull under the morning sun. She raised a hand.

"Hello, Jim," she said. "I've been up since four. And I called room service because your dining room is never opened so early. You should look into that, you know."

He tucked his empty tray under his arm and promised he would. She told him she had yet to see Halla Mountain, and he offered her suggestions on reliable drivers, who appeared at the entrance to the hotel every hour. To all of this she nodded vaguely. "Yes, yes," she added. "Tell me what else you know of this place."

Jim began to describe it as best as he could. If you were to think of the island in terms of circles, then the outer circle was mostly residential, including the resorts, and also used to farm fruit and care for livestock; behind that were forests, and at the very center was the national park and the mountain that stood behind them. She had only glanced at it through the taxi window on her way here. And although it was always visible, she made no effort to take the time to observe it. She wasn't interested. Not in its presence or its impressive height or how most guests were determined to hike along its trails. For her, it was simply what identified Cheju Island. She had come to the right place. That was all.

"It takes no longer than one hour to get from here to anywhere," Jim said.

"Anywhere," she repeated, then smiled, although Jim didn't join in the merriment.

She concluded that the boy was tired, that he had been up late and needed sleep. She could tell from the redness of his eyes, the way his shoulders slouched. There was a question she wanted to ask him but decided it could wait. Instead, she pointed her head as discreetly as possible toward the Canadians and said, "Terrible business. I suspect you won't look fondly on Americans after this."

The expression on his face was that of confusion.

"My husband. He was here, you know. Many years ago. Not here, exactly, but over there." She lifted a finger toward the coast. "Somewhere over there, I think. I'm not really sure, to be perfectly honest. But I can imagine it. And it would take exactly one hour. That's what I think, Jim. Like you said. Exactly one hour, and we'd find it."

The boy asked whether he could get her anything else.

"Oh, I'm just fine," the woman said. "And you work too hard. Get some rest."

And here, before being conscious of it, she took his hand between hers and patted his knuckles. His skin was warm, his circulation excellent. She imagined the blood that flowed underneath these fingers, rivers of it, splitting like highway systems. How healthy he must be with such warm hands. He was a boy, she was certain, who didn't grow cold easily.

It wasn't hope he felt. That God was merciful. No, that was his parents, praying that their older son had found a piece of wood. Found the belly of a whale. He was, rather, unable to accept. There was a difference. Because for him, the event never happened. Not until the body was recovered. Until then, his brother was still fishing. On a boat in the Pacific casting nets the size of mountains.

The manager offered a leave of absence. His parents wanted him to fly back home. But Jim declined the offer. And so he continued to do his work. The staff was not yet aware of the circumstances. He made the manager promise. And in this way every day was like all the days. He wiped lint off his jacket. Tightened the knot of his black tie. Washed his hands before serving. His cowaiters called, "Hey, Jim!" and he walked over to their tables to speak to the tourists about the scenic hiking trails and the best waterfall for swimming. There was much talk, of course, about the submarine incident over dinner, but it was conversation that wasn't directed in any way toward him. He lingered for a moment above their heads while pouring wine or refilling their water glasses, and the more they talked, the more it seemed it had nothing to do with him at all. As though the event, once escaped from mouths, was no longer his, now fanned across the air in the realm of static.

When he could spare a moment, he often stood by the American widow because he had done so for what seemed like a long time before. Her shedding white hair and linen outfits were a recurring fixture on the long porch, where he, with a form of reverence, served plates of the country's finest cuisine. She was the one who stayed long after the other guests retired. Her fingers tapped the stem of a wineglass or the candleholder as she addressed the scenery in front of her — she always ate facing the sea — all the while knowing that behind her right shoulder there stood Jim as the busboys cleared the tables and the rest of the waiters took their cigarette breaks.

And he listened. Listened to her describe a photograph of a young man — younger than Jim — in uniform with a stern expression and his hair cut short (how she mourned for his hair when they cut it), and the large fields through which they walked, passing silos and a stable where they once sneaked in and tried to feed carrots to a stubborn pony, who, instead, bit her knuckle.

He remained behind her, listening, without knowing exactly why. Perhaps it was her voice. The calm of it. The sudden laughter. Or her scent: the smell of lemongrass. Or because it felt, facing that distant coast, as if it weren't her voice at all but one that originated from the sea. He waited until she finished, and only then did he respond by way of a brief comment or a simple nod, and she would, as it grew to be her habit, take his hand between hers and tap his fingers.

"I have never been to your country," he confessed to her.

"You will if you want to," she answered. "I have no doubt."

He didn't tell her whether or not he wanted to. He wasn't sure himself. It seemed this place would suffice. Or maybe it wasn't an issue of sufficiency. Maybe going somewhere else was an act of remembrance, of where you were from. A world of mirrors in which you witnessed a countless number of things that could have occurred at home or anywhere. And maybe, just maybe, that in itself was worth doing now and again. Perhaps he already was. Like this woman who decided to come to this island of all places and now spent her days looking out toward the sea, at times with a finger pointed at a single spot on the horizon with the utmost certainty.

His brother used to take him out on a small motorboat their uncle owned. This was when they were all living by the eastern coast of the peninsula, when Jim was eleven, his brother four years his senior. Their mother packed lunches for them, adamant in her rule that they should never stray far from shore. They were to raise their hands, palms facing land, and if the beach was hidden from their view, then they had gone too far.

They never followed this rule. His brother went where he pleased. And Jim trusted him with confidence, the way he hooked his arm over the rudder and leaned back as though he were reclining on a chaise longue. He smoked an unfiltered cigarette he had stolen from their father, and the scent of it reminded Jim of damp wood. When they were far enough away his brother stripped to his underwear and shut his eyes, the midday sun on his chest, which was broad, a man's chest of which Jim was envious, as smooth and dark as the calm sea they floated over. He always took his clothes off on the boat rather than before they departed, as though he were only capable of doing so farther from the coast.

"We're going to find the middle of this ocean," his brother said.

They were pushing hard, perpendicular to the waves, and Jim sat toward the bow, tightening his legs against the constant pressure of the water as it split beside the hull. He sat facing his brother, the shoreline receding behind the level of the older boy's shoulders. They sped onward. Twenty minutes perhaps. Maybe longer. And then all of a sudden he cut the engine and elbowed the rudder and Jim held on to the edge as they spun, fast, the boat rocking, and then slowing, slower, in their sight a single straight line that divided sky and sea, a line that traced their movements like the unraveling of a ball of string until, gradually, they were still.

Above them there hung a quiet. Save for water lapping against the hull, there existed no sound, not even of a bird or of a distant horn. And around them there was the ocean, a great wide ring of it with just that thin line of the color gray with the boat its very center, and his brother then stood and raised a hand to his brows in the manner of a salute, and he said, "There. We've done it," and Jim followed his brother's gaze, and where there was once the shore there was now water, and where west once lay was now north, east, south, any one of them. How many rotations the boat had spun Jim couldn't recall.

The panic came in the form of an arc. Slowly rising until the boy felt his heart clench and the joints of his legs loosen, and when his brother began to laugh in triumph, hopping and whooping, he knew then what it was to be afraid. It was the feeling of diminishment. And he didn't know what to do so he sat there gripping the sides of the boat as his brother, in his underwear, dove into the water and surfaced and shouted for him to come on down, he said, come on down, and he would not, shaking his head, his jaw set and his gaze fixed at that gray line. He heard his brother's breathing. And he saw, in his periphery, what resembled a fish arc up into the air and bite down on his wrist and all at once that line tilted and he felt the cold and the warmth, and he shut his eyes and opened them to see that the sky was now a glowing haze of thick water.

This was when he screamed. Opened his mouth as the sea entered the passage of his throat, and he could hear the dull vibration of it against his ears and then all at once he felt a rising, a lifting as water gave way to the heat of the sun, and all he saw then was a pair of thick, dark arms that enveloped his chest and he leaned back and listened to a soft laughter and felt a palm pressed against his soaked hair and heard the words, I was just playing, I was just playing, it's all right now, everything is fine. And then a hand appeared in front of him and within the thumb and index finger there lay a compass, suspended just above the horizon.

"Here's our sun," the older boy said.

Jim reached up and took hold of the compass and, as the sound of the engine returned and they headed west, slowly this time, he fell asleep in the arms of his brother.

They reached shore just as the sun was setting.

"You're not going tell anyone?" his brother said, waking him. "Promise? You won't tell anyone?"

He remembered walking up the beach, his clothes still wet, and the look on his brother's face which, to his surprise, seemed so young then, so much younger than himself, his eyes as wide as a child's, his shoulders not so confident anymore, and he couldn't help but smile.

He promised. And then they held each other's hands for a moment, the way a shy couple would do, and by the time they returned home and into the kitchen to their mother shouting about their whereabouts and ordering them to their room until their father returned to give them a proper punishment, their afternoon was already far in their memory, where it took the shape of not only a grinning secret, not only the conspiracy of two brothers, but of a campaign against the sea.

The Spaniard lived in a cave. That was the rumor she had heard from the boy Jim. For how long no one was certain. But he had been coming to the resort property lately to receive leftover food in exchange for God knows what. She saw him once, against the slope of a distant hill, with a walking stick, and pointed at his figure, and that was how the boy responded — that he lived in a cave. Almost at once the American widow drew a mental picture of this man, outfitted in bearskin and smelling of lard, perhaps, or a week-old fish. Hairy. She quickly dismissed this fantasy. It was, after all, the cave she was interested in.

"There are many," Jim said.

"I'm speaking of ones close to shore," the woman said.

"Many there as well."

She pondered this. Her hand covered the folded newspaper on her dining table. It was evening, the candles lit. A single body had been recovered. A man in his forties. The search continued.

She wondered if, among the missing, there were husbands. And she thought of the wives and whether they caught themselves in the late afternoons unable to remember what they had been doing or were going to do. She thought of the waiting. Of images of the sea that, years ago, dominated her dreams — the water more terrifying in its emptiness, vast and quiet and gray. Of how she prayed for her husband's safety, for his return, and how, in his absence, her love for him grew through memory, in constant repetition, images circling so that the effect was that time paused. And yet, time did not because a single day turned into another. She slept, woke. It was a feeling of both immobility and motion. This was waiting. She knew it well. And it was how the wives of the fishermen spent their days, she was certain, with the conviction that they were alone, regardless of the publicity, the news, the interviews, condolences.

A couple from Boston had shortened their stay on the island lest the incident provoke anti-American sentiment, which was developing on the mainland. A group of college students had formed a rally in front of the walls of a U.S. Army base outside of Seoul. There had been a skirmish at a bar involving a G.I. and a teenager. Jeeps had been vandalized with words painted on the windshields: *Go Home.*

But she would not. Now that Jim had mentioned the caves. Afterward, perhaps. Or maybe she would stay. It felt very possible to do so.

During some time off from the aircraft carrier, her husband and a friend joined a fishing crew and sailed to Cheju Island. They spent the day there swimming and walking up the beach. In the distance, their ship, a sentinel in the shape of a fingertip. But other than that, there were no reminders of what they would soon return to. Not even the distant roar of fighter jets. On that morning, it was as if the war had paused for a day, and while the fishermen rounded the island he collected coral and urchin shells, took photographs of the hills and the forest inland, and chased crabs.

There, on that coast, he found a cave. A wide mouth that drank shallow seawater at low tide, its walls as tall as the entrance to a fortress within the earth. He waded in. Not too far, for it was dark. Far enough so that he could still see his own hands, daylight concentrated into the shape of an egg behind him. He picked up a stone. And against the right wall, he inscribed his initials and hers and drew a heart around them.

There it would remain for the rest of their days, he told her. On an island at the opposite end of the world he knew was waiting after all this. Four letters and the shape of a heart etched in stone.

The first few times he told this story she believed him. And loved him for it, pressing her cheek down against his chest without speaking. They were in their thirties then, and life seemed as they imagined, living in a town in upstate New York with enough fields to walk across in the evenings. Her letters to him during the war had gone unanswered. He had never received them, he said. But it didn't matter anymore. Because he had written against the wall of a cave. To her. Somehow, though she couldn't explain why, that was worth more than a lifetime of correspondences.

But when she asked him one day to see the photographs of the island he hesitated. He lost the camera, he said. Stolen by a little Korean boy. And as the years progressed his story began to change. Not dramatically, but enough to make her wonder, pause, repeat the story in her mind. It wasn't a fishing boat. It was a small motorboat. Three friends instead of one. They were AWOL. It wasn't a stone but a shard of coral. And the more the story changed, the more she wasn't sure herself what she heard on that first night.

He was getting older. Age transformed memory. That is what she told herself. And why say such a thing if it never happened? It was her inability to answer this that allowed her to forgive him. She wasn't angry. No. Just puzzled.

Later, she would find in a drawer a stack of photographs. Pictures of a stranger beside a fighter jet spray-painted with the words: *Eat This MiG*. A group of young girls smiling shyly. One of the girls in another photograph bending over as her husband pointed a pistol at her rear. And one of the sea, flat and emerald, and set against the horizon a wide island with a mountain at its center.

She rushed outside where he was changing a tire, her duster in one hand with feathers the color of a rainbow, saying, "Is this it? Is this it?" until he snatched the photograph and told her to never go through his possessions again.

It was only in the evening, in bed, that he nodded, said, "Yes, yes, that was the island. That was it, baby. That was where I wrote to you." And he pulled her shoulders to him, and she felt a quickening and shut her eyes and imagined herself folding, refolding, growing smaller, and she turned then, away from him, pretended to sleep, and felt as though she were sinking.

So when Jim answered that there were many caves she wasn't surprised. In any case, she told him her husband's story. About the initials.

"You would like to find them," he said.

In his voice there lay a trace of skepticism. Or perhaps it was her own sentiment that she heard behind his words. Strips of the sea shone silver from the stars. A busboy blew out the votive candles around them.

"I would like to find him," she said.

Silence. She heard him sigh, shift his feet behind her.

She went on: "To wait. It is a fever. And I waited for him. But the man whom I knew, he never came. So I want to remember him. Not the one who returned. But the one who never left."

A breeze came in from the ocean, and she watched the shadow of the candle flame swing across the tablecloth. It was late. She noticed the busboy lingering, waiting for her to leave.

"I would like to see a cave," she said. "Close to shore. A tall one. Before I leave. That's all."

And it was then she managed to ask Jim the question that had been on her mind since her first day on Cheju Island. Why she waited so long — she had been here for almost two weeks now — she wasn't sure. Perhaps she didn't want to go at all, she thought. Perhaps the question was waiting for the right person. And so she asked him and no one else. And he, after a short pause, leaned over so that his face hung beside her hair like a moon and quietly responded.

"I will take you," he said.

It wasn't a secret that Jim had grown an affinity toward the American widow, the Madame, they joked, who, they were sure, came from royalty. No one in their right minds would spend more than two weeks at the Shilla Resort. Not with these prices.

"But a woman who has nothing?" one waiter conjectured. "What does it matter to her?"

"What do you think, Jim?" another said. "Has she told you about her fortune?"

"Will you marry her, Jim?"

"All she'll do in bed is tell you about her husband!"

They had gathered outside the back entrance to the kitchen, on the dimly lit gravel lot where the shipments of food were delivered every morning by way of a narrow dirt road that cut through a forest and around the resort property. Jim remained silent, smiling on occasion at their well-intentioned humor. For that was what it was. Their teasing wasn't out of spite. Perhaps a little envy. That was possible. Jim had found some other form of amusement rather than watching movies late at night in the conference room or smoking hashish.

They also knew of his brother. Word had, of course, spread among the staff. They offered to take his tables so that he could leave. But Jim thanked them politely and refused, which at once confused them and brought a certain respect for the boy's dedication to his work. In short, they weren't at all sure how to proceed. In the end, they chose distance. They joked with him, as they always did, and never mentioned the news updates or their opinions on the matter — which ranged from rage to a shrug of a shoulder — although they saw him every morning in the bar watching television, skimming the reports in the paper, and speaking on his cellular phone to whom they presumed to be his mother.

And whether or not they knew it, Jim was grateful. Glad, he admitted, for the company and the harmless words and the patterns of these days, including the nightly gathering of the waiters, which always began at the back entrance of the kitchen.

They heard the footsteps first and then from the road a figure appeared with a walking stick. He was tall with short bright hair and wore shorts and hiking boots, his wool socks rolled about his shins. He stopped a few feet away from them and leaned against his walking stick in the manner of one who had traveled from afar. From his pocket he handed over a small paper bag, and Jim, who was carrying a Tupperware container filled with leftover food, walked toward him and asked if he could have a word.

"Gracias, Luis!" the waiters called.

The two stopped some distance away from the kitchen entrance, right where the road began.

"You know about the caves," Jim said. "Along the coast."

"Yes. Many of them."

"There's one that's very tall and wide," Jim said.

"Many," Luis said again.

"But you know the best?"

"The best?"

"Yes, the best. The biggest."

"The most magnificent," Luis said, and extended his arms.

Jim nodded. He then told the man that he had promised to show a woman a cave. "A family relation," Jim added.

He hadn't planned on saying that. But it came out naturally, and so he repeated it. She was a friend of his mother's. An American. She wanted to see a cave by the sea.

Luis stood in contemplation. After some time, he agreed to meet them at a campsite on the southeastern coast, and from there he would lead them to the cave.

"Sunrise," Luis said. "That will be best. Tomorrow."

With the container of food in his possession, he was about to walk away but then paused and tapped his fingers against his walking stick. He looked at Jim in a way that was indecipherable to the boy's eyes. He shook his container in front of him and said, "There is nothing more beautiful than eating with a full view of the sun at the very edge of this world. On the days I come here. To pick up this. That is what I miss."

And then he left, and Jim watched him for some time, under the glow of a tall lamp, and wondered whether he really did live in a cave. And if he did, it was no different, he supposed, than living in a house. Perhaps his brother had found a cave, he thought, as Luis's figure faded. He could imagine it. With a front entrance that was always open.

"It is all set," the boy had said when he called her room. They would leave before sunrise. She woke early anyway. At four o'clock. Starving long before the dining room opened. She asked him up for tea. She would stay up a little later if he wanted to chat. "I have to prepare for our expedition" was how he replied, then told her she wouldn't have time to eat. Then he gave a short laugh and said good night. It was to be a surprise. How old his voice sounded on the telephone.

"Good night," she said, perplexed.

And now she lay on a king-sized bed in the dark, unable to sleep. He was so kind, the boy. A kindness she imagined he had brought with him from infancy. She wondered about his family. His answers were always so nondescriptive. What she knew was that he was born in a place called Pusan and now his family lived in Seoul. He grew up on the coast. And siblings? She had forgotten to ask about that. She grew angry at herself for not asking such a simple question, but then the feeling subsided. There lay many more opportunities to speak with Jim. A lovely name. One that she always admired. James. For its strength. For its sensitivity.

Before sleeping, she thought of a great flat field. This was when her husband returned. They had yet to marry. In the dark they wandered, careful of their steps, for it had rained the day before. He led with a small flashlight and for every dry spot he placed a foot she imitated with such exactness that all they heard on that night was a single body in the midst of cicadas and the distant rumble of a truck on the freeway, its headlights filtered through the forest in the distance, shredded and fading like a frosted breath.

It was her blanket he carried. Light blue, pulled from her bed and folded and folded until what hung beneath his arms was a square, a pillow, a sack filled with a mysterious treasure, one that he revealed in the middle of that dark field. He placed the flashlight on the grass, and as it lit a fallen dome of white beside their feet, he lifted his arms and the cloth unfurled and paused for a brief instant in midair, then floated like a parachute over the surface of the plain. There, in the middle, lay their shape, their shadows already congregating. It resembled a tortoise. Their arms around each other. Their two heads meeting.

"There we are," he said, and pointed down at their silhouettes.

In that dark under a night spread with unknown constellations and the warmth that gathered at the very bottom of her stomach — there she made her promise. Because he had come home and this time wouldn't ever go away. Afterward, lying there, she grabbed the flashlight and twirled the beam over his pale body.

They had known each other since high school. Three lives they led. The first, she would always think of as the evenings when he appeared at her house with his hair wet and groomed and they walked without touching, a good distance between them, as they discussed books or what they wanted to be. He always phrased it that way: what she wanted to be. The second was right after the war, when she thought of him as a swimming tortoise. And then that faded as the years passed, and it was replaced by something she couldn't, to this day, articulate. It was the longest of the three. Though in retrospect, it didn't seem that way at all. In fact, the opposite. It was the first that lasted. For a good while. When his scent was of soap. When he would have done such an act as pick up a stone and write their initials in the mouth of a cave. Caged in the loose sketching of a heart.

They were to have a service for him. Without a body. A photograph instead. Jim received the call from his mother the day before. He would go. He had decided. His brother wouldn't forever be fishing, although he could always think of him in that way. Regardless of a service, a formality. It made no difference. He knew that now. So he would go. In two days, he would fly to the mainland and return home. How long he would stay he was unsure. But there was one thing he was now sure of. He would stand there, in that room, beside the photograph of his brother, in front of a small group of the city's citizens, neighbors, family friends, anyone — he didn't care — and recount the story of finding the middle of the ocean. He would share that. And in doing so, he would regain his brother, pull him back down from the static of the sea and air. From the mouths of strangers.

And when the widow asked him, "Will you take me?" he said yes. He would do that as well.

He recruited two other waiters. Three was enough. They agreed in amusement, slapping him on his back and shaking their heads and describing it as the farewell party.

So at four in the morning they stole the keys of a resort truck and loaded it with the necessary products and, with the American widow, they sped away down the dirt road and through the forest and around the hills toward the southeastern coast. Their headlights spotted the foliage, a luminous lime color, the stars still clear and distinguishable against a paling sky. The woman remained silent throughout the journey, her hands against her lap, squished between Jim and another waiter. She was wearing one of her linen outfits, a light blue, with a white scarf draped over her arms. They all bumped shoulders whenever the truck skimmed over rocks.

It took less than an hour, as Jim predicted, and by the time they reached the beach, the sun was lifting above the horizon line. Jim, with a hand on the woman's elbow, took her to an old log at the edge of the forest and told her to wait. From his pocket he took out a handkerchief and reached over toward the woman's head.

"It's a surprise," Jim said. "I promise. Just for a short time."

The woman nodded, staring up at his tanned face. Behind him, toward the boundary of the beach, the sea was red and the sky thinned toward morning. She felt her heart. And the last thing she saw before her vision was covered in darkness was the boy's T-shirt with the image of a sailboat printed on his chest.

When her eyes were covered, he took her hand and squeezed once quickly and then ran toward the truck where the three waiters carried the table and a chair down to the middle of the beach. They covered the table with a white cloth. Jim set down a plate, flanked by a napkin, forks, knives, and a teaspoon. He placed a saucer and a coffee cup to the left and two glasses on the right. The chair faced the sea. From the back of the truck they ignited Bunsen burners to heat the small silver trays that contained scrambled eggs, fried potatoes, and sausages. They opened the icebox to reveal a bottle of water, cream, pineapple, melons, and strawberries. The thermos of coffee was still warm. They changed into their outfits, black jackets instead of their usual white.

It was all set. They stood beside the truck barefoot. Jim began to roll up his pants.

"One more thing," he said.

He treaded down to shore. The waiters paused behind him, hesitant. The tide rose up to his shins. He looked back at the distant canopy of the forest, the flat peak of Halla Mountain. It was possible, he considered, that this island lay at the center of the ocean, a place he and his brother had never found. And thinking this, he wept, covering his mouth, rubbing his eyes with his knuckles. He waited for the feeling to cease. He breathed, slowly, then slipped his hand into his breast pocket and produced against the light of the sun what resembled a harmonica. It shone amber. Leaning forward, he dipped the object he was holding into the sea, like the beak of a bird, and then lifted it in a slow arc toward the length of his hair.

She had heard of fishermen in the ancient days, lost at sea, delirious and pushing hard toward the horizon and the half sphere of a sun in pursuit of illusions. The opposite of a mirage. A vision of not water but of land or anything attributed to the earth and the soil and the possibility of your feet touching a surface without sinking. She imagined that for the men who fell into the sea over a week ago now, perhaps one of them, if only for the briefest of moments, considered this as the water beneath them parted and there rose the skin of what could very well have been a continent. That perhaps, before they keeled, there was this sense of a waking dream and, through it, a descending of peace akin to slipping into sleep. She hoped that it happened too quickly for them to feel otherwise. That by the time they knew this was the last of their days, they had already entered the sea and shut their eyes and given themselves to its depths.

That was what she thought of in the covered darkness of the handkerchief. And how, every night, she sent them a prayer. Not to a god but to their ghosts, whom she envisioned forever on a boat, riding the cusps of the East China Sea, in search of images that existed only in the mind.

Like the one she saw at dawn as she smelled potatoes and heard footsteps and Jim uncovered her eyes, forcing her to squint, her vision blurred. There in the distance: penguins. Tall and slim, rising out of the ocean. Then they evolved into black-suited men walking on the beach, their clothes dry but their hair wet and combed and before them a table and a chair. She gasped and placed her hands to her chest, her hair silver against sunrise. One of the men carried a thermos of coffee. Another a water bottle. Jim helped her toward her chair and then leaned over to tell her of the menu. He then picked up her plate and carried it to the back of a truck and proceeded to arrange her requested breakfast. When he returned, he stood behind her. She picked up her fork and knife and then changed her mind and took his hand and tapped him lightly before she began to eat, slowly, the sun reddening her skin and the tide beginning to reach up close to the table legs.

Afterward, Jim and the American widow greeted a man approaching them with a walking stick. They shook hands. With a nod, Luis led them around the coast to a cave by the shore. He gestured toward it with his arms spread, indicating that it was, in his mind, the best. He would wait for them by the truck, collecting the leftovers. "Careful," he told them. And they were.

Jim held her by her elbow as they waded in through its tall entrance, the ends of the woman's skirt forming a ring in the water.

"There is a myth," he said. His voice echoed the farther they entered. "That this island has a network of underground passageways, used as meeting points for scholars who were persecuted for their religious and political beliefs. In the middle of the night, by candlelight, they would travel from all parts of the island and speed through the tunnels toward a room somewhere. There they discussed the future of the island, its people, and how they would spread culture. They wrote speeches and prepared pamphlets for distribution. No one knows where the room is. But perhaps this is one of the passageways."

They hadn't gone far. To each other they were still visible. They listened to the rush of streaming water. And Jim, his hair dry now, presented his hand to the woman. Within his palm there lay a small flat stone that she reached for and rubbed with the tips of her old fingers. He stepped away, stood behind her. Water cool and thin around his toes. He watched her. Her thin shoulders. Her shedding gray hair. Her arm rising. With that stone she speared the wall of the cave and began what could have been a sketch, calligraphy, some form of design — Jim was not yet sure — or the words of a language long forgotten.

TOBIAS WOLFF

Awaiting Orders

FROM THE NEW YORKER

SERGEANT MORSE was pulling night duty in the orderly room when a woman called, asking for Billy Hart. He told her that Specialist Hart had shipped out for Iraq a week earlier. She said, "Billy Hart? You sure? He never said a word about shipping out."

"I'm sure."

"Well. Sweet Jesus. That's some news."

"And you are . . . ? If you don't mind my asking."

"I'm his sister."

"I can give you his e-mail. Hang on, I'll find it for you."

"That's O.K. There's people waiting for the phone. People who don't know any better than to breathe down other people's neck."

"It won't take a minute."

"That's O.K. He's gone, right?"

"Feel free to call back. Maybe I can help."

"Hah," she said, and hung up.

Sergeant Morse returned to the paperwork he'd been doing, but the talk of Billy Hart had unsettled him. He got up and went to the water cooler and drew himself a glass. He drank it and filled the glass again and stood by the door. The night was sullenly hot and still: just past eleven, the barracks quiet, only a few windows glowing in the haze. A meaty gray moth kept thumping against the screen.

Morse didn't know Billy Hart well, but he'd had his eye on him. Hart was from the mountains near Asheville and liked to play the hick for the cover it gave him. He was always running a hustle, Hart, engaged elsewhere when there was work to be done but on hand to fleece the new guys at poker or sell rides to town in his Mustang convertible. He was said to be dealing but hadn't got caught at it. Thought everyone else was dumb — you could see him thinking it, that little smile. He would trip himself up someday, but he'd do fine for now. Plenty of easy pickings over there for the likes of Billy Hart.

A good-looking troop, though. Some Indian there, those high cheekbones, deep-set black eyes; beautiful, really, and with that slow, catlike way about him, cool, aloof, almost contemptuous in the languor and ease of his movements. Morse had felt the old pull despite himself, knowing Hart was trouble but always a little taut in his presence, fighting the stubborn drift of his gaze toward Hart's face, toward that look of secret knowledge playing on his lips. Hart was approachable, Morse felt sure of it, open to whatever might offer both interest and advantage. But Morse kept his distance. He didn't give advantage, and couldn't take the gamble of a foolish entanglement — not now, anyway.

Morse had spent twenty of his thirty-nine years in the army. He was not one of those who claimed to love it, but he belonged to it as to a tribe, bound to those around him by lines of unrefusable obligation, love being finally beside the point. He was a soldier, no longer able to imagine himself as a civilian — the formlessness of that life, the endless petty choices to be made.

Morse knew that he belonged where he was, yet he had often put himself in danger of scandal and discharge through risky attachments. Just before his tour in Iraq, there'd been the Cuban waiter he met in a restaurant downtown; the waiter turned out to be married, and a gambling addict, and, finally, when Morse broke it off, a blackmailer. Morse would not be blackmailed. He wrote down his commanding officer's name and telephone number. "Here," he said, "go on, call him" — and though he didn't think the man would actually do it, Morse spent the next few weeks inwardly hunched as if against a blow. Then he shipped out and soon came to life again, ready for the next excitement.

This turned out to be a young lieutenant who joined Morse's unit the week Morse arrived. They went through orientation together, and Morse saw that the lieutenant was drawn to him, though the lieutenant himself seemed unsure of his own disposition, even when he surrendered to it — with an urgency only heightened by the near impossibility of finding private time and space. In fact, he was just discovering himself, and in the process he suffered fits of self-loathing so cruel and dark that Morse feared he would do himself harm, or turn his rage outward, perhaps onto Morse himself, or bring them both to grief by bawling out a drunken confession to a fatherly colonel in some officers' bar.

It didn't come to that. The lieutenant had adopted a mangy one-eared cat while they were on patrol; the cat scratched his ankle and the scratch got infected, and instead of going for treatment he played the fool and tried to tough it out and damn near lost his foot. He was sent home on crutches five months into his tour. By then, Morse was so wrung out that he felt not the slightest stirrings of pity — only relief.

He had no cause for relief. Not long after returning stateside, he was called to battalion headquarters for an interview with two smooth, friendly men in civilian clothes who claimed to be congressional aides from the lieutenant's home district. They said that there was a sensitive matter before their congressman that required closer knowledge of the lieutenant's service in Iraq — his performance in the field, his dealings with other officers and with the troops who served under him. Their questions looped around conversationally, almost lazily, but returned again and again to the lieutenant's relations with Morse. Morse gave nothing away, even as he labored to appear open, unguarded. He figured these men for army narcs, whatever else they said. They let several weeks go by before calling him to another meeting, which they canceled at the last minute. Morse was still waiting for the next summons.

He had often wished that his desires served him better, but in this he supposed he was not unusual — that it was a lucky man indeed whose desires served him well. Yet he had hopes. Over the last few months Morse had become involved with a master sergeant in division intelligence — a calm, scholarly man five years older than he. Though Morse could not yet think of himself as anyone's "partner," he had gradually forsaken his room in the N.C.O. quarters to spend nights and weekends at Dixon's townhouse off post. The place was stuffed with ancient weapons and masks and chess sets that Dixon had collected during his tours overseas, and at first Morse had felt a sort of nervous awe, as if he were in a museum, but that had passed. Now he liked having these things around him. He was at home there.

But Dixon was due to rotate overseas before long, and Morse would soon receive new orders himself, and he knew it would get complicated then. They would have to make certain judgments about each other and about themselves. They would have to decide how much to promise. Where this would leave them, Morse didn't know. But all that was still to come.

Billy Hart's sister called again at midnight, just as Morse was turning over the orderly room to another sergeant. When he picked up and heard her voice, he pointed at the door and the other man smiled and stepped outside.

"Would you like the address, then?" Morse asked.
"I guess. For all the good it'll do."
Morse had already looked it up. He read it to her.
"Thanks," she said. "I don't have a computer, but Sal does."
"Sal?"
"Sally Cronin! My cousin."
"You could just go to an Internet café."
"Well, I suppose," she said skeptically. "Say — what'd you mean, maybe you could help?"
"I don't know, exactly," Morse said.
"You said it, though."
"Yes. And you laughed."
"That wasn't an actual laugh."
"Ah. Not a laugh."
"More like . . . I don't know."
Morse waited.
"Sorry," she said. "Look, I'm not asking for help, O.K.? But how come you said it? Just out of curiosity."
"No reason. I didn't think it out."
"Are you a friend of Billy's?"
"I like Billy."
"Well, it was nice. You know? A real nice thing to say."

After Morse signed out, he drove to the pancake house she'd been calling from. As agreed, she was waiting by the cash register, and when he came through the door in his fatigues he saw her take him in with a sharp measuring glance. She straightened up — a tall woman, nearly as tall as Morse himself, with close-cut black hair and a long, tired-looking face, darkly freckled under the eyes. Her eyes were black, but otherwise she looked nothing like Hart, nothing at all, and Morse was thrown by the sudden disappointment he felt and the impulse to escape.

She stepped toward him, head cocked to one side, as if making a guess about him. Her eyebrows were dark and heavy. She wore a sleeveless red blouse and hugged her freckled arms against the chill of the air conditioning. "So should I call you Sergeant?" she said.

"Owen."

"Sergeant Owen."

"Just Owen."

"Just Owen," she repeated. She offered him her hand. It was dry and rough. "Julianne. We're over in the corner."

She led him to a booth by the big window looking out on the parking lot. A fat-faced boy, maybe seven or eight, sat drawing a picture on the back of a place mat among the congealed remains of eggs and waffles and sausages. Holding the crayon like a spike, he raised his head as Morse slid onto the bench across from him. He had the same fierce brows as the woman. He gave Morse a long, unblinking look, then he sucked in his lower lip and returned to his work.

"Say hello, Charlie."

He went on coloring for a time. Then he said, "Howdy."

"Won't say hello, this one. Says howdy now. Don't know where he got it."

"That's all right. Howdy back at you, Charlie."

"You look like a frog," the boy said. He dropped the crayon and picked up another from the clutter on the table.

"Charlie!" she said. "Use your manners," she added mildly, beckoning to a waitress pouring coffee at the neighboring table.

"It's O.K.," Morse said. He figured he had it coming. Not because he looked like a frog — though he was all at once conscious of his wide mouth — but because he'd sucked up to the boy. *Howdy back at you!*

"What is wrong with that woman?" Julianne said as the waitress gazed dully around the room. Then Julianne caught her eye, and she came slowly over to their table and refilled Julianne's cup. "That's some picture you're making," the waitress said. "What is it?" The boy ignored her. "You've got yourself quite the little artist there," she said to Morse, then moved dreamily away.

Julianne poured a long stream of sugar into her coffee.

"Charlie your son?"

She turned and looked speculatively at the boy. "No."

"You're not my mom," the boy murmured.

"Didn't I just say that?" She stroked his round cheek with the back of her hand. "Draw your picture, nosy. Kids?" she said to Morse.

"Not yet." Morse watched the boy smear blue lines across the place mat, wielding the crayon as if out of grim duty.

"You aren't missing anything."

"Oh, I think I probably am."

"Nothing but back talk and mess," she said. "Charlie's Billy's. Billy and Dina's."

Morse would never have guessed it, to look at the boy. "I didn't know Hart had a son," he said, and hoped she hadn't heard the note of complaint that was all too clear and strange to him.

"Neither does he, the way he acts. Him and Dina both." Dina, she said, was off doing another round of rehab in Raleigh — her second. Julianne and Bella (Julianne's mother, Morse gathered) had been looking after Charlie, but they didn't get along, and after the last blowup Bella had taken off for Florida with a boyfriend, putting Julianne in a bind. She drove a school bus during the year and worked summers cooking at a Girl Scout camp, but with Charlie on her hands and no money for child care she'd had to give up the camp job. So she'd driven down here to try and shake some help out of Billy, enough to get her through until school started, or Bella decided to come home and do her share, fat chance.

Morse nodded toward the boy. He didn't like his hearing all this, if anything could penetrate that concentration, but Julianne went on as if she hadn't noticed. Her voice was low, growly, but with a nasal catch in it, like the whine of a saw blade binding. She didn't have the lazy music that Hart could play so well, but she seemed more truly of the hollows and farms of their home; she spoke of the people there as if Morse must know them, too — as if she had no working conception of the reach of the world beyond.

At first, Morse was expecting her to put the bite on him, but she never did. He did not understand what she wanted from him, or why, unprompted, he had offered to come here tonight.

"So he's gone," she said finally. "You're sure."

"Afraid so."

"Well. Good to know my luck's holding. Wouldn't want it to get worse." She leaned back and closed her eyes.

"Why didn't you call first?"

"What, and let on I was coming? You don't know our Billy."

Julianne seemed to fall into a trance then, and Morse soon followed, lulled by the clink of crockery and the voices all around, the soft scratching of the crayon. He didn't know how long they sat like this. He was roused by the tapping of raindrops against the window, a few fat drops that left oily lines as they slid down the glass. The rain stopped. Then it came again in a rush, sizzling on the asphalt, glazing the cars in the parking lot, pleasant to watch after the long, heavy day.

"Rain," Morse said.

Julianne didn't bother to look. She might have been asleep but for the slight nod she gave him.

Morse recognized two men from his company at a table across the room. He watched them until they glanced his way, then he nodded and they nodded back. Money in the bank — confirmed sighting of Sergeant Morse with woman and child. Family. He hated thinking so bitter and cheap a thought, and resented whatever led him to think it. Still, how else could they be seen, the three of them, in a pancake house at this hour? And it wasn't just their resemblance to a family. No, there was the atmosphere of family here, in the very silence of the table: Julianne with her eyes closed, the boy working away on his picture, Morse himself looking on like any husband and father.

"You're tired," he said.

The tenderness of his own voice surprised him, and her eyes blinked open as if she, too, were surprised. She looked at him with gratitude; and it came to Morse that she had called him back that night just for the reason she gave, because he had spoken kindly to her.

"I am tired," she said. "I am that."

"Look. Julianne. What do you need to tide you over?"

"Nothing. Forget all that stuff. I was just blowing off steam."

"I'm not talking about charity, O.K.? Just a loan, that's all."

"We'll be fine."

"It's not like there's anyone waiting in line for it," he said, and this was true. Morse's father and older brother, finally catching on, had gone cold on him years ago. He'd remained close to his mother, but she died just after his return from Iraq. In his new will, Morse named as sole beneficiary the hospice where she'd spent her last weeks. To name Dixon seemed too sudden and meaningful and might draw unwelcome attention, and anyway Dixon had made some sharp investments and was well fixed.

"I just can't," Julianne said. "But that is so sweet."

"My dad's a soldier," the boy said, head still bent over the place mat.

"I know," Morse said. "He's a good soldier. You should be proud."

Julianne smiled at him, really smiled, for the first time that night. She had been squinting and holding her mouth in a tight line. Then she smiled and looked like someone else. Morse saw that she had beauty, and that her pleasure in him had allowed this beauty to show itself. He was embarrassed. He felt a sense of duplicity that he immediately, even indignantly, suppressed. "I can't force it on you," he said. "Suit yourself."

The smile vanished. "I will," she said, in the same tone he had used, harder than he'd intended. "But I thank you anyhow. Charlie," she said, "time to go. Get your stuff together."

"I'm not done."

"Finish it tomorrow."

Morse waited while she rolled up the place mat and helped the boy collect his crayons. He noticed the check pinned under the saltshaker and picked it up.

"I'll take that," she said, and held out her hand in a way that did not permit refusal.

Morse stood by awkwardly as Julianne paid at the register, then he walked outside with her and the boy. They stood together under the awning and watched the storm lash the parking lot. Glittering lines of rain fell aslant through the glare of the lights overhead. The surrounding trees tossed wildly, and the wind sent gleaming ripples across the asphalt. Julianne brushed a lock of hair back from the boy's forehead. "I'm ready. How about you?"

"No."

"Well, it ain't about to quit raining for Charles Drew Hart." She yawned widely and gave her head a shake. "Nice talking to you," she said to Morse.

"Where will you stay?"
"Pickup."
"A pickup? You're going to sleep in a truck?"
"Can't drive like this." And in the look she gave him, expectant and mocking, he could see that she knew he would offer her a motel room, and that she was already tasting the satisfaction of turning it down. But that didn't stop him from trying.

"Country-proud," Dixon said when Morse told him the story later that morning. "You should have invited them to stay here. People like that, mountain people, will accept hospitality when they won't take money. They're like Arabs. Hospitality has a sacred claim. You don't refuse to give it, and you don't refuse to take it."

"Never occurred to me," Morse said, but in truth he'd had the same intuition, standing outside the restaurant with the two of them, wallet in hand. Even as he tried to talk Julianne into taking the money for a room, invoking the seriousness of the storm and the need to get the boy into a safe dry place, he had the sense that if he simply invited her home with him she might indeed say yes. And then what? Dixon waking up and playing host, bearing fresh towels to the guest room, making coffee, teasing the boy — and looking at Morse in that way of his. Its meaning would be clear enough to Julianne. What might she do with such knowledge? Out of shock and disgust, perhaps even feeling herself betrayed, she could ruin them.

Morse thought of that but didn't really fear it. He liked her; he did not think she would act meanly. What he feared, what he could not allow, was for her to see how Dixon looked at him, and then to see that he could not give back what he received. That things between them were unequal, and himself unloving.

So that even while offering Julianne the gift of shelter he felt false, mealy-mouthed, as if he were trying to buy her off; and the unfairness of suffering guilt while pushing his money at her and having his money refused proved too much for Morse. Finally, he told her to sleep in the damned truck then if that was what she wanted.

"I don't want to sleep in the truck," the boy said.

"You'd be a sight happier if you did want to," Julianne said. "Now come on — ready or not."

"Just don't try to drive home," Morse said.

She put her hand on the boy's shoulder and led him out into the parking lot.

"You're too tired!" Morse called after her, but if she answered he couldn't hear it for the drumming of the rain on the metal awning. They walked on across the asphalt. The wind gusted, driving the rain so hard that Morse had to jump back a step. Julianne took it full in the face and never so much as turned her head. Nor did the boy. Charlie. He was getting something from her, ready or not, walking into the rain as if it weren't raining at all.

DONNA TARTT

The Ambush

FROM TIN HOUSE

BEFORE I MET TIM — who, in spite of everything I'm about to tell you, would be my best friend for the next four or five years — my mother warned me on the way over to his grandmother's house that I had to be nice to him. "I mean it, Evie. And don't mention his father."

"Why?" I said. I was expecting to hear: *Because his parents are divorced.* (This was why I had to be nice to John Kendrick, whom I couldn't stand.)

"Because," my mother said, "Tim's father was killed in Vietnam."

"Did he get shot?"

"I don't know," said my mother. "And don't you ask him."

I was eight, and small for my age. Tim was seven. As my mother and his grandmother chatted above my head in the doorway of his grandmother's house, we looked at each other silently, from a distance, like two little animals: me, standing in the bright doorway between the grownups; Tim, from the remote, wood-paneled darkness of the hallway. I couldn't see him clearly, but he was my height, which pleased me.

My mother put her hand on my shoulder. "Did you know," she said to me, in the stagy voice she used when she spoke to me in front of other people, "that Mrs. Cameron is good friends with your grandmother?"

I twisted away, shyly, under the broad pink-gummed smile of Mrs. Cameron. Every old lady in town was friends with my grandmother: if she didn't play cards with them, she went to church with them. The card-playing friends dyed their hair and dressed more stylishly, with cocktail rings and handbags that matched their shoes. The church friends were stouter, and friendlier to children; they wore flower prints, and pearls instead of diamonds, if they wore jewelry at all. Mrs. Cameron was clearly a church friend: compact, pony-built, with shiny pink cheeks. Her hair was gray and she had very black eyebrows, but they were naturally black, like a man's — not drawn on with pencil.

"Hello, honey," she said to me. "I've got a nice swing set out in the backyard. Tim, why don't you take her out to see it?"

As soon as we were alone, the very first thing Tim said to me was: "My dad's dead."

"I know," I said.

He didn't seem surprised that I knew. We stood facing each other, over the water hydrant in his grandmother's backyard: a long way away from the house. He was a snub-nosed, well-rounded little boy, burned brown from the sun, with eerie yellow-brown eyes and a plump, satisfied tummy like a rabbit's. He reached inside his shirt and showed me some dog tags on a metal chain.

"These were his," he said. "They're mine now."

The dog tags had a name stamped on them that was Tim's last name, and they said U.S. MARINES, but didn't look like they really belonged to his dad. They looked like something he'd had made at a fair or at a booth at the mall.

"See, my dad was trying to chase down this Vietnamese that shot his friend," said Tim. "And then the Vietnamese killed him too. I can act it out for you if you want. I'll be my dad, and you be his buddy. O.K. Here we are in the jungle." He walked away a few steps, and then looked back at me. "You're walking with me. Keep up. We can't get separated."

"What's my name?"

"Hank," he said, with gratifying swiftness. "Hank Madigan. All right, here we go. We're walking down the path toward camp, we're talking, O.K.?"

"O.K.," I said. I caught up with him, and together we crept — heads down, a pair of cautious infantrymen — toward a tangle of shrubbery at the edge of his grandmother's yard. He'd said we were supposed to be talking, and I wondered if maybe I should ask something soldierly ("How far to camp, sir?"), but Tim had such a grim, determined look on his face that I was slightly afraid to say anything at all, even in character. He plowed straight ahead, toward the shrubbery, while I kept my eyes on the side of his face.

"Now — all of a sudden, these shots come out the jungle, *eck eck eck boom.* You're dead," he said after a moment or two, when I still stood looking at him.

Obediently, I clutched my chest and crumpled to the grass. Tim dropped to his knees beside me and began to shake my shoulders.

"Oh my God!" he said. "Stay with me, Hank! You can't die, you son of a bitch!"

I grimaced and tossed my head from side to side in agony as Tim — in a desperate effort to revive me — pounded on my chest. I was impressed by his profanity, but even more impressed that he had taken the Lord's name in vain on my behalf.

Far away, from the back porch, Tim's grandmother called out to us in a thin, irritating voice: "Do you all want lemonade?"

"No," shouted Tim, plainly annoyed. He sat back on his heels, on the grass, and looked at me. "You're hurt too bad to live," he said to me matter-of-factly. "There's nothing I can do for you."

I coughed a little and said: "Good-bye." Then I shut my eyes and fell back on the lawn.

In the silence following my death, as I lay still with my cheek against the scratchy warm grass, I heard Tim's grandmother call: "Why don't y'all go play on the swings?"

"Because we don't want to," screamed Tim.

I raised up on my elbows obligingly. "Wait until she leaves," said Tim under his breath. He was angry, staring fixedly into the yard next door.

At last, Tim's grandmother called: "All right." The childish quiver of her voice as it trailed away made me feel bad. She went back inside the house, and I heard the door shut with a forlorn, final sound.

I started to get up, but Tim pushed me down on the grass again. "You're dead," he said, and his voice wasn't unkind or rude — just matter-of-fact. "You can't raise up on your elbow or talk to me or do anything like that. Anyway. So then" — Tim unslung a pretend rifle from his shoulder — "my dad screams: *You shot my buddy! I'm gonna get you!*" He ran across the grass to the bank of privet hedge that bordered the lawn: mouth twisted, fanning his imaginary rifle, spitting imaginary bullets: *eck eck eck eck eck.*

"Ha! Got you!" he cried. And then his face went empty; he reeled back, winced, and jerked under a burst of automatic gunfire, then clutched his own chest and went down.

We lay there in silence for a few moments, staring blankly at the sky, before Tim got up and looked at me. "That's how my dad died," he said.

I sat up. Then I looked back at his grandmother's house — and saw a hand parting a curtain at a tiny upstairs window.

"Somebody's up there watching us," I said, and pointed. "See?"

"Oh, don't worry," said Tim without looking, "that's just my mother," and as he spoke, I saw the curtain drop back down slowly over the window.

"Let's act it out again," said Tim.

From then on, I ran down the street to play with Tim almost every day — in his grandmother's yard but also in the tall weeds of an empty lot next door. If for some reason I was late slipping away to his house in the morning, he came down the street and pounded manfully on the back door for me. Then we ran away together down the bright sidewalk without speaking, crashing through backyards and hedges down to the jungle-flanked path where the assassin waited for us. All day long we dodged bullets in rank suburban tangles of elderberry and ailanthus and day lilies run wild, scrambling on our hands and knees, running doubled over, darting in breathless zigzags from point to point, cover to cover, running and freezing and running again, barraged by fire from an enemy we never saw. And again and again we staggered and fell before him — first me, then Tim; for though our battles became daily more elaborate and complicated (firefights, booby traps, mortar-rocket attacks), the end of the game was always the same. Contorted in our separate agonies, we lay face-up in the buzzing heat, just long enough for our deaths to settle over us and soak in. And even after we rubbed our eyes, stretched, and sat up again, we sometimes sat quietly for a little while without saying much.

"One more time," Tim would say, standing suddenly, breaking the spell. "But better this time."

I was used to playing with children like Tim — holiday visitors whose grandparents were friends with my grandparents — and when it was time for them to go home it was easy for me to say good-bye and run down the street without looking back. For a week every Christmas I played chess with timid Robby Millard, whose parents were missionaries in Mexico, and who had all kinds of stomach problems and took all kinds of medicine because he'd gotten an intestinal parasite from eating improperly washed fruit in Mexico City. And every Easter vacation I looked forward to Jackie and Sherilyn — twins, blond and freckled, older than I — who loved little kids and were constantly begging their parents for a baby brother or sister. The first time they'd met me, they had each taken me by a hand and led me up to the remote attic bedroom in their grandmother's house where they had set up housekeeping, kindly explaining that we were destitute orphans and I was their baby sister ("Hannah") whom they were bringing up on their own. So every spring, for a few days, I was "Hannah," and Jackie and Sherilyn cooked and washed and swept and sewed for me and sang me to sleep in the "garret" where we all lived.

But Tim was different. We were the same size. His yellow-brown eyes were like the eyes of an intensely interested house cat. There was nothing silly or frivolous about him, and I felt that his seriousness made him my natural soul mate. I felt too — intuitively — that somehow he wasn't quite as temporary as Jackie and Sherilyn and the others, and as it turned out, I was right.

Tim's father — the Lieutenant Robert Allan Cameron whose name was printed on the dog tags — had been Mrs. Cameron's only son. But what had been announced by Mrs. Cameron (at church) as a postfuneral visit from her grandson and daughter-in-law soon stretched beyond the usual two-week limit. A month passed; then two months. Painters were seen trooping into Mrs. Cameron's house. Then a child's bed was ordered from the furniture store downtown. My mother — in an overly casual tone that did not conceal her curiosity — asked me if I knew when Tim and his mother were going back to Dallas (which was where they lived) or if I ever saw Tim's mother when I went over to Mrs. Cameron's house.

"No," I said, and ran off. I was still little enough that I could deal with questions I didn't want to answer or didn't know how to answer by literally turning and running away.

Vietnam. The war was on the news every night, but I couldn't understand it, even when my mother tried to explain it to me. The pictures flashed by in no particular order: bad roads, explosions, fires burning in jungle blackness, schoolgirls riding bicycles, and deserted-looking cities where paper blew down the street. An American prisoner of war bowed from the waist in all four directions like a maniac. The place names (Haiphong, Dak To, Ia Drang, Dong Ha) were like something from a ghost story. Some of the far country places didn't even have names, only numbers, and some of the soldiers — mud-caked, grinning, staggering and falling, their helmets scrawled with ugly black writing — looked crazy.

There was something nightmarish about the dusty green gloss of the camellia bushes, deep, deep cover where our sniper lay and waited for us. Every day, he drew us in as if by a poisonous charm; every day, we dove from the trap and crawled for cover, as round after round of fire cracked over our heads. The skirmish took on very different moods, depending on the time of day: damp, overcast mornings, with dew and frantic birdsong; shadowless noons where the sun beat down empty and white; violent afternoon downpours that swept in on us in moments, no warning but a sudden blackening of the sky, and then a gust that sent the leaves flying. Together we hid under the trees as Tim's grandmother called us uselessly from the back porch, the strong wind snatching the words from her mouth. But the rains blew over us and pattered away almost as quickly as they came — sometimes in less than a minute — and then the sun poured out with almost unimaginable brilliance on the rain-washed greenery. With dripping hair, clothes plastered to our bodies, we dropped to our knees and crawled from beneath our tree and commenced our battle again. It was only a matter of time before I was struck, then Tim, before we clutched the grass and died on the ground together in blood-smeared agony — but still we fought every day until the fireflies came out, until it was almost too dark to see. And even when I was supposed to be dead, sometimes I opened my eyes to sneak a look over at Tim, because he was so locked-in, face turned up and staring raptly over the twilit garden and out into some different reality, and though I was never sure exactly what he saw (white smoke? incoming helicopters? tracer rounds, orange sparks?), whatever it was, it shone off his face and left it luminous, like reflected light from a movie screen.

I began to grow bold around Mrs. Cameron. Though I didn't dare shout at her or order her around as Tim did, I often ran past her without answering when she spoke to me, and — following Tim's lead — no longer bothered with thank you or please. If I'd behaved so badly at my own house, I would have got a spanking — but somehow I understood that Mrs. Cameron wasn't going to tell. When Tim and I burst thundering into the house, with mud and leaves in our hair and dirty knees from crawling on the ground, she often looked up at us with a bright, slightly alarmed smile, all long teeth and pink gums, as if we were a pair of snappy terriers who might bite. We gulped down her lemonade without a word, snatched away the oatmeal cookies she offered us and stuffed them into our pockets, and ran back out to the field again.

Then one day we galloped into the kitchen, hot and dirty, and there — at the table with Mrs. Cameron, glancing up at us with a quick, flinching movement — was Tim's mother. She was young and very thin, with pale lipstick and a nervous mouth. Her collarbone stood out at the neckline of her sleeveless top; her hair was teased stiff and combed back; and her eyes (heavily done, with lots of dark makeup) had a bruised and slightly pleading look. She was the kind of mother that made you want to jump at her from behind a door and yell, "Boo!"

I stopped. "Hello," I said, for I still hadn't quite forgotten my manners.

Tim's mother looked over at me and smiled, with a sort of grateful surprise, and something about the smile made me angry. It was a comradely, confidential smile, as if she assumed that I was her ally and not Tim's.

"Hiya, cutie," she said. "You're a little doll, aren't ya?" Her voice was warm and rough and startling, entirely at odds with her frail-looking person. I'd never heard a Brooklyn accent before, except on *The Honeymooners* or *The Jackie Gleason Show*.

"What's wrong, doll? Cat gotcha tongue? Listen up, buddy," she said to Tim, "what's with all the screaming and yellin' out there?"

"Oh, Gali!" said Mrs. Cameron. "Let him play. He's just a little boy!" But as she reached around and drew Tim close to her I noticed — with surprise — that her eyes were pink, that she was blinking back the tears.

Tim shrugged away from her and turned to me with an expression that meant: *let's go*. And out we ran from the kitchen, clattering down the back steps, running faster than usual because we were both embarrassed by the scene (though I doubt either of us could have said quite why) and because we wanted to get back down to our palmy little Vietnam, where our ambush awaited.

"Wonder what Mrs. Cameron thought," my father said at dinner a few nights later, "when Bobby Cameron come back from up north married to a Jewish girl?"

I started to ask what *Jewish* meant, but before I could, my mother gave me a quick glance and said: "Well, I expect Mrs. Cameron's glad enough to have her now that Bobby's dead."

My father reached for the salt. "Roger Bell over at the barbershop?" he said pleasantly. "He was in for a root canal the other day, and *he* said she used to sell newspapers and magazines from a stand on the street. That's how Bobby met her."

"What's wrong with selling newspapers?" I said.

"Nothing," said my mother. "There's nothing wrong with working for a living."

"I'm just *saying*." Busily, my father shook salt over his food. "You know it's got to kill Mrs. Cameron. If Bobby had stayed home and married Kitty Teasdale, I can tell you Ogden Teasdale would have kept him out of it. Ogden's in the legislature," he said, when my mother kept on looking at him like she wanted him to shut up. "He isn't going to have any son-in-law of his going off to Vietnam."

"Well," said my mother, "all I can say is, if you went to Vietnam and got killed, I sure wouldn't be taking the children and going to live with *your* mother."

My father shrugged. "You might," he said. "If you didn't have anyplace else to go."

Both my mother and my grandmother seemed vaguely troubled that Tim and his mother were living at Mrs. Cameron's, but for reasons I didn't understand. Mainly they seemed bothered that Mrs. Cameron hadn't given an official explanation or made a formal announcement of any sort. ("Why hasn't anybody met her yet?" I heard my mother's friend Virginia ask. "It looks like Mrs. Cameron would throw a little party or something for her, doesn't it?")

Some days, Tim's mother stayed in her room and listened to the radio — baseball games, Motown hits turned up so loud that we could hear them outside. But she was also starting to spend a lot more time downstairs. She and Mrs. Cameron called each other by their first names: Rose and Gali. They sat together at the kitchen table; they drank coffee and tea; they talked, mostly in voices too low to hear. ("Sure, I was poor, growing up," I heard her say to Mrs. Cameron, her husky voice rising louder than usual. "But not poor poor.") They looked at magazines and cookbooks; they looked at a scrapbook of things Tim's father had done in high school. Once or twice, Tim and I ran in the kitchen while Mrs. Cameron was trying to teach Tim's mother how to knit, but she couldn't seem to get the hang of it. ("Nah," she said, flopping her hands at the tangle of yarn, "looka this thing, I got it all screwed up. I mean, all *fouled* up," she added, when she saw the expression on Mrs. Cameron's face.)

By now it was full summer, and the days were almost unbearably hot. And maybe it was only the heat, but the old adrenaline punch of the game wasn't nearly so strong anymore. So Tim and I played even harder, trying to pump it all up again, anything to draw fire and beat back our boredom. We tore pickets from the fence to build a stockade; we lobbed mud-clod grenades into the enemy stronghold; we trampled the garden in our desperate retreats, knocked over flowerpots and broke them. Sometimes Tim's mother got up from the kitchen table and came to watch us from the back porch with a strange expression on her face — but once or twice, when it looked like she was about to come out and say something, Mrs. Cameron came over and took her by the arm and whispered in her ear. Then they both went inside, back to the kitchen table again.

"You see?" said Tim triumphantly, as we were carrying the "stakes" we'd torn from Mrs. Cameron's cherry tree back to our position, in order to lay a trap for our enemy. "They don't mind. It's because my dad's dead."

One evening, when my grandmother came over to our house to return a book she'd borrowed, she announced: "Mrs. Cameron brought that little daughter-in-law of hers to the Garden Club party yesterday."

"Oh really?" said my mother. She put down her needlework; she looked at my grandmother. "And how was that?"

"She's a pretty little thing," said my grandmother, "with a trim little figure, but my Lord! Of course she's perfectly *pleasant*."

"What do you mean?"

"It's just —" My grandmother's voice trailed away, and she made a sort of vague, meaningless gesture. We were used to these pauses of hers; she was one of those ladies who tried never to say anything about anybody if it wasn't nice.

"Well, she tries very hard indeed," she said at last, as if that was an end to it.

It took awhile, but finally my mother managed to get a bit more information out of her. For one thing: Tim's mother had worn black stretch pants and spike-heeled shoes, and she had also used some coarse language, though my grandmother wouldn't repeat it. Moreover, Tim had been brought to the party (my mother looked startled; this wasn't something people did), and his mother and Mrs. Cameron had had a hard time controlling him.

"They won't lay a hand on him, either one of them," my grandmother said. "He ran wild all over the garden. The mother is lax, but it's not all her fault. Rose Cameron won't let her touch him."

"I wonder why?"

"Well, I don't know if you remember, but Bobby Cameron was spoiled too."

I listened uneasily as my mother and my grandmother talked about how hard things must be for poor Mrs. Cameron, and how terrible they felt for her. Then, with an uncomfortable start, I realized that my mother was giving me a look.

"What exactly do you and Tim do over at Mrs. Cameron's all day?" she said.

"Nothing."

"You don't ever play rough or misbehave over at her house, do you?"

"No, ma'am," I said.

"I'd better not find out that you do."

I was troubled all the rest of that evening, and that night as I lay in bed I resolved to act better at Mrs. Cameron's house. Even if Tim was bad, I would be good. But by the next day — when Tim and I dragged out house paint and brushes from Mrs. Cameron's garage and began to paint a landing strip on the grass — I had forgotten all about it.

"I'm bored," said Tim one hot afternoon in July.

It was the first time either of us had said it aloud. But I was starting to get bored too. Our firefights had slowed. Now when we died, we took longer and longer getting up to fight again. Sometimes now, in Mrs. Cameron's wrecked yard, we lay on the ground for hours, as still as a pair of fallen trees, as clouds of tiny black bugs hummed all around us.

"Without an enemy," said Tim, "it's not a real war."

I knew what he meant. The problem with the artillery barrages we endured all day long was that they weren't actually coming from anywhere; we had ground fire, plenty of it, but no shooter. And what was the fun of that? We had tried splitting up, chasing each other, but we were already too much of a team: it felt fake. There were other kids in the neighborhood, but they were all much older or much younger; the younger kids were no fun to play with, and the older ones wouldn't have anything to do with us, even when we threw pebbles and tried to make them chase us.

"Let's go play under the hose," I said. I was forbidden to touch the hose and the outdoor faucets at my own house, and I couldn't understand Tim's lack of interest in water fights, especially since it was so hot.

"What about that little kid Brannon who lives in the white brick house?" suggested Tim.

"He's *way* too little. His mother doesn't let him go out of his own yard."

There was a long silence. Up front, we heard the door creak open — and all of a sudden, Tim's face lit up.

"Hey!" he said, in a hushed voice. He sat up; he listened. I sat up too. A flash of excitement crackled through me at the tense, bright expression on his face. And when we looked at each other, I realized that we were thinking the same thing.

Tim — trembling all over — put a finger to his lips. Then, silently, he motioned for me to follow. Quickly — in his doubled-up marine crouch — he ran out of our brushy cover and onto the bright green lawn, and I ran out behind him, blood pounding with a fierce joy.

I've played and replayed this moment a lot in my mind over the years, and it all happened so quickly that even in memory it goes by too fast, I wince at it, knowing I can't stop it. We rounded the corner of the house — and then Tim, with his imaginary machine gun, charged up the stairs to the front porch with me rushing in tight at his flank, bearing in fast, both of us spraying fire, *eck eck eck eck eck*. Of course, we knew very well that we were rushing either

The Ambush

Tim's mother or Mrs. Cameron, and we meant to scare the hell out of them. But what we didn't know was that Mrs. Cameron wasn't on the porch, but halfway down the front stairs, and she was coming down them rather carefully, because she was wearing shoes with heels and carrying a plate of white frosted cake in both hands.

We stopped short, but we didn't stop short enough. Her eyes rounded in horror, and she reached for a railing that wasn't there, and then Mrs. Cameron — with a faint gasping cry — fell backwards and slid down the stairs, all the way down to the concrete walk at the bottom, as the plate crashed on the ground.

Tim — as if it was all just part of the game — immediately dropped to his knees beside her: the perfect little field medic. "Don't worry," he said to her, bending low, in the tender but businesslike voice he sometimes used with me when I got hit. "Lie still. We'll get you to a doctor."

Frozen beside the foot of the stairs, I found myself staring hard at the cake plate, which lay broken in big pieces on the ground. Blood pooled darkly on the gritty concrete walk and — in a sick daze — I noticed that the pool was spreading out bigger and bigger every second.

Tim raised his head. "Mother?" he shouted. Then, to me, with admirable cool, he said: "Go get her."

I ran up the steps — bold with my mission, but also with a weird, exhilarating sense of putting some sort of hard-earned emergency training into action — and collided with Tim's mother, who grabbed me by the shoulders and shoved me aside. As soon as she saw Mrs. Cameron lying all bloody on the ground, she pressed her hands on both sides of her head and shrieked: "Oh my God!"

Mrs. Cameron was crying too, but in a way I didn't think grownups ever cried: wetly, noisily, with big gulps of air. Her forearm was cut, on the tender white underside; she'd cut it on the cake plate. That was where all the blood was coming from. The blood pumped out from it in a diagonal slash, streamed down her arm, and dripped red off her fingertips, so much red it looked like Mrs. Cameron was wearing a scarlet elbow glove.

"Oh my God!" screamed Tim's mother, looking frantically up into the tree branches, as if she expected to find help there.

"Go call, Evie!" said Tim, over his mother's shrieks. "Nine-one-one!"

I ducked behind Tim's mother — there was a telephone on a table in the front hall — but much to my shock, she caught me by the arm and whirled me around. "Don't you dare go in there!" Her face was bright red. I tried to pull my wrist away, but — almost before I could blink — she whacked me hard with her open hand across the face.

"*Little* goyische *girl,*" she screamed. "Run around over here like you own the damn place, eh? Lemme tell you something, girlie." She prodded me in the chest with her sharp forefinger. "Ya no good. This boy was never bad a day in his life."

Mrs. Cameron, at the bottom of the steps, was raising a frightened cry: "Gali? Gali?" She was struggling to get up. Tim was trying to hold her down.

"Ah, the hell with it." Tim's mother kicked the board game (Operation) that Tim and I had left spread out on the porch, and the pieces went flying — plastic funny bone, wishbone, heart.

She let go of me, and I backed away from her, down the stairs. She was crying too.

"It's an ugly world," she said. "An ugly, stinking world."

Edging away from her — edging away from them all — at the bottom of the stairs, I felt something slick touch my bare ankle, and I jumped. It was Mrs. Cameron, her hand all bloody. She didn't say anything, but the look on her face was enough. I turned away from them and ran, out from Mrs. Cameron's yard and the shadows of the oak trees into the hard, shimmering heat of the sidewalk, no cover, just open space and open sky, streets so hostile in the midday sun that even my panic was drowned in all that emptiness and shrunk down to something flimsy and ridiculous.

Later people said I'd been smart to run up to Main Street for help instead of toward my own house, which was blocks farther away. I never told anybody the truth: that my fear had spun me around and thrown me blindly off in the wrong direction.

But it wasn't just fear; it was a sick, bitter exaltation. And as I ran, the word she'd shouted at me pounded in my head: *goyische goyische goyische,* a strange word, screamed in a high, bad voice, a word that sounded like it had to mean something terrible, even if I didn't know what it was. Saigon would not fall for another year. And I was only eight, and Mrs. Cameron would be home from the hospital in a couple of days with seventeen stitches in her arm, but still — I knew it even then — I was as close at that moment to the real war as I was ever going to get.

MAXINE SWANN

Secret

FROM PLOUGHSHARES

It was through our friend Shirley that we met the Kalowski boys. I was eleven that summer, and my sister, Lila, was thirteen. Shirley used to live in the hollow down below us, but had recently moved up the road, where there were more houses, closer to the hard road and the still faraway town. For years, in our little enclave in the woods, Shirley had lorded it over my sister and me and our other friend, Trish, who lived over the hill.

Shirley was my sister's age. She didn't have a father. She had sandy hair and small eyes that almost closed up when she smiled. She had a rich fantasy life to which we were all meant to adhere. All games, as long as we remembered, had been under her dominion, in the pasture, on the ponies, lounging on the creek bank in the sun: "O.K., I'm the empress, you're the lady in waiting, you're the messenger." "O.K., I'm the prettiest, you're the second prettiest." Lila had spaces between her teeth and always carried her head tilted to one side. I thought she was the prettiest. But it didn't matter what we thought. Shirley was in charge.

She staged her dark dream life with us as actors. Death was everywhere. She taught us how to make each other faint. One person leans over and hyperventilates, while the other grips her from behind and holds tight across her diaphragm, then drops her in the pasture grass out cold. You'd come to, head spinning, thinking hours had passed. Shirley was obsessed at different times with the Manson murderers — "They kill you, whole families, and hang your bodies on the clothesline" — whom she assured us would soon be coming here, and Henry VIII and his wives. Another game was to have one of us go into a dark closet and turn around eight times saying "Mary Walker." It didn't always work, but it could happen sometimes that the ghost of Mary Walker would come out and kill you.

I can see Shirley singing Donna Summer — *"Toot, toot, yeah, beep, beep"* — and swirling her hips. Standing by the mailbox of her new house along the road, still a dirt road, but wider and more trafficked than the tiny path that trickled by our house, and waiting for the chance to catch someone's eye. She flourished in this new environment, where there were people driving by, eyes to catch, and she soon got to know all the neighborhood characters — Michael Melton, Bonnie Rider, Marcy, the Lyalls. My sister and I were now like the country cousins, while Shirley had been out and seen the world. She'd ride her pony over to our house to give a report, delighting in the ambassadorial role.

Michael Melton's father sat on the porch of their low ranch house drinking all day with a gun in his hands and shot at things that passed by on the road, squirrels, stray dogs, cars. Michael's mother dressed herself and Michael's sister, Mindy, exactly the same, in skirts or patterned pants suits, like two dolls. Michael was older than Mindy, fourteen or so, very tall, with gray teeth. He was an amazing athlete, and his name was familiar to Lila and me since we'd heard it mentioned over the loudspeaker for winning sports prizes at school.

Bonnie Rider was adopted. She had a pale, grave, watchful face and gray-brown hair. Behind her house was a pond full of weeds. Bonnie was friends with Marcy. "Marcy's cool," Shirley said offhandedly, as if she and Marcy were now very close. Lila and I knew enough who Marcy was — the coolest girl in school — to know this couldn't be true. But we were used to Shirley's lies. She lied about everything.

The Lyalls had a blue plastic out-of-ground swimming pool. Everyone spent as much time at their house as possible. They kept a cooler filled with sodas in the dark garage. All the Lyalls had Renaissance faces, dark shoulder-length hair that curled at the ends, along their temples or lower cheeks, and clear, soft features. They were slim and retiring in manner and had a yard full of trash and flower bushes right at the corner where the bus stop was.

But the big news that summer was the arrival of the Kalowski boys, two brothers from the city. Their parents took the farm up the road from Shirley's. There were rumors that they'd moved because there'd been trouble in the city, nobody knew exactly what. The Kalowski boys wore city clothes and smoked cigarettes. They were twelve and fourteen. They were soon tight with Michael Melton, friends with Tim Lyall. This whole business of country life was strange to them — their farm had come with two ponies and a cow — but the boys took it in stride, flipping their legs over the ponies as if they were motorbikes, congregating in the woods instead of on street corners, thinking up new ways to vandalize.

Shirley had gone out riding with them more than once. An expert herself on all things "equestrian" (that was the word she liked to use), she said that their ponies were much too small for them, and, besides that, they didn't know how to ride. When she'd tried to give them pointers, they wouldn't listen. They'd veer off instead to spray-paint a driveway or topple the statues on Ed Trout's pristine lawn. Shirley had told the boys about my sister and me, and they were eager to meet us, not so much for the reason she'd thought, because we had ponies, too, but because they'd heard from Tim Lyall that our mother and her boyfriend were hippies and would go swimming naked at our swimming hole.

One day, Shirley arranged for us all to meet up on ponies outside her house.

Shirley made the introductions. "Lila's my age," she explained, "but four months younger. Trish and Rinnie are both eleven, but Rinnie's younger by a month and a half." (As usual, I was always the less or least.)

The older boy, Sid, was wiry, with chicken-like arms and legs and one dark tooth on the side. His legs dangled off his tiny pony. He couldn't stop jittering.

"You know, in the future human beings won't have bodies anymore," he said.

"Why?" Shirley said.

"Because they won't need them. They hardly need them now. Most everything they can do with their minds."

The younger one, Jesse, had an angelic face and a small paunch, his blond hair curling in his eyes and ears. "You know, our brother, Lee, lives on a nuclear submarine."

"Why?" Trish asked. While Lila and I looked at the boys without really looking — Lila took her ponytail out and put it in again; I pretended to scratch my insect bites — Trish looked directly. She had a pointed nose and thin, sleek hair. She stared at the boys' mouths, not their eyes, her own lips parted somewhat. When she acted like this, I thought she was dumb, but later I realized there were other reasons.

Jesse noticed her looking at him and looked back, languorously, rubbing his stomach with one hand. "Because he's in the army," he said. "There's a war on with the Russians. Didn't you know?" Suddenly, his face lit up. "Oh, shit, Sid, there he is!"

Ed Trout's white pickup truck had appeared, coming slowly down the road. "Let's go, go, go!" Jesse said. He kicked his pony hard. The pony, taken by surprise, shot out across the road and plunged straight into the field of wheat on the other side. Jesse slipped to one side, pulled himself up, then slipped to the other, clinging to his pony's neck for dear life. Sid followed Jesse. I saw a stroke of confusion, then elation, cross Lila's face. She kicked her pony. I kicked mine. We all plunged after the boys into the wheat, cutting pathways, running blindly.

When we came out again, over by the Ballards' farm, I looked over my shoulder. You could see in the distance the white pickup coming after us. My heart was racing.

"This way!" Sid said.

We galloped down the road, then ducked into the woods behind the Lyalls' house. We waited there, panting, hiding. The smell of a lilac bush was very strong. Off to one side were the ruins of an old house. A rusted metal bedstand still stood in one of the rooms.

We heard the pickup pass by. A moment later, it turned and came back the same way, then the sound of it grew fainter and fainter. We waited until the sound had disappeared altogether and then walked out through the trees until we got to the Lyalls' yard.

We tied our ponies up on the little straggly trees beside the mounds of trash with enough rein so they could eat grass. The grass was very lush, maybe from the garbage. There was already a crowd in the Lyalls' yard. Michael Melton, his toes gripping the thin metal edge of the pool, did swan dives — you could see the hair in his armpits as he lifted his arms — or cannonballs. The whole point was to hit someone. He'd aim right for your head.

We all got in the pool. Shirley didn't have her bathing suit on so she climbed in in her clothes. She tried to organize one of her games, this one about King Arthur and the Knights of the Round Table — she would play Guinevere — but no one listened. Not even Trish and I, the little ones, listened. The truth was we were pretty sick of listening to her, and now, besides, there was so much else to see. Only Tim Lyall listened, very politely, his clear Renaissance face never swerving from hers. He seemed to listen to anyone who spoke forcefully and with conviction and had, it seemed, maybe precisely for this reason, a particular crush on Shirley. She soon settled down to just addressing him. They edged over to the side of the pool.

Marcy came by. She wore tight blue jeans, though it was summer, and a see-through shirt with silver thread in it. She was thirteen, same as Lila. She leaned her elbows up against the pool and asked Sid if he had cigarettes. Shivering, blue, he climbed up out of the water, more than happy to oblige. Marcy's hair, the glossiest blue-black I'd ever seen, was shoulder-length, swept back in feathers. She wasn't getting wet. She'd be in eighth grade next year. Her bra showed through her shirt — we all looked at it. She wandered off again, a vacant look on her face, completely conscious of the effect she made, and went to talk to Denise Lyall, who was even older than Marcy, but had been held back a year, and was sitting inside with a perm in her hair. A little bit later, Bonnie Rider came by. She stared into the pool for a few minutes, saying nothing, her grave, motionless face showing just above the edge. Then she, too, went into the house.

As far as swimming went, it was much more satisfying to be in the creek. Here in this plastic cubicle world there was no space whatever to move around. The water was stagnant and full of human fluids. You could be hit at any moment by a human cannonball. But the scene was riveting to watch. I could see Lila watching, pressed against the edge, head tilted to the side, a strand of hair caught in her mouth.

That night Lila and I lay awake, picturing Marcy's bra through her shirt, Sid's one dark tooth, Ed Trout coming after us, our hearts pounding with excitement.

From then on, we went out riding with the boys nearly every day. Sometimes we went by their house to pick them up. Their yard was always quiet. There was a rose of Sharon bush, a clothesline, upturned cars, a few dark kittens here and there. Their father, a mechanic with a blond cowlick, would peer out from behind one of the cars. Their mother was nearly always inside. She had an angelic face, like Jesse's, and hair wrecked by treatments. Inside, the house was dark and filled with stuffed sofas and chairs. Their mother spent most of her time sitting on the couch with her eight-year-old daughter, watching TV. Like the father, she was very young. They slept upstairs in a large heart-shaped bed. When a neighbor came by to complain about the boys, their father would hide behind the hood of one of his cars. Their mother would come out of the house and listen, nodding, perplexed, like a little girl, then go back inside. There was a photo of the older brother propped up on the TV.

Or the boys came to our house. Although our father had moved out awhile ago and our house had changed a lot since — an addition had been built; there were now rooms and doors — it still had the reputation of being a hippie house, or so Shirley had told us, with rumors circulating about walls painted all sorts of funny colors, and weird experiments and wild parties going on. The first time the Kalowski boys came over, they couldn't but be disappointed. The walls were wood-colored, and there was no one around. But there were a few things to marvel at, all the same: the swing hanging from the center of the ceiling — Lila got up on it and did all the tricks she knew — and the paintings done by a friend of our mother's of naked people. The boys went over and stood in front of the naked paintings, whispering and jabbing each other with their elbows. They were very eager to see our mother swimming naked, as Tim Lyall had. What they didn't know is that our mother had changed, too. Although she still went swimming naked, and had spent a night in jail not long ago for protesting at a nuclear plant, she'd also recently done a stint as head of the PTA. The boys hung around waiting for her to appear and, when she did, looked her up and down. Since it was summer, and she was mostly in the garden, she had bare feet and wore cutoff shorts. Lila and I knew what they were thinking.

We took them down to the swimming hole, where we plunged right in, still on our ponies' backs, hot and sticky, without even taking off our clothes. The ponies wobbled at first, hooves sinking into the mud, then, necks long, heads pulsing forward, began to swim. I gripped my pony's back with my legs. The water made everything feel different. Lila let her legs free so they streamed out behind her, just clinging with both hands to her pony's mane.

The boys came out of the water. Sid was shivering. He had a little sneer whenever he was wet and partially dressed, as if he were frightened or disgusted by his body. "Did you see the movie *2001: A Space Odyssey?*" he asked.

Lila and I shook our heads.

"Me, neither. But there's a computer in there that tries to take over from humans."

Jesse, fresh, white-skinned, went to scratch his back on a nearby tree.

Our parents' figures faded. I could see it on my sister's face. We were no longer thinking so much about them, our father's feeling abandoned, our mother's new boyfriend. And we weren't worrying, either, about the other things we worried about, school next year. Our minds were elsewhere, out riding with the boys, tearing through the trees. The creek water clung to our skin, hair, clothes. We dove headlong into the world and then back headlong into bed. We woke smelling of creek water or pool water and ponies.

Soon Trish wasn't allowed to play with us and the Kalowski boys. They were "bad boys," her parents said. Their older brother, Lee, was in jail. Now she sat alone in her house, watching out the windows. It was a charity gesture to go and see her when we could be having so much fun.

The boys lied. They told stories about their brother. ("The submarine he's on has made it over to Russia now," Jesse said. "They're spying off the coast.") Shirley lied. The lies gave a surreal quality to the world.

I had the first little nubs of breasts. Lila, older by two years, had nothing. Shirley had actual boobs. When she had first started to get them, too soon, Lila had been delighted still to be flat. "You'll be sorry later," Shirley had said. Now Lila was. I heard the boys walking behind us one day and whispering about our breasts. I saw them staring at our shirts. They were curious and less shy around Shirley. Once they took her aside and questioned her, a conversation that she reported afterward:

"Does Lila have hair down there?"

"No."

"Does Rinnie?"
"No."
"Do you?"
"I told them I did."

We were curious about them, too. We could see their erections through their shorts. Sid's voice was changing. He had some hair in his armpits.

The boys bragged about this or that, but nothing happened. Not yet. At the Lyalls' pool, everyone was squirming, jittering, pushing the envelope. Shirley was part of this, too. My sister and I watched. We knew quite a bit about adult sex from seeing our parents' friends frolic at parties. We were a little bit behind, and at the same time far ahead. What had been forbidden to them hadn't been forbidden to us. We'd seen more grownups swimming naked than we cared to think about. What we hadn't seen, though, were things like Michael Melton's dad, red-eyed, hurling insults, firing a shotgun blindly from his porch at the road. The boys said that Michael Melton came over to their house at night and had sex with their ponies, surely another lie. We hadn't been exposed to violence or cruelty of that kind, the way, for example, Michael Melton would hurl a kitten hard against a tree, breaking its skull.

When my pony got hurt one day, I rode along behind Sid on his, leg to leg, my arms around his bony chest. I could have felt a lot of things, like laying my head down on his back, the hot, thin T-shirt against my face.

The summer sky spiraled upward. It cast a fantasy light over the wheat, the pasture grass, and trees. Lila and I lay awake, hearts pounding. The world was different now. We were thinking about other things, the future, outer space, not our parents, not Shirley and her hierarchical games.

We'd go riding in the pouring rain, under lightning. Or we'd wait it out awhile under the trees. Sid, skin and bones, was shivering, his face blue. My sister lay back along the spine of her horse. Her yellow shirt clung to her skin. The trees sheltered us almost completely from the rain. A roll of thunder crossed the sky. Then lightning. Lila sat up.

That year, when school began, things were different, too. We were all by now in the middle school. While our elementary school had been a small pink building with rows of trees and a playground outside, the middle school, in contrast, was huge and angular, built from cinder blocks, with almost no windows. Instead of a playground, there was a vast indoor gym. All the elementary schools in the area, including ours, fed into the middle school. In the broad concrete hallways, the fluorescent lights blared down. Crowds accumulated. There were far too few teachers to control all the kids. The principal seemed to relish all the paddling he did.

For the Kalowski boys, school provided a whole new set of opportunities to misbehave. Although they started out in the sixth and eighth grades, they were soon put into the "retarded" class, a class for both the mentally retarded and simply very bad. The boys and their friends from the retarded class traveled the hallways in a marauding horde, throwing things, shouting, knocking on doors as they went by. Lila and I were in the "gifted and talented group." The boys' friends would make comments about us. They would grab us between the legs as we passed by in the halls. The Kalowski boys wouldn't dare do these things themselves, but we couldn't help wondering if they weren't directing operations. One friend of theirs in particular, Marshall, always grabbed me between the legs. I would turn my back to the wall and slide along it whenever I saw him coming my way.

Sid stole things, jackknives or hats from kids' lockers, science magazines from the library. He was so skinny he could slip the magazines down the back of his pants. Jesse was more flamboyantly bad. He'd pinch the Social Studies teacher's butt — Miss Dandy had lovely, large curves everywhere, including her butt, and a limp because of one leg that dragged — or pick a fight with another kid in the gym. As he was hauled off to the principal's office, he had his usual look of fear mixed with delight. The boys were kept in for detention all the time. They were paddled. The principal, Mr. Loehmann, was a medium-sized man with wire-framed glasses and teeth with jagged edges. He wore shirts with small colored stripes. His rounded shoulders were too large for the rest of his body. He must have had, or at least acquired, strength from all the paddling he did.

At the end of the day, the yellow round-nosed buses lined up in front of the school. The Kalowski boys would come to the bus after having been paddled, holding their butts in their hands. One day, when the long line of buses was just beginning to move, Marcy stood up and yelled, "Wait!" We looked over and saw Jesse running out of the front door of the school with the principal, Mr. Loehmann, on his tail. Jesse ran for the bus, the principal right behind him. The bus driver, Mr. Hershey, a red-haired man with a beard who, every few minutes along the road to and from school, looked up into the large tilted mirror above his head and yelled, "Keep it down!" or "In your seats!," waited just a second longer, as Jesse neared, and opened the door. Jesse leapt on, Mr. Hershey closed the door, and the bus pulled away, leaving Mr. Loehmann out on the pavement. Everyone went berserk. Mr. Hershey pretended not to understand anything, but a moment later, as we turned out of the school driveway, Trish and I saw him smile.

The bus was a world unto itself. It was like being in a room where everything was too loud, music playing, people yelling, the TV on, and then outside the silent landscape streaming by, wheat fields, corn fields, farms, and clumps of trees. Everyone was squirming, straining, either to hide away or make himself heard. The windows fogged over with breath and sweat. Jesse snapped Marcy's bra strap. Michael Melton hulked down the aisle to grab the retarded boy. Shirley was telling Bonnie Rider about past lives, turned around in her seat, propped up on one knee, screaming above the noise. Sometimes one or another of the bad boys peed, and, depending on whether we were going up or down a hill, the pee would run forward or back along the aisle.

It was a relief to step off the bus out into the air, which felt cool and clear, late fall now, though our ears were still ringing. The Lyalls and the Meltons scattered to their houses. Trish's parents were waiting to pick her up. Marcy and Bonnie Rider walked a ways with us.

Shirley went on with what she was saying. "I was Queen Elizabeth the First."

"But how do you know?" Bonnie asked.

Lila was walking beside them, carrying her violin. The days were getting shorter, the pink-yellow light of sundown already in the air.

"You just know."

"And so that means in the next life you'll be someone else?" Bonnie asked.

"Yeah, sure," Shirley said.

"You'll definitely come back and be someone else with a different life?"

Shirley shrugged, delighted to have Bonnie Rider hanging on her every word. "Of course."

Sid came up beside me. He had a science magazine tucked into the back of his pants. "You know a nuclear war would mean the end of the world," he said. "Everything, the whole planet, would be destroyed."

Marcy was eyeing Jesse. She was about a head taller, walking beside him. "Hey, do you have a cigarette?" she asked.

Jesse dug into his pocket and pulled out a bent cigarette. He found some matches and lit it for her. He watched Marcy lean down, her face near his hands.

"You know, our brother, Lee, was captured by the Russians," he said. He put his hand inside his jacket to touch his stomach.

Marcy inhaled. She flipped her hair coolly. "What do they want from him?" she asked.

"They're trying to get him to tell nuclear secrets."

"Really? Does he know nuclear secrets?"

"Of course! He knows everything."

We still went riding sometimes on the weekends, but it had grown cold, and Lila and I had other things to do, like homework.

Sid and Jesse never did their homework and didn't even always go to school. One day, Jesse's mother promised him twenty dollars if he got an A on a test. He asked Lila and me if we could help him. It was a geography test, and he had to memorize the continents and oceans on the globe. He came over to our house to study and was distracted only momentarily by the sight of our mother. The following day, he came home from school holding the test paper high in his hand. He'd gotten an A. His mother was beaming. Jesse clearly could have gone on like this, with just minimal studying, and done well. But this wasn't what interested him. The rewards elsewhere were more gratifying. He had it in his blood, the thrill of being bad, much more intoxicating than any A.

Lila and I went about our school days. To combat any weird rumors about our house, we tried to act as normal as we could. We carried combs in our back pockets, flipped our hair back, trying to imitate the cooler girls. The rewards for us were in getting A's. We got A's. But we were also torn about it. We had always been debilitated by this penchant of ours to get A's, because getting A's wasn't cool. We tried to stop but couldn't. We were caught in a bind. We walked around with our friends. In the halls, we ducked to avoid being thrown against the lockers by a teacher, too enraged and helpless to see whom he was hitting. We skirted along against the wall to avoid having our pussies grabbed by Sid and Jesse's friends. We played instruments in the orchestra, my sister the violin, me the cello. My sister changed her part to the middle — mine was still on the side — and soon afterward became a cheerleader, an enormous step toward being cool. I went on getting A's, debilitating myself.

Shirley was not that cool, either, but her big boobs helped her a lot in other ways. She and Lila were still friends. They walked around carrying their books up near their chests. But Lila had other friends, too, especially now that she was a cheerleader, and Shirley had found other acolytes to listen to her. She could always find acolytes to listen to her. Trish, twelve now like me, who hadn't been able to ride with us and the Kalowski boys, because her parents were terrified she'd get pregnant young, had suddenly out of nowhere begun making out with boys between the lockers. Though she was pretty occupied with this, we were still friends.

And Lila and I were still friends with the Kalowski boys, though it was a strange sort of communication — as if we were spies meeting on the border of foreign territories, speaking in code. We'd exchange confidences in the hall. Lila and I both at different times covered for them. Once Sid came speeding by me and passed off a jackknife, which I didn't know what to do with and stuffed into the front pocket of my jeans. He was being chased. All day, the jackknife stayed there, pressing against my thigh.

Another time, in the hall, Lila lied for Jesse, saying she'd seen him go one way when he'd gone the other. A few minutes later, as Lila was walking down the hall talking to her cheerleader friend, the science teacher, Miss Lehr, who had a rough manner and a boxy face, grabbed Lila from behind by the hair.

"You know what that's called?" she said, bringing her large square head close to Lila's. She had a scratchy, sensual voice. "Aiding and abetting." She still had Lila's head yanked back, Lila's neck exposed. She seemed to be relishing this, and to want to keep Lila in this position for as long as she could. That day, after school, Lila, her face burning and the roots of her hair still sore, had to stay for detention.

I would sometimes run into Marcy, usually in the bathroom. She'd be looking in the mirror putting eyeliner on — she wore it very dark along the lower lid — and singing softly to herself, *"Welcome to the Hotel California . . ."* Once I was in a stall when she and Denise Lyall and Bonnie Rider came in. They were loud, in a mood. Or at least Denise and Marcy were. Marcy had colored pieces of chalk, probably stolen from the science room. I was in a stall peering out. They were talking about boys. Bonnie wrote "Fuck" with the chalk in big letters on the wall. For some reason, I felt scared and stayed where I was in the stall. Denise was giggling a lot. Bonnie watched. She smiled. She seemed to have a secret.

Then something wonderful happened. Marcy decided that she wanted to "go with" Jesse, even though he was younger than her and in the retarded class. She had the message conveyed to him by Denise.

Jesse's delight was immeasurable. Now Marcy walked down the hall with him, his hand on her butt. They sat together on the bus. It was clear from Jesse's expression, sitting there, his arm hooked around her shoulder, that he couldn't believe his luck, and none of the rest of us could, either. Denise and Bonnie Rider sat in the seat in front of them so the three girls could still talk. Denise tried to flirt with Sid, but it didn't work. He was too shy. Bonnie Rider watched gravely. Once off the bus, Jesse and Marcy went into the woods behind the Lyalls' to do things on the abandoned bed out there. They'd hauled out a foam mattress and a stash of blankets, Tim Lyall said. But they also couldn't wait. They did things at school. Marcy would wear no underwear if he asked her. She'd let him unhook her bra behind the gym. Once I passed them making out between the lockers and heard Marcy moan. For a long time I couldn't get that sound out of my head.

One day when we were walking home from the bus stop, after Marcy and Jesse had slipped off into the woods, Sid came up to me. Lila and Shirley were walking ahead. He was jittery, glancing around as if he was afraid of something.

"I could kiss you," he said.

I looked at him, too surprised even to blush. He moved off, a science magazine tucked into the back of his pants.

After that, he came up to me every once in a while, passing by me in the hall at school or on the way home from the bus stop, and said very softly so no one could hear, "I'll kiss you soon."

At first, when he said it, I felt confused. I wasn't actually sure if I wanted to kiss him or anyone at all. When I saw Trish kissing boys between the lockers, her cheeks long and contorted, it didn't look like something I wanted to do. But even though I wasn't sure I wanted to kiss Sid, I began to look forward to him saying that to me. He said it like a threat, but it wasn't threatening. And the more he said it and didn't do anything, the more curious I got.

Once, on the walk home from the bus stop, he grabbed my wrist and whispered it, his lip grazing my ear. I turned my face to his, but he quickly moved off again.

Finally, I couldn't stand it anymore, and one day, a Saturday in early spring, I went down to the pasture to get my pony and, without telling anyone, rode up the street alone. I took the back way so as to avoid passing in front of Shirley's house. Though the ground was still frozen, there were the first green buds on the trees.

The Kalowski boys' yard, as usual, was still. I rang the bell. Their mother came out, her hair wrapped in blue plastic.

"Is Sid here?" I asked.

She called up to him. He answered. Jesse, as I figured, wasn't around, off somewhere with Marcy.

"One of the girls is here to see you."

Sid appeared on the stairs. He saw me and immediately looked scared, as if he knew what I'd come for. He ducked his face. "I'll be right there," he said, and went back upstairs.

But he didn't come. His mother invited me to sit down with her and her daughter and watch TV, but I said I'd wait outside. I waited and waited, but Sid didn't come. I began to get cold from just standing there. I saw Sid's face in an upstairs window, ducking as I glanced up.

But I wouldn't leave.

Finally, reluctantly, Sid stepped outside. I was standing by my pony.

"What are you doing?" he asked, kicking at a chunk of frozen ground. He seemed to have a hard time getting the words out.

I shrugged. I felt a rush of discomfort. I hardly knew why I was there anymore. But then I acted, as if blindly. "Come on," I said. I led my pony across the yard toward the back of the barn.

I felt that I was moving blindly. I didn't know what I was doing. I didn't want to do this. Sid looked worried. He glanced around and followed me, his expression unhappy.

At the back of the barn were stables, facing out to the pasture. I stopped here.

Sid stopped, too. He was jittering.

"You know, there are two billion black holes in the universe," he said.

"What's a black hole?" I asked, putting my pony's reins on a hook.

"It's an empty dark hole with nothing in it, no light or air or bottom." He snickered nervously. "If you fall in, you just disappear."

I stepped toward him. He leaned back away from me, then even stepped backwards. His face was scared, cloudy. His back was now pressed against the stable wall.

I was moving without thinking. I leaned up and put my lips on his. He jerked his head back a little. He laughed nervously, looked around. Then, as if he had no other option, he bent near and put his mouth on mine, trying it. His lips were soft. When he brought his face away, his eyes were already different. He came near and kissed me again, then to my surprise, pressed his tongue inside my mouth, at first a little bit, then deeper, then all the way in. I felt something wiggle up from between my legs all the way to my throat.

Afterward, we walked back across the frozen yard, past a pile of old motors. Sid was acting different. He lit a cigarette. His step was jauntier. I felt happier, too. We passed the rose of Sharon bush, now just a skeleton. I pictured how it would be in the summer, bursting with hand-sized purple flowers.

That spring, Bonnie Rider killed herself one morning. She had it all planned in advance, went out by the pond behind her house, tied rocks on her feet, and stepped in. It happened over the weekend. We found out because they announced it over the loudspeaker at school. "We regret to inform you that Bonnie Rider passed away over the weekend."

Four days later, Marcy and Denise decided to do the same. They were on the telephone together, both with their fathers' hunting guns in their hands. In the notes they left they said they did it because they "wanted to be with Bonnie." When they weren't on the bus, we thought it was because they were upset about Bonnie. But then the announcement played over the loudspeaker that Marcy was also dead. Denise had changed her mind at the last minute.

For a moment, on the bus, the jittering, pulsing, jamming, stopped. It actually felt, for a split second, like the end of the world. Then it started again, but differently. Shirley explained in a quiet voice about all the historical figures she knew of who had killed themselves. "Suicide," she explained, "is an ancient practice." Though we'd grown tired of listening to her, we felt in that moment that we'd never been so relieved to hear a person's voice.

Summer came, and we all still went out riding, we still had a great time. The boys' voices were changing, our breasts were growing, they had more hair in their armpits, yet it was still possible. Jesse was a little different, his face heavier, less angelic-looking. Something really inexplicably bad had happened. The boys lied less. What was the point? Reality this time had outstretched fantasy. We still went to the Lyalls' pool. The boys collected dog turds and put them in people's mailboxes. They knocked over road signs. But things were changing all around us, we were changing. Time was moving forward, we couldn't stop it. Lila and I were going one way, the Kalowski boys the other.

The following year at school, we'd all drift further apart. Lila and Shirley would be waiting for their boyfriends, going out on dates. The Kalowski boys would start committing their first petty crimes. (At one point, there was some suspicion that they'd broken into our house and stolen things, a painting with naked people in it and a tin of our mother's boyfriend's pot.) And the year after that, we'd move away. Although our father didn't live with us, our parents still made decisions together. They had decided that we should go to a different school, that school wasn't good for us. Our parents were so-called hippies, but they were thinking of our future. They had set aside money for us. My sister and I would go to college. While the Kalowski boys would go on to other things. Since we'd moved away, we didn't know exactly what, but there were rumors — prison on drug charges, fathering children young.

But we still had this summer. Sid and I still kissed sometimes in secret behind the barn. I thought a lot about kissing him. His mouth was soft and voluminous. He'd put his finger in my bellybutton. "Give me your tongue," he'd say. In the pasture, out riding, I'd look over at him. Since that day I'd gone to find him, he was different, I could tell. He wasn't so afraid. And I was different, too. I knew it. I had a secret. It had nothing to do with anyone, not my parents, not the girls. I wasn't anymore less or the least. I had a secret, out of sight of everyone, blooming inside me. I would carry it with me out into the world.

MARK SLOUKA

Dominion

FROM TRIQUARTERLY

THEY'D ALWAYS SLEPT with the windows open. Even now, late into the season, with the husks of the cicadas dangling like Chinese lanterns in the webs below the eaves, they'd swing the frames up to the ceiling, mating hook to eye: one toward the dirt road, another toward the up-sloping woods, two toward the old pasture wall that ran straight into the lake and disappeared like a man determined to drown himself. Not that you could see any of these things — on moonless nights opening the windows was like punching holes into a barrel — but they were there. They always had been.

He didn't know where the coyotes had come from, or how long they'd been there. A season, maybe two. The dairy farms were falling fast, replaced by things named after whatever had been destroyed to make room for them, but there were still enough open woods left to allow for a pack or two. Now, with the leaves almost down, you could hear them all the way out toward the state park. It always started the same way: a series of quick, laughing yips that pulled you out of your sleep, three, four, five voices, almost joyful, falling over one another like pups until one would suddenly catch and hold, as though impaled, in mid-laugh, and then the others would follow, stricken in turn, rising, barking, screaming, a braided chorus of hilarity and pain. These were not dogs.

He didn't know what it was. He'd awoken the first time in a well of fear, unable to breathe.

"Hear that?" he'd whispered into the dark, needing to wake her.

"What on earth . . . ?"

Her voice was sanity, bottom, ground. The world corrected itself.

"What am I listening to?" she asked.

"I think they're coyotes," he said, slipping back inside himself, resuming his place.
"Since when do we have coyotes?" she whispered back.

He hadn't known what he was listening to at first, what it was he was hearing — hadn't been able to place it at all. He'd been dreaming something . . . bad, and for a few moments it had been as though the dream, the madness of it, had followed him out into the waking world, clinging to him like a piece of tape stuck to the middle of his back.
They lay side by side, listening. At the base of the wall of voices he could now make out a simple screaming — something being killed.
"Good God," she said.
"Sounds like they got something," he said. The screams changed into a high, repetitive keening, like a broken mechanism.
"We have to do something," she said.
"Like what?"
"Make a noise or something."
"They're a quarter of a mile away."
Outside in the blackness something was choking wetly. It was oddly embarrassing to listen to it. He had to say something, cover this.
"I saw in the paper they found one in Central Park," he said, and that instant saw a small, blue motel room sixty years ago, the two of them trying to talk over the cries and grunts coming from the landscape hanging over the bed as their daughter colored in a picture on a round table. "Said it had to have walked over one of the bridges during the night."
"Into Manhattan?"
"That's where they keep Central Park."
"I don't believe it. Sounds like alligators in the sewers to me."
"Said they're cunning little bastards. Tough as a shovel. That they'll go anywhere."
"Did it say where they came from?"
"Didn't say. I think . . ."
They were going, dropping quickly into silence. The quiet spread: thick, cool paint on glass.
"I think it's over," she said.
"I think it is," he said.

He could feel himself beginning to unclench. He wished he could remember now what the article had said — whether they had come out of the west, spreading east through the plains and the cornfields as the predators died before them, or whether they had always been there, right from the beginning, and only been squeezed into visibility by the loss of their space. He seemed to recall that both theories had their backers. It hardly mattered. Domestic or imported, they were here.

"I've never heard anything like that before in my life," she said, turning over on her side.

They hunted like cats, he remembered now, stalking and leaping on the backs of their prey rather than running it down like wolves.

He lay awake for an hour after that, listening, waiting for them to return, trying to understand what had happened to him. In the first few moments, as he'd plunged from sleep like a swimmer rushing from the water, he'd distinctly imagined a giant muzzle crashing through the roof of the cabin, snuffing and snatching at flesh as though they were voles in a burrow. The madness of that image, so uncharacteristic of him, troubled him now. He had never been particularly bothered by the ferocity of nature before, had always known, and accepted the fact, that the border between life and death was a porous thing, the two sides bleeding into each other everywhere and always. And yet, though he understood all this and more, having served in France at a time when the borders had been fixed and hard and the bleeding pretty much all one way, there was something else going on here.

Sometimes, lately, he'd wake up in the middle of the night and lean over her to see if she was breathing. Twice in the last year, unable to hear anything, he'd shaken her awake, fighting off the panic tightening his chest and rising into his throat like glue. "What's wrong? What is it?" she'd cried out both times, bolting up into the dark, and both times he'd had to invent some absurd story, once that he'd had a nightmare, the other, more shamefully, that he had no idea what she was talking about, that she was the one who had woken him. "What? What is it?" he'd begun yelling the instant she sprang awake, making a big show of being disoriented and confused. When she asked him what this was all about, and whether he had finally lost his mind, waking her up in the middle of the night, he'd allowed himself to get angry. "Why the hell would I want to wake you?" he'd demanded, and spent the next few minutes arguing so convincingly, so self-righteously, that by the time he'd rolled over on his other side he half believed that it was she who had woken him, and resented her for it.

At night he would lie looking up into the cedar planks or out through the open windows into the dark, weighing his life, adding a little dust here, a little there, shaking it in his palm, then raining it out like salt. The scales tipped and creaked.

Harold Prochaska had been a journalist with the *Hartford Courant* for fifty-nine years. He'd think about that sometimes. He'd started there when he was sixteen, two years after armistice, less than three after his father died — a tough, ringwormy-looking kid in borrowed shoes who did whatever was asked of him. The old guys, who didn't like anybody, had taken a shine to him right off. It had all been an accident, the way it had turned out. A noisy argument had broken out around O'Connor's desk, where the boys had gathered, as usual, to shoot the shit and pass judgment on whomever seemed in need of it. God how he'd loved the place.

"Hell, any kid off the street could tell you that," he heard someone say, as he walked to the mailroom.

"Hey, you," O'Connor had called out to him. "Yeah, you. What's your name?" Harold told him. O'Connor waved it away. "Jesus, all right, get over here. You can read, right?" He snapped a sheet of paper at him. "Read this."

And seventeen-year-old Harold Prochaska, who hadn't even gotten laid yet though he'd thought about it a good deal, who didn't know shit from shittola, who had nothing but a pair of oversized shoes and a bit of moxie with which to front the world, opened his mouth and a legend flew out — a miracle of deadpan delivery and Swiss-watch timing. Everyone was there: Franks, with his leg up over the corner of the desk; Maroni, looking like the bagged-out welterweight he was; old Ralph Simmes, forever rolling a spit-black inch of stogie between his teeth. All of them, including himself, blissfully unaware that they were calcifying into newsroom clichés, becoming in some basic way unbelievable. "Well?" O'Connor had growled after some seconds had passed. "Not too bad," the kid pronounced, still looking at the paper. "What's his first language?"

And there it was. Just like that. Afterward, all he'd had to do was not smile or, when he did, make it look like it hurt. The old guard protected him, laughed at his mistakes, created openings: "Give it to the kid. What about the kid? Let the kid take a whack at it." Maroni, seeing him reading something, would call: "Hey, kid, what do you think — French?" and all he would have to do was not look up but stare at the paper a moment, considering it. "Well . . ." And it was in the bag. His line, which owed everything to the gods of chance, who could turn the world on its head in an instant, became as much a part of the atmosphere as the ring-and-smack of the carriage returns. One generation passed it to the next like a well-fingered baton.

A blessed life, in many ways. He'd enjoyed the newsroom, resisted all attempts to move him up and away from it. He'd loved everything about it: the smell, like smoke and sweat and something very much like the inside of a brass pot; the harsh, industrial lighting; the immovable metal-topped desks . . . loved getting up to go to the cooler just to see the room sit up and tighten, so to speak, the younger men hunching over their typewriters or pulling pencils from behind their ears, the older ones deliberately leaning back in their swivel chairs and leafing through some papers to show that, like him, they didn't need to look busy to get the job done. He liked this generalized awareness of himself, this constant reflecting back. He hadn't realized how much. Once or twice, after he'd left, he'd felt as though he'd disappeared.

Which he had, really. On the day he retired he'd received a plaque, a pen, a bottle of champagne, and a rectangular black jewelry box in which a row of printer's type, buried up to the pin mark in cotton, spelled out "Thank You, Harold P." He drank the champagne, kept the pen, tossed the plaque and the jewelry box in the kitchen garbage. Whose bright idea had *that* been?

And that was that. He was gone, yanked, pulled like a hair. Off the radar. A butterfly flaps its wings, he thought, and not a goddamned thing happens in China. He recognized himself for what he was — a retirement cliché — and ridiculed himself for it, but that didn't make it go away. He still felt thin somehow — transparent. He couldn't help it. Less than a month later, walking through the midday crowd along Main Street, he had been overcome by the sense that he could do anything he wanted — take out his dick and piss in his hat, run out of a store with an armful of brassieres — and no one would notice. No one. Everything around him had grown strangely quiet, the sounds of voices and traffic receding as though they were all on the back of an invisible truck moving steadily away from him. He'd stood there in the hot sun until he became aware of the fact that he was breathing very high and fast, as though his lungs had shrunk to the size of a fist, and then, not knowing what else to do, had sat down on a nearby bench. It passed. The next day he had had himself checked out, thinking it might have been a stroke of some kind, but nothing.

He'd decided not to say anything to Janice. It wasn't that he was worried she'd overreact — she'd always been a practical woman, good at seeing what was there and no more — just that he didn't much care for the picture of himself going on. That was never the way it had been between them — he'd never played the child with her — and he wasn't about to start changing things now.

They'd been married for damn near sixty years. At night when they went to sleep he'd press up against her back and reach around and cup one of her big, soft breasts with his right hand, then move down to her stomach, whose skin was soft and foldy like the fur on those socklike dogs that had been so fashionable a few years back. She would reach behind and give him an affectionate squeeze, and though it didn't lead to anything anymore like it used to, that was all right.

God in Heaven, but how he used to ride her. In this very room, in fact, though the beds had changed over the years, rocked out of joint one after the other, including one that had actually crashed to the floor in the middle of things, scaring the hell out of them both. Janice Vaculik — who would have believed it? Seemed like that first year they couldn't get enough of each other — she was always grabbing at him, sneaking a squeeze even under her parents' dinner table or whispering in his ear, making him hard on the bus — but even after, when imagination had taken over and they had begun to dare each other further and further into thinking things that shamed and excited them, it had been good. Very good. He still remembered it — the stored-up feeling of it, the anticipation of it.

Harold Prochaska rolled over on his back. The antique scales on his chest, their base nestled down into the mat of hair, rose and fell. The first house, the second, the view from the bedroom window, the faces of the kids ... They'd done all right. Better than all right. He had no complaints, nor any right to any.

But right has no claim in the court of our fears. As Harold Prochaska was sliding sideways into sleep, the inevitability of his own death suddenly slipped up and seized him by the throat. He struggled and thrashed, knowing it would pass, brought his usual weapons to bear: Everyone had to die. Others died young, or in pain, or alone. He himself could have died half a century ago in France. He called himself names: He was an ungrateful bastard, a coward, the worst kind of egotist, whining for a special dispensation, unable to imagine the world without him. Sit up, you fool, he said to himself, and sat up in bed in the dark, and then, like a man pushing back a great dark wall on rollers, began to think of other things, moving the thing inch by inch from his mind. He got up and walked to the kitchen, his toes curling up from the cold floor, and poured himself a drink. Fuck it. He was fine. When he came back to bed his wife was still sleeping.

It was such a simple thing. You really had to laugh. He was eighty-seven years old, with spots on his temples and odd little tags of skin on his arms and legs and neck, and he didn't want to die. But that wasn't it, exactly. It wasn't so much that he didn't want to die — who would? — as that he simply couldn't conceive of it. It had been a problem, off and on, for as long as he could remember. How could the moment come when he would no longer be conscious of the world? He understood death. He'd written about it, seen more than his share of it. And yet, when it came right down to it, he didn't understand it at all. How could you be alive, and then not? How could the great doors close forever, sweeping over the sky, the trees ... ?

He had always thought it was something he'd understand once he got closer to it, like algebra. That his occasional episodes (for that was what he thought of them as) would pass with age. That like a forest, which seems solid from a distance but is actually filled with paths, death would explain itself on closer acquaintance. It hadn't happened that way. And now here he was. Bummer, as the young people said.

It wasn't until he'd seen it go by with the cat that he knew it was death. Lowercase death, unemphatic and certain. It was just after lunch, a strangely warm November afternoon. He was sitting at the too tall desk by the window, trying to work, when it appeared, a long-legged, unhealthy-looking creature at once arrogant and supplicant, and looked at him — that is, looked at him as he sat there in dreaming disbelief as it trotted straight across the yard and along the wall, then disappeared out of sight into the undergrowth. There had been a hand-sized patch of fur missing on its right flank. A rusty cat was hanging from its jaws.

Janice had been in the other room, reading by the window. "Oh my God, I just . . ." he started to call out, still half believing what he'd seen, and then for some reason stopped himself. He heard the chair springs in the other room. "Harold?"

"Right here," he said. "I swear to God I just had it right here. Not five seconds ago." He heard her settle back in the chair. "You want some more coffee?" she said, and he heard the newspaper. Some days later, when a young couple who lived down the road came by asking whether they had seen their cat, he didn't have the heart or the courage to tell them. It was like a secret he'd pledged to keep. And anyway it was done.

He was fine during the days, reading in the hammock, carrying small bundles of kindling into the cabin, cleaning out the shed. A late fall. When they went for their walks now, the walls that marked the old pastures were visible everywhere, and yet during the afternoons sometimes he would still hear the high trill of crickets that should have been gone long ago. A cold sound, thin and perfect. The lake was tea-black and still. On warm days he could hear the wasps under the eaves and one morning nearly bit into one that was walking carefully along the edge of his toast.

And yet it was always there now, like a shape hidden in a drawing. He could sense it in the trees and the lichened boulders of the walls, in the late light on the water, in the black rim of shore reflected in the pond. An absurd conceit. During the days it was deniable, laughable. At night it wasn't. He was exhausted now. Every night he'd snap awake and lie there listening, clammy with sweat and self-disgust, unable to escape that ridiculous equation: they were it. It was as though, once imagined, the thing had taken on a life that could not be denied. He didn't know what he was afraid of, exactly, and yet he was afraid. Again and again it trotted through his world, its head turned to the window behind which he sat frozen, and disappeared over the wall. There was the ugly hand-sized patch of skin on its haunch. It looked at him over the floppy-legged body in its mouth, then leaped the stones, the cat's head swinging back and forth like a child's doll with its stuffing removed. And there it was again. It trotted past the window. There was the ugly patch of hairless skin, the cat's head swinging . . . And again.

It did no good to argue. Once it had taken hold, there was nothing he could do. Getting up didn't help; reading didn't help. He knew they weren't a threat — not literally. And yet it didn't matter. It was as though everything had been turned upside down inside of him, reason itself revealed as a lifelong artifice, a reef of tiny lies and rationalizations. They were coming back. He was going to die. It scared him witless. It broke his heart.

He said nothing. He unscrewed the ladder from the dock, dragged it into the shed, then pushed dirt over the two narrow furrows he'd dug into the grass. The weather had turned. A windless gloom had settled over the water, the stones, the hills. Everything seemed emptied out now, an exercise in perspective: The three dead trees by the dam, the wooden float. The day had dawned so dark that hearing Janice in the kitchen, he thought she had gotten up early. It was almost ten.

By noon it was dusk. He busied himself bringing in more wood, then took a phone call from his son in the city. Everything was fine. At four it started to rain, a thick, soaking rain, and he made a fire. He tried to read but couldn't. He always loved a fire on rainy days: the crack and spit of the wood, the sweet, sharp smell. It filled him with sadness now. Once or twice he had a glimpse of himself, trapped in a peculiar box of his own making, but it passed like a scent, like the idlest whimsy, like an offhand remark, and was gone. At nine-thirty, he went to bed.

He fell asleep almost immediately — a deep, drowning sleep. It was night, and something was in the lake. He couldn't reach it. He dragged the heavy ladder back to the water, lowered it down, felt something grasp it in the dark. Somebody was calling his name from the cabin. Just a minute, he called. He had to do this. He struggled to pull the ladder from the water, to save this thing. It was working. He grabbed a lower rung, hauled up with all his strength. Something was wrong — it was up too quickly. He grasped another rung, and another. The ladder had never been this long. Even before he saw it, he was struggling to run, unable to unclench his hands from the wet wood: a paleness, a hand-sized circle, rising out of the water, screaming.

And suddenly he was awake and it was all around him: a continent of sound, shoving in from the dark. It seemed to be everywhere at once, a guttural, howling chorus, just beyond the open window. He couldn't move, he couldn't breathe. There was nothing out there. Nothing, just darkness, endless, interminable. My God, he thought: so this is how it is.

Something soft fell across his chest. There was a small jostling crash, a quick curse, then a rush to the window. A beam like a sword flashed into the darkness, cut along the wall, the woods, the dripping trees, even as an infuriated voice yelled into the void: "Shut up, you stupid mutts!"

Silence, as abrupt as a slammed door.

The beam clicked off. He listened to her walk back around to her end of the bed knowing her body, feeling it negotiating the obstacles as though it were his own. "Goddamn it, I'm going to have this bruise for a week," he heard her say. "When are you going to put some padding on that corner like I keep asking you to?" She climbed back in, turned on her side. "Next time it's your turn," she said.

A great clarity, like cold water, like oxygen. Harold Prochaska lay on his back. He wanted to laugh. It was gone, cracked like an egg. "Boo!" he whispered to himself.

He looked around the room. There was the sloping ceiling, the hanging coat, the mirror to the other bedroom in which they lay. There were the four windows, open like mouths. And beyond them? Beyond them was the known world: the lake, the boulder of the wall, the endless, shoreless forest.

PATRICK RYAN

So Much for Artemis

FROM ONE STORY

AT THE BEGINNING OF THE SUMMER Jennifer hypnotized Frankie with her MedicAlert bracelet. "You are in my power," she said. "You will do exactly as I say." She told him to bark like a dog, and he barked. She told him he was a car, and, sitting across from her on her bed with his eyes closed, he honked and lurched forward, screeched and reared back. "Now you're a beggar," she said. "Go ask my mother for a dollar."

Frankie got up and walked out of her room and down the hall, fluttering his eyelids, his arms raised in front of him like a zombie. Now that school was out, Jennifer's mother was Frankie's babysitter on the weekdays. She was in the above-ground pool in the backyard, floating in a tire-shaped raft that had a holder for her plastic iced tea cup. Her hair was piled onto her head with bobby pins, and she was reading a book through a pair of large, round sunglasses. At the top of the metal steps, his arms still raised, Frankie said, "Mrs. Woodrow, I need a dollar, for I am a beggar."

"You certainly are," Mrs. Woodrow said.

Standing next to Frankie on the deck, Jennifer told her mother she'd hypnotized him.

"Well, I don't go swimming with my purse," Mrs. Woodrow said.

"You can promise," Jennifer said. "You can give it to us later."

Mrs. Woodrow promised and asked them to please go do something else.

Back in her bedroom, Frankie sat cross-legged on the floor and said, "Half that dollar's mine, right?"

"You will have no memory of this," Jennifer said, and snapped her fingers.

He was never, ever to push her, hit her, or throw things at her. He didn't want to do any of that, but his mother had told him not to anyway, saying it was Mrs. Woodrow's rule for any child she babysat. "And don't ever ask Jennifer if she's sick," his mother had told him. "Mrs. Woodrow said other children have done that, and it isn't nice. Jennifer's not sick. She's just . . . fragile." Frankie was seven and small for his age, but Jennifer was eight, and smaller. Her nose came to a sharp tip and her jaw was almost not there at all, as if it had been pushed into her neck. Her skin was wrinkled and dry-looking, like a thin layer of papier-mâché. She always wore some kind of hat, indoors or out — a cowboy hat, a plastic fireman's helmet, or, most often, a soft, white fishing cap with the NASA logo and an elastic strap that hung loosely over her throat. That afternoon, when Frankie asked if they could take turns hypnotizing each other, she led him into the bathroom and took off the cap, showing him her bare head for the first time. She was almost entirely bald. Her scalp was dimpled with pink and gray spots and had just a few strands of white hair. "You have to be very smart to hypnotize a person," she said, looking at herself in the mirror. "My brain is so big, there's hardly room for hair roots." Frankie stared at her too, and then the two of them looked at Frankie's head, which was covered in dark, wavy hair. "The less hair you have," Jennifer said, "the more brains. It's just a fact of nature."

During dinner that evening, Frankie, the youngest, looked at the five other heads around the table, each one covered with hair, and said, "Do you think we'd be a smarter family if we were bald?"

Matt and Joe burst out laughing, and Katherine, who was eleven, bucked forward and pinched her nose. "God!" she said. "I almost snorted milk!"

Frankie's mother had more hair than any of them; it was straight and the color of palm bark. She frowned while they were laughing, and her mouth started moving soundlessly, as if she didn't know what she wanted to say. Finally she snapped, "All right, that's enough, now. Your father's had a *very* rough day."

At the other end of the table, Frankie's father kept his head down and his hands close to his plate, sliding his knife through his

Salisbury steak. When he put a piece in his mouth, his jaw moved like a machine with a worn-down battery. He glanced at Frankie's mother, and between bites he said, "Why don't you tell them?"

She swallowed and pushed her napkin against her lips. "Let's just have a nice dinner."

"They're going to find out anyway," his father said.

Matt, who was fourteen and the eldest, said, "You don't have to tell me. I already know."

"Oh, Matt, be quiet," his mother said. "You *don't* know."

"Yes, I do," Matt insisted. "Paul Krieger's father is in the same boat. He told Paul, and Paul told me."

"Why does Matt get to know and I don't?" Katherine asked.

"There's nothing to know," Frankie's mother said, glaring at Matt. "Everything is fine." She glared at Katherine and at Joe, too, and finally at Frankie, whose mouth was full of food. "Just eat," she said.

The next morning, she got dressed and left for work without taking Frankie to Mrs. Woodrow's house. His father was at the table for breakfast, as usual, but he didn't go anywhere afterward. He stayed in his robe and pajamas, reading the newspaper.

An hour later, Frankie was sitting on the couch, and Matt and Joe were on the living room floor, watching *Ultraman*. Frankie's father was still at the table. Katherine stood between the two rooms, holding a glass of milk, staring at him. "Aren't you going to work?" she asked.

"No." He lit a cigarette and turned a page of the newspaper.

Matt looked at Katherine and Joe. "Told you."

"I'm supposed to go to Mrs. Woodrow's house," Frankie said.

"You don't have to go today," his father said without looking up. "I'm going to be here."

"Are you sick?" Katherine asked.

"No, I'm not sick. I'm just going to be here."

Frankie heard Katherine groan softly as she walked toward the back of the house. When their television show ended, both his brothers followed.

By lunchtime, the three of them were gone. Matt and Joe had ridden their bicycles to the mall, and Katherine had walked to the end of the street to play foursquare with her friends. Frankie's father made him a bologna sandwich, and Frankie sat on the couch eating it and watching *Andy Griffith*. His father ate his own sandwich standing up. Chewing slowly, he crossed the living room and stood at the window. He stared out at the front lawn for a while. Then he turned around. "Do they usually do that? Just go somewhere like that?"

"Who?"

"Matt and Joe. Katherine."

"I don't know," Frankie said. "I'm supposed to go to Mrs. Woodrow's."

His father looked at him, chewing. He turned back to the window. "Why is the grass so pale?"

"I'm supposed to be playing with Jennifer."

"It looks awful," his father said. "Probably the soil. Who's Jennifer?"

"*Jen*nifer," Frankie said.

"Oh, that little girl with — that's Mrs. Woodrow's daughter?"

Frankie nodded.

"Well, you're not going over there today, I told you that. Wouldn't you rather be here with me for a change? Have some fun?"

The walls on either side of the front window were lined with pictures from his father's job. He worked with cameras at the Space Center, and after each big launch he'd been given photographs, framed in thin black metal, that hung like award certificates all over the living room: trios of smiling, orange-suited astronauts; the enormous building where they constructed the rockets; silver capsules drifting down over the ocean beneath orange-and-white-striped parachutes. Above the television was a large picture of Neil Armstrong standing on the surface of the moon, saluting a stiff American flag. His father ate dinner most nights with his NASA badge still dangling from his shirt pocket. He liked reading the paper and working on the lawn, and his favorite television show was the news, which seemed, lately, to be on all the time and had turned into nothing but men sitting around in suits and talking to one another about the president. Frankie couldn't picture what kind of fun the two of them might have.

"So," his father said, turning away from the window. "What do you want to do?"

They looked at each other. His father raised his eyebrows and held them that way for a moment. Then he let them drop, took his hand off the curtain, and walked over to the television. *Andy Griffith* was over, and he turned the dial to the men in suits, one of whom was frowning and speaking very slowly. Lowering himself into the armchair next to the couch, he said, "You let me know when you think of something."

The next morning, Frankie begged his mother to take him to Mrs. Woodrow's. She was standing in the kitchen, about to leave for work, and she looked toward Frankie's father at the dining room table. His father turned his eyes down to the newspaper and lifted one hand with the fingers spread wide, which somehow conveyed that it was fine with him.

They played Mouse Trap. They played Battleship and Don't Break the Ice. They played Lava, a game Jennifer had invented, which involved stepping cautiously around her room with their arms raised while she determined which pieces of furniture and which parts of the floor would incinerate them. Mr. Woodrow came home in the middle of the day and ate lunch with his yellow realtor's blazer hanging over the back of his chair, and when he was gone, Mrs. Woodrow set up her card table next to the television and worked on her decoupage. Jennifer and Frankie watched *The Big Blue Marble* and sang along with its eerie theme song. "That song says the planet's turning slowly, but it's really spinning at a million miles per hour," Jennifer told Frankie. "If it stopped, we'd all fly off into space."

"That's not true," Frankie said.

"It is true. Isn't it true, Mom?"

Mrs. Woodrow was leaning over a plaque of wood, spreading shellac onto the picture of a long-necked crane she'd cut from a magazine. "It's true," she confirmed.

"Let's play Science," Jennifer said. "You can be my assistant."

In the kitchen, they mixed baking soda with mustard and red food coloring and spooned the result into a glass filled with pickle juice. "It might be poisonous," Jennifer said. "But it might be a cure for the most deadly disease in the world. Test it." She pushed the glass toward him.

"You test it," he said, nudging it back toward her.

"If it's poison, I'm the only one who could make the antidote. It has to be you."

So Much for Artemis

Frankie took the smallest sip he could from the glass. It tasted awful, and he swallowed it with his head shuddering.

"Your vital signs are good," Jennifer said, resting her tiny, shriveled fingers on his wrist. "Let's play Wild Kingdom."

Their neighborhood sat alongside a patch of swamp, and armadillos and opossums sometimes crept out of it and came waddling down the sidewalk. Glass snakes and black snakes wound across the road and curled up against doorsteps. There were palmetto bugs, slugs, rollie-pollies, and dragonflies that hovered right in front of your face like miniature helicopters. A turtle as big as a suitcase lived in a cavern beneath the house at the end of Jennifer's street. But when they played Wild Kingdom, it was about the lizards, which were everywhere. Jennifer had developed a very specific tracking system for the ones they caught in her backyard. They would name them, tag them by tying bits of colored string to their legs, and use index cards to record the information: *Zeus, 5 inches long, lime green, white belly, found near back fence next to magnolia bush. Red string on right foreleg.* They had never caught the same lizard twice, but if it ever happened, they were prepared to record its new location and note any changes in its appearance.

"Herman," Frankie said, holding up a lizard he'd caught against the warm, metal side of the swimming pool. Its torso felt spongy between his fingers.

Jennifer peered at it and shook her head. "Artemis," she said, and wrote the name down on an index card. She pulled a couple of inches of blue thread from the spool her mother had given her, and bit it off. Frankie cupped his hands around Artemis and felt the lizard charging against his palms, ricocheting back and forth like a miniature SuperBall. Lizards were so fast, they sometimes seemed to vanish before his eyes: one moment they'd be clinging to the side of the house, or to the edge of the patio, or to a slat in the fence — and the next moment, they'd be gone. "We should do a magic show," he said. "We could be a husband-and-wife magic team, and we could have the Amazing Vanishing Lizard, and put Artemis in a box, and when we opened the box, he'd run away so fast, it would look like he disappeared."

"Red ants," Jennifer said.

"What would they do?"

"You're standing in red ants," she explained, pointing down.

He bent over and saw at least a dozen of them crawling over his sneakers and around the folds in his socks, heading for his bare calves. When he finished jumping and kicking his feet and smacking at his legs, the lizard was gone.

"So much for Artemis," Jennifer said, still holding the piece of string.

"Sorry."

She shrugged. "I don't like magic, anyway. It's silly. If we're husband and wife, we're an explorer team doing a study on Bigfoot."

"O.K.," Frankie said.

"There's been one spotted right over there" — she pointed to a corner of the yard where a thatch of bamboo stood higher than the fence behind it — "and they have to go investigate the sighting."

Frankie nodded. They started across the grass.

"The husband's always rescuing the wife from quicksand," Jennifer said.

"O.K."

"And she's his assistant."

He nodded.

As they neared the bamboo, Jennifer put one of her bird-claw hands against Frankie's chest and stepped ahead of him. She said, "You be the wife."

For the next couple of weeks, Frankie continued to go to Mrs. Woodrow's during the day. In the mornings his father would be at the dining room table, reading the paper. In the afternoons, when Frankie and his mother walked through the front door, he would be on the couch in front of the television. He stayed in his pajamas some days, and if he had a cowlick at breakfast, it would still be poking up at dinner.

One afternoon Frankie and his mother came home, and the living room looked bigger. It took Frankie a moment to realize that all of the NASA pictures had been taken down from the walls. The nails were gone and the holes had been dabbed with white putty.

Frankie's mother stood next to him holding her purse and looking at the walls. Then she walked out of the room. His father was standing at the sliding glass door in the dining room, staring out at the backyard. He was turning a book of matches in his hand.

"Where'd all the pictures go?" Frankie asked.

"Away," his father told him.

"Where?"

"Just away." He looked over his shoulder at Frankie. His jaw was turning dark with stubble.

"What do you say we go to the library tomorrow?"

"I'm supposed to go to Mrs. Woodrow's house."

"I know. But let's go to the library. I have to look up some information. We have a project to do, you and me."

"What kind of project?"

"The lawn," his father said.

The next day they drove to the library, a squat, one-story building made of large, flat rectangles of concrete. His father opened a drawer in the card catalogue and Frankie headed for the children's section, but he never made it past the curved, carpeted wall that held tanks of gerbils and garden snakes and a frowning, putty-colored iguana hugging a plastic branch. Before long his father was tapping his shoulder. He didn't have any books, but he was tucking a folded piece of paper into his pocket and there was a ballpoint pen behind his ear. "You ready?"

They drove from the library to Mr. Krieger's house, in the neighborhood next to theirs, and parked in his driveway. Frankie waited in the car while his father knocked on the front door. Mr. Krieger stepped outside wearing a dress shirt and a baggy bathing suit. He was growing a beard. Frankie's father did most of the talking, motioning toward Mr. Krieger's chalk-red pickup truck and then planing a hand out purposefully in front of him with his palm down. Mr. Krieger shrugged, said something, and disappeared back into his house. Frankie's father came back to the car. "That's all set, then," he said, getting behind the wheel. He glanced at Frankie. "Isn't this fun?"

At dinner that night, someone had a Gas Attack. It was either Matt or Joe, and they both clutched their throats and leaned sideways while Katherine pretended to throw up and Frankie pressed his hands against his face.

"Can we please?" Frankie's mother said.

"Please what?" Katherine asked.

"Have a quiet meal, young lady."

"Why? Did Dad have another rough day watching TV?"

"That'll do."

Matt said, "Dad watches more TV than we do."

"That's *enough*."

Frankie's father cleared his throat. "I don't know how you'd know that because you're never home during the day."

"I'm just saying," Matt said. "It was on when I left and it was on when I got home."

Frankie's mother set her fork down. "You'll clean up that sass mouth, Mr. Man, or you'll spend the rest of the summer in your room, with no television at all."

Matt was silent for a moment. Then he said, "Fine with me." He reached out to the Parmesan cheese shaker and picked at its green foil wrapper with his fingernail. "Maybe I'll just hitchhike up to Utica and spend the summer with my real dad."

Matt and Katherine had a second father who lived up north. Frankie didn't understand it, and he'd been told, by his mother, that he didn't need to.

"*Hitchhike?*" his mother asked Matt.

"Yeah." Matt stared at the cheese shaker. "Up to Utica."

She looked down and turned her spaghetti with a fork. "As if he'd want to see you."

Frankie's father leaned over his plate. "It just so happens that *fake* dad, here, has been busy. I've been working with Frankie on a little home improvement project."

Joe looked at Frankie and crossed his eyes.

"Can kids get married?" Frankie asked.

His mother set her fork down and touched her temple. "What are you talking about?"

"Me and Jennifer. We want to get married and be an explorer team that investigates Bigfoots."

Katherine and Joe broke into laughter. "Good one!" Katherine said, and Joe held up an imaginary scorecard: "Ten points!" Katherine leaned into Frankie. "I mean, that would be like marrying your *grandmother.*"

"Enough!" Frankie's mother nearly shouted. "Enough, enough, enough!"

The next day his father watched the news all morning and through lunch. When he and Frankie had finished their sandwiches, he changed out of his pajamas into shorts and a white T-shirt, walked out to the storeroom at the end of the carport, and came back into the living room with a shovel. "Time to get to work," he said.

They walked to the end of their block and down the next street, where a little concrete bridge crossed a ditch into the next neighborhood. His father smoked along the way, occasionally tapping the blade of the shovel against the sidewalk. At Mr. Krieger's house, he let Frankie hold the shovel and knocked on the door. This time Mr. Krieger came out wearing only his bathing suit. His chest was broad and pale and covered with gray hairs, and he had a can of beer in his hand. "AC died," he told Frankie's father. "How's that for timing?"

"Real bad," Frankie's father said.

Mr. Krieger looked down at Frankie. "You must be who is it. Joseph."

"I'm Frankie," Frankie said.

Mr. Krieger said, "I don't know, Roy. It's not looking good out there. The Apollo program's been dying a slow death for a while now, but the big boys are finally starting to get scared. I thought they'd take a few of us back, maybe pawn us off on Quality Control. But it's a contract situation. Technicolor's shaking in its boots."

Frankie's father nodded. "I thought we'd borrow that truck now, if it's all right."

Mr. Krieger sucked his teeth. He took the keys from a hook inside the door and handed them over. "Take your time with it. I'm not going anywhere."

The truck was old and noisy and dirty. Its grille was speckled with smashed love bugs. Frankie's half of the wide front seat was swollen and bounced him up and down in front of the glove compartment. They took the road that ran behind the two neighborhoods and alongside the patch of swamp, then followed the edge of the swamp to where the Publix sat at the corner of the mall parking lot. Behind the Publix was a small, sandy jut of land that stuck out like an elbow into Newfound Harbor and was dotted with palmetto bushes. Frankie's father slowed the truck down and turned off the pavement into the sand. He rolled forward a little ways, looking out both sides of the cab, humming to himself. Then he shut off the engine. "Let's steal some beach," he said, opening his door.

It wasn't a beach; the sand dropped almost immediately into the brown-green water of the inlet, and there was no place where Frankie would have wanted to put a blanket. He stood at the back of the truck and watched his father open the tailgate and then stab the shovel into the ground and toss a blade's worth of sand into the bed, where it scattered across the ribbed metal. "You watch the road for cops," he directed, winking at Frankie. "What we're doing is technically illegal. There's nothing wrong with it, we're just relocating a little bit of land, but the cops wouldn't see it that way."

He scooped and tossed, slowly covering the bottom of the truck bed.

After a while, he said, "There's a man I know up at the Space Center, his name is Mr. Swilly, and he used to work at the Chamber of Commerce. He's seen pictures of Merritt Island when it was nothing but swamp. Then people came along and did just what we're doing. They relocated soil — brought it over from Cocoa and spread it around so they could build houses and roads." He looked at Frankie. "Mr. Swilly told me something else, too. You know what this whole island used to be covered with?"

Frankie glanced toward the road. He shook his head.

"Take a guess," his father said.

"Cops."

"Nope." His father kept shoveling. "You're just one letter off, though. *Cows*. It was cattle country. There were ranchers who used to let their cows just wander through the swamp. You know that big, concrete bridge we take to get into Cocoa? It used to be just a little wooden bridge. When it came time to take the cows away, they'd round them up and herd them across that bridge. A cattle drive right across the Indian River. Can you imagine that?" He was starting to breathe heavily. His arms and neck were shiny with sweat. "We went from land cowboys to space cowboys, all on the same island," he said. His T-shirt had turned flesh-colored. "What kind of cowboys do you think will come next?"

Frankie looked at the truck bed. It wasn't even half-filled. He said, "Sea cowboys."

His father snapped his head to get the sweat off his face. "We already have those. They're called sailors."

"Sky cowboys?"

"We have them, too — airline pilots," he said. "There may not be any cowboys left."

It took a long time to fill the truck bed. Frankie sat down on the ground and was drawing Bigfoot prints in the sand with his finger when his father announced that they were finished and motioned him back into the cab. On the way home they stopped at the Minute Mart and got Freezies. Frankie's father pinched his cup between his legs so that he could steer the truck and shift gears at the same time. Glancing at Frankie across the wide, bulging front seat, he said, "I don't know about you, but I'm having fun."

At home, he unloaded the sand at the side of the carport. Then they went back for another load. They kept Mr. Krieger's truck overnight, and the following day they did it all over again, twice, only this time when they got home he drove the truck right up onto the lawn at the opposite end of the house and shoveled both loads of sand over the fence into the backyard. The mound reached halfway to Katherine's bedroom window.

All his father would tell any of them, when they asked about the sand, was that it was part of the project he and Frankie were working on. They were a team, he said, and it was a secret.

"So," Katherine said to Frankie that night while he was brushing his teeth, "fess up."

"Huh?" Frankie said through a mouthful of toothpaste.

She took hold of the skin over his Adam's apple and twisted it. "What's with all the sand, dingus?"

"I don't know!" He leaned into her hand and dipped his head, dripping toothpaste down his chin.

Matt walked into the bathroom and reached around the two of them for his hairbrush.

"He won't talk," Katherine said.

"Let him go. Talk about what?"

She let go of Frankie's throat and wiped a drop of toothpaste from her arm onto his shirt. "The sand."

"I don't know anything!" Frankie said.

"Who cares about the sand?" Matt looked at himself in the mirror. He drew the hairbrush across each side of his head, reestablishing his part. "I'm just glad he's not my real dad. No job. No friends. *And* he voted for Nixon."

Frankie asked his father the next day if he could *please* go to Mrs. Woodrow's house to play with Jennifer. His father looked irritated. "We're a team. You're not going to quit on me now, are you?" He got Frankie a can of Pix soda and handed him an entire bag of potato chips and told him to sit on the front porch and keep an eye out for squad cars. Frankie sat in the middle of the porch and ate the potato chips while his father distributed the first two piles of sand across the lawn one shovelful at a time.

"So," Frankie's mother said when they were all at the table that night, her eyes tired-looking and her mouth bent into a smile, "I thought it might be nice if your father told us about what's happening with the yard." She shrugged as if it didn't matter one way or the other.

"We're replenishing the soil," he said. He glanced around the table as if he were waiting for an argument, or a burst of laughter. "This island's technically three feet below sea level. I don't know if you know that. There's a lot of dampness in the ground, and then we get all that rain on top of it. Over time, the soil gets washed away and the roots get exposed, so the soil needs to be replenished. I've researched this."

"Don't the Petersons have the same soil we do?" Matt asked.

"Yes."

"Their grass looks great. It's like a golf course."

"That's because the Petersons have WonderLawn come out and hose their yard down with expensive chemicals. And their grass is St. Augustine. Ours is Bahaya. It's thinner."

"And," Frankie's mother said, shrugging again, "how long will the sand be there?"

"Until it sinks into the ground. It's for the *soil.* It'll sink in on its own, and the grass will look a thousand times better." He reached for a slice of bread. "Two weeks, tops."

The next day was devoted to distributing the two remaining piles of sand over the backyard. Frankie knew by now that it was no use asking if he could go anywhere. His father told him after breakfast that it was another project day for the two of them, and that it was Frankie's job to sit on the back patio and keep an eye out for police helicopters while he worked. Frankie didn't see any helicopters, or police of any kind, though later that afternoon several neighbors slowed their cars down while passing the house and stared at the sand-covered lawn as if they were witnessing a crime, or an accident. One of the cars belonged to Mrs. Woodrow. She rolled to a stop next to the sidewalk and brought down the passenger window. "Hello, Frankie," she said. "We're just on our way home from the doctor's. It was checkup day. What on earth's happened to your yard?"

"We're fixing the soil," Frankie said. He looked at Jennifer in the back seat and waved. She waved back, then scooted over to the open window and leaned out, peering at the lawn from under the bill of her cap. She said, "There's *sand* all over the grass."

"I know," Frankie said. "My dad says it's good for it."
"That's stupid. Grass needs sunlight. Anyone knows that."
"Frankie," Mrs. Woodrow said, "we miss having you around. Come back and see us."
"I'll try," Frankie said.
The window went up and the car began to roll. Frankie waved again as they rounded the corner.

The sand remained right where it was. The sky was clear and the air stayed hot, day after day, until what little grass there was, poking above the surface, began to curl and turn brown. His father added a soap opera to his afternoons, and several times a day he got up and stood at the front window, or at the sliding glass doors that opened onto the backyard, smoking and staring outside. They were sitting on the couch when they heard a rumble in the distance that grew until it nearly blocked out the sound of the TV. The door knocker rattled like a telegraph knob. Frankie looked toward the front window, then at his father. His father's eyes didn't leave the screen, but his nose twitched and his nostrils flared, and, as if he'd identified the rocket by smell alone, he said, "Weather satellite."

One morning, after Matt, Joe, and Katherine had cleared out of the house, he stood in the kitchen talking to Frankie's mother, who was calling from work, and Frankie heard him say that he'd figured out the lawn problem, and that he and Frankie were going to get to work on it that day. "We just haven't had enough rain, that's all. If this were last summer, with all the rain we had, everything would be fine. But we're going to take care of it — give it a little jump-start. We're working out a whole sprinkler thing." He paused, listening. He began tapping a finger against the kitchen counter. "Teresa, I go through that paper every day," he said. "But the fact is, there's nothing out there . . . Yes, I do . . . Yes, I have, but it's not going to happen overnight. That's a lot of people they let go, and there are only so many jobs in one county. I mean, I'm looking at a whole career change. Do you really want to get into this now? Here, talk to Frankie." He waved Frankie over to the phone.

"Hi," Frankie said into the receiver.
"Hi, honey," his mother said. "Are you having fun?"
"I guess," Frankie said.
"Can I talk to your father?"
Frankie held up the phone.

They drove to the hardware store and bought a sprinkler that sat on a spike and spit water and shook its head *no* continuously.

The sand turned to mud, dried out, and turned to mud again; but it didn't go anywhere.

His father still made Frankie sandwiches for lunch but stopped making them for himself, grazing instead on whatever snack foods he found in the cabinets. Some nights he didn't eat dinner with the rest of the family, claiming he wasn't hungry, and there were mornings when Frankie came out into the living room and found him asleep on the couch.

One evening, just after they'd finished a meal without him, Frankie's mother was doing the dishes and his father walked into the kitchen and started eating a piece of bologna. A fight broke out. They didn't hit each other; they just yelled, and then whispered, and then yelled for a long time. Katherine and Matt closed themselves up in their bedrooms and turned on their record players, and Joe dropped down onto his bed to read a comic book, but Frankie stood and listened in the doorway of the room they shared. He heard his mother shouting about how embarrassed she was, how tired she was, how frightened, and his father shouting about which boat he was in, what didn't fly with him, what was driving him up a tree. Frankie waited to hear the word *sand*, but he never did.

His father yanked at the garden hose and stretched it across the yard until the sweep of the sprinkler was just short of the fence. He dodged the water, making footprints in the sand. A neighbor came out of the house behind them and walked slowly over to the chainlink fence that ran between the two yards. He was old. His head hovered in front of his body, between his shoulders. He pointed at the sand and started talking to Frankie's father. Frankie couldn't make out anything the old man was saying, but eventually his father straightened up, dried his hands on his pants, and folded his arms, listening.

Frankie was stretched out flat on the patio. He closed his eyes for a while and looked at the sun through his lids; then he rolled onto his side and turned a SuperBall in front of his face and sang *The Big Blue Marble* song. Finally, he got up and walked to the side of the house, where the gate stood open and a thin band of living grass ran between the fence posts. Lifting his arms out in front of him, his fingertips stretched toward the street, he stepped over the grass and, as if hypnotized, walked across the sandy front yard until he'd reached the sidewalk.

Two streets later he was at Jennifer's house. He rang the bell, and she answered the door wearing a plastic Viking helmet. "Who brought you?" she asked, looking past him down the driveway.

"Nobody."

"Oh. I'm Poseidon, Ruler of Atlantis. Do you want to be the citizens?"

Atlantis was at the bottom of the tub in her bathroom. She'd filled the tub with water and submerged several overturned cereal bowls and coffee cups, along with the upright, plastic cover for the tissue box, and grouped them together to make a city. Lined up along the edge of the tub were the citizens: wavy-armed, rubber finger puppets from the quarter machines at the grocery store, plastic monster figurines she'd gotten out of cereal boxes, a Pez dispenser with a clown head. Frankie knelt down on the floor next to the tub, and Jennifer sat on the lid of the toilet. "Poseidon's problem is that the citizens are being unruly," she said. "They're refusing to stay underwater." She reached over and flicked one of the monsters into the tub. It sank an inch or so, but then rose to the surface. Frankie poked at it with his finger.

"See?" Jennifer said. "That behavior is unacceptable. There's a curfew, and everyone is supposed to be indoors, asleep."

Frankie put on one of the finger puppets and jiggled it up and down, making its rubber arms flap. In a high, squeaky voice, he said, "We can't help it!"

"Yes, you can," Jennifer said. "You're being unruly, and you're all going to be punished."

"Have mercy!" Frankie said, jiggling the puppet. "Give us one more chance!"

"Poseidon is not a patient god," Jennifer replied.

Frankie looked at the submerged city, and at the row of citizens. He reached into the water, covered the opening in the tissue box, and tilted it back. With his other hand he took the citizens one by one and made them jump into the water and swim under the bottom edge of the box. When they were all inside, he replaced his hand with one of the overturned coffee cups, so that the cup became a domed roof. He sat back, then, his hands dripping, and smiled proudly.

"Poseidon is not pleased," Jennifer said.

"Why?"

"Because you've changed the whole kingdom around without permission."

"Just one building."

"It's a serious offense," she decreed. "I'm afraid everyone will have to be banished to the Outer Sea."

"Where's that?"

"Gather your people," she said, "and follow me."

Frankie pretended to weep as he removed the cup and the citizens rose to the surface. He collected them in one of the cereal bowls and followed Jennifer out to the backyard.

Mrs. Woodrow had just gotten out of the pool when they climbed the metal steps. Her book and her iced tea cup were on the deck next to the ladder, and the tire-shaped raft was drifting away from the side. She took her towel from the white, metal railing and wrapped it around her body just below her arms. "Hello, Frankie," she said, pushing her sunglasses up the bridge of her nose. "I didn't know you were here."

"He's leading the citizens of Atlantis to the shores of the Outer Sea, by order of Poseidon," Jennifer said. "They're all being banished."

"All right, then," Mrs. Woodrow said. "Would you kids like something to eat?"

Frankie nodded.

"I'll make PBJs." She carried her book and her cup down the steps and disappeared into the house.

"Phineas L. Wigglethorp," Jennifer proclaimed.

"Who's that?" Frankie asked.

"The first citizen to be banished. We're doing it one by one."

Frankie looked into the bowl. He took one of the finger puppets and tossed it into the middle of the pool.

"William B. Kootchapapa," Jennifer said.

They kept on until the bowl was empty. Then, because Jennifer deemed that punishment not severe enough, they took turns holding the citizens down against the bottom with the pool net. Mrs. Woodrow reappeared, still wrapped in her towel and carrying a tray that held two sandwiches, two glasses of Kool-Aid, and a bowl of potato chips. She set the tray on the picnic table next to the patio, called them over, and went back into the house.

They were eating when Frankie's father came into the backyard through the side gate. He was walking slowly, holding a cigarette down next to his hip, with his head cocked as if he were listening for a particular sound. When he spotted Frankie, he frowned open-mouthed.

"What are you doing?" he asked.

Frankie felt his stomach tighten up. He swallowed and said, "Eating."

"You just walked over here, without saying anything?"

"You were talking to that old man."

"So you just *left*? You don't do that! What were you thinking? How was I supposed to know where you were?"

"He's eating his lunch," Jennifer said. She was still wearing the Viking helmet. The horns teetered as she gazed up at him.

"No, he's not. He's done."

Frankie pushed the last bite of sandwich into his mouth.

"He hasn't finished his potato chips," Jennifer said. She dug into the bowl and took a small handful of chips and dropped them onto Frankie's plate.

"Stop that," his father said.

"You're not the boss of me," she said.

Frankie glanced up nervously. His father's face was drawn tight against his skull.

The Viking helmet tipped forward, and Jennifer reached up to lift it away from her eyes. "How come you're killing your lawn? You *are* killing it, you know. Grass needs sunlight. And air."

"You don't know what you're talking about."

"No plant can live buried under a bunch of sand." She dropped another handful of chips onto Frankie's plate.

"*Stop* that," his father said. "Frankie, I'm not going to tell you again — "

Just then the back door opened, and Mrs. Woodrow stepped out, holding the chlorine tester in one hand.

"Who are you?"

"I'm Frankie's father."

"Oh! You're Mr. Kerrigan," she said. "I'm Jill Woodrow. It's nice to finally meet you." She stepped across the patio, extending her free hand.

"Let's go," Frankie's father said to him. "I don't know what you were thinking, coming over here, but you're in big trouble."

Mrs. Woodrow lowered her hand. "He's been perfectly well behaved."

"Excuse me, but — I'm talking to my son. And no, he hasn't been well behaved, because he left the house without permission, and I didn't know where he was."

"He isn't through *eating*," Jennifer told her mother. "Does he have to go with this lawn-killer?"

"*Frankie,*" his father said. He put the cigarette in a corner of his mouth and set his hand on Frankie's shoulder.

Frankie felt his eyes going damp. "I'm not finished yet."

"Well, then, I'm going to stand here until you decide just how much trouble you want to be in."

"I'm sorry," Mrs. Woodrow said, approaching the other end of the picnic table, "but I don't allow smoking around my daughter."

Frankie's father frowned, causing the cigarette to droop. Around it he said, "We're outside."

"She doesn't have a normal resistance to pollution, and I don't allow smoking anywhere in my house, or on my property. It's a rule."

"A rule," his father said. He inhaled through the cigarette, then blew smoke around his words. "You know, if you're so concerned about kids, you might think to call us when our son just shows up by himself, without an adult."

"I think," Mrs. Woodrow said, "that I do a *very* good job of baby-sitting your son and that it's your responsibility to make sure he stays in your house when you're home with him. Now would you *please* put out that cigarette?"

His father peeled his lips back and in one swift motion plucked the cigarette from his teeth as if it had roots, threw it down onto the grass, and stepped on it.

Jennifer put a single chip onto Frankie's plate.

"That's it," his father said. "Come on."

Frankie ate the chip.

She dug into the bowl again and brought another chip across the table. His father was reaching down to haul Frankie up by the arm, but he hissed, "*Stop* it," and closed his hand over Jennifer's arm instead.

"Hey!" Mrs. Woodrow snapped.

He let go.

Jennifer looked startled. She pulled her hand back and looked at Frankie and stuck the chip into her mouth.

"You don't touch my daughter!"

"I didn't hurt her," Frankie's father said.

"Who do you think you are? Do you realize how frail she is?" Mrs. Woodrow stepped forward, waving the chlorine tester in front of her body. "Get off my property!"

"Jesus," his father said. And then, more loudly, "That's what I'm trying to do."

"Then go!"

Frankie looked across the table at Jennifer. "Bye," he said.

"Bye," Jennifer said. The expression on her face, dwarfed by the Viking helmet, made her look different to Frankie. For the first time, she looked more like a little girl than an old lady.

His father tapped the back of his head, and he got up from the picnic table.

They didn't talk during the short ride home. In their driveway his father turned off the car, but instead of getting out, he just sat there, one hand resting on top of the steering wheel, his gaze fixed on something beyond Frankie's side window.

Frankie said, "Sorry."

"You know," his father said, "I'm just trying to do my job here."

Frankie nodded.

"You're the one who's supposed to stick around. You're the one I can depend on. Your brothers and your sister, every day they're off somewhere — "

"They're allowed," Frankie said.

"Yes. *They're* allowed. But you're not, because you're not old enough. And you know that. I thought we had a project going on here. I thought we were a team."

"Is Mrs. Woodrow still my babysitter?"

His father slid his palm back and forth across the top of the steering wheel. He tilted his head to one side and rifled air through his nose. "I don't think so, Frankie. That woman . . . if her daughter . . .

what's her name? Jennifer? If she's so sick, then maybe it's not such a good idea for you to be playing with her."

"She's not sick," Frankie said. "Mom said she wasn't sick."

His father blinked and looked at him, one brow hitched up. "She *is* sick. You should know that, Frankie. She has an illness. It makes her very old, even though she's just a little girl."

"Will she get better?"

"I don't think so," his father said, frowning. "Plus, you saw what just happened. People like that, if you hurt them? Even by accident? They'll sue you. You know what that means? They'll take you to court. The cops will come, and they'll take you to court and *make* you give people like that a whole lot of money. And if you don't have a whole lot of money, then what do you do?"

Frankie didn't know the answer to the question. His father was looking past him again, out the passenger side of the car, at the sand-covered lawn and the row of houses beyond it.

"I don't want to be on your team," Frankie said.

His father pulled his focus in and looked at him as if he'd uttered a swear word. "Get in the house. We'll talk about this later."

Frankie stayed where he was.

"Go on," his father said. "Get in the house." Frankie didn't move. His father reached down and unbuckled Frankie's seat belt for him. Then he stretched over, unlatched the passenger door, and shoved it open.

Frankie didn't want to stay in the car; he didn't want to go inside, either. He didn't feel like doing anything his father told him to do.

Finally, growling under his breath, his father opened his own door and got out of the car.

But instead of going into the house, he walked out to the middle of the yard and stood with his back to Frankie and the driveway. Surrounded by sand, he looked like a man standing on a beach.

A breeze moved through the open windows of the car. Frankie smelled salt in the air. He imagined he heard the sound of the ocean carried on the breeze. The citizens of Atlantis had been sad as they'd stood on the shore and heard their names called out, one by one, but his father didn't look sad. He looked angry and impatient. He had his hands on his hips and was tapping a foot against the sand, as if ready to march into the waters of the Outer Sea the next time someone said his name.

BENJAMIN PERCY

Refresh, Refresh

FROM THE PARIS REVIEW

WHEN SCHOOL LET OUT the two of us went to my backyard to fight. We were trying to make each other tougher. So in the grass, in the shade of the pines and junipers, Gordon and I slung off our backpacks and laid down a pale green garden hose, tip to tip, making a ring. Then we stripped off our shirts and put on our gold-colored boxing gloves and fought.

Every round went two minutes. If you stepped out of the ring, you lost. If you cried, you lost. If you got knocked out or if you yelled stop, you lost. Afterward we drank Coca-Colas and smoked Marlboros, our chests heaving, our faces all different shades of blacks and reds and yellows.

We began fighting after Seth Johnson — a no-neck linebacker with teeth like corn kernels and hands like T-bone steaks — beat Gordon until his face swelled and split open and purpled around the edges. Eventually he healed, the rough husks of scabs peeling away to reveal a different face from the one I remembered — older, squarer, fiercer, his left eyebrow separated by a gummy white scar. It was his idea that we should fight each other. He wanted to be ready. He wanted to hurt those who hurt him. And if he went down, he would go down swinging as he was sure his father would. This is what we all wanted: to please our fathers, to make them proud, even though they had left us.

This was in Crow, Oregon, a high desert town in the foothills of the Cascade Mountains. In Crow we have fifteen hundred people, a Dairy Queen, a BP gas station, a Food4Less, a meatpacking plant, a bright green football field irrigated by canal water, and your standard assortment of taverns and churches. Nothing distinguishes us from Bend or Redmond or La Pine or any of the other nowhere towns off Route 97, except for this: we are home to the Second Battalion, Thirty-fourth Marines.

The marines live on a fifty-acre base in the hills just outside of town, a collection of one-story cinder-block buildings interrupted by cheatgrass and sagebrush. Throughout my childhood I could hear, if I cupped a hand to my ear, the lowing of bulls, the bleating of sheep, and the report of assault rifles shouting from the hilltops. It's said that conditions here in Oregon's ranch country closely match the mountainous terrain of Afghanistan and northern Iraq.

Our fathers — Gordon's and mine — were like the other fathers in Crow. All of them, just about, had enlisted as part-time soldiers, as reservists, for drill pay: several thousand a year for a private and several thousand more for a sergeant. Beer pay, they called it, and for two weeks every year plus one weekend a month, they trained. They threw on their cammies and filled their rucksacks and kissed us good-bye, and the gates of the Second Battalion drew closed behind them.

Our fathers would vanish into the pine-studded hills, returning to us Sunday night with their faces reddened from weather, their biceps trembling from fatigue, and their hands smelling of rifle grease. They would talk about ECPs and PRPs and MEUs and WMDs and they would do pushups in the middle of the living room and they would call six o'clock "eighteen hundred hours" and they would high-five and yell, "Semper fi." Then a few days would pass, and they would go back to the way they were, to the men we knew: Coors-drinking, baseball-throwing, crotch-scratching, Aqua Velva–smelling fathers.

No longer. In January the battalion was activated, and in March they shipped off for Iraq. Our fathers — our coaches, our teachers, our barbers, our cooks, our gas station attendants and UPS deliverymen and deputies and firemen and mechanics — our fathers, so many of them, climbed onto the olive green school buses and pressed their palms to the windows and gave us the bravest, most hopeful smiles you can imagine and vanished. Just like that.

Nights, I sometimes got on my Honda dirt bike and rode through the hills and canyons of Deschutes County. Beneath me the engine growled and shuddered, while all around me the wind, like something alive, bullied me, tried to drag me from my bike. A dark world slipped past as I downshifted, leaning into a turn, and accelerated on a straightaway — my speed seventy, then eighty — concentrating only on the twenty yards of road glowing ahead of me.

On this bike I could ride and ride and ride, away from here, up and over the Cascades, through the Willamette Valley, until I reached the ocean, where the broad black backs of whales regularly broke the surface of the water, and even farther — farther still — until I caught up with the horizon, where my father would be waiting. Inevitably, I ended up at Hole in the Ground.

A long time ago a meteor came screeching down from space and left behind a crater five thousand feet wide and three hundred feet deep. Hole in the Ground is frequented during the winter by the daredevil sledders among us and during the summer by bearded geologists interested in the metal fragments strewn across its bottom. I dangled my feet over the edge of the crater and leaned back on my elbows and took in the black sky — no moon, only stars — just a little lighter than a raven. Every few minutes a star seemed to come unstuck, streaking through the night in a bright flash that burned into nothingness.

In the near distance Crow glowed grayish green against the darkness — a reminder of how close to oblivion we lived. A chunk of space ice or a solar wind could have jogged the meteor sideways and rather than landing here it could have landed there at the intersection of Main and Farwell. No Dairy Queen, no Crow High, no Second Battalion. It didn't take much imagination to realize how something can drop out of the sky and change everything.

This was in October, when Gordon and I circled each other in the backyard after school. We wore our golden boxing gloves, cracked with age and flaking when we pounded them together. Browned grass crunched beneath our sneakers, and dust rose in little puffs like distress signals.

Gordon was thin to the point of being scrawny. His collarbone poked against his skin like a swallowed coat hanger. His head was too big for his body, and his eyes were too big for his head, and football players — Seth Johnson among them — regularly tossed him into garbage cans and called him E.T.

He had had a bad day. And I could tell from the look on his face

— the watery eyes, the trembling lips that revealed in quick flashes his buckteeth — that he wanted, he *needed,* to hit me. So I let him. I raised my gloves to my face and pulled my elbows against my ribs and Gordon lunged forward, his arms snapping like rubber bands. I stood still, allowing his fists to work up and down my body, allowing him to throw the weight of his anger on me, until eventually he grew too tired to hit anymore and I opened up my stance and floored him with a right cross to the temple. He lay there, sprawled out in the grass with a small smile on his E.T. face. "Damn," he said in a dreamy voice. A drop of blood gathered along the corner of his eye and streaked down his temple into his hair.

My father wore steel-toed boots, Carhartt jeans, and a T-shirt advertising some place he had traveled to, maybe Yellowstone or Seattle. He looked like someone you might see shopping for motor oil at Bi-Mart. To hide his receding hairline he wore a John Deere cap that laid a shadow across his face. His brown eyes blinked above a considerable nose underlined by a gray mustache. Like me, my father was short and squat, a bulldog. His belly was a swollen bag, and his shoulders were broad, good for carrying me during parades and at fairs when I was younger. He laughed a lot. He liked game shows. He drank too much beer and smoked too many cigarettes and spent too much time with his buddies, fishing, hunting, bullshitting, which probably had something to do with why my mother divorced him and moved to Boise with a hairdresser and triathlete named Chuck.

At first, after my father left, like all of the other fathers, he would e-mail whenever he could. He would tell me about the heat, the gallons of water he drank every day, the sand that got into everything, the baths he took with baby wipes. He would tell me how safe he was, how very safe. This was when he was stationed in Turkey. Then the reservists shipped for Kirkuk, where insurgents and sandstorms attacked almost daily. The e-mails came less frequently. Weeks of silence passed between them.

Sometimes, on the computer, I would hit refresh, refresh, *refresh,* hoping. In October I received an e-mail that read: "Hi, Josh. I'm O.K. Don't worry. Do your homework. Love, Dad." I printed it and hung it on my door with a piece of Scotch tape.

For twenty years my father worked at Nosier, Inc. — the bullet manufacturer based out of Bend — and the Marines trained him as an ammunition technician. Gordon liked to say his father was a gunnery sergeant, and he was, but we all knew he was also the battalion mess manager, a cook, which was how he made his living in Crow, tending the grill at Hamburger Patty's. We knew their titles, but we didn't know, not really, what their titles meant, what our fathers *did* over there. We imagined them doing heroic things: rescuing Iraqi babies from burning huts, sniping suicide bombers before they could detonate on a crowded city street. We drew on Hollywood and TV news to develop elaborate scenarios where maybe, at twilight, during a trek through the mountains of northern Iraq, bearded insurgents ambushed our fathers with rocket launchers. We imagined them silhouetted by a fiery explosion. We imagined them burrowing into the sand like lizards and firing their M-16s, their bullets streaking through the darkness like the meteorites I observed on sleepless nights.

When Gordon and I fought we painted our faces — black and green and brown — with the camo grease our fathers left behind. It made our eyes and teeth appear startlingly white. And it smeared away against our gloves just as the grass smeared away beneath our sneakers — and the ring became a circle of dirt, the dirt a reddish color that looked a lot like scabbed flesh. One time Gordon hammered my shoulder so hard I couldn't lift my arm for a week. Another time I elbowed one of his kidneys, and he peed blood. We struck each other with such force and frequency that the golden gloves crumbled and our knuckles showed through the sweat-soaked, blood-soaked foam like teeth through a busted lip. So we bought another set of gloves, and as the air grew steadily colder we fought with steam blasting from our mouths.

Our fathers had left us, but men remained in Crow. There were old men, like my grandfather, whom I lived with — men who had paid their dues, who had worked their jobs and fought their wars and now spent their days at the gas station, drinking bad coffee from Styrofoam cups, complaining about the weather, arguing about the best months to reap alfalfa. And there were incapable men. Men who rarely shaved and watched daytime television in their once white underpants. Men who lived in trailers and filled their shopping carts with Busch Light, summer sausage, Oreo cookies.

And then there were vulturous men like Dave Lightener — men who scavenged whatever our fathers had left behind. Dave Lightener worked as a recruitment officer. I'm guessing he was the only recruitment officer in world history who drove a Vespa scooter with a Support Our Troops ribbon magnet on its rear. We sometimes saw it parked outside the homes of young women whose husbands had gone to war. Dave had big ears and small eyes and wore his hair in your standard-issue high-and-tight buzz. He often spoke in a too loud voice about all the insurgents he gunned down when working a Fallujah patrol unit. He lived with his mother in Crow, but spent his days in Bend and Redmond trolling the parking lots of Best Buy, ShopKo, Kmart, Wal-Mart, Mountain View Mall. He was looking for people like us, people who were angry and dissatisfied and poor.

But Dave Lightener knew better than to bother us. On duty he stayed away from Crow entirely. Recruiting there would be too much like poaching the burned section of forest where deer, rib-slatted and wobbly legged, nosed through the ash, seeking something green.

We didn't fully understand the reason our fathers were fighting. We understood only that they *had* to fight. The necessity of it made the reason irrelevant. "It's all part of the game," my grandfather said. "It's just the way it is." We could only cross our fingers and wish on stars and hit refresh, *refresh,* hoping that they would return to us, praying that we would never find Dave Lightener on our porch uttering the words *I regret to inform you . . .*

One time, my grandfather dropped Gordon and me off at Mountain View Mall, and there, near the glass-doored entrance, stood Dave Lightener. He wore his creased khaki uniform and spoke with a group of Mexican teenagers. They were laughing, shaking their heads and walking away from him as we approached. We had our hats pulled low, and he didn't recognize us.

"Question for you, gentlemen," he said in the voice of telemarketers and door-to-door Jehovah's Witnesses. "What do you plan on doing with your lives?"

Gordon pulled off his hat with a flourish, as if he were part of some *ta-da!* magic act and his face was the trick. "I plan on killing some crazy-ass Muslims," he said and forced a smile. "How about you, Josh?"

"Yeah," I said. "Kill some people, then get myself killed." I grimaced even as I played along. "That sounds like a good plan."

Dave Lightener's lips tightened into a thin line, his posture straightened, and he asked us what we thought our fathers would think, hearing us right now. "They're out there risking their lives, defending our freedom, and you're cracking sick jokes," he said. "I think that's sick."

We hated him for his soft hands and clean uniform. We hated him because he sent people like us off to die. Because at twenty-three he had attained a higher rank than our fathers. Because he slept with the lonely wives of soldiers. And now we hated him even more for making us feel ashamed. I wanted to say something sarcastic, but Gordon was quicker. His hand was out before him, his fingers gripping an imaginary bottle. "Here's your maple syrup," he said.

Dave said, "And what is that for?"

"To eat my ass with," Gordon said.

Right then a skateboarder type with green hair and a nose ring walked from the mall, a bagful of DVDs swinging from his fist, and Dave Lightener forgot us. "Hey, friend," he was saying. "Let me ask you something. Do you like war movies?"

In November we drove our dirt bikes deep into the woods to hunt. Sunlight fell through tall pines and birch clusters and lay in puddles along the logging roads that wound past the hillsides packed with huckleberries and on the moraines where coyotes scurried, trying to flee from us and slipping, causing tiny avalanches of loose rock. It hadn't rained in nearly a month, so the crabgrass and the cheatgrass and the pine needles had lost their color, as dry and blond as cornhusks, crackling beneath my boots when the road we followed petered out into nothing and I stepped off my bike. In this waterless stillness, it seemed you could hear every chipmunk within a square acre rustling for pine nuts, and when the breeze rose into a cold wind the forest became a giant whisper.

We dumped our tent and our sleeping bags near a basalt grotto with a spring bubbling from it, and Gordon said, "Let's go, troops," holding his rifle before his chest diagonally, as a soldier would. He dressed as a soldier would too, wearing his father's overlarge cammies rather than the mandatory blaze-orange gear. Fifty feet apart, we worked our way downhill through the forest, through a huckleberry thicket, through a clear-cut crowded with stumps, taking care not to make much noise or slip on the pine needles carpeting the ground. A chipmunk worrying at a pinecone screeched its astonishment when a peregrine falcon swooped down and seized it, carrying it off between the trees to some secret place. Its wings made no sound, and neither did the blaze-orange-clad hunter when he appeared in a clearing several hundred yards below us.

Gordon made some sort of SWAT-team gesture — meant, I think, to say, stay low — and I made my way carefully toward him. From behind a boulder we peered through our scopes, tracking the hunter, who looked, in his vest and earflapped hat, like a monstrous pumpkin. "That cocksucker," Gordon said in a harsh whisper. The hunter was Seth Johnson. His rifle was strapped to his back and his mouth was moving — he was talking to someone. At the corner of the meadow he joined four members of the varsity football squad, who sat on logs around a smoldering campfire, their arms bobbing like oil pump jacks as they brought their beers to their mouths.

I took my eye from my scope and noticed Gordon fingering the trigger of his 30.06. I told him to quit fooling around, and he pulled his hand suddenly away from the stock and smiled guiltily and said he just wanted to know what it felt like having that power over someone. Then his trigger finger rose up and touched the gummy white scar that split his eyebrow. "I say we fuck with them a little."

I shook my head no.

Gordon said, "Just a little — to scare them."

"They've got guns," I said, and he said, "So we'll come back tonight."

Later, after an early dinner of beef jerky and trail mix and Gatorade, I happened upon a four-point stag nibbling on some bear grass, and I rested my rifle on a stump and shot it, and it stumbled backwards and collapsed with a rose blooming from behind its shoulder where the heart was hidden. Gordon came running, and we stood around the deer and smoked a few cigarettes, watching the thick arterial blood run from its mouth. Then we took out our knives and got to work. I cut around the anus, cutting away the penis and testes, and then ran the knife along the belly, unzipping the hide to reveal the delicate pink flesh and greenish vessels into which our hands disappeared.

The blood steamed in the cold mountain air, and when we finished — when we'd skinned the deer and hacked at its joints and cut out its back strap and boned out its shoulders and hips, its neck and ribs, making chops, roasts, steaks, quartering the meat so we could bundle it into our insulated saddlebags — Gordon picked up the deer head by the antlers and held it before his own. Blood from its neck made a pattering sound on the ground, and in the half-light of early evening Gordon began to do a little dance, bending his knees and stomping his feet.

"I think I've got an idea," he said, and he pretended to charge at me with the antlers. I pushed him away and he said, "Don't pussy out on me, Josh." I was exhausted and reeked of gore, but I could appreciate the need for revenge. "Just to scare them, right, Gordo?" I said.

"Right."

We lugged our meat back to camp, and Gordon brought the deer hide. He slit a hole in its middle and poked his head through so the hide hung off him loosely, a hairy sack, and I helped him smear mud and blood across his face. Then, with his Leatherman, he sawed off the antlers and held them in each hand and slashed at the air as if they were claws.

Night had come on, and the moon hung over the Cascades, grayly lighting our way as we crept through the forest imagining ourselves in enemy territory, with tripwires and guard towers and snarling dogs around every corner. From behind the boulder that overlooked their campsite, we observed our enemies as they swapped hunting stories and joked about Jessica Robertson's big-ass titties and passed around a bottle of whiskey and drank to excess and finally pissed on the fire to extinguish it. When they retired to their tents we waited an hour before making our way down the hill with such care that it took us another hour before we were upon them. Somewhere an owl hooted, its noise barely noticeable over the chorus of snores that rose from their tents. Seth's Bronco was parked nearby — the license plate read SMAN — and all their rifles lay in its cab. I collected the guns, slinging them over my shoulder, then I eased my knife into each of Seth's tires.

I still had my knife out when we were standing beside Seth's tent, and when a cloud scudded over the moon and made the meadow fully dark I stabbed the nylon and in one quick jerk opened up a slit. Gordon rushed in, his antler-claws slashing. I could see nothing but shadows, but I could hear Seth scream the scream of a little girl as Gordon raked at him with the antlers and hissed and howled like some cave creature hungry for man-flesh. When the tents around us came alive with confused voices, Gordon reemerged with a horrible smile on his face, and I followed him up the hillside, crashing through the undergrowth, leaving Seth to make sense of the nightmare that had descended upon him without warning.

Winter came. Snow fell, and we threw on our coveralls and wrenched on our studded tires and drove our dirt bikes to Hole in the Ground, dragging our sleds behind us with towropes. Our engines filled the white silence of the afternoon. Our back tires kicked up plumes of powder and on sharp turns slipped out beneath us, and we lay there in the middle of the road bleeding, laughing, unafraid.

Earlier, for lunch, we had cooked a pound of bacon with a stick of butter. The grease, which hardened into a white waxy pool, we used as polish, buffing it into the bottoms of our sleds. Speed was what we wanted at Hole in the Ground. We descended the steepest section of the crater into its heart, three hundred feet below us. We followed each other in the same track, ironing down the snow to create a chute, blue-hued and frictionless, that would allow us to travel at a speed equivalent to free fall. Our eyeballs glazed with frost, our ears roared with wind, and our stomachs rose into our throats as we rocketed down and felt as if we were five again — and then we began the slow climb back the way we came and felt fifty.

We wore crampons and ascended in a zigzagging series of switchbacks. It took nearly an hour. The air had begun to go purple with evening when we stood again at the lip of the crater, sweating in our coveralls, taking in the view through the fog of our breath. Gordon packed a snowball. I said, "You better not hit me with that." He cocked his arm threateningly and smiled, then dropped to his knees to roll the snowball into something bigger. He rolled it until it grew to the size of a large man curled into the fetal position. From the back of his bike he took the piece of garden hose he used to siphon gas from fancy foreign cars and he worked it into his tank, sucking at its end until gas flowed.

He doused the giant snowball as if he hoped it would sprout. It didn't melt — he'd packed it tight enough — but it puckered slightly and appeared leaden, and when Gordon withdrew his Zippo, sparked it, and held it toward the ball, the fumes caught flame and the whole thing erupted with a gasping noise that sent me staggering back a few steps.

Gordon rushed forward and kicked the ball of fire, sending it rolling, tumbling down the crater, down our chute like a meteor, and the snow beneath it instantly melted only to freeze again a moment later, making a slick blue ribbon. When we sledded it, we went so fast our minds emptied and we felt a sensation at once like flying and falling.

On the news Iraqi insurgents fired their assault rifles. On the news a car bomb in Baghdad blew up seven American soldiers at a traffic checkpoint. On the news the president said he did not think it was wise to provide a time frame for troop withdrawal. I checked my e-mail before breakfast and found nothing but spam.

Gordon and I fought in the snow wearing snow boots. We fought so much our wounds never got a chance to heal, and our faces took on a permanent look of decay. Our wrists felt swollen, our knees ached, our joints felt full of tiny dry wasps. We fought until fighting hurt too much, and we took up drinking instead. Weekends, we drove our dirt bikes to Bend, twenty miles away, and bought beer and took it to Hole in the Ground and drank there until a bright line of sunlight appeared on the horizon and illuminated the snow-blanketed desert. Nobody asked for our IDs, and when we held up our empty bottles and stared at our reflections in the glass, warped and ghostly, we knew why. And we weren't alone. Black bags grew beneath the eyes of the sons and daughters and wives of Crow, their shoulders stooped, wrinkles enclosing their mouths like parentheses.

Our fathers haunted us. They were everywhere: in the grocery store when we spotted a thirty-pack of Coors on sale for ten bucks; on the highway when we passed a jacked-up Dodge with a dozen hay bales stacked in its bed; in the sky when a jet roared by, reminding us of faraway places. And now, as our bodies thickened with muscle, as we stopped shaving and grew patchy beards, we saw our fathers even in the mirror. We began to look like them.

Our fathers, who had been taken from us, were everywhere, at every turn, imprisoning us.

Seth Johnson's father was a staff sergeant. Like his son, he was a big man but not big enough. Just before Christmas he stepped on a cluster bomb. A U.S. warplane dropped it and the sand camouflaged it and he stepped on it and it tore him into many meaty pieces. When Dave Lightener climbed up the front porch with a black armband and a somber expression, Mrs. Johnson, who was cooking a honeyed ham at the time, collapsed on the kitchen floor. Seth pushed his way out the door and punched Dave in the face, breaking his nose before he could utter the words *I regret to inform you* . . .

Hearing about this, we felt bad for all of ten seconds. Then we felt good because it was his father and not ours. And then we felt bad again, and on Christmas Eve we drove to Seth's house and laid down on his porch the rifles we had stolen, along with a six-pack of Coors, and then, just as we were about to leave, Gordon dug in his back pocket and removed his wallet and placed under the six-pack all the money he had — a few fives, some ones. "Fucking Christmas," he said.

We got braver and went to the bars — the Golden Nugget, the Weary Traveler, the Pine Tavern — where we square-danced with older women wearing purple eye shadow and sparkly dreamcatcher earrings and push-up bras and clattery high heels. We told them we were Marines back from a six-month deployment, and they said, "Really?" and we said, "Yes, ma'am," and when they asked for our names we gave them the names of our fathers. Then we bought them drinks and they drank them in a gulping way and breathed hotly in our faces and we brought our mouths against theirs and they tasted like menthol cigarettes, like burnt detergent. And then we went home with them, to their trailers, to their waterbeds, where among their stuffed animals we fucked them.

Midafternoon and it was already full dark. On our way to the Weary Traveler we stopped by my house to bum some money off my grandfather, only to find Dave Lightener waiting for us. He must have just gotten there — he was halfway up the porch steps — when our headlights cast an anemic glow over him, and he turned to face us with a scrunched-up expression, as if trying to figure out who we were. He wore the black band around his arm and, over his nose, a white-bandaged splint.

We did not turn off our engines. Instead we sat in the driveway, idling, the exhaust from our bikes and the breath from our mouths clouding the air. Above us a star hissed across the moonlit sky, vaguely bright like a light turned on in a day-lit room. Then Dave began down the steps and we leapt off our bikes to meet him. Before he could speak I brought my fist to his diaphragm, knocking the breath from his body. He looked like a gun-shot actor in a Western, clutching his belly with both hands, doubled over, his face making a nice target for Gordon's knee. A snap sound preceded Dave falling on his back with blood coming from his already broken nose.

He put up his hands, and we hit our way through them. I punched him once, twice, in the ribs while Gordon kicked him in the spine and stomach and then we stood around gulping air and allowed him to struggle to his feet. When he righted himself, he wiped his face with his hand, and blood dripped from his fingers. I moved in and roundhoused with my right and then my left, my fists knocking his head loose on its hinges. Again he collapsed, a bloody bag of a man. His eyes walled and turned up, trying to see the animal bodies looming over him. He opened his mouth to speak, and I pointed a finger at him and said, with enough hatred in my voice to break a back, *"Don't* say a word. Don't you dare. Not one word."

He closed his mouth and tried to crawl away, and I brought a boot down on the back of his skull and left it there a moment, grinding his face into the ground so that when he lifted his head the snow held a red impression of his face. Gordon went inside and returned a moment later with a roll of duct tape, and we held Dave down and bound his wrists and ankles and threw him on a sled and taped him to it many times over and then tied the sled to the back of Gordon's bike and drove at a perilous speed to Hole in the Ground.

The moon shone down and the snow glowed with pale blue light as we smoked cigarettes, looking down into the crater, with Dave at our feet. There was something childish about the way our breath puffed from our mouths in tiny clouds. It was as if we were imitating choo-choo trains. And for a moment, just a moment, we were kids again. Just a couple of stupid kids. Gordon must have felt this, too, because he said, "My mom wouldn't even let me play with toy guns when I was little." And he sighed heavily as if he couldn't understand how he, how we, had ended up here.

Then, with a sudden lurch, Dave began struggling and yelling at us in a slurred voice and my face hardened with anger and I put my hands on him and pushed him slowly to the lip of the crater and he grew silent. For a moment I forgot myself, staring off into the dark oblivion. It was beautiful and horrifying. "I could shove you right now," I said. "And if I did, you'd be dead."

"Please don't," he said, his voice cracking. He began to cry. "Oh fuck. Don't. Please." Hearing his great shuddering sobs didn't bring me the satisfaction I had hoped for. If anything, I felt as I did that day, so long ago, when we taunted him in the Mountain View Mall parking lot — shameful, false.

"Ready?" I said. "One!" I inched him a little closer to the edge. "Two!" I moved him a little closer still, and as I did I felt unwieldy, at once wild and exhausted, my body seeming to take on another twenty, thirty, forty years. When I finally said *"Three,"* my voice was barely a whisper.

We left Dave there, sobbing at the brink of the crater. We got on our bikes and we drove to Bend and we drove so fast I imagined catching fire like a meteor, burning up in a flash, howling as my heat consumed me, as we made our way to the U.S. Marine Recruiting Office, where we would at last answer the fierce alarm of war and put our pens to paper and make our fathers proud.

EDITH PEARLMAN

Self-Reliance

FROM LAKE EFFECT

WHEN CORNELIA FITCH RETIRED from the practice of gastroenterology she purchased — on impulse, her daughter thought — a house beside a spring-fed pond in New Hampshire. She did not relinquish the small apartment of her widowhood, though — three judicious rooms with framed drawings on the gray walls. This apartment, in the Boston suburb of Godolphin, was a twenty-minute walk from the hospital where Cornelia had worked; and her daughter lived nearby, as did both of her friends; and at Godolphin Corner she could visit a good secondhand bookstore and an excellent seamstress. One of Cornelia's legs was slightly longer than the other, a fault concealed by the clever *tailleur*. "Do you think there's anybody what's perfect," her aunt Shelley had snorted when, at fifteen, Cornelia's defect became apparent. Aunt Shelley lived with the family; where else could she live? "You're a knucklehead," added that gracious dependent.

The place by the water — Cornelia had had her eye on it for years. It reminded her of the cottage of a gnome. "Guhnome," Aunt Shelley used to miscorrect. The other houses in the loose settlement by the pond were darkly weathered wood; but Cornelia's was made of the local mauve granite. It had green shutters. There was one room downstairs and one up, an outdoor toilet, a small generator. Aquatic vines climbed the stones. Frogs and newts inhabited the moist garden.

She spent more and more time there. At the bottom of the pond, turtles inched their way to wherever they were going. Minnows traveled together, the whole congregation turning this way and then that, an underwater flag flapping in an underwater wind. Birches, lightly clothed in leaves, leaned toward the pond.

There was no beach. Most people had a rowboat or a canoe or a sunfish. They were retirees like Cornelia, who passed their days as she did — reading, watching the mild wildlife, sometimes visiting each other. Their dirt road met the main road a mile away, where a Korean family kept a general store. Thompson the geezer — Cornelia thought of him as a geezer, though he was, like her, in his early seventies — sat on his porch all day, sketching the pond. Two middle-aged sisters played Scrabble at night, and Cornelia joined them once in a while.

"I worry about you in the middle of nowhere," Nancy said. But the glinting stones of the house, its whitewashed interior, summer's greenness and winter's pale blueness seen through its deep windows, the mysterious endless brown of the peaked space above her bed . . . and pond and trees and loons and chipmunks . . . not nowhere. Somewhere. Herewhere.

"Cornelia, good sense demands that we treat this," the oncologist said. "A course of chemo, some radia ———" He paused. "We can beat it back."

She stretched her legs — the long one, the longer. She liked her doctor's old-fashioned office with its collection of worn books in a glass-fronted case. The glass now reflected her own handsome personage: short hair dyed bark, beige linen pants suit, cream shirt. A large sapphire ring was her one extravagance. And only a seeming extravagance, since the stone, though convincing, was glass. The ring had been Aunt Shelley's, probably picked up at a pawnshop. But the woman who now wore this fake article was a woman to trust. People *had* trusted her. They'd trusted her with their knotty abdomen, their swollen small bowel, their bleeding cecum, their tortuous lower bowel. Meekly they presented their anuses so she could insert the scope and guide it in, past the rectum, the sigmoid, the descending colon . . .

"Cornelia?" He too was reliable — ten years younger than she, a slight man, a bit of a fop, but no fool. Yes, together they could beat back this recurrence, and wait for the next one.

"Well, what else can we do?" she said in a reasonable tone. "Will you ask your nurse to schedule me?"

He gave her a steady look. "I will. Next week, then."
She nodded. "Write a new pain-med scrip, please. And the sleeping stuff, too."

On the way north she stopped at Nancy's house. The children were home from day camp — two enchanting little girls. Nancy hugged her. "How nice it's summer, I'm not teaching, I can be with you for the infusions."
"Bring a book." She hated chatter.
"Of course. Some lunch now, what do you say?"
"No, thanks." She touched her hair.
"And there's that lovely wig, from the last time," said Nancy shyly.
They waved good-bye: younger woman and children in the doorway, older woman in the car. It *was* a lovely wig. A bumptious genius of an artisan had exactly reproduced Cornelia's style and color, meanwhile recommending platinum curls — hey, doc, try something new! But she wanted the old, and she'd gotten it. There wasn't much she'd wanted that she hadn't gotten: increasing professional competence, wifedom, motherhood; papers published; even an affair years ago, when she was chief resident — she could hardly remember what he'd looked like. Well, if Henry had been less preoccupied . . . She had failed to master French and had lost her one-time facility with the flute. She was unlikely to correct those defects even with a remission. She had once perforated a colon, early in her career — it had been repaired right away, no complications, and the forgiving woman remained her patient. She'd had a few miscarriages after Nancy, then given up. Her opinions had been frequently requested. She'd supported Aunt Shelley in that rooming house, so messy; but the old lady, who liked bottle and weed, refused to go into a home. At retirement Cornelia had been given a plaque and an eighteenth-century engraving. Novels were O.K., but she preferred biographies. If she hadn't studied medicine, she might have become an interior designer, though it would have been difficult to accommodate to some people's awful taste.

She stopped at the general store and bought heirloom tomatoes, white grape juice, a jug of water. "The corn is good," advised the proprietor, his smile revealing his gold tooth.
"I'll bet it is. I'll be in again tomorrow."

The tomatoes nestled in her striped bowl. For a moment she regretted leaving them, their rough scars, their bulges. Then, eyes wide open, the knowledgeable Cornelia endured a vision: emaciation, murky awakenings, children obediently keeping still. She squinted at a bedside visitor, she sat dejectedly on the commode, she pushed a walker to the corner mailbox and demanded a medal for the accomplishment, she looked at a book upside down. The mantle of responsible dependency . . . it would not fit. With one eye still open, she winked the other at the tomatoes.

She changed into her bathing suit and took a quick swim, waving to the Sisters Scrabble and the geezer. Back in her house she put on jeans and a T-shirt, tossed the wet suit onto the crotch of a chokecherry tree. What should a person take for a predinner paddle? Binoculars, sun hat against insidious sidelong rays, towel, and the thermos she'd already filled with its cocktail. Pharmacology had been a continuing interest. "I'll swallow three pills a day and not a gobbet more," Aunt Shelley had declared. "You choose them, rascal."

She pushed off vigorously, then used a sweep stroke to turn the canoe and look at slate roof and stone walls. Just a little granite place, she realized; not fantastical after all; she had merely exchanged one austerity for another. She thought of the tomatoes, and turned again, and stroked, right side, left, right . . . Then, as if she were her own passenger, she opened a backrest and settled herself against it and slid the paddle under the seat. She drank her concoction slowly, forestalling nausea.

Sipping, not thinking, she drifted on a cobalt disk under an aquamarine dome. Birches bent to honor her, tall pines guarded the birches. She looked down the length of her body. She had not worn rubber boat shoes, only sandals, and her ten toenails winked Flamingo.

The spring was in the middle of the roughly circular pond. Usually a boat given its freedom headed in that direction. Today, however, the canoe was obeying some private instructions. It had turned eastward; the lowering sun at her back further brightened her toenails. Her craft was headed toward the densely wooded stretch of shore where there were no houses. It was picking up speed. Cornelia considered shaking herself out of her lethargy, lifting the paddle, resuming control; but instead she watched the prow make its confident way toward trees and moist earth. It would never attain the shore, though, because there seemed to be a gulf between pond and land. No one had ever remarked on this cleavage. Perhaps it had only recently appeared, a fault developing in the last week or two; perhaps the land had receded from the pond or the pond recoiled from the land; at any rate, there it was: fissure, cleft . . . falls.

Falls! And she was headed directly toward them. All at once a sound met her ears . . . plashing not roaring, inviting not menacing, but still. As the canoe was riding the lip of the new waterfall she stood up, never easy to do in a boat, more difficult now with substances swirling in her veins. She grabbed an overhanging bough, and watched in moderate dismay as her vessel tipped and then fell from her, carrying its cargo of towel, paddle, binoculars, sun hat, and almost empty thermos.

What now? She hung there, hands, arms, shoulders, torso, uneven legs, darling little toenails. She looked down. The rent in the fabric of the water was not, after all, between water and shore: it was between water and water. It was a deep, dark rift, like a mail slot. She dropped into it.

Into the slot she dropped. She fell smoothly and painlessly, her hair streaming above her head. She landed well below the water's surface on a mossy floor. Toenails still there? Yes, and the handkerchief in the pocket of her jeans. A small crowd advanced, some in evening clothes, some in costume.

"Cornailia," whispered her Dublin-born medical school lab partner. How beautifully he hadn't aged. "Dr. Flitch," said her cleaning woman, resplendent in sequins. "Granny?" said a child. "Cornelia," said a deer, or perhaps it was an antelope or a gazelle. She leaned back; her feet rose. She was horizontal now; she was borne forward along a corridor toward a turning; the rounded walls of this corridor were sticky and pink. "Rest, rest," said the unseen animal whose back was below her back — an ox, maybe, some sort of husband. They turned a corner with difficulty — she was too long, the ox was too big — but they managed; and now they entered a light-filled room of welcome or deportation, trestle tables laden with papers. She was on her feet. "Friends," she began. "Sssh," said a voice. Some people were humbly hooked up to IVs hanging from pine branches. They ate tomatoes and sweet corn and played Scrabble.

Some were walking around. I'm chief here, she tried to say. She lay with a feathered man. "Don't you recognize me, Connie?" He presented his right profile and then his left. That boiled eye . . . well, yes, but now she couldn't remember his name. She was on her back again, her knees raised and separated; ah, the final expulsion of delivery. Nancy . . . She was up, dancing with a rake, holding it erect with lightly curled fists. Its teeth smiled down at her. She saw her thermos rolling away; she picked it up and drank the last mouthful. She kissed a determined creature whose breath was hot and unpleasant. "I'm a wayward cell," it confided. The talons of a desperate patient scratched her chest. Then the breathable lukewarm water enveloped her, and she felt an agreeable loosening.

A sudden rush of colder fluid, and the room was purged of people, apparatus, creatures, animals. Everyone gone but Dr. Fitch. Her tongue grew thick with fear. And then Aunt Shelley shuffled forward, wearing that old housedress, her stockings rolled below her puffy knees, a cigarette hanging from her liver-colored mouth. How Cornelia and her sisters had loved climbing onto Shelley's fat thighs; how merrily they had buried their noses in her pendant flesh. "Scamp," she'd say with a chuckle. "Good-for-nothing." No endearment was equal to her insults, no kiss as soothing as the accidental brush of her lips, no enterprise as gratifying as the attainment of her lap.

A scramble now, a rapturous snuggle. One of Cornelia's sandals fell off. Her forehead burrowed into the familiar softness between jaw and neck.

"Stay with me," she whispered. Something was pawing at her . . . Regret? Reproval? Oh, get lost. This was bliss, this sloppy and forgiving hug. Bliss, again, after six dry decades. "Stay."

It could not last. And now there was no one, no relative, no friend, no person, no animal, no plant, no water, no air. Cornelia was not alone, though; she was in the company of a hard semi-transparent sapphire substance, and, as she watched, it flashed and then shattered, and shattered again, and again, all the while retaining its polyhedrality, seven sides exactly, she examined a piece on her palm to make sure, and it shattered there on her lifeline. Smaller and smaller, more and more numerous grew the components. Expanding in volume, they became a tumulus of stones, a mound of pebbles, a mountain of sand, a universe of dust, always retaining the blue color that itself was made up of royal and turquoise and white like first teeth. The stuff, finer still, churned, lifted her, tossed her, caressed her, entered her orifices, twirled and turned her, polished her with its grains. It rose into a spray that threw her aloft; it thickened into a spiral that caught her as she fell. She lay quiet in its coil. Not tranquil, no; she was not subject to poetic calm. She was spent. She was elsewhere.

Sometime later the geezer rowed out to the middle of the pond. He had been watching the drifting canoe for the last hour. A person's business was a person's business. He saw that his neighbor was dead. He tied the prow of the canoe to the stern of his rowboat and towed her ashore.

ALICE MUNRO

The View from Castle Rock
FROM THE NEW YORKER

ON A VISIT TO EDINBURGH with his father when he is nine or ten years old, Andrew finds himself climbing the damp, uneven stone steps of the castle. His father is in front of him, some other men behind — it's a wonder how many friends his father has found, standing in cubbyholes where there are bottles set on planks, in the High Street — until at last they crawl out on a shelf of rock, from which the land falls steeply away. It has just stopped raining, the sun is shining on a silvery stretch of water far ahead of them, and beyond that is a pale green and grayish blue land, a land as light as mist, sucked into the sky.

"America," his father tells them, and one of the men says that you would never have known it was so near.

"It is the effect of the height we are on," another says.

"There is where every man is sitting in the midst of his own properties and even the beggars is riding around in carriages," Andrew's father says, paying no attention to them. "So there you are, my lad" — he turns to Andrew — "and God grant that one day you will see it closer, and I will myself, if I live."

Andrew has an idea that there is something wrong with what his father is saying, but he is not well enough acquainted with geography to know that they are looking at Fife. He does not know if the men are mocking his father or if his father is playing a trick on them. Or if it is a trick at all.

Some years later, in the harbor of Leith, on the fourth of June, 1818, Andrew and his father — whom I must call Old James, because there is a James in every generation — and Andrew's pregnant wife, Agnes, his brother Walter, his sister Mary, and also his son James, who is not yet two years old, set foot on board a ship for the first time in their lives.

Old James makes this fact known to the ship's officer who is checking off the names.

"The first time, serra, in all my long life. We are men of the Ettrick. It is a landlocked part of the world."

The officer says a word that is unintelligible to them but plain in meaning. *Move along.* He has run a line through their names. They move along or are pushed along, Young James riding on Mary's hip.

"What is this?" Old James says, regarding the crowd of people on deck. "Where are we to sleep? Where have all these rabble come from? Look at the faces on them — are they the blackamoors?"

"Black Highlanders, more like," Walter says. This is a joke, muttered so that his father cannot hear, Highlanders being one of the sorts the old man despises.

"There are too many people," his father continues. "The ship will sink."

"No," Walter says, speaking up now. "Ships do not often sink because of too many people. That's what the fellow was there for, to count the people."

Barely on board the vessel and this seventeen-year-old whelp has taken on knowing airs; he has taken to contradicting his father. Fatigue, astonishment, and the weight of the greatcoat he is wearing prevent Old James from cuffing him.

The business of life aboard ship has already been explained to the family. In fact, it has been explained by the old man himself. He was the one who knew all about provisions, accommodations, and the kinds of people you would find on board. All Scotsmen and all decent folk. No Highlanders, no Irish.

But now he cries out that it is like the swarm of bees in the carcass of the lion.

"An evil lot, an evil lot. Oh, that ever we left our native land."

"We have not left yet," Andrew says. "We are still looking at Leith. We would do best to go below and find ourselves a place."

More lamentation. The bunks are narrow planks with horsehair pallets that are both hard and prickly.

"Better than nothing," Andrew says.

"Oh, that ever I was enticed to bring us here, onto this floating sepulcher."

Will nobody shut him up? Agnes thinks. This is the way he will go on and on, like a preacher or a lunatic, when the fit takes him. She cannot abide it. She is in more agony herself than he is ever likely to know.

"Well, are we going to settle here or are we not?" she says.

Some people have hung up their plaids or shawls to make a half-private space for their families. She goes ahead and takes off her outer wrappings to do the same.

The child is turning somersaults in her belly. Her face is as hot as a coal, her legs throb, and the swollen flesh in between them — the lips the child must soon part to get out — is a scalding sack of pain.

Her mother would have known what to do about that. She would have known which leaves to mash to make a soothing poultice. At the thought of her mother, such misery overcomes her that she wants to kick somebody.

Why does Andrew not speak plainly to his father, reminding him of whose idea it was, who harangued and borrowed and begged to get them just where they are now? Andrew will not do it, Walter will only joke, and as for Mary she can hardly get her voice out of her throat in her father's presence.

Agnes comes from a large Hawick family of weavers, who work in the mills now but worked for generations at home. Working there they learned the art of cutting one another down to size, of squabbling and surviving in close quarters. She is still surprised by the rigid manners, the deference and silences in her husband's family. She thought from the beginning that they were a queer sort and she thinks so still. They are as poor as her own folk, but they have such a great notion of themselves. And what have they got to back it up?

Mary has taken Young James back up to the deck. She could tell that he was frightened down there in the half dark. He does not have to whimper or complain — she knows his feelings by the way he digs his little knees into her.

The sails are furled tight. "Look up there, look up there," Mary says, and points to a sailor who is busy high up in the rigging. The boy on her hip makes his sound for bird — "peep." "Sailor-peep, sailor-peep," she says. She and he communicate in a half-and-half language — half her teaching and half his invention. She believes that he is one of the cleverest children ever born into the world. Being the eldest of her family, and the only girl, she has tended to all her brothers, and been proud of them all at one time, but she has never known a child like this. Nobody else has any idea how original and independent he is. Men have no interest in children so young, and Agnes, his mother, has no patience with him.

"Talk like folk," Agnes tells him, and if he doesn't she gives him a clout. "What are you?" she says. "Are you a folk or an elfit?"

Mary fears Agnes's temper, but in a way she doesn't blame her. She thinks that women like Agnes — men's women, mother women — lead an appalling life. First with what the men do to them — even as good a man as Andrew — and then with what the children do, coming out. She will never forget the way her own mother lay in bed, out of her mind with a fever, not knowing anyone, till she died, three days after Walter was born. She screamed at the black pot hanging over the fire, thinking it was full of devils.

Mary — her brothers call her "poor Mary" — is under five feet tall and has a tight little face with a lump of protruding chin, and skin that is subject to fiery eruptions that take a long time to fade. When she is spoken to, her mouth twitches as if the words were all mixed up with her spittle and her crooked teeth, and the response she manages is a dribble of speech so faint and scrambled that it is hard for people not to think her dimwitted. She has great difficulty looking anybody in the eye — even the members of her own family. It is only when she gets the boy hitched onto the narrow shelf of her hip that she is capable of some coherent and decisive speech — and then it is mostly to him.

She hears the cow bawling before she can see it. Then she looks up and sees the brown beast dangling in the air, all caged in ropes and kicking and roaring frantically. It is held by a hook on a crane, which now hauls it out of sight. People around her are hooting and clapping their hands. A child cries out, wanting to know if the cow will be dropped into the sea. A man tells him no — she will go along with them on the ship.

"Will they milk her, then?"

"Aye. Keep still. They'll milk her," the man says reprovingly. And another man's voice climbs boisterously over his.

"They'll milk her till they take the hammer to her, and then ye'll have the blood pudding for yer dinner."

Now follow the hens, swung through the air in crates, all squawking and fluttering in their confinement and pecking one another when they can, so that some feathers escape and float down through the air. And after them a pig trussed up like the cow, squealing with a human note in its distress and shifting wildly in midair, so that howls of both delight and outrage rise below, depending on whether they come from those who are hit or those who see others hit.

James is laughing, too. He recognizes shite, and cries out his own word for it, which is "gruggin."

Someday he may remember this, Mary thinks. *I saw a cow and a pig fly through the air.* Then he may wonder if it was a dream. And nobody will be there — she certainly won't — to tell him that it was not, that it happened on this ship. It's possible that he will never see a ship like this again in all his waking life. She has no idea where they will go when they reach the other shore, but she imagines that it will be someplace inland, among the hills, someplace like the Ettrick.

She does not think that she will live long, wherever they go. She coughs in the summer as well as the winter, and when she coughs her chest aches. She suffers from sties, and cramps in the stomach, and her bleeding comes rarely but may last a month when it does. She hopes, though, that she will not die while James is still in need of her, which he will be for a while yet. She knows that the time will come when he will turn away, as her brothers did, when he will become ashamed of the connection with her. At least, that is what she tells herself will happen, but like anybody in love she cannot believe it.

On a trip to Peebles, Walter bought himself a notebook to write in, but for several days he has found too much to pay attention to and too little space or quiet on the deck even to open it. Finally, after some investigating, he has discovered a favorable spot, near the cabins on the upper deck.

The View from Castle Rock

We came on board on the 4th day of June and lay the 5th, 6th, 7th, and 8th in the Leith roads getting the ship to a place where we could set sail, which was on the 9th. We passed the corner of Fifeshire all well nothing occurring worth mentioning till this day the 13th in the morning when we were awakened by a cry, John o'Groat's House. We could see it plain and had a fine sail across the Pentland Firth having both wind and tide in our favour and it was in no way dangerous as we had heard tell. There was a child had died, the name of Ormiston and its body was thrown overboard sewed up in a piece of canvas with a large lump of coal at its feet.

He pauses in his writing to think of the weighted sack falling down through the water. Would the piece of coal do its job, would the sack fall straight down to the very bottom of the sea? Or would the current of the sea be strong enough to keep lifting it up and letting it fall, pushing it sideways, taking it as far as Greenland or south to the tropical waters full of rank weeds, the Sargasso Sea? Or might some ferocious fish come along and rip the sack and make a meal of the body before it had even left the upper waters and the region of light?

He pictures it now — the child being eaten. Not swallowed whole as in the case of Jonah but chewed into bits as he himself would chew a tasty chunk from a boiled sheep. But there is the matter of a soul. The soul leaves the body at the moment of death. But from which part of the body does it leave? The best guess seems to be that it emerges with the last breath, having been hidden somewhere in the chest, around the place of the heart and the lungs. Though Walter has heard a joke they used to tell about an old fellow in the Ettrick, to the effect that he was so dirty that when he died his soul came out his arsehole, and was heard to do so with a mighty explosion.

This is the sort of information that preachers might be expected to give you — not mentioning anything like an arsehole, of course, but explaining something of the proper location and exit. Yet they shy away from it. Also they cannot explain — at least, he has never heard one explain — how the souls maintain themselves outside of bodies until the Day of Judgment and how on that day each one finds and recognizes the body that is its own and reunites with it, though it be not so much as a skeleton at that time. *Though it be dust.* There must be some who have studied enough to know how all this is accomplished. But there are also some — he has learned this recently — who have studied and read and thought till they have come to the conclusion that there are no souls at all. No one cares to speak about these people, either, and indeed the thought of them is terrible. How can they live with the fear — indeed, the certainty — of Hell before them?

On the third day aboard ship Old James gets up and starts to walk around. After that, he stops and speaks to anybody who seems ready to listen. He tells his name, and says that he comes from Ettrick, from the Valley and Forest of Ettrick, where the old kings of Scotland used to hunt.

"And on the field at Flodden," he says, "after the battle of Flodden, they said you could walk up and down among the corpses and pick out the men from the Ettrick, because they were the tallest and the strongest and the finest-looking men on the ground. I have five sons, and they are all good strong lads, but only two of them are with me. One of my sons is in Nova Scotia. The last I heard of him he was in a place called Economy, but we have not had any word of him since and I do not know whether he is alive or dead. My eldest son went off to work in the Highlands, and the son that is next to the youngest took it into his head to go off there, too, and I will never see either of them again. Five sons and, by the mercy of God, all grew to be men, but it was not the Lord's will that I should keep them with me. A man's life is full of sorrow. I have a daughter as well, the oldest of them all, but she is nearly a dwarf. Her mother was chased by a ram when she was carrying her."

> On the afternoon of the 14th a wind from the North and the ship began to shake as if every board that was in it would fly loose from every other. The buckets overflowed from the people that were sick and vomiting and there was the contents of them slipping all over the deck. All people were ordered below but many of them crumpled up against the rail and did not care if they were washed over. None of our family was sick however and now the wind has dropped and the sun has come out and those who did not care if they died in the filth a little while ago have got up and dragged themselves to be washed where the sailors are splashing buckets of water over the decks. The women are busy too washing and rinsing and wringing out all the foul clothing. It

is the worst misery and the suddenest recovery I have seen ever in my life.

A young girl ten or twelve years old stands watching Walter write. She is wearing a fancy dress and bonnet and has light brown curly hair. Not so much a pretty face as a pert one.

"Are you from one of the cabins?" she says.

Walter says, "No. I am not."

"I knew you were not. There are only four of them, and one is for my father and me and one is for the captain and one is for his mother, and she never comes out, and one is for the two ladies. You are not supposed to be on this part of the deck unless you are from one of the cabins."

"Well, I did not know that," Walter says, but he does not bestir himself to move away.

"I have seen you before writing in your book."

"I haven't seen you."

"No. You were writing, so you didn't notice. I haven't told anybody about you," she adds carelessly, as if that were a matter of choice and she might well change her mind.

When she leaves, Walter adds a sentence.

And this night in the year 1818 we lost sight of Scotland.

The words seem majestic to him. He is filled with a sense of grandeur, solemnity, and personal importance.

16th was a very windy day with the wind coming out of the SW the sea was running very high and the ship got her gib-boom broken on account of the violence of the wind. And our sister Agnes was taken into the cabin.

"Sister," he has written, as if she were all the same to him as poor Mary, but that is not the case. Agnes is a tall well-built girl with thick dark hair and dark eyes. The flush on one of her cheeks slides into a splotch of pale brown as big as a handprint. It is a birthmark, which people say is a pity, because without it she would be handsome. Walter can hardly bear looking at it, but this is not because it is ugly. It is because he longs to touch it, to stroke it with the tips of his fingers. It looks not like ordinary skin but like the velvet on a deer. His feelings about her are so troubling that he can speak to her only unpleasantly, if he speaks at all. And she pays him back with a good seasoning of contempt.

Agnes thinks that she is in the water and the waves are heaving her up and slamming her down. Every time they slap her down it is worse than the time before, and she sinks farther and deeper, the moment of relief passing before she can grab it, for the next wave is already gathering its power to hit her.

Then sometimes she knows that she is in a bed, a strange bed and strangely soft, but it is all the worse for that because when she sinks down there is no resistance, no hard place where the pain has to stop. People keep rushing back and forth in front of her. They are all seen sideways and all transparent, talking very fast so she can't make them out, and maliciously taking no heed of her. She sees Andrew in the midst of them, and two or three of his brothers. Some of the girls she knows are there, too — the friends she used to lark around with in Hawick. And they do not give a poor penny for the plight she is in now.

She never knew before that she had so many enemies. They are grinding her down and pretending they don't even know it. Their movement is grinding her to death.

Her mother bends over her and says in a drawling, cold, lackadaisical voice, "You are not trying, my girl. You must try harder." Her mother is all dressed up and talking fine, like some Edinburgh lady.

Evil stuff is poured into her mouth. She tries to spit it out, knowing it is poison.

I will just get up and get out of this, she thinks. She starts trying to pull herself loose from her body, as if it were a heap of rags on fire.

She hears a man's voice, giving some order. "Hold her," he says, and she is split and stretched wide open to the world and the fire.

"Ah — ah — anh," the man says, panting as if he had been running in a race.

Then a cow that is so heavy, bawling heavy with milk, rears up and sits down on Agnes's stomach.

"Now. Now," the man says, and he groans at the end of his strength as he tries to heave it off.

The fools. The fools, ever to have let it in.

She was not better till the 18th when she was delivered of a daughter. We having a surgeon on board nothing happened. Nothing occurred till the 22nd this was the roughest day we had till then experienced. Agnes was mending in an ordinary way till the 29th we saw a great shoal of porpoises and the 30th (yesterday) was a very rough sea with the wind blowing from the west we went rather backwards than forwards.

"In the Ettrick there is what they call the highest house in Scotland," Old James says, "and the house that my grandfather lived in was a higher one than that. The name of the place is Phauhope — they call it Phaup. My grandfather was Will O'Phaup, and fifty years ago you would have heard of him if you came from any place south of the Forth and north of the Debatable Lands."

There are people who curse to see him coming, but others who are glad of any distraction. His sons hear his voice from far away, amid all the other commotion on the deck, and make tracks in the opposite direction.

For the first two or three days, Young James refused to be unfastened from Mary's hip. He was bold enough, but only if he could stay there. At night he slept in her cloak, curled up beside her, and she wakened aching along her left side because she had lain stiffly all night so as not to disturb him. Then in the space of one morning he was down and running about and kicking at her if she tried to hoist him up.

Everything on the ship calls out for his attention. Even at night he tries to climb over her and run away in the dark. So she gets up aching not only from her position but from lack of sleep altogether. One night she drops off and the child gets loose, but most fortunately stumbles against his father's body in his bid for escape. Henceforth, Andrew insists that he be tied down every night. He howls, of course, and Andrew shakes him and cuffs him and then he sobs himself to sleep. Mary lies by him softly explaining that this is necessary so that he cannot fall off the ship into the ocean, but he regards her at these times as his enemy, and if she puts out a hand to stroke his face he tries to bite it with his baby teeth. Every night he goes to sleep in a rage, but in the morning when she unties him, still half-asleep and full of his infant sweetness, he clings to her drowsily and she is suffused with love.

Then one day he is gone. She is in the line for wash water and she turns around and he is not beside her. She was just speaking a few words to the woman ahead of her, answering a question about Agnes and the infant, she had just told the woman its name — Isabel — and in that moment he got away.

Everything in an instant is overturned. The nature of the world is altered. She runs back and forth, crying out James's name. She runs up to strangers, to sailors who laugh at her as she begs them, "Have you seen a little boy? Have you seen a little boy this high, he has blue eyes?"

"I seen fifty or sixty of them like that in the last five minutes," a man says to her. A woman trying to be kind says that he will turn up, Mary should not worry herself, he will be playing with some of the other children. Some women even look about, as if they would help her search, but of course they cannot, they have their own responsibilities.

This is what Mary sees plainly in those moments of anguish: that the world, which has turned into a horror for her, is still the same ordinary world for all these other people and will remain so even if James has truly vanished, even if he has crawled through the ship's railings — she has noticed everywhere the places where this would be possible — and been swallowed by the ocean.

The most brutal and unthinkable of all events, to her, would seem to most others like a sad but not extraordinary misadventure. It would not be unthinkable to them.

Or to God. For in fact when God makes some rare and remarkable, beautiful human child is He not particularly tempted to take His creature back, as if the world did not deserve it?

Still, she is praying to Him all the time. At first she only called on the Lord's name. But as her search grows more specific and in some ways more bizarre — she is ducking under clotheslines that people have contrived for privacy, she thinks nothing of interrupting folk at any business, she flings up the lids of their boxes and roots in their bedclothes, not even hearing them when they curse her — her prayers also become more complicated and audacious. She tries to think of something to offer, something that could equal the value of James being restored to her. But what does she have? Nothing of her own — not health or prospects or anybody's regard. There is no piece of luck or even a hope that she can offer to give up. What she has is James.

And how can she offer James for James?
This is what is knocking around in her head.
But what about her love of James? Her extreme and perhaps idolatrous, perhaps wicked love of another creature. She will give up that, she will give it up gladly, if only he isn't gone.
If only he can be found. If only he isn't dead.

She recalls all this an hour or two after somebody has noticed the boy peeping out from under a large empty bucket, listening to the hubbub. And she retracts her vow at once. Her understanding of God is shallow and unstable, and the truth is that, except in a time of terror such as she has just experienced, she does not really care. She has always felt that God or even the idea of Him was more distant from her than from other people. There is a stubborn indifference in her that nobody knows about. In fact, everybody may imagine that she clings secretly to religion because there is so little else available to her. They are quite wrong, and now that she has James back she gives no thanks but thinks what a fool she was and how she could not give up her love of him any more than stop her heart beating.

After that, Andrew insists that James be tied down not only by night but also by day, to the post of the bunk or to their clothesline on the deck. Andrew has trounced his son for the trick he played, but the look in James's eyes says that his tricks are not finished.

Agnes keeps asking for salt, till they begin to fear that she will fuss herself into a fever. The two women looking after her are cabin passengers, Edinburgh ladies, who took on the job out of charity.

"You be still now," they tell her. "You have no idea what a fortunate lassie you are that we had Mr. Suter onboard."

They tell her that the baby was turned the wrong way inside her, and they were all afraid that Mr. Suter would have to cut her, and that might be the end of her. But he had managed to get it turned so that he could wrestle it out.

"I need salt for my milk," says Agnes, who is not going to let them put her in her place with their reproaches and their Edinburgh speech. They are idiots, anyway. She has to explain to them how you must put a little salt in the baby's first milk, just place a few grains on your finger and squeeze a drop or two of milk onto it and let the child swallow that before you put it to the breast. Without this precaution there is a good chance that it will grow up half-witted.

"Is she even a Christian?" one of them says to the other.

"I am as much as you," Agnes says. But to her own surprise and shame she starts to weep aloud, and the baby howls along with her, out of sympathy or hunger. And still she refuses to feed it.

Mr. Suter comes in to see how she is. He asks what all the grief is about, and they tell him the trouble.

"A newborn baby to get salt in its stomach — where did she get the idea?"

He says, "Give her the salt." And he stays to see her squeeze the milk on her salty finger, lay the finger to the infant's lips, and follow it with her nipple.

He asks her what the reason is and she tells him.

"And does it work every time?"

She tells him — a little surprised that he is as stupid as they are, though gentler — that it works without fail.

"So where you come from they all have their wits about them? And are all the girls strong and good-looking like you?"

She says that she would not know about that.

Sometimes visiting young men, educated men from the town, used to hang around her and her friends, complimenting them and trying to work up a conversation, and she always thought that any girl who allowed it was a fool, even if the man was handsome. Mr. Suter is far from handsome — he is too thin, and his face is badly pocked, so that at first she took him for an old fellow. But he has a kind voice, and if he is teasing her a little there is no harm in it. No man would have the nature left to deal with a woman after looking at her spread wide, her raw parts open to the air.

"Are you sore?" he asks, and she believes there is a shadow on his damaged cheeks, a slight blush rising. She says that she is no worse than she has to be, and he nods, picks up her wrist, and bows over it, strongly pressing her pulse.

"Lively as a racehorse," he says, with his hands still above her, as if he did not know where to put them next. Then he decides to push back her hair and press his fingers to her temples, as well as behind her ears.

She will recall this touch, this curious, gentle, tingling pressure, with an addled mixture of scorn and longing, for many years to come.

"Good," he says. "No sign of a fever."

He watches, for a moment, the child sucking.

"All's well with you now," he says with a sigh. "You have a fine daughter, and she can say all her life that she was born at sea."

Andrew arrives later and stands at the foot of the bed. He has never looked on her in such a bed as this (a regular bed, even though bolted to the wall). He is red with shame in front of the ladies, who have brought in the basin to wash her.

"That's it, is it?" he says, with a nod — not a glance — at the bundle beside her.

She laughs in a vexed way and asks what did he think it was. That is all it takes to knock him off his unsteady perch, to puncture his pretense of being at ease. Now he stiffens up, even redder, doused with fire. It isn't just what she said. It is the whole scene — the smell of the infant and the milk and the blood, and most of all the basin, the cloths, the women standing by, with their proper looks that might seem to a man both admonishing and full of derision.

He looks as if he can't think of another word to say, so she has to tell him, with rough mercy, to get on his way, there's work to be done here.

Some of the girls used to say that when you finally gave in and lay down with a man — even granting he was not the man of your first choice — it gave you a helpless but calm and even sweet feeling. Agnes does not recall that she felt that with Andrew. All she felt was that he was an honest lad and the right one for her in her circumstances, and that it would never occur to him to run off and leave her.

Walter has continued to go to the same private place to write in his book and nobody has caught him there. Except the girl, of course. One day he arrives at the place, and she is there before him, skipping with a red-tasseled rope. When she sees him she stops, out of breath. And no sooner does she catch her breath than she begins to cough, so that it is several minutes before she can speak. She sinks down against the pile of canvas that conceals the spot, flushed, her eyes full of bright tears from the coughing. He simply stands and watches her, alarmed at this fit but not knowing what to do.

"Do you want me to fetch one of the ladies?"

He is on speaking terms with the Edinburgh women now, on account of Agnes. They take a kind interest in the mother and baby and Mary and Young James, and think that the old father is comical. They are also amused by Andrew and Walter, who seem to them so bashful.

The coughing girl is shaking her curly head violently.

"I don't want them," she says, when she can gasp the words out. "I have never told anybody that you come here. So you mustn't tell anybody about me."

"Well, you are here by rights."

She shakes her head again and gestures for him to wait till she can speak more easily.

"I mean that you saw me skipping. My father hid my skipping rope, but I found where he hid it."

"It isn't the Sabbath," Walter says reasonably. "So what is wrong with you skipping?"

"How do I know?" she says, regaining her saucy tone. "Perhaps he thinks I am too old for it. Will you swear not to tell anyone?"

What a queer, self-important little thing she is, Walter thinks. She speaks only of her father, so he thinks it likely that she has no brothers or sisters and — like himself — no mother. That condition has probably made her both spoiled and lonely.

The girl — her name is Nettie — becomes a frequent visitor when Walter tries to write in his book. She always says that she does not want to disturb him, but after keeping ostentatiously quiet for about five minutes she interrupts him with some question about his life or a bit of information about hers. It is true that she is motherless and an only child. She has never even been to school. She talks most about her pets — those dead and those living at her house in Edinburgh — and a woman named Miss Anderson, who used to travel with her and teach her. It seems that she was glad to see the back of this woman, and surely Miss Anderson, too, was glad to depart, after all the tricks that were played on her — the live frog in her boot and the woolen but lifelike mouse in her bed.

Nettie has been back and forth to America three times. Her father is a wine merchant whose business takes him to Montreal.

She wants to know all about how Walter and his people live. Her questions are, by country standards, quite impertinent. But Walter does not really mind. In his own family he has never been in a position that allowed him to instruct or teach or tease anybody younger than himself, and it gives him pleasure.

What does Walter's family have for supper when they are at home? How do they sleep? Are animals kept in the house? Do the sheep have names, and what are the sheepdogs' names, and can you make pets of them? What is the arrangement of the scholars in the schoolroom? Are the teachers cruel? What do some of his words mean that she does not understand, and do all the people where he is from talk like him?

"Oh, aye," Walter says. "Even His Majesty the Duke does. The Duke of Buccleuch."

She laughs and freely pounds her little fist on his shoulder.

"Now you are teasing me. I know it. I know that dukes are not called Your Majesty. They are not."

One day she arrives with paper and drawing pencils. She says that she has brought them to keep herself busy, so she will not be a nuisance to him. She offers to teach him to draw, if he wants to learn. But his attempts make her laugh, and he deliberately does worse and worse, till she laughs so hard she has one of her coughing fits. Then she says that she will do some drawings in the back of his notebook, so that he will have them to remember the voyage by. She draws the sails up above and a hen that has somehow escaped its cage and is trying to travel like a sea bird over the water. She sketches from memory her dog that died. And she makes a picture of the icebergs she saw, higher than houses, on one of her past voyages with her father. The setting sun shone through these icebergs and made them look — she says — like castles of gold. Rose-colored and gold.

Everything that she has drawn, including the icebergs, has a look that is both guileless and mocking, peculiarly expressive of herself.

"The other day I was telling you about that Will O'Phaup that was my grandfather, but there was more to him than I told you. I did not tell you that he was the last man in Scotland to speak to the fairies. It is certain that I have never heard of any other, in his time or later."

Walter is sitting around a corner, near some sailors who are mending the torn sails, but by the sounds that are made throughout the story he can guess that the out-of-sight audience is mostly women.

There is one tall well-dressed man — a cabin passenger, certainly — who has paused to listen within Walter's view. There is a figure close to this man's other side, and at one moment in the tale this figure peeps around to look at Walter and he sees that it is Nettie. She seems about to laugh, but she puts a finger to her lips as if warning herself — and Walter — to keep silent.

The man must, of course, be her father. The two of them stand there listening quietly till the tale is over. Then the man turns and speaks directly, in a familiar yet courteous way, to Walter. "Are you writing down what you can make of this?" the man asks, nodding at Walter's notebook.

Walter is alarmed, not knowing what to say. But Nettie looks at him with calming reassurance, then drops her eyes and waits beside her father as a demure little miss should.

"I am writing a journal of the voyage," Walter says stiffly.

"Now, that is interesting. That is an interesting fact, because I, too, am keeping a journal of this voyage. I wonder if we find the same things worth writing of."

"I only write what happens," Walter says, wanting to make clear that this is a job for him and not an idle pleasure. Still, he feels that some further justification is called for. "I am writing to keep track of every day so that at the end of the voyage I can send a letter home."

The man's voice is smoother and his manner gentler than any address Walter is used to. He wonders if he is being made sport of in some way. Or if Nettie's father is the sort of person who strikes up an acquaintance in the hope of getting hold of your money for some worthless investment.

Not that Walter's looks or dress would mark him out as a likely prospect.

"So you do not describe what you see? Only what, as you say, is happening?"

Walter is about to say no, and then yes. For he has just thought, if he writes that there is a rough wind, is that not describing? You do not know where you are with this kind of person.

"You are not writing about what we have just heard?"

"No."

"It might be worth it. There are people who go around now pry-ing into every part of Scotland and writing down whatever these old country folk have to say. They think that the old songs and stories are disappearing and that they are worth recording. I don't know about that — it isn't my business. But I would not be surprised if the people who have written it all down will find that it was worth their trouble — I mean to say, there will be money in it."

Nettie speaks up unexpectedly.

"Oh, hush, Father. The old fellow is starting again."

This is not what any daughter would say to her father in Walter's experience, but the man seems ready to laugh, looking down at her fondly.

And indeed Old James's voice has been going this little while, breaking in determinedly and reproachfully on those of his audience who might have thought it was time for their own conversations.

"And still another time, but in the long days in the summer, out on the hills late in the day but before it was well dark . . ."

Walter has heard the stories his father is spouting, and others like them, all his life, but the odd thing is that until they came onboard this ship he had never heard them from his father. The father he knew until a short while ago would, he is certain, have had no use for them.

"This is a terrible place we live in," his father used to say. "The people is all full of nonsense and bad habits, and even our sheep's wool is so coarse you cannot sell it. The roads are so bad a horse cannot go more than four miles an hour. And for plowing here they use the spade or the old Scotch plow, though there has been a better plow in other places for fifty years. 'Oh, aye, aye,' they say when you ask them. 'Oh, aye, but it's too steep hereabouts, the land is too heavy.'

"To be born in the Ettrick is to be born in a backward place," he would say, "where the people is all believing in old stories and seeing ghosts, and I tell you it is a curse to be born in the Ettrick."

And very likely that would lead him on to the subject of America, where all the blessings of modern invention were put to eager use and the people could never stop improving the world around them.

But hearken at him now.

"You must come up and talk to us on the deck above," Nettie's father says to Walter when Old James has finished his story. "I have business to think about, and I am not much company for my daughter. She is forbidden to run around because she is not quite recovered from the cold she had in the winter, but she is fond of sitting and talking."

"I don't believe it is the rule for me to go there," Walter says in some confusion.

"No, no, that is no matter. My girl is lonely. She likes to read and draw, but she likes company, too. She could show you how to draw, if you like. That would add to your journal."

So they sit out in the open and draw and write. Or she reads aloud to him from her favorite book, which is *The Scottish Chiefs*. He already knows the story — who does not know about William Wallace? — but she reads smoothly and at just the proper speed and makes some things solemn and others terrifying and others comical, so that soon he is as much in thrall to the book as she is. Even though, as she says, she has read it twelve times already.

He understands a little better now why she has so many questions to ask him. He and his folk remind her of the people in her book, such people as there were out on the hills and in the valleys in the olden times. What would she think if she knew that the old fellow, the old tale-spinner spouting all over the boat and penning people up to listen as if they were sheep — what would she think if she knew that he was Walter's father?

She would be delighted, probably, more curious about Walter's family than ever. She would not look down on them, except in a way that she could not help or recognize.

> We came on the fishing bank of Newfoundland on the 12th of July and on the 19th we saw land and it was a joyful sight to us. It was a part of Newfoundland. We sailed between Newfoundland and St. Paul's Island and having a fair wind both the 18th and the 19th we found ourselves in the river on the morning of the 20th and within sight of the mainland of North America. We were awakened at about 1 o'clock in the morning and I think every passenger was out of bed at 4 o'clock gazing at the land, it being wholly covered with wood and quite a new sight to us. It was a part of Nova Scotia and a beautiful hilly country.

*

The View from Castle Rock 131

This is the day of wonders. The land is covered with trees like a head with hair and behind the ship the sun rises, tipping the top trees with light. The sky is clear and shining as a china plate and the water playfully ruffled with wind. Every wisp of fog has gone and the air is full of the resinous smell of the trees. Sea birds are flashing above the sails all golden like creatures of Heaven, but the sailors fire a few shots to keep them from the rigging.

Mary holds Young James up so that he may always remember this first sight of the continent that will be his home. She tells him the name of this land — Nova Scotia.

"It means New Scotland," she says.

Agnes hears her. "Then why doesn't it say so?"

Mary says, "It's Latin, I think."

Agnes snorts with impatience. The baby was woken early by all the hubbub and celebration, and now she is miserable, wanting to be on the breast all the time, wailing whenever Agnes tries to take her off. Young James, observing all this closely, makes an attempt to get on the other breast, and Agnes bats him off so hard that he staggers.

"Suckie-laddie," Agnes calls him. He yelps a bit, then crawls around behind her and pinches the baby's toes.

Another whack.

"You're a rotten egg, you are," his mother says. "Somebody's been spoiling you till you think you're the Laird's arse."

Agnes's roused voice always makes Mary feel as if she were about to catch a blow herself.

Old James is sitting with them on the deck, but pays no attention to this domestic unrest.

"Will you come and look at the country, Father?" Mary says uncertainly. "You can have a better view from the rail."

"I can see it well enough," Old James says. Nothing in his voice suggests that the revelations around them are pleasing to him.

"Ettrick was covered with trees in the old days," he says. "The monks had it first and after that it was the Royal Forest. It was the king's forest. Beech trees, oak trees, rowan trees."

"As many trees as this?" Mary says, made bolder than usual by the novel splendors of the day.

"Better trees. Older. It was famous all over Scotland. The Royal Forest of Ettrick."

"And Nova Scotia is where our brother James is," Mary continues.

"He may be or he may not. It would be easy to die here and nobody know you were dead. Wild animals could have eaten him."

Mary wonders how her father can talk in this way, about how wild animals could have eaten his own son. Is that how the sorrows of the years take hold of you — turning your heart of flesh to a heart of stone, as it says in the old song? And if it is so, how carelessly and disdainfully might he talk about her, who never meant to him a fraction of what the boys did?

Somebody has brought a fiddle onto the deck and is tuning up to play. The people who have been hanging on to the rail and pointing out to one another what they can all see on their own — likewise repeating the name that by now everyone knows, Nova Scotia — are distracted by these sounds and begin to call for dancing. Dancing, at seven o'clock in the morning.

Andrew comes up from below, bearing their supply of water. He stands and watches for a little, then surprises Mary by asking her to dance.

"Who will look after the boy?" Agnes says immediately. "I am not going to get up and chase him." She is fond of dancing, but is prevented now not only by the nursing baby but by the soreness of the parts of her body that were so battered in the birth.

Mary is already refusing, saying she cannot go, but Andrew says, "We will put him on the tether."

"No. No," Mary says. "I've no need to dance." She believes that Andrew has taken pity on her, remembering how she used to be left on the sidelines in school games and at the dancing, though she can actually run and dance perfectly well. Andrew is the only one of her brothers capable of such consideration, but she would almost rather he behaved like the others and left her ignored as she has always been. Pity galls her.

Young James begins to complain loudly, having recognized the word "tether."

"You be still," his father says. "Be still or I'll clout you."

Then Old James surprises them all by turning his attention to his grandson.

"You. Young lad. You sit by me."

"Oh, he will not sit," Mary says. "He will run off and then you cannot chase him, Father. I will stay."

"He will sit," Old James says.

"Well, settle it," Agnes says to Mary. "Go or stay."

Young James looks from one to the other, cautiously snuffling.

"Does he not know even the simplest word?" his grandfather says. "Sit. Lad. Here."

Young James lowers himself, reluctantly, to the spot indicated.

"Now go," Old James says to Mary. And all in confusion, on the verge of tears, she is led away.

People are dancing not just in the figure of the reel but quite outside of it, all over the deck. They are grabbing anyone at all and twirling around. They are even grabbing some of the sailors, if they can get hold of them. Men dance with women, men dance with men, women dance with women, children dance with one another or all alone and without any idea of the steps, getting in the way — but everybody is in everybody's way already and it is no matter.

Mary has caught hands with Andrew and is swung around by him, then passed on to others, who bend to her and fling her undersized body about. She dances down at the level of the children, though she is less bold and carefree. In the thick of so many bodies she is helpless, she cannot pause — she has to stamp and wheel to the music or be knocked down.

"Now, you listen and I will tell you," Old James says. "This old man, Will O'Phaup, my grandfather — he was my grandfather as I am yours — Will O'Phaup was sitting outside his house in the evening, resting himself. It was mild summer weather. All alone, he was. And there was three little lads hardly bigger than you are yourself, they came around the corner of Will's house. They told him good evening. 'Good evening to you, Will O'Phaup,' they says. 'Well, good evening to you, lads. What can I do for you?' 'Can you give us a bed for the night or a place to lie down?' they says. And 'Aye,' he says. 'Aye, I'm thinking three bits of lads like yourselves should not be so hard to find room for.' And he goes into the house with them following, and they says, 'And by the bye, could you give us the key, too, the big silver key that you had of us?' Well, Will looks around, and he looks for the key, till he thinks to himself, What key was that? For he knew he never had such a thing in his life. Big key or silver key, he never had it. 'What key are you talking about?' And turns himself around and they are not there. Goes out of the house, all around the house, looks to the road. No trace of them.

Looks to the hills. No trace. Then Will knew it. They was no lads at all. Ah, no. They was no lads at all."

James has not made any sound. At his back is the thick and noisy wall of dancers, to the side his mother, with the small clawing beast that bites into her body. And in front of him is the old man with his rumbling voice, insistent but remote, and his blast of bitter breath.

It is the child's first conscious encounter with someone as perfectly self-centered as he is.

He is barely able to focus his intelligence, to show himself not quite defeated. "Key," he says. "Key?"

Agnes, watching the dancing, catches sight of Andrew, red in the face and heavy on his feet, linked arm to arm with various jovial women. There is not one girl whose looks or dancing gives Agnes any worries. Andrew never gives her any worries, anyway. She sees Mary tossed around, with even a flush of color in her cheeks — though she is too shy, and too short, to look anybody in the face. She sees the nearly toothless witch of a woman who birthed a child a week after her own, dancing with her hollow-cheeked man. No sore parts for her. She must have dropped the child as slick as if it were a rat, then given it to one or the other of her weedy-looking daughters to mind.

She sees Mr. Suter, the surgeon, out of breath, pulling away from a woman who would grab him, ducking through the dance and coming to greet her.

She wishes he would not. Now he will see who her father-in-law is; he may have to listen to the old fool's gabble. He will get a look at their drab, and now not even clean, country clothes. He will see her for what she is.

"So here you are," he says. "Here you are with your treasure."

It is not a word that Agnes has ever heard used to refer to a child. It seems as if he is talking to her in the way he might talk to a person of his own acquaintance, some sort of a lady, not as a doctor talks to a patient. Such behavior embarrasses her, and she does not know how to answer.

"Your baby is well?" he says, taking a more down-to-earth tack. He is still catching his breath from the dancing, and his face is covered with a fine sweat.

"Aye."

"And you yourself? You have your strength again?"

The View from Castle Rock

She shrugs very slightly, so as not to shake the child off the nipple.

"You have a fine color, anyway. That is a good sign."

He asks then if she will permit him to sit and talk to her for a few moments, and once more she is confused by his formality but tells him that he may do as he likes.

Her father-in-law gives the surgeon — and her as well — a despising glance, but Mr. Suter does not notice it, perhaps does not even realize that the old man and the fair-haired boy who sits straight-backed facing the old man have anything to do with her.

"What will you do in Canada West?" he asks.

It seems to her the silliest question. She shakes her head — what can she say? She will wash and sew and cook and almost certainly suckle more children. Where that will be does not much matter. It will be in a house, and not a fine one.

She knows now that this man likes her, and in what way. She remembers his fingers on her skin. What harm can happen, though, to a woman with a baby at her breast? She feels stirred to show him a bit of friendliness.

"What will you do?" she says.

He smiles and says that he supposes he will go on doing what he has been trained to do, and that the people in America — so he has heard — are in need of doctors and surgeons, just like other people in the world.

"But I do not intend to get walled up in some city. I'd like to get as far as the Mississippi River, at least. Everything beyond the Mississippi used to belong to France, you know, but now it belongs to America and it is wide open — anybody can go there, except that you may run into the Indians. I would not mind that, either. Where there is fighting with the Indians, there'll be all the more need for a surgeon."

She does not know anything about this Mississippi River, but she knows that Mr. Suter does not look like a fighting man himself — he does not look as if he could stand up in a quarrel with the brawling lads of Hawick, let alone red Indians.

Two dancers swing so close to them as to put a wind into their faces. It is a young girl, a child, really, whose skirts fly out — and who should she be dancing with but Agnes's brother-in-law Walter. Walter makes some sort of silly bow to Agnes and the surgeon and his father, and the girl pushes him and turns him around and he laughs at her. She is dressed like a young lady, with bows in her hair. Her face is lit up with enjoyment, her cheeks are glowing like lanterns, and she treats Walter with great familiarity, as if she had got hold of a large toy.

"That lad is your friend?" Mr. Suter says.

"No. He is my husband's brother."

The girl is laughing quite helplessly, as she and Walter — through her heedlessness — have almost knocked down another couple in the dance. She is not able to stand up for laughing, and Walter has to support her. Then it appears that she is not laughing but coughing. Walter is holding her against himself, half carrying her to the rail.

"There is one lass that will never have a child to her breast," Mr. Suter says, his eyes flitting to the sucking child before resting again on the girl. "I doubt if she will live long enough to see much of America. Does she not have anyone to look after her? She should not have been allowed to dance."

He stands up so that he can keep the girl in view as Walter holds her by the rail.

"There, she has stopped," he says. "No hemorrhaging. At least not this time."

Agnes can see that he takes a satisfaction in the verdict he has passed on this girl. And it occurs to her that this must be because of some condition of his own — that he must be thinking that he is not so bad off by comparison.

There is a cry at the rail, nothing to do with the girl and Walter. Another cry, and many people break off dancing and rush to look at the water. Mr. Suter rises and goes a few steps in that direction, following the crowd, then turns back.

"A whale," he says. "They are saying there is a whale to be seen off the side."

"You stay here!" Agnes shouts in an angry voice, and he turns to her in surprise. But he sees that her words are meant for Young James, who is on his feet.

"This is your lad, then?" Mr. Suter exclaims, as if he had made a remarkable discovery. "May I carry him over to have a look?"

And that is how Mary — happening to raise her face in the crush of passengers — beholds Young James, much amazed, being carried across the deck in the arms of a hurrying stranger, a pale and determined dark-haired man who is surely a foreigner. A child stealer, or child murderer, heading for the rail.

She gives so wild a shriek that anybody would think she was in the Devil's clutches herself, and people make way for her as they would for a mad dog.

"Stop, thief! Stop, thief!" she is crying. "Take the boy from him. Catch him. James! James! Jump down!"

She flings herself forward and grabs the child's ankles, yanking him so that he howls in fear and outrage. The man bearing him nearly topples over but doesn't give him up. He holds on and pushes at Mary with his foot.

"Take her arms," he shouts to those around them. He is short of breath. "She is in a fit."

Andrew has pushed his way in, through people who are still dancing and people who have stopped to watch the drama. He manages somehow to get hold of Mary and Young James and to make clear that one is his son and the other his sister and that it is not a question of fits.

All is shortly explained with courtesies and apologies from Mr. Suter.

"I had just stopped for a few minutes' talk with your wife, to ask her if she was well," the surgeon says. "I did not take time to bid her good-bye, so you must do it for me."

Mary remains unconvinced by the surgeon's story. Of course he would have to say to Agnes that he was taking the child to look at the whale. But that does not make it the truth. Whenever the picture of that devilish man carrying Young James flashes through her mind, and she feels in her chest the power of her own cry, she is astonished and happy. It is still her belief that she has saved him.

> We were becalmed the 21st and 22nd but we had rather more wind the 23rd but in the afternoon were all alarmed by a squall of wind accompanied by thunder and lightning which was very terrible and we had one of our mainsails that had just been mended torn to rags again with the wind. The squall lasted about 8 or 10 minutes and the 24th we had a fair wind which sent us a good way up the River, where it became more strait so that we saw land on both sides of the River. But we becalmed again till the 31st when we had a breeze only two hours.

*

Nettie's father's name is Mr. Carbert. Sometimes he sits and listens to Nettie read or talks to Walter. The day after the dancing, when many people are in a bad humor from exhaustion and some from drinking whiskey, and hardly anybody bothers to look at the shore, he seeks Walter out to talk to him.

"Nettie is so taken with you," he says, "that she has got the idea that you must come along with us to Montreal."

He gives an apologetic laugh, and Walter laughs, too.

"Then she must think that Montreal is in Canada West," Walter says.

"No. No. I am not making a joke. I looked out for you on purpose when she was not with me. You are a fine companion for her, and it makes her happy to be with you. And I can see that you are an intelligent lad and a prudent one and one who would do well in my office."

"I am with my father and my brother," Walter says, so startled that his voice has a youthful yelp in it. "We are going to get land."

"Well, then. You are not the only son your father has. There may not be enough good land for all of you. And you may not always want to be a farmer."

Walter tells himself that this is true.

"My daughter, now, how old do you think she is?"

Walter cannot think. He shakes his head.

"She is fourteen, nearly fifteen," Nettie's father says. "You would not think so, would you? But it does not matter — that is not what I am talking about. Not about you and Nettie, anything in years to come. You understand that? There is no question of years to come. But I would like for you to come with us and let her be the child that she is and make her happy now with your company. Then I would naturally want to repay you, and there would also be work for you in the office, and if all went well you could count on advancement."

Both of them at this point notice that Nettie is coming toward them. She sticks out her tongue at Walter, so quickly that her father apparently does not notice.

"No more now. Think about it and pick your time to tell me," her father says. "But sooner rather than later would be best."

Walter does not take long to make up his mind. He knows enough to thank Mr. Carbert, but says that he has not thought of working in an office, or at any indoor job. He means to work with his family until they are set up with land to farm and then when they do not need his help so much he thinks of being a trader to the Indians, a sort of explorer. Or a miner for gold.

"As you will," Mr. Carbert says. They walk several steps together, side by side. "I must say I had thought you were rather more serious than that. Fortunately, I said nothing to Nettie."

But Nettie has not been fooled as to the subject of their talks together. She pesters her father until he has to let her know how things have gone and then she seeks out Walter.

"I will not talk to you anymore from now on," she says, in a more grown-up voice than he has ever heard from her. "It is not because I am angry but just because if I go on talking to you I will have to think all the time about how soon I'll be saying good-bye to you. But if I stop now I will have already said good-bye, so it will all be over sooner."

She spends the time that is left walking sedately with her father, in her finest clothes.

Walter feels sorry to see her — in these fine cloaks and bonnets she looks more of a child than ever, and her show of haughtiness is touching — but there is so much for him to pay attention to that he seldom thinks of her when she is out of sight.

Years will pass before she will reappear in his mind. But when she does he will find that she is a source of happiness, available to him till the day he dies. Sometimes he will even entertain himself with thoughts of what might have happened had he taken up the offer. He will imagine a radiant recovery, Nettie's acquiring a tall and maidenly body, their life together. Such foolish thoughts as a man may have in secret.

> Several boats from the land came alongside of us with fish, rum, live sheep, tobacco, etc. which they sold very high to the passengers. The 1st of August we had a slight breeze and on the morning of the 2nd we passed by the Isle of Orleans and about six in the morning we were in sight of Quebec in as good health I think as when we left Scotland. We are to sail for Montreal tomorrow in a steamboat.

> My brother Walter in the former part of this letter has written a large journal which I intend to sum up in a small ledger. We have had a very prosperous voyage being wonderfully preserved in health. We can say nothing yet about the state of the country. There is a great number of

people landing here but wages is good. I can neither advise nor discourage people from coming. The land is very extensive and very thin-peopled. I think we have seen as much land as might serve all the people in Britain uncultivated and covered with wood. We will write you again as soon as settled.

When Andrew has added this paragraph, Old James is persuaded to add his signature to those of his two sons before the letter is sealed and posted to Scotland from Quebec. He will write nothing else, saying, "What does it matter to me? It cannot be my home, it can be nothing to me but the land where I will die."

"It will be that for all of us," Andrew says. "But when the time comes we will think of it more as a home."

"Time will not be given to me to do that."

"Are you not well, Father?"

"I am well and I am not."

Young James is now paying occasional attention to the old man, sometimes stopping in front of him and looking straight into his face, with a sturdy insistence.

"He bothers me," Old James says. "I don't like the boldness of him. He will go on and on and not remember a thing of Scotland, where he was born, or the ship he traveled on. He will get to talking another language the way they do when they go to England, only it will be worse than theirs. He looks at me with the kind of look that says he knows that me and my times is all over with."

"He will remember plenty of things," Mary says. Since the dancing and the incident of Mr. Suter she has grown more forthright within the family. "And he doesn't mean his look to be bold," she says. "It is just that he is interested in everything. He understands what you say, far more than you think. He takes everything in, and he thinks about it."

Her eyes fill with tears of enthusiasm, but the others look down at the child with sensible reservations.

Young James stands in the midst of them — bright-eyed, fair, and straight. Slightly preening, somewhat wary, unnaturally solemn, as if he had indeed felt descend upon him the burden of the future.

The adults, too, feel the astonishment of the moment. It is as if they had been borne for these past six weeks not on a ship but on one great wave, which has landed them with a mighty thump on this bewildering shore. Thoughts invade their heads, wheeling in with the gulls' cries, their infidel commotion.

Mary thinks that she could snatch up Young James and run away into some part of the strange city of Quebec and find work as a sewing woman (talk on the boat has made her aware that such work is in demand). Then she could bring him up all by herself, as if she were his mother.

Andrew thinks of what it would be like to be here as a free man, without wife or father or sister or children, without a single burden on his back. What could he do then? He tells himself that it is no harm, surely, it is no harm to think about it.

Agnes has heard women on the boat say that the officers you see in the street here are surely the best-looking men anywhere in the world, and that they are ten or twenty times more numerous than the women. Which must mean that you can get what you want out of them — that is, marriage. Marriage to a man with enough money that you could ride in a carriage and send presents to your mother. If you were not married already and dragged down with two children.

Walter thinks that his brother is strong and Agnes is strong — she can help him on the land while Mary cares for the children. Who ever said that he should be a farmer? When they get to Montreal he will go and attach himself to the Hudson's Bay Company and they will send him to the frontier, where he will find riches as well as adventure.

Old James has sensed defection and begins to lament openly, "How shall we sing the Lord's song in a strange land?"

These travelers lie buried — all but one of them — in the graveyard of Boston Church, in Esquesing, in Halton County, Ontario, almost within sight, and well within sound, of Highway 401, which at that spot, just a few miles from Toronto, may be the busiest road in Canada.

Old James is here. And Andrew and Agnes. Nearby is the grave of Mary, married after all and buried beside Robert Murray, her husband. Women were scarce and so were prized in the new country. She and Robert did not have any children together, but after Mary's early death he married another woman and with her he had four sons who lie here, dead at the ages of two, and three, and four, and thirteen. The second wife is here, too. Her stone says "Mother." Mary's says "Wife."

Agnes is here, having survived the births of many children. In a letter to Scotland, telling of the death of Old James in 1829 (a cancer, not much pain until near the end, though "it eat away a great part of his cheek and jaw"), Andrew mentions that his wife has been feeling poorly for the past three years. This may be a roundabout way of saying that during those years she bore her sixth, seventh, and eighth children. She must have recovered her health, for she lived into her eighties.

Andrew seems to have prospered, though he spread himself less than Walter, who married an American girl from Montgomery County, in New York State. Eighteen when she married him, thirty-three when she died after the birth of her ninth child. Walter did not marry again, but farmed successfully, educated his sons, speculated in land, and wrote letters to the government complaining about his taxes. He was able, before he died, to take a trip back to Scotland, where he had himself photographed wearing a plaid and holding a bouquet of thistles.

On the stone commemorating Andrew and Agnes there appears also the name of their daughter Isabel, who, like her mother, died an old woman.

Born at Sea.

Here, too, is the name of Andrew and Agnes's firstborn child, Isabel's elder brother.

Young James was dead within a month of the family's landing at Quebec. His name is here, but surely he cannot be. They had not yet taken up their land when he died; they had not even seen this place. He may have been buried somewhere along the way from Montreal to York or in that hectic new town itself. Perhaps in a raw temporary burying ground now paved over, perhaps without a stone in a churchyard, where other bodies would someday be laid on top of his. Dead of some mishap in the busy streets, or of a fever, or dysentery, or any of the ailments, the accidents, that were the common destroyers of little children in his time.

KEVIN MOFFETT

Tattooizm

FROM TIN HOUSE

DIXON DRIVES. Andrea attends to the beachside drifters pushing shopping carts along the sidewalk. She calls them "Cajuns." She likes how it sounds when yelled. Cajun! She likes that the drifters have no idea why she chooses this, of all things, to yell. She and Dixon drive past a restaurant that sells only hot dogs, past a giant rocking chair made of cockleshells, which you can pay to sit on. Cajun! Andrea wants to throw something. A ripe pear, a stuffed animal maybe, something not too hard.

Dixon is excited. He sings along with "Afternoon Delight" on the radio, smiling without smiling, something in the squint of his eyes. Andrea isn't bothered by his singing — his voice is soft, nonintrusive, nearly pleasant — but she finds herself waiting for him to stop. In a few hours she has to babysit for her brother. She thinks: *Something has always just happened or is about to happen. Nothing is ever* happening.

She is nineteen, Dixon, twenty-four. He has red, tightly curly hair, red eyelashes, red hair on his arms, his chest, red hair all over, except on the top part of his legs, which is shaved. He is training to be a tattoo artist by practicing on his thighs, covering them with flames, leaves, wings, cartoon characters, hearts, crosses, squiggles, spirals, and other meaningless designs. When she first met him there were freckles and soft red hair on his thighs. Now it's a mess, a tattoo stew. He is wearing shorts, and if Andrea looked away from the street and at his right leg she would see a purple tiger paw pulling scratch marks across his thigh.

A man pulling two clear plastic bags steps into the crosswalk. "Cajun!" Andrea yells. The man jerks his head forward, then sidelong like a fish extending for a worm, hooked.

He has to practice on somebody, Dixon tells her.

He is singing again, to a song that goes, "I want it," over and over — *it* being, Andrea guesses, sex. Dixon is excited because they are going to see a building he wants to turn into a tattoo studio. He drives exactly thirty-five miles an hour. He thinks the streetlights are timed so that if you maintain the speed limit you won't get any red lights. Every few blocks he's proven wrong.

Early this morning, they were naked in his bed. "Maybe you could allow me your right shoulder," Dixon said, tracing a finger along her clavicle. Andrea told him that at the end of August, on their first anniversary, she'd let him tattoo a small roman numeral *I* on her thigh. She's mad at herself for saying it. She doesn't want a small roman numeral *I* on her thigh. It seemed reasonable when they were naked. Anyway, it didn't satisfy Dixon at all. "I need practice," he told her. "I'm running out of room on my legs. All I've got is my arm."

They pull up next to a stucco two-storied shop with dry-rotted awnings and a FOR LEASE sign on the front door. It used to house, Andrea can read in the dust and sand collecting on the torn-off window stickers, the Fun Shack. The building looks slightly nonplused, as if someone has just asked it a question.

"Look inside," Dixon says. "Imagine chairs and artwork on the walls. A big dog walking around." He sprints across the street, kneels to one knee, and holds a camera to his face. Andrea waits for the flash's wink, but it doesn't come. The sun is shining.

She cups her hands over her eyes and leans against a window: pair of sawhorses, balled-up tarps, barstools. The blond pine floor shines in parallelograms where the afternoon sun comes in through the windows. Andrea tries to imagine a big dog walking around.

"It's expensive," Dixon says when he gets back. "And the location is no good. We'll have to lure people down here."

She should offer something pleasant. She should compliment him on finding this Fun Shack. He is sitting on the hood of the car, deep green tattoos sneaking out of the hem of his shorts. "Tattooizm," he says. "There'll be an orange neon sign in the front window. Tattooizm with a *Z*, indicating impatience with the way things are."

She could say she likes the pine floors, that he has managed to find a building with the loveliest pine floors she's ever seen. "Aren't there licenses you need?" she asks. "How are you going to afford it?"

"Loans. Business loans."

"Didn't you ruin your credit, Dixon?"

"Come here and enjoy our building." He pats the hood of the car. It makes a solid, unsociable sound. "Let me worry about the particulars."

She walks over and sits beside him. He reaches his hand inside the waistband of her shorts and underwear, rests it casually atop her thigh. Whenever she hears what kind of person Dixon thinks he is, it causes her to wonder what else he is mistaken about. Does he realize that lately he uses *we* when talking about his plans for the tattoo business, and that she feels pretty much indifferent to the whole thing?

His hand is just *sitting* on her thigh, as inert as a cicada's vacated husk. Stillness unbothered by anticipation — it makes her jittery. She grips his elbow and moves his hand higher and to the right, closes her eyes while he maneuvers his fingers up, searching for her, slowly, finding her. He rubs with two fingers, rests his thumb in her navel.

Her new favorite answer when her next boyfriend asks what Dixon was like: he could draw a really good Yosemite Sam.

She looks forward to some rest when school starts in three months. Dixon's an increasingly demanding lover. In the morning he picks her up and they drive around or go to his house and have sex three, four times before she has to babysit her brother in the evening. Dixon lights candles, burns sage oil, turns his bedroom into a little shrine. He keeps his shirt off, his hair wet from repeated showers. They watch a lot of TV together: Dixon has a lot of channels. Sometimes while a woman in an apron, say, is praising a no-wipe oven cleaner, the TV goes black and Andrea looks over to see Dixon's rapt face moving toward her lap. She helps him slip off her underwear, leans back on the sofa, tunnels her fingers through his tight red curls. He has a certain appeal, she'll be the first to admit.

Now, on the hood of his car, she shudders from her tailbone ahead toward Dixon's hand. Once the feeling passes, she's left fogged by momentary cheerfulness. Dixon slowly slips his hand out of her shorts. Her eyes are closed. The sun backlights the blood vessels in her eyelids. She opens them and sees Dixon holding his hand aloft and still, as if it's about to be fitted with a special glove.

"Well," he says.

The air smells very suddenly like orange blossoms.

"It's a nice building," she says.

Dixon smiles, hops off the hood of the car. "I wish that expression were permanent. I wish it would stick around a few days at least."

"What are you talking about?"

He kneels, pulls the camera out of his pocket, and snaps a picture of her. "Satisfied. I've satisfied you."

She lets whatever expression was on her face go slack.

"And away it goes," he says. "Hope it sends me a postcard."

He drops her off at the security gate to the Grove, where she lives with her mother and brother, and where the guard has told Dixon that since his car is no doubt leaking oil, he can't drive in, where there are children and wading birds and endangered cypresses. The second he pulls away, Andrea feels untethered. Never has someone's absence exerted such influence on her. When they're apart she is nagged by the certainty that she neglected to say the thing that would have set things right. She's been dishonest in her silence.

"We could live on the top floor," Dixon said as they were pulling into the Grove. Andrea was too surprised by the suggestion to laugh, which would have been the correct response. Whereas she imagines living above a tattoo parlor by the beach as akin to being nailed into an attic and having food passed to her through a slot, Dixon happily refuses to bother an idea like this past speculation. There was an old *Pennysaver* on the seat between them, and she should have rolled it up and swatted him across the chest, or put it to his ear and yelled, "You aren't my future!"

She's been out of school for more than a year. In the fall she begins classes at the junior college. She looks forward to paying attention again, to being rewarded for listening and remembering. She needs to buy folders and pens, some new clothes. Most people are unhappy about going to the junior college, but Andrea is not. Or she is, but only slightly. She is determined not to be.

Her little brother, Cory, meets her at the front door and tells her that their mother has already left for work. He begs Andrea to hurry taking off her shoes so they can microwave some nachos. Cory finds intense satisfaction in watching the cheese melt and bubble and congeal on the chips. He is part boy, part savage. Andrea wants to encourage the boy so she gladly microwaves the nachos. She gladly does any old moronic thing to make him happy.

She layers the chips in a collapsed-domino pattern on the platter. "We found a plumber," he says when Andrea asks how his day was. "Mommy cut my hair while I stood in the tub. We hanged another feeder."

Cory's hair looks exactly as it did last night: ragged around his ears and neck and pasted in a straight, straight line above his eyebrows. He has a barely kempt look to him, like a parolee on a job interview. A dubious boy's face has replaced the vacant infant's.

"You were gone when I woke up," he says. "Were you in school?"

Andrea opens a bag of pregrated cheese. *Three Cheeses in One!* the bag says. "I haven't started yet, remember? I was out with a friend."

"Mommy says you want to marry a man from the circus."

Andrea pours the cheese over the chips. It comes out in three colors: white, orange, and very orange.

"The Human Sketch Pad," Cory says.

"She knew you'd tell me that," Andrea says, wiping her hands on the front of her shorts. "Mom thinks things are one way when really they're another."

"I thought she was gonna tell me a joke." He lays a hand on the platter. "Don't microwave them yet. I want them to be like this for a while."

Andrea misses childhood. Her childhood ended the morning she bled from her vagina, according to Miss Moten, her eighth-grade health teacher. Miss Moten also said that having sex was like being tickled from the inside out. One day in class she removed her shirt to demonstrate the correct way to apply deodorant. Some parents complained, but it turned out Miss Moten had obtained necessary clearance from the county to remove her shirt in class. Since then, things have gotten considerably less wondrous in Andrea's view. She supposes Miss Moten was more or less right about everything.

"Left side, right, middle, middle," Cory sings as the nachos cook. It's a song from a TV show which he's adapted for the nachos.

Andrea touches the pause button on the microwave and her brother shrieks with delight. When the nachos are sufficiently scorched, she dumps them into the garbage.

The phone rings while she and Cory are playing checkers with canned food on the kitchen's checkerboard linoleum floor. "The forearm," Dixon says, as if answering a trivia question, "is deceptively small." Andrea sits on the countertop with a dented can of butter beans in her lap. Cory has run off somewhere. "I just put a roman numeral *I* above my wrist. Wait till you see it. It's perfection."

Dixon is probably playing with himself. Often he does while they talk on the phone. He probably hasn't even taken off his surgical gloves. His penis is drooped like a sunburned mushroom out of the fly of his boxer shorts while he handles it carelessly, probably.

"What's your middle name?" he asks.

"Olive," she says, though this is not true. Her mother didn't give her a middle name.

"Spelled in the traditional way?"

"Don't put *Olive* on your arm, Dixon. Why can't we talk about normal things?"

"My arm, your middle name, we're talking about normal things." He sighs. "Listen, I took a nap when I got home and dreamt that you let me tattoo strings along your spine and an f-hole on each side of your back. When I made love to you from behind, it was like plucking a cello. I awoke and, well, I guess it goes without saying . . ."

Made love to you from behind, Andrea repeats to herself. It is perhaps the worst attempt at delicacy she's ever heard. She plans to tell her next boyfriend that Dixon had a foot-shaped gas pedal in his car. That he was fond of movies in which an adult and a child switch bodies. That he meant well, but emotionally he wasn't her equal. She's always been mature for her age. The next boyfriend will already have started to surmise this.

She tells Dixon she has to go find her brother.

"Sometimes," he concludes, "I think you and I are wilting from our own need."

Out back, Cory is refilling the new bird feeder. It's a test tube–shaped container with flower-shaped holes through which red liquid leaks onto the deck. Cory tears open a sugar packet and pours it into the feeder. "Mommy says that a hummingbird's tongue soaks up nectar like a paper towel with juice," he says. "Its tongue is shaped like a *W*."

How entirely beside the point! Andrea is too young to be smothered by Dixon's longing. He seemed so self-contained when she met him at the art-supply store. She was buying markers for Cory. Dixon was waiting for her, or someone like her, it's clear now. Someone who acted more experienced than she was. Someone who'd had sex maybe a dozen times with a surfer boy who, she's presently reminded, claimed he could tie a cherry stem into a knot with his tongue, but who broke up with her before he showed her, and who used to talk about Costa Rica, and who laid a Quiksilver towel over his bedspread before they began kissing.

"Squirrels are smarter than birds," Cory is saying. He walks around checking the other feeders, which are topped with wooden squirrels to deter real squirrels.

"I was having trouble finding anything I want in here," Dixon said when she met him at the art-supply store. "Are you an artist?"

Andrea will allow Dixon this summer. He had last fall, he has had winter and spring. Summer will be a nice end of the cycle. She will start college and meet nice boys with manageable obsessions. Of course she intends to remember Dixon fondly, like an old toy or a book that she read in bed when she was sick.

One day she wakes up thinking: *I am becoming what I wasn't.* It seems terribly ominous in the haze of sleep, but really it doesn't make much sense. Or it does make sense, but it's too obvious to think about. She isn't sure. Sex is draining her, turning her into a dull and contented cow. Away from Dixon, when she is able to consider, really stop to soberly consider, the physical act of sex, she decides it is overrated. Just because it feels good doesn't mean she should spend all day doing it! Soon it won't be special anymore. Dixon doesn't know anything. If he weren't around, she could easily be happy without having sex three, four times a day.

She misses her friends. She had just two: Jamie and Erin. Jamie was earnest and creative, and Erin was sarcastic and good with her hands. Both met Dixon once and said he was nice. Nice, even when Andrea barely knew Dixon, seemed wrong. Either they hated him or they weren't too perceptive. Jamie said he had a nice voice; Erin thought he was too skinny. Really, they thought he was old and weird and gross. Andrea has stopped calling her friends, because what's the point? She has stayed and they have left. Jamie is attending culinary school, and Erin plans to become a merchant marine. Andrea has no clue what, exactly, being a merchant marine involves, but she loves the sound of it. She is jealous of Erin. In ten years Erin will be able to say: *Back when I was a merchant marine* . . .

A substantial part of life, Andrea thinks, is finding and wanting things you like the sound of.

Dixon picks her up, and they drive to his house, along the beachside. "Cajun!" Andrea yells at a woman reading a newspaper on a park bench. The woman looks up from the paper, and she isn't a drifter at all, just a normal woman with windblown hair.

"The junior college was on TV last night," Dixon says. "They asked some foreign students what they liked about the college, and one of them said, 'Every day is discovery.'"

They drive past the deserted hotel's parking lot, where kids from the high school used to gather on weekends. A vinyl banner attached to a flagpole says PARDON OUR PROGRESS. Though Andrea never went to the parking lot, she feels nostalgic driving past. Mondays at school she would hear about fistfights and arrests in the parking lot. Once someone with a pitchfork threatened someone else.

"I've never been anywhere," Dixon says.

Andrea yells at a black man on roller skates carrying a rake and a pail. She's not sure why she has continued yelling at the drifters, she means them no harm. Their lives, she knows, are difficult enough without being yelled at by someone in a passing car. It is something she and Erin started doing in high school. Andrea would yell, "Cajun!" and Erin would yell, "Rubble!" It was very funny. They would never yell something overtly mean like "Bum!" or "Loser!" For starters, neither, when yelled, sounds as good as "rubble" or "Cajun." Probably it is the nicest-sounding thing the drifters will hear yelled at them all day. Erin used to call the people who hung out in the deserted hotel's parking lot "combers," because the hotel was called the Beachcomber. Probably Andrea's nostalgic about the parking lot because she can't go there anymore, even if she wanted to, which she does not.

Later, naked in bed, Dixon strokes her thigh. Candles cast roving shadows on the walls: excited arms, retreating animals. Andrea watches the shadows and tries to discern a pattern, but there is no pattern. Dixon's sheets are sandy. His pillowcases smell like his scalp.

"Flex," he says. His hand, moving upward along her leg, stops on the crease of skin where thigh meets pubic bone. He rubs it. "Does that feel good?"

"Sort of," she says. "Not overly." In the candlelight, his forearm looks meticulously bruised, or gangrened. Andrea knows what is there: in the center, written in dark and elaborate cursive like a formal declaration, is *Olive,* followed by an exclamation mark. The *O* is set apart from the *L* so it looks like *O live!* The rest of the arm is beset by roman numerals, dozens of tiny *I*s and *X*s and *V*s scattered at random.

The lines on the new tattoos are more assured, the shading more delicate. Clearly he is improving his technique. But oh! Andrea cannot look at the new tattoos. They are indisputably, noisily, mistakenly about *her* — and permanent, permanent, permanent. She instead looks at Dixon's thighs, at the symbols that have nothing to do with her. She can look at the thighs without feeling anxious. The thighs, compared to the forearm, are Disneyland.

"Does that feel good?" he says.

Today in the gas station the cashier pointed to Dixon's arm and said, "Those aren't *real,* are they?"

Andrea thought this the worst response that one with tattoos could hope for, but Dixon seemed pleased by it, as if he thinks he's defying reality or something.

He's still pleased. His face, lit from below by the candles, looks hollow and evangelical. He tucks his hand between the fleshy part of her thighs. "I want to fall asleep with my hand between your thighs," he says. "I won't pull it out till morning."

She has decided to break up with him on August 25, which will be a week before their first anniversary and one day before classes begin at the junior college. There is no way she's letting him touch her with the tattoo gun, which sits beneath a T-shirt on his nightstand, and looks nothing like a gun. It looks like a dart attached to an engine. "Tattoo *machine,*" he says when she calls it a gun.

She has registered for four classes: Calculus, Argumentative Writing, Geology Lab, and Volleyball. They offer a class in volleyball! She is going to be polite and astute, the most hopeful student on campus. She plans to join clubs, form study groups. She'll volunteer to help deaf students take notes. She'll bring extra pens to class. She'll be reluctantly popular. She'll wear a sweatband and those cool little canvas kneepads to play volleyball.

Dixon goes to the kitchen, returns with a bowl of blackberries, and watches Andrea eat them. When she finishes, he puts the bowl on his nightstand. She rolls over onto her side and he rubs himself into her. She exhales a forced breath. He seizes her ear, her entire ear, with his mouth and gently bites the cartilage. It feels good. Almost everything he does to her feels good. He grips her hand, brings it around, and puts it between her legs. She touches herself, but it seems a bit redundant, so she reaches behind and clutches his hip, which is sweaty. He is working hard. Her hand follows the thrust and pop of his hip. He whispers what sounds like *little tin pans*. The shadows on the ceiling have gone crazy. The sheets are still sandy. She makes long, low sounds, smeared, overrun.

In the shower Dixon scrubs her back with a sponge. Her eyes are closed beneath the showerhead. The water is too hot, Dixon is scrubbing too hard, and for now everything is righteously O.K.

While they towel off, he tells her he is taking her home early because he has an appointment to talk to someone about a workspace.

"What's happening with the building?"

"A new plan," he says. "I haven't told you about our new plan?"

"You haven't told me about any plan."

"I guess that's because it's a *surprise* plan." His big laugh reveals a space between his canines, a word missing a letter. His chest, covered in freckles, is orangy from the hot water. "I'm doing research right now. But soon enough, this new plan is going to happen. Prepare yourself."

She thinks: *Soon enough a lot of things are going to happen.* The muscles in her nose twitch, like a rabbit nose. She sneezes.

As Dixon dries the top of his forearm gingerly, Andrea looks at his thigh, at a cluster of blue spheres above a semitruck hauling a bolt of lightning. Above the spheres, below a thicket of red hair, is his penis. It looks beleaguered. Andrea feels sorry for it. Flushed, crooked, not knowing what will happen next.

Dixon towels off her back. When he's done he says, "You are immaculate."

He drops her off at the entrance to the Grove. The security guard is new, but Dixon doesn't try to sneak past. Andrea's walk back to the apartment is nice — past gnarled oaks with osprey nests that look like steel wool — long enough to collect her thoughts but not so long that she starts to doubt them. She makes nachos for Cory. She sleeps. She hasn't seen her mom in days. Her mom leaves notes on tiny scraps of paper, tapes them to the front door: *Remember Cory's teeth.* And: *Get melon.* Before Cory and her mom are awake the next morning, Andrea leaves the house. Dixon picks her up at the security gate, his hair wet, new tattoos on his forearm. They go to the drugstore and buy condoms for Dixon and folders and pens for Andrea. She needs to buy a rock kit for her geology lab, but she wants to see if she likes the class first. They eat lunch in Dixon's bed. They watch TV again. They get naked again. They stay naked for hours.

Dixon sits on the edge of the bed with the tattoo gun. "This *I* looks like a *T*," he says. "*T* isn't a roman number."

A week goes by. Another week. Andrea has trouble keeping track of what day it is. Naked, everything is pretty much the same as the day before, and after.

Except: Dixon has stopped mentioning the anniversary tattoo. He's not any less physically attentive, but he hasn't mentioned that his forearm is now fully covered with tattoos. She appreciates the consideration. She appreciates it and is suspicious of it.

One day, on the way back to the Grove, she says, "I don't want a tattoo, Dixon. I know I told you I'd let you give me — "

"I know," he interrupts. "Nobody's going to give you something you don't want." He turns to the open window. Did he spit? His head lurched slightly as if he did. "We can't want what we don't want," he says.

She laughs without meaning to. He sounds so earnest, like their conversation really means something. She can tell she's disappointed him. She'll continue to disappoint him.

"It's so fake!" Cory says. This is Cory the savage. Andrea sits next to him on the couch, beneath a Superman blanket, watching two wrestlers on television karate-chop each other. The crowd cheers when the man in black tights karate-chops the man in red tights, and boos when the man in red tights karate-chops the man in black tights. Both men glisten with oil. The man in red tights jumps on the back of the man in black tights and pulls his chin from behind. The camera cuts to a Japanese man in a tuxedo running with a folding chair toward the ring. "All he has to do is wiggle his way free. And then — " Cory jabs his elbow upward.

The Japanese man swings the chair at the man in red tights but instead hits the man in black tights, who cringes and stands up. He and the Japanese man begin karate-chopping each other.

Beneath the Superman blanket, Andrea has slipped her hand into her shorts. She intended to scratch an itch on her thigh, but once she moved her hand the itch disappeared. Now she has begun playing with herself. She pulls the blanket higher on her shoulders and massages wet folds between her fingers. At first she didn't realize what she was doing, she was just rubbing herself without ambition, but now she realizes what she's doing.

"It's so fake!" Cory shouts, accidentally kicking her arm. "It's so retarded!"

Now the man in red tights is struggling with the referee, trying to prevent him from stopping the match. Andrea fingers herself more vigorously. She rubs side to side, moving just her fingers; the rest of her body is perfectly still. It is like typing a single letter. She watches Cory. His mouth is open in an expression of pure malevolent joy. Rarely does she imagine anything sexual when she plays with herself. *This feels nice,* she'll think. *This is pleasurable.* Dixon could be a thousand miles away, on a Pacific island, tattooing himself with a bird quill. The important thing is that Cory is happy; she loves even Cory the savage: this is what she is thinking, or feeling, while she watches him watch wrestling. She fingers herself fondly and more intently. Dixon could be in Iceland, in Greenland, encased in ice, grinning as if he's performing a public service . . .

She moans loudly, twice, before she thinks to suppress it. She tightens up, and a shudder passes through her, unaided.

Opening her eyes, she sees Cory staring at her. "Are you gonna pass out?"

"I'm dizzy," she says. "I think I might have food poisoning."

She runs to the bathroom, locks the door, and pumps soap onto her hands. She squeezes them together under the running water until they hurt. She is frantic, crying. What was she doing? Why couldn't she have waited until she was alone? Dixon's torn some seal or protective covering or something, and now she can't control herself.

"Are you O.K.?" Cory says on the other side of the bathroom door. "Can I help you throw up?"

Andrea tells him she'll be all right. She lets the faucet run, sits on the toilet, and cries a little more. When she's done, she feels emptied, better. She decides to paint her toenails copper red. She collects all the supplies from the medicine cabinet and sets them in front of her. Applying the nail polish, she imagines she's being evaluated. She's careful. Her strokes are smooth, no streak marks, no polish, not a drop, on her cuticles. How efficient her technique! How not-ugly her toes! Another vision of Dixon: shirtless in his bedroom, squinting, aiming the needle at his arm.

August 25, she reminds herself. Then Calculus, Geology Lab, Argumentative Writing, Volleyball. Volleyball!

In the living room, Cory is watching *Xtreme Animal Challenge*, which shows footage of animals stalking, chasing, catching, and eating other animals. The host says, "Does anyone have some jelly? Because this gazelle is *toast*!" A gazelle, pulled down in midstride by some lions, folds onto itself like an empty sleeve.

Andrea sits down next to her brother, who watches the lion eat the gazelle. The lion tosses a hunk of flesh aside. "Picky, picky," the host says. Why does everything have to be so hostile and funny? When she was Cory's age, she used to watch a woman tell stories using a series of hand puppets. At the end of the show the woman would hold up a mirror, turn around, and say, "Magic Mirror, tell me today, are all my friends at home at play?"

"This is tedious," Andrea says. "Do you know what tedious is?"

Cory considers it for a second. "No. Do you know that there are some plants that will eat ground beef?"

Later, Dixon calls. He tells her to be ready in the morning for a surprise. For the rest of the night Andrea doesn't know what to do with herself. She reads a book to Cory, who lies on the carpet with his eyes closed. She studies her toenails, which, dry, are more ruby red than copper red. Oh, the little disappointments. She imagines she is still being evaluated, but now she isn't doing so well. She's being penalized for diminishing congeniality. Dixon should know that saying get ready for a surprise makes the surprise unsurprising. There's still the surprise, but not the surprise of the surprise.

"Cory?" she says.

He has fallen asleep on the carpet. Asleep, he looks like Cory the boy again.

In the morning, when Andrea locks the front door and starts down the driveway, she sees Dixon's car coming up the street. It moves slowly and low to the ground, scurrying forward like a cockroach. When she gets in she sees that Dixon is wearing tan slacks and a striped shirt with a button-down collar. His hair is wet, he's clean-shaven. There are small red bumps along his jawline. "The guard let you in?" she asks.

"I replaced my oil pan. He said I'm free to enter and exit at my discretion."

Turning out of the Grove, Dixon salutes the security guard. Cuff links, Andrea notices. She wears a tank top and a pair of shorts with a bad waistband. She feels gloomy and slack, inadequately prepared for the day; on her way to the front gate is when she usually prepares. Dixon, in that outfit, is going to expect something from her, she is sure.

On the beachside, they pass a water park: chainlink fences around yellow slides named after natural disasters. The Typhoon, the Tsunami. The early morning sun casts everything in blushing light, peach and sea foam green like a yard sale sofa. The hotels, the houses, the streets. Dixon is excited today, singing with the radio. He smiles by squinting. He drives exactly thirty-five miles an hour. Every few blocks he's proven wrong.

A bearded man at the street corner points accusingly at a newspaper machine, argues with it. "Cajun!" Andrea yells out the open window.

Dixon turns down the radio. "Don't do that. Not today."

"Why?"

"It's childish. Plus, today's different."

As if for proof, he pulls into the parking lot of a two-storied cinder-block motel with yellow doors and a yellow sign: SIDE-O-SEA MOTEL. He leaves the car running while he goes into the office. Suede loafers, Andrea notices. She imagines he's attempting a romantic gesture by dressing up and bringing her here. She feels sorry for him, for herself. Wedged into the dashboard is a picture of her sitting on the hood of the car, taken when they went to see the Fun Shack building. In the picture she appears pleased with herself, sloppily.

Their motel room is dark and cold with ugly, palm-patterned drapes closed across a sliding glass door, which, presumably, looks out onto the ocean. The floor is silver terrazzo, polished to dullness. Dixon sets a duffel bag on one of the beds, unzips it, and pulls out gloves, towels, disinfectant, tubing, his tattoo gun.

"What are you doing?" she says. She looks at the door, at him, at the door again. The door isn't yellow on this side, but brown.

"Unpacking," he says.

He stands between her and the door. "What are *we* doing? With your tattoo gun."

"Tattoo *machine*," he says. He's tricked her! He reaches into the duffel bag again — twine? handcuffs? — and pulls out a flyer. TATTOOIZM ENTERPRIZES, it says at the top. She scans the rest of it: something about free demonstrations, something about a variety of designs available. She's relieved, though not totally relieved.

"Do you realize that there are people who want tattoos but can't afford them?"

"You're kidding."

"No."

"This is the surprise? Tattoos for the underprivileged?"

"Do I look like I'm kidding?"

No, he doesn't look like he's kidding.

There's a knock at the door. Dixon opens it and a tentative-acting drifter enters holding the same flyer Andrea is holding. Andrea sits on the bed while Dixon negotiates with the drifter. The man wants the Mitsubishi logo tattooed on his upper arm, his favorite car is a Mitsubishi. Dixon needs a picture of the Mitsubishi logo. The man doesn't have one, maybe there's a Mitsubishi out in the parking lot? "Listen," Dixon says. "I'll do a nice yin-yang for you. The yin-yang's been around for several thousand years."

The man considers it for a moment, shrugs.

Dixon unbuttons his cuff links and rolls up his sleeves while the man sits down with a cough on the other bed. The man smells like spray paint and stale beer. Dixon wipes the man's arm with disinfectant, then carefully assembles his tattoo gun. Andrea turns on the TV, lies on her stomach, and gets very interested in a special about famous despots. No reason to leave now: the special has just started. Most despots, but not all, are failed students, it says. Most, not all, love dogs. Most, not all, worry about their height. The more Andrea learns about despots, the less historic her presence in the motel room feels. She relaxes. The man on the bed next to hers coughs a scuffed-leather cough.

"Did yours hurt like this?" he asks after a while. Andrea waits for Dixon's answer, then realizes the man is addressing her.

"I don't have any tattoos," she says.

"It feels like I'm being chewed. No, friends, I don't think I like this one bit."

Dixon bears down over him. When he's finished, his gloves are spotted with dark blood. He conceals the yin-yang under a bandage and throws the gloves onto the floor. "Drink plenty of water," he says. "In about four days, the yin-yang will start to itch: don't scratch it. A slap, a light slap, will suffice."

Andrea imagines a great fog lifting when she starts school. She'll tell her next boyfriend that Dixon was avid about his work. *So few have such passion!* she'll say. So few do. When Dixon concentrates he looks like a boy. She likes him most when he is concentrating, when his expression is guileless and imperturbable. He is sexiest when he's at his most unaware. She probably won't tell her next boyfriend this.

A woman knocks on the door and asks for a red rose on her shoulder. Dixon didn't bring any red ink, so she settles for a palm tree. The woman falls asleep while he's working. The next man, who wants the Marine Corps bulldog on his stomach, settles for a palm tree also. "The palm is our most sophisticated tree," Dixon says.

The man has a blue tear tattooed on his cheek. When he leaves, Dixon tells Andrea that the tear means he has killed someone.

A woman in a Jaguars sweatsuit comes in and says, "I came for some praying hands, but there's a dude downstairs talking about his arm being manhandled."

"He had sensitive skin," Dixon says. "Why don't I give you a sample with white ink. If it hurts too much I can stop and no damage done."

"I don't want no half tattoo."

"It's not a tattoo," Dixon says. "It's the tattoo *feeling.*"

A tan boy in flip-flops comes in with a picture of a flag with a blue stripe at the top and bottom. Dixon studies the picture while Andrea studies the boy's toes: the hair on them is blond, almost white. Around his right ankle is an inch-wide tan line from his surfboard leash. He's a surfer, Andrea's age. He is watching her. She turns back to the television.

Most despots, but not all, die in uniform.

"You're Andrea, right?" the boy says.

Andrea looks up from the television.

"You used to date Bobby. He's always talking about you."

Bobby was, is, the surfer. "What do you mean?" she says.

"Bobby, when he's talking, a lot of the time it's about you. Does that make sense? 'Andrea told me blah, but she meant blah-blah.' 'Andrea acted like she didn't like anything.' Bobby can't figure you out."

"Bobby wasn't too observant. I like plenty of things."

"Yeah. I'll be sure to let him know I saw you here. In this motel room. Bobby and I are leaving for Costa Rica in a few weeks."

It seems unfair that, now that they aren't together, Bobby always talks about her. When they were together, Bobby always talked about Costa Rica. "Tell Bobby people aren't supposed to be figured out," she says.

Dixon, who's been staring at the picture, hands it back to the boy. "I'm here for the needy," he says.

The boy looks at Andrea, then at Dixon, and seems to swallow whatever retort he had. When he leaves, Dixon bolts the door and sits down next to Andrea while she watches the closing credits. She singles out the nice-sounding names: Mira, Sven, Lamar, Katya.

The boy is going to tell everyone she's unhappy, jealous of him and Bobby on their way to Costa Rica. "For a few thousand dollars it's possible to live like a sultan in Costa Rica," Bobby used to say. He said it with such greedy certainty. "Who wants to live like a sultan?" Andrea would ask. What does Costa Rica have to do with anything? She isn't unhappy. What makes her unhappy is the fact that the boy thinks she's unhappy.

She rolls over and lets Dixon kiss her. He tastes familiar. He rubs her hips, then scoots down on the bed and removes her shorts and underwear in a single tug. He takes off his shirt and kisses her breasts, her navel, strokes her neck with his left hand. *O live!* she sees. Really, the tattoos don't look that bad. The lines are assured, the shading delicate. At least he's passionate about something.

He turns off the TV and removes his pants.

"Let's lie here for a little while," she says. Since the episode with Cory, she has begun refusing sex once per day. One has to make rules, even arbitrary rules. Refusing sex usually means delaying it for forty-five minutes.

"Whatever you want," Dixon says. He lies on his back and puts his hand in his underwear, where it remains. "I'm exhausted," he says. "We've done some good! I mean, let's not rest on our laurels, but let's not fail to recognize obvious truths."

Her heart beats erratically. Given the right wording, she thinks Dixon could persuade her to get a tattoo, a very small one, on her ankle. She thinks she could be persuaded, given the right wording, to do just about anything.

"Tell me about Bobby," he says. "We know he's a surfer. And that he's on his way to Costa Rica with another surfer. That he spends all his time thinking about you, like I do."

"I barely remember him," she says. This is true, and also insufficient. Once, she had a conception of how she would describe him to her next boyfriend, but she's forgotten it. Dixon has never asked about him. She says, "He drank a lot of water."

Dixon adjusts himself. "Everyone's a mystery."

"He liked summer."

"Most do."

She feels sad. She has long suspected that, behind her back, people were reaching a consensus about her. Soon Bobby and his friends will agree on her past, present, and future unhappiness. Andrea will concede the past, concede the present, but she is *not* destined to be unhappy! She's just overly hopeful. When reality fails to meet expectation, she's disappointed! Isn't everyone?

"Can I satisfy you now?" Dixon asks.

Yes, she tells him.

As he bites her ear, there's another knock at the door. They lie still until they hear footsteps retreating.

Later, Dixon says, "I've been thinking, Andrea. You said you don't want a tattoo, but do you realize I can put one anywhere, on your armpit, on the inside of your lip?"

She doesn't know the wording she was thinking of earlier, but she knows this is not it. She tells him she doesn't want a tattoo.

"You start school in a few weeks," he says. "Then what? We spend less and less time together. You're tired all the time. I call you and you're in class or at the library, studying with Ashley and Chad. 'Can I take a message?' your mom says. But there is no message. I'll go out of my way to drive past the college, imagining you in class, raising your hand, asking questions just to ask questions, trying so hard. I never raised my hand. I'm not stupid. How can I convince you how happy I'd be if you'd allow me to put a tattoo on your thigh? A remembrance, a tribute, small?"

Her first impulse is to argue with the prediction, to tell him that her starting school doesn't mean they'll break up, who knows what will happen. She's annoyed. Partly by the assumption that she's so easily distractible, partly by the fact that she and Dixon have been imagining futures so similar.

"How bad will it hurt?" she asks.

He says he can put the tattoo on the back of her thigh, which will hurt less because there's so much fatty tissue. "No offense," he says. "It'll take twenty minutes, tops."

He stands up before she says anything, puts on his underwear and a pair of surgical gloves, and begins cleaning the ink tube in the sink. She looks at the bedside clock: two hours until she has to babysit Cory. Dixon in the daytime, Cory at night. She is being pulled from both ends. The other day Cory said, "If I got a tattoo, it would be a word only I knew the meaning of."

She lies on her stomach while Dixon sterilizes her leg. The cloth is cool, and then the gun buzzes, and her thigh feels slightly hot, but she can see Dixon hasn't started yet. He stares at her thigh. "I can do a letter, a shape, anything you want."

"Where are you going to put it?"

"I'll center it. It'll look like it's been there all your life."

She tells him to give her a small asterisk on the side of her thigh, then explains what an asterisk looks like. Dixon nods, still staring at her thigh, memorizing it. He is excited. Andrea feels buoyed by his excitement. Finding the right things to want is easy, she decides. Actually wanting them, this is the difficult part.

She stares at the ugly drapes, waits for the needle. She thinks, *It's just as easy to make drapes pretty as drapes ugly.* She thinks, *Another contented cow thought.*

August 25. Calculus, Geology Lab, Argumentative Writing, and Volleyball. She'll get to know her professors. She'll buy terry cloth running shorts, a shirt with stripes down the sleeves. She'll befriend people because of their interesting-sounding names. She'll take notes with one of those four-color ink pens, changing ink color for each class.

Dixon dabs at her leg with a towel. He is leaning over her so purposefully, attending to her. "Almost there," he says. "You all right?"

She'll miss Dixon, she already misses him. The fog will lift, and Dixon will be gone and she will miss him. She will tell her next boyfriend that Dixon, poor Dixon, was very nice, that she has nothing but nice things to say about him. The next boyfriend will understand. He will offer to scratch her back, or apply lotion to her back, or whatever the occasion calls for.

Dixon dabs at her thigh some more, then sets the tattoo gun on the end table. "I'm finished," he says.

"That's it?" Andrea says. "That didn't feel like being chewed."

"Fatty tissue," he says.

"Can I look at it? What's it look like?"

"It's lovely. A perfect souvenir."

She walks over to the full-length mirror. In her bare feet, over the dull terrazzo.

"It didn't feel like anything," she says. She turns around and looks for the tattoo. In the center of her thigh are a few beads of blood around a colorless star, a tiny patch of skin faded to white.

Dixon removes his gloves. They snap off his fingers.

"It isn't," he says.

THOMAS McGUANE

Cowboy

FROM THE NEW YORKER

THE OLD FELLA makes me go into the house in my stocking feet. The old lady's in a big chair next to the window. In fact, the whole room is full of big chairs, but she's only in one of them — though, big as she is, she could fill up several. The old man says, "I found this one in the loose-horse pen at the sale yard."

She says, "What's he supposed to be?"

He says, "Supposed to be a cowboy."

"What's he doin' in the loose horses?"

I says, "I was lookin' for one that would ride."

"You was in the wrong pen, son," the old man says. "Them's canners. They're goin' to France in cardboard boxes."

"Soon as they get a steel bolt in the head." The big old gal laughs in her chair.

Now I'm sore. "There's five in there broke to death. I rode 'em with nothin' but binder twine."

"It don't make a shit," the old man says. "Ever' one of them is goin' to France."

The old lady don't believe me. "How'd you get in them loose horses to ride?"

"I went in there at night."

The old lady says, "You one crazy cowboy, go in there in the dark. Them broncs kick your teeth down your throat. I suppose you tried them bareback?"

"Naw, I drug the saddle I usually ride at the Rose Bowl Parade."

"You got a horse for that?"

"I got Trigger. We unstuffed him."

The old lady addresses the old man. "He's got a mouth on him. This much we know."

"Maybe he can tell us what good he is."

I says, "I'm a cowboy."

"You're a outta-work cowboy."

"It's a dying way of life."

"She's about like me — she's wondering if this ranch's supposed to be some kinda welfare agency for cowboys."

I've had enough. "You're the dumb honyocker drove me out here."

I think that'll be the end of it, but the old lady says, "Don't get huffy. You got the job. You against conversation or something?"

We get outside and the old sumbitch says, "You drawed lucky there, son. That last deal could've pissed her off."

"It didn't make me no nevermind if it did or didn't."

"She hadn't been well. Used to she was sweet as pudding."

"I'm sorry for that. We don't have health, we don't have nothin'."

She must have been afflicted something terrible, because she was ugly morning, noon, and night for as long as she lasted — she'd pick a fight over nothing, and the old sumbitch got the worst of it. I felt sorry for him, little slack as he cut me.

Had a hundred seventy-five sweet-tempered horned Herefords and fifteen sleepy bulls. Shipped the calves all over for hybrid vigor, mostly to the South. Had some go clear to Florida. A Hereford that still had its horns was a walking miracle, and the old sumbitch had a smart little deal going. I soon learned to give him credit for such things, and the old lady barking commands offen the sofa weren't no slouch neither. Anybody else seen their books might've said they could be wintering in Phoenix.

They didn't have no bunkhouse, just a LeisureLife mobile home that had lost its wheels about thirty years ago, and they had it positioned by the door of the barn so it'd be convenient for the hired man to stagger out at all hours and fight breech births and scours and any other disorder sent us by the cow gods. We had some doozies. One heifer got pregnant, and her calf was near as big as she was. Had to reach in with a saw and take it out in pieces. When we threw the head out on the ground, she turned to it and lowed like it was her baby. Everything a cow does is designed to turn it into meat as fast as possible so that somebody can eat it. It's a terrible life.

The old sumbitch and I got along good. We got through calving and got to see them pairs and bulls run out onto the new grass. Nothing like seeing all that meat feel a little temporary joy. Then we bladed out the corrals and watched them dry under the spring sun at long last. Only mishap was when the manure spreader threw a rock and knocked me senseless and I drove the rig into an irrigation ditch. The old sumbitch never said a word but chained up and pulled us out with his Ford.

We led his cavvy out of the hills afoot with two buckets of sweet feed. Had a little of everything, including a blue roan I fancied, but he said it was a Hancock and bucked like the National Finals in Las Vegas, kicking out behind and squalling, and was just a man-killer. "Stick to the bays," he said. "The West was won on a bay horse."

He picked out three bays, had a keg of shoes, all ones and oughts, and I shod them best I could, three geldings with nice manners, stood good to shoe. About all you could say about the others was they had four legs each, and a couple, all white-marked from saddle galls and years of hard work, looked like no more summers after this. They'd been rode many a long mile. We chased 'em back into the hills and the three shod ones whinnied and fretted. "Back to work," the old sumbitch says to them.

We shod three 'cause one was going to pack a ton of fencing supplies — barb wire, smooth wire, steel T-posts, old wore-out Sunflower fence stretchers that could barely grab on to the wire, and staples — and we was at it a good little while where the elk had knocked miles of it down, or the cedar finally give out and had to be replaced by steel. That was where I found out that the old sumbitch's last good time was in Korea, where the officers at the front would yell over the radio, "Come on up here and die!" Said the enemy was coming in waves. Tells me all this while the stretcher's pulling that wire squealing through the staples. The sumbitch was a tough old bastard. "They killed a pile of us and we killed a pile of them." *Squeak.*

We hauled the mineral horseback, too, in panniers — white salt and iodine salt. He didn't have no use for blocks, so we hauled it in sacks and poured it into the troughs he had on all these bald hilltops where the wind would blow away the flies. Most of his so-called troughs were truck tires nailed onto anything flat — plywood, old doors, and suchlike — but they worked good. A cow can put her tongue anywhere in a tire and get what she needs, and you can drag one of them flat things with your horse if you need to move it. Most places we salted had old buffalo wallers where them buffalo wallered. They done wallered their last — had to get out of the way for the cow and the man on the bay horse.

I'd been rustling my own grub in the LeisureLife for quite some time when the old lady said it was time for me to eat with the white folks. This was not necessarily a good thing. The old lady's knee replacements had begun to fail, and both me and the old sumbitch was half-afraid of her. She cooked as good as ever, but she was a bomb waiting to go off, standing bowlegged at the stove and talking ugly about how much she did for us. When she talked, the old sumbitch would move his mouth as though he was saying the same words, and we had to keep from giggling, which wasn't hard. For if the old lady caught us at that there'd a been hell to pay.

Both the old sumbitch and the old lady was heavy smokers, to where a oxygen bottle was in sight. So they joined a Smoke-Enders deal the Lutherans had, and this required them to put all their butts in a jar and wear the jar around their necks on a string. The old sumbitch liked this O.K. because he could just tap his ash right under his chin and not get it on the truck seat, but the more that thing filled up and hung around her neck the meaner the old lady got. She had no idea the old sumbitch was cheating and setting his jar on the woodpile when we was working outside. She was just more honest than him, and in the end she give up smoking and he smoked away, except he wasn't allowed to smoke in the house no more, nor buy ready-mades, 'cause the new tax made them too expensive and she wouldn't let him take it out of the cows, which come first. She said it was just a vice and if he was half the man she thought he was he'd give it up as a bad deal. "You could have a long and happy old age," she said, real sarcastic-like.

One day me and the old sumbitch is in the house hauling soot out of the fireplace, on account of they had a chimbley fire last winter. Over the mantel is a picture of a beautiful woman in a red dress with her hair piled on top of her head. The old sumbitch tells me that's the old lady before she joined the motorcycle gang.

"Oh?"

"Them motorcycle gangs," he says, "all they do is eat and work on their motorcycles. They taught her to smoke, too, but she's shut of that. Probably outlive us all."

"Looks to me she can live long as she wants."

"And if she ever wants to box you, tell her no. She'll knock you on your ass. I guarantee it. Throw you a damn haymaker, son."

I couldn't understand how he could be so casual-like about the old lady being in a motorcycle gang. When we was smoking in the LeisureLife, I asked him about it. That's when I found out that him and the old lady was brother and sister. I guess that explained it. If your sister wants to join a motorcycle gang, that's her business. He said she even had a tattoo — "Hounds from Hell," with a dog shooting flames out of his nostrils and riding a Harley.

That picture on the mantel kind of stayed in my mind, and I asked the old sumbitch if his sister'd ever had a boyfriend. Well, yes, quite a few, he told me, quite a damn few. "Our folks run them off. They was just after the land."

He was going all around the baler hitting the zerks with his grease gun. "I had a lady friend myself. She'd do anything. Cook. Gangbusters with a snorty horse, and not too damn hard on the eyes. Sis run her off. Said she was just after the land. If she was, I never could see it. Anyway, went on down the road long time ago."

Fall come around and when we brought the cavvy down two of them old-timers who'd worked so hard was lame. One was stifled, one was sweenied, and both had crippling quarter cracks. I thought they needed to be at the loose-horse sale, but the old sumbitch says, "No mounts of mine is gonna feed no Frenchman," and that was that. So we made a hole, led the old-timers to the edge, and shot them with a elk rifle. First one didn't know what hit him. Second one heard the shot and saw his buddy fall, and the old sumbitch had to chase him around to kill him. Then he sent me down the hole to get the halters back. Lifting those big heads was some chore.

I enjoyed eating in the big house that whole summer until the sister started giving me come-hither looks. They was fairly limited except those days when the old sumbitch was in town after supplies. Then she dialed it up and kind of brushed me every time she went past the table. There was always something special on the town days — a pie, maybe. I tried to think about the picture on the mantel, but it was impossible, even though I knew it might get me out of the LeisureLife once and for all. She was getting more and more wound up, while I was pretending to enjoy the food or going crazy over the pie. But she didn't buy it — called me a queer and sent me back to the trailer to make my own meals. By calling me a queer, she more or less admitted what she'd been up to, and I think that embarrassed her, because she covered up by roaring at everyone and everything, including the poor old sumbitch, who had no idea what had gone sideways while he was away. It was two years before she made another pie, and then it was once a year on my birthday. She made me five birthday pies in all — sand cherry, every one of them.

I broke the catch colt, which I didn't know was no colt, as he was the biggest snide in the cavvy. He was four, and it was time. I just got around him for a couple of days, then saddled him gently as I could. The offside stirrup scared him, and he looked over at it, but that was all it was to saddling. I must've had a burst of courage, 'cause next minute I was on him. That was O.K., too. I told the old sumbitch to open the corral gate, and we sailed away. The wind blew his tail up under him, and he thought about bucking but rejected the idea and that was about all they was to breaking Olly, for that was his name. Once I'd rode him two weeks, he was safe for the old sumbitch, who plumb loved this new horse and complimented me generously for the job I'd did.

We had three hard winters in a row, then lost so many calves to scours we changed our calving grounds. The old sumbitch just come out one day and looked at where he'd calved out for fifty years and said, "The ground's no good. We're movin." So we spent the summer building a new corral way off down the creek. When we's finished, he says, "I meant to do this when I got back from overseas and now it's finished and I'm practically done for, too. Whoever gets the place next will be glad his calves don't shit themselves into the next world like mine done."

Neither one of us had a back that was worth a damn, and the least we could do was get rid of the square baler and quit hefting them man-killing five-wire bales. We got a round baler and a DewEze machine that let us pick up a bale from the truck without laying a finger on it. We'd tell stories and smoke in the cab on those cold winter days and roll out a thousand pounds of hay while them old-time horned Herefords followed the truck. That's when I let him find out I'd done some time.

"I figured you musta been in the crowbar hotel."

"How's that?"

"Well, you're a pretty good hand. What's a pretty good hand doin' tryin' loose horses in the middle of the night at some Podunk sale yard? Folks hang on to a pretty good hand, and nobody was hangin' on to you. You want to tell me what you done?"

I'd been with the old sumbitch for three years and out of jail the same amount of time. I wasn't afraid to tell him what I done 'cause I had started to trust him, but I sure didn't want him telling nothing to his sister. I told him I rustled some yearlings, and he chuckled like he understood entirely. I had rustled some yearlings, all right, but that's not what I went up for.

The old man paid me in cash, or, rather, the old lady did, since she handled anything like that. They never paid into workmen's comp, and there was no reason to go to the records. They didn't even have my name right. You tell people around here your name is Shane, and they'll always believe you. The important thing is I was working my tail off for that old sumbitch, and he knew it. Nothing else mattered, even the fact that we'd come to like each other. After all, this was a goddamn ranch.

The old fella had several peculiarities to him, most of which I've forgotten. He was one of the few fellas I ever heard of who would actually jump up and down on his hat if he got mad enough. You can imagine what his hat looked like. One time he did it 'cause I let the swather get away from me on a hill and bent it all to hell. Another time a Mormon tried to run down his breeding program to get a better deal on some replacement heifers, and I'll be damned if the old sumbitch didn't throw that hat down and jump on it, right in front of the Mormon, causing the Mormon to get into his Buick and ease on down the road without another word. One time when we was driving ring shanks into corral poles I hit my thumb and tried jumping on my hat, but the old sumbitch gave me such an odd look I never tried it again.

The old lady died sitting down. I went in, and there she was, sitting down, and she was dead. After the first wave of grief, the old sumbitch and me fretted about rigor mortis and not being able to move her in that seated position. So we stretched her onto the couch and called the mortician and he called the coroner and for some reason the coroner called the ambulance, which caused the old sumbitch to state, "It don't do you no nevermind to tell nobody nothing." Course he was right.

Once the funeral was behind us, I moved out of the LeisureLife, partly for comfort and partly 'cause the old sumbitch fell apart after his sister passed, which I never would've suspected. Once she's gone, he says, he's all that's left of his family and he's alone in life, and about then he notices me and tells me to get my stuff out of the LeisureLife and move in with him.

We rode through the cattle pritnear ever' day year round, and he come to trust me enough to show how his breeding program went, with culls and breedbacks and outcrosses and replacements, and took me to bull sales and showed me what to expect in a bull and which ones were correct and which were sorry. One day we's looking at a pen of yearling bulls on this outfit near Luther and he can't make up his mind and he says he wished his sister was with him and he starts snuffling and says she had an eye on her wouldn't quit. So I stepped up and picked three bulls out of that pen, and he quit snuffling and said damn if I didn't have an eye on me, too. That was the beginning of our partnership.

One whole year I was the cook, and one whole year he was the cook, and back and forth like that, but never at the same time. Whoever was cook would change when the other fella got sick of his recipes, and ever once in a while a new recipe would come in the *AgriNews*, like that corn chowder with the sliced hot dogs. I even tried a pie one time, but it just made him lonesome for days gone by, so we forgot about desserts, which was probably good for our health, as most sweets call for gobbing in the white sugar.

The sister never let him have a dog 'cause she had a cat and she thought a dog would get the cat. It wasn't much of a cat, anyhow, but it lived a long time, outlived the old lady by several moons. After it passed on, we took it out to the burn barrel and the first thing the old sumbitch said was "We're gettin' a dog." It took him that long to realize that his sister was gone.

Tony was a Border collie we got as a pup from a couple in Miles City that raised them. You could cup your hands and hold Tony when we got him, but he grew up in one summer and went to work and we taught him "down," "here," "come by," "way to me," and "hold 'em," all in one year or less, 'cause Tony would just stay on his belly and study you with his eyes until he knew exactly what you wanted. Tony helped us gather, mother up pairs, and separate bulls, and he lived in the house for many a good year and kept us entertained with all his tricks. Finally, Tony grew old and died. We didn't take it so good, especially the old sumbitch, who said he couldn't foresee enough summers for another dog. Plus that was the year he couldn't get on a horse no more and he wasn't about to work no stock dog afoot. There was still plenty to do and most of it fell to me. After all, this was a goddamn ranch.

The time had come to tell him why I went to jail and what I did, which was rob that little store at Absarokee and shoot the proprietor, though he didn't die. I had no idea why I did such a thing — then or now. I led the crew on the prison ranch for a number of years and turned out many a good hand. They wasn't nearabout to let me loose until there was a replacement good as me who'd stay awhile. So I trained up a murderer from Columbia Falls, could rope, break horses, keep vaccine records, fence, and irrigate. Once the warden seen how good he was, they paroled me out and turned it all over to the new man, who was never getting out. The old sumbitch could give a shit less when I told him my story. I could've told him all this years before when he first hired me, for all he cared. He was a big believer in what he saw with his own eyes.

I don't think I ever had the touch with customers the old sumbitch had. They'd come from all over looking for horned Herefords and talking hybrid vigor, which I may or may not have believed. They'd ask what we had and I'd point to the corrals and say, "Go look for yourself." Some would insist on seeing the old sumbitch, and I'd tell them he was in bed, which was pritnear the only place you could find him now that he'd begun to fail. Then the state got wind of his condition and took him to town. I went to see him there right regular, but it just upset him. He couldn't figure out who I was and got frustrated 'cause he knew I was somebody he was supposed to know. And then he failed even worse. The doctors told me it was just better if I didn't come round.

The neighbors claimed I was personally responsible for the spread of spurge, Dalmatian toadflax, and knapweed. They got the authorities involved and it was pretty clear that I was the weed they had in mind. If they could get the court to appoint one of their relatives ranch custodian while the old sumbitch was in storage they'd get all that grass for free till he was in a pine box. The authorities came in all sizes and shapes, but when they were through they let me take one saddle horse, one saddle, the clothes on my back, my hat, and my slicker. I rode that horse clear to the sale yard, where they tried to put him in the loose horses 'cause of his age. I told them I was too set in my ways to start feeding Frenchmen and rode off toward Idaho. There's always an opening for a cowboy, even a old sumbitch like me if he can halfway make a hand.

JACK LIVINGS

The Dog

FROM THE PARIS REVIEW

AFTER LI YAN PUT THE BABY DOWN, she joined her husband at the rough table. He was reading *People's Daily* in the brown light of a bare bulb dangling from the ceiling. Li Yan opened her English textbook and began to read a dialogue. It was still early, but she was worn out and had trouble focusing on the words.

Pretty soon she looked up and said, "Chen Wei, do you want some tea?"

From behind the paper he said no.

"O.K. It's no trouble. I'll make you some anyway."

"Fine," he said. "Just not too many leaves."

Li Yan filled the kettle and turned on the coil. The light buzzed and the room took on a subterranean murk. Chen Wei rattled his paper at her.

"Hello there," she said. The paper rose again. She unwrapped the tea package and put leaves in a cup for herself, then sprinkled some in another cup for her husband. She thought for a moment about taking a dumpling back to the table for him, then decided against it. She'd sworn never to stuff him the way his mother had. No wonder he didn't like to eat.

It was dusk, warm out, and street noise came in through the open doorway. Occasionally a leaf or a scrap of paper would drift across the threshold. Next door, pensioners slapped their chess pieces on the board outside Old Feng's house. They could get rowdy, sometimes playing until dawn when they had enough to drink, and then Old Feng would sing opera in a warbling voice. Old Feng's wife was head of the neighborhood committee, but no one had the courage to confront her about the noise. She was paranoid and sharp-tongued, especially when it came to defending Old Feng. No one crossed her. In a way, Li Yan admired the woman's harsh reputation. She'd seen some things in her life.

"Hope they don't wake up the baby tonight," Li Yan said.

"What am I supposed to do about it?" Chen Wei said. He adjusted his reading glasses. He kept them low on his nose and peered over the top of the lenses because his vision was fine. Li Yan made him wear them.

"Just thinking out loud," she said. She turned off the coil. The light bulb above Chen Wei's head flickered, burned intensely yellow for a moment, then resigned itself to a dingy glow. She carried the teacups to the table and set one in front of the newspaper.

"If you were more of a chess player, you might have some pull with them," she said.

"You know, not everything you think is worth saying out loud," he said.

"Very wise," she said.

She went back to her dialogue, sounding out the words in a whisper. The book was filled with ink drawings of Alex and Mary, a stylish young American couple. Mary always wore high heels and a tweedy skirt, and Alex a dark blazer, unless they were at the beach or an embassy ball. They bore no resemblance to Li Yan's English teacher, an American college student who sometimes touched his students on the shoulder and wore the same flannel shirt and dirty blue jeans every week. He laughed at his own jokes. She suspected that he had never been away from home before. During free-talk hour, she and her classmates usually tried to ask him questions about his family to determine whether he was homesick. Everyone agreed that he was terribly lonely so far away from his parents.

I would like to buy a computer. I would like to buy a stereo. She paused every couple of sentences for a sip of tea, and had fallen into a meditative rhythm when her husband grunted and threw down the paper. His teacup spiraled across the table. Li Yan caught the cup before it tumbled off the edge. A thin pool of water steamed on the table.

"Look at this," he said, stabbing at the paper with his finger.

"What now?" she said in English.

"Read what it says," he said. "There, on page six."

The Dog

She peeled the paper off the table and stared at the puddle of water.

"I'll clean it up," he said. "Just read."

"What am I looking at?"

"There, look there."

She read the block of characters he was pointing to. The Beijing Municipal Government had cracked down on dog racing. The paper quoted a cadre: "We are committed to stamping out corruption," he said. "As we all know, gambling spoils even the most steadfast heart. Fines will go toward cultural improvement programs."

"Politicians. If I had five minutes with one of those guys," Chen Wei said. He shook his fist at the wall. "It's unbelievable. Everything I do goes up in flames."

Li Yan took the cotton rag from his hand and started swabbing at the spilled tea. "I get it," she said. "You're a funny guy." Chen Wei worked for the Public Utilities Bureau. He burned bodies at the Number 7 Crematorium.

"Greedy bastards," he said.

"Would you be quiet? Everyone will hear you."

"I have to go see Zheng tomorrow. Don't expect me home."

"Don't be so dramatic. There's nothing he can do about this."

"I'll take the train after work and be back in the morning." He paused. "If I'm not robbed or killed on the way there." He drew a finger across his throat and bugged his eyes.

"That's very brave of you," she said. "Why don't you just call him from work? Life isn't a movie, you know. Sometimes it's best to stay calm."

"I don't have time to stand around all day yapping on the phone," he said. "Why don't you call him?"

"You're funny," she said. Li Yan was a tailor's apprentice. She had to ask permission just to use the bathroom.

"I'm serious. My work is time-sensitive. The dead are pesky that way," he said.

"Yeah, they're a demanding bunch," she said.

Li Yan actually liked Chen Wei's flair for the dramatic. He didn't have much else to recommend him — he wasn't rich and he smelled of greasy smoke and he looked as plain as a flap of burlap, but he had shown up at the gates of her high school every afternoon with a flower clutched in his chemical-stained hand. He'd spotted her walking in the market nearby, and he said he'd fallen in love instantly. Right there in the street he'd sung a pop ballad to her. A crowd had gathered, and some peasants watching the proceedings from a fruit stand had screamed "Young Love" over and over, as though a call to arms. At first Li Yan thought Chen Wei was crazy, and she'd told him so, and added that she hadn't appreciated being embarrassed in the middle of the street like that. *It will never happen again,* he'd said, his eyes so stricken that she realized he must have been serious. Three years later, she still hadn't figured out how to tell his moods apart. He was strange, but there was nothing wrong with that. He worked for a living. That was good. And in the weeks after they'd met, he was always waiting there at the gate, peering through the iron bars like a monkey in the zoo.

Chen Wei told her wild stories about working with his cousin, Zheng, in the western provinces, tales that involved dismemberment, knives, and, too often for her to believe, barefisted combat with wild animals. Later, Cousin Zheng — at the time, just a name Chen Wei waved around like a red scarf — had procured a dress for him to give her. It had a silk rose embroidered on the thigh.

Zheng was Chen Wei's first cousin, and, since his parents' deaths, his closest living relative. Zheng had always been a real operator. A stint in the army hadn't reformed him at all, and now he lived near Yulin, where he was in import-export. He made money, but still lived like a peasant.

It had been Zheng's idea to purchase a racing dog, and because he lived in the countryside, he boarded the dog. Every weekend he traveled to Beijing for races. Though Li Yan had seen the dog only once — and then in its cage — she wasn't surprised that it won. It was muscled like a horse. The snout was as sleek as a bullet.

The dog had cost six hundred yuan. Then, for a license, another six hundred to the government. And three hundred yearly to maintain the license. After the dog won enough to cover the debts, Zheng declared it a good investment. Li Yan wasn't so sure. Zheng moved in dangerous circles, and though she couldn't forbid Chen Wei from partnering with him, she knew something would go wrong. Zheng had lost a chunk of Chen Wei's money a few years ago in a cigarette importing scheme — they'd met a shipper from Shenzhen who'd cooked up a plan to import American Marlboros secreted in false-bottomed cargo crates. But he needed investors up front. Chen Wei handed over his share. Two months later, Zheng told him the ship had been hit by a cyclone. "Lucky only one of us bought in," Zheng said. This was Chen Wei's lot in life. Li Yan hoped the man from Shenzhen had gone down with the ship.

There had been other catastrophes. A stock scheme. A plan to export artifacts from Suzhou. She'd argued with Chen Wei about the dog, but he'd told her the animal would pay for itself, and for once he'd been right. It was hard to argue with extra money.

That night she lay awake thinking about the swift dog sleeping three hundred li to the northwest. It had provided them with the spoils of a wealthier household — new wool sweaters, silk long underwear, and a grass-stroke scroll depicting the character for good luck, which hung opposite their bed. Chen Wei said the scroll spoke to him. Li Yan thought a microwave would have made better sense.

A few years ago she would have attributed his choice to his romantic streak, but now she wondered if he'd purchased it out of cowardice. They could have just as easily bought a microwave, but Chen Wei worried about attracting the attention of Old Feng's wife, a woman reputed to have the ear of a local cadre. They weren't doing anything illegal, but even today you had to watch out for the old guard. There was no point making people jealous. Perhaps it was better that they should go back to a modest life. They'd had the extra income for only a few months, not long enough to change their habits drastically. They had enough to eat, a healthy child, a place to live. No one could ask for more than that, Li Yan told herself.

Li Yan nudged Chen Wei with her leg. He sighed deeply and rolled over. She nudged him again.

"What?" he said.

"Don't you think Zheng mistreats you?" she said.

"Not now," he moaned.

"It's keeping me up. Why does Zheng take a bigger cut?"

"It's a business deal."

"Zheng's your partner. You're entitled to an equal share."

"It's a complex arrangement."

"Are you joking with me?" she said. "I can't see your face. Are you joking around?"

Chen Wei propped himself up on one elbow and cleared his

throat. Elm leaves rattled in the wind and threw ragged patterns across the wall of their room. Old Feng and his friends were still out there.

"As a husband, I would say that, as a wife, you're really hard to satisfy," Chen Wei said. He tickled her foot with his toe.

"It's not a hard question," she said.

"You're smarter than I am," Chen Wei said. "You tell me why he takes more. What difference does it make now?"

She listened to Old Feng and his friends push their chessmen around the board. They were behaving themselves tonight, voices muted but lively, like a clutch of girls passing around a secret. At one point the baby yodeled, and Li Yan tensed, but it was just a cry from a dream, and Li Yan settled back into her pillow.

"You should be more confident in life," Li Yan said.

"Aye, comrade."

"I'm not kidding. You possess the capacity for improvement. Everybody does. But you're too content."

"I do what I can. I have what I need."

"That's not true. Look at Zheng. He is a man of action. Don't you want to act?" It had occurred to Li Yan that those like Zheng — the boors, the idiots, the drooling slobs — in short, those worst equipped to navigate the slick world of commerce — were somehow the very people who reaped the hugest rewards. People forced to survive on ingenuity and pure will seemed to have luck on their side. She herself could never envy Zheng, but she thought her husband ought to. After all, Zheng was, in a way, a good role model for Chen Wei, who just couldn't seem to figure out how to put his talents to good use. Even at the crematorium he was the number two guy. She wanted him to be a number one guy.

"I do my best, you know," he said.

"I know," she said.

"There's more to me than meets the eye," he said.

"Let's go to sleep," she said.

"Tired of thinking out loud?"

"Let's go to sleep."

After work the next evening, Li Yan rode her bicycle to her parents' house. It was usually Chen Wei's duty to pick up the baby after work, but he'd packed a bag that morning and left the house with-

The Dog

out saying good-bye. She'd given it some thought, and she was glad he was on the train to see Zheng. But when she arrived at her parents' compound, Chen Wei's bicycle was parked outside. She pushed open the heavy door and walked into the dirt courtyard. Chen Wei was bouncing the baby on his knee, and Li Yan's father was puffing thoughtfully on his pipe. They were sitting on sacks of concrete by the clothesline. Wet clothes were piled in a basket, abandoned by her father when Chen Wei showed up, and Li Yan began draping shirts over the line. Both men looked at her, but didn't break the stride of their conversation. Someone was playing basketball nearby. The hollow sound of the ball clanging off the rim echoed through the maze of alleys surrounding the house.

"This is foolish," her father said. He expelled a bowl of smoke and shook his head. "I know your people are from the north, but this isn't how things are done. It's bad business sense. There must be someone willing to buy the dog."

"Who wants a racing dog you can't race?" Chen Wei said.

"You're thinking too small," the old man said.

Li Yan squatted down beside them and wrung out a pair of socks. The water formed muddy blisters on the courtyard floor. "Everyone on embassy row has a dog," she said. "Sell it to a foreigner." Her comment didn't seem to register with the two men.

"Look," her father said, "you live in the city now. Your own daughter is going to grow up here. Beijingers don't eat dog."

"Some restaurants in the Yuyuantan are serving it," Chen Wei said. "It's gaining acceptance."

"There is a great difference between acceptable behavior and civilized behavior," the old man said.

"Easy for you to say. Zheng doesn't approach problems the way you or I do."

"I know that," Li Yan's father said. "He thinks like a bandit."

"He's really got me over a barrel this time. That's the trouble with being an investor."

The old man looked to Li Yan for the first time, as if to ask how she could have brought such a weakling into the family. "Look, man, you still have a say," her father said.

Li Yan tossed the socks back into the basket and took her daughter from Chen Wei. "Zheng's selling the dog to a restaurant?" she said.

"Not exactly," Chen Wei said.
"This should be good."
"We're going to eat it."
She stared at him.

Chen Wei shrugged. "He wants to obliterate every trace of the dog. That's what he said."

"What did you say? You're still his partner," she said. "Even bandits talk things over."

"That's uncalled for," her father said, but Chen Wei waved it off.

"Zheng's already told the entire family there'll be a feast. You should have heard him. He was furious."

"What's he taking it out on the dog for?" she said.

"He doesn't react well to resistance. I can't tell him what to do."

Li Yan said, "He's got a screw loose."

"It's already decided."

Li Yan studied his face for some sign that he might consider opposing Zheng, but she only saw resignation in his hooded eyes.

"He's family," Chen Wei said. "We have a long history."

"Do you want me to call him? I'll give him a piece of my mind," she said.

Her father sucked on his pipe and mumbled, "Behave like a wife," but he didn't put much force behind his words.

"No," Chen Wei said. "I'll deal with it." But she knew he wouldn't.

Early that Saturday morning, Li Yan, Chen Wei, and their daughter crowded into a hard-seat car of the Number 44 train to Yulin. Four of the hard-seat cars were reserved for soldiers, young men who moved with dazed absence, as though they had been sleeping in the hot sun for a long time. That left only one hard-seat car for civilians — families traveling to see relatives in the country, merchants transporting goods to provincial markets, businessmen too poor to travel in soft-seat. Bundles the size of refrigerators blocked the aisle. There were no seats for Li Yan or her husband, so they fought their way to the back of the car and squatted by the bathroom door. The car was already filling with the low haze of cigarette smoke as the train pulled out of the West Station. Tinny revolutionary songs squawked from speakers in the corners of the car.

Chen Wei laid a leaf of newsprint on the floor between them and took out the playing cards. Li Yan beat him at Catch the Pig and

Struggling Upstream before they finally settled on Looking for Friends, which required less strategy. After their third game, the baby woke and cried some, but Li Yan got her back to sleep with a song. As she sang, a farmer wearing rags emerged from behind a bundle of vegetables. He crouched against the bathroom door and hummed along with her, then clapped when the song ended. Chen Wei shooed him, and the farmer drifted back into the car.

At the Xuanhua Station, they got off and found a bus going to Yulin. They had been in transit two hours already, and it was another hour before they reached Yulin, where they boarded a van traveling into the countryside. The driver's crony tried to gouge them once they were on the road, saying the baby counted as a person and needed a ticket, but the other passengers shouted him down. One old woman called him a wolf and shook her fist at him.

"I've known him a long time," she said. "He'd screw his own mother."

As thanks, Li Yan let her hold the baby until they disembarked at the dirt road leading to the village where Chen Wei had grown up. Hot, their clothes stained with dust and sweat, they arrived at his cousin's house just before noon. Zheng met them at the door and embraced them both. He was a barrel-chested man who looked something like a frog — bulbous eyes and wide lips that seemed barely able to contain his tongue. A cluster of dark hair sprouted from his chin.

"She's really getting fat," he said, pinching the baby's legs. "She'll make a good side dish." He spat out a sharp laugh.

Chen Wei laughed, too, but Li Yan could hear the discomfort in his voice. He would never come right out and say it, but she knew he was ashamed of his family's rough manners, their rugged faces and wide brown feet. She looked at his dust-creased face and saw a refugee. In the country, he drank heavily to disguise his shame, but she never chastised him when he was hung-over the next day. She leaned close to her husband while Zheng was rounding up the rest of the family and said, "You are a good cousin. Don't worry, we'll be back in Beijing tomorrow night." He looked puzzled.

Chen Wei spent the afternoon drinking and talking with the men. Aunties floated in and out of the house, an interchangeable cast of thickset women clad in blue cotton who ferried off the baby and left their own children with Li Yan. The children wouldn't stop talking about the dog, acting out great victories they'd heard about from Zheng, scampering in and out of the house on their hands and knees, barking and licking each other on the face. They pestered her to follow them into the backyard to see the dog, but she refused. She wanted to ask the children if they understood the dog would be killed, but couldn't bring herself to ruin their fun. As the afternoon wore on, she felt a dreadful unease set in, a misgiving mixed with disdain for her husband's run-down village. Meanwhile, her husband matched Zheng drink for drink, told bawdy jokes he'd heard at work, toasted his uncles, made a spectacle of himself. She could see that he was trying to liquor himself up for the slaughter. Zheng was a hardhearted man whose only goal in life was to become wealthy, but her husband wasn't so naturally equipped for the bloody work that lay ahead. He didn't fit in with these people.

Late in the afternoon, Zheng rose stiffly and raised his glass in an official toast. "To the Beijing Municipal Government, which has brought the family together again!" All the men raised their glasses and shouted "Gangbei." One of the uncles fell out of his chair. Outside, the aunties had dug a fire pit and assembled a tripod for the cauldron. Everyone moved into the walled yard where the dog was caged. Zheng held out a butcher knife to Chen Wei, who grasped it like a sword, with two hands, stiff-armed. Zheng produced a long carving knife from his belt and swung it overhead.

There was no breeze, and it was the hour before birds and bats come out for insects. The golden grass in the hills around them stood still. Everything was quiet.

"Release the beast," Zheng shouted. A little cousin rattled the dog's cage, then unfastened the latch. The door swung open and the dog trotted out. He stood outside his cage and wagged his tail. The little cousin slapped the dog's rump and yelled, "Run!" Whether out of shock or compliance, the dog's claws scrabbled over the hard earth, and he was off. The dog ran directly at Chen Wei but at the last second broke left and charged along the wall. The children chased after the dog, but it was too fast for them, cutting a jagged path through several of the older girls and boys who tried to intercept it at the corner. Zheng waited with Chen Wei, still gripping his butcher knife with two hands. Li Yan watched from the doorway. Beside her an aunt rocked the baby in her ropy arms.

The Dog

The dog outwitted the children at every turn, doubling back and twisting through their small hands, running with a hint of terror, as though it could smell menace on the air. The children wore down, moving now like a school of fish, unable to block the dog's unpredictable path, parting when it doubled back and ran directly at them, going down in a tangle of legs but quickly forming up again. The dog ran a circuit around the yard, its paws whipping up eddies of dust. Once, it appeared to be readying itself to leap clear of the fence altogether, but Zheng bellowed a command and the dog stopped dead in its tracks. Then he shouted, "Go!" and the dog was off again.

Even though the dog's eyes were wild with terror, he obeyed. If Zheng threw his knife across the yard, the dog would probably return it to his master's hands. There was, for him, sport in this. Li Yan understood that. She watched Chen Wei's face as the dog ran, and knew he was unprepared. She knew her husband, and she knew what he was feeling.

Eventually the animal got tired. Its jukes became predictable, its speed sapped, and it cowered against a corner of the wall, fangs bared, sleek hair spiked the length of its spine. The band of children closed in.

"Don't go any closer," Zheng said. "We'll take over." He punctuated this declaration with a slap to Chen Wei's back, and walked toward the children, who scattered, squealing in mock horror as he swung the knife above their heads. "Come on," he said to Chen Wei. They bore down upon the dog together, their knives raised. The dog snarled. Spittle dripped from its muzzle. "Sit," Zheng said. The dog sat.

Li Yan couldn't bear to watch any longer. She leapt from the doorway and forced her way through the children.

"Stop," she shouted. "Stop." She was waving her arms over her head.

Zheng turned toward her, his butcher knife still raised, and to someone watching from beyond the fence, it might have appeared that he meant to threaten Li Yan's life. But she moved forward, unafraid, until she stood between the two men and the dog. Her husband lowered his knife and hooked his thumbs through his belt loops. He tried to slouch like a gunfighter.

"I should have known," Zheng said.

Li Yan said nothing.

"Move over," Zheng said.

"I'm sorry, Chen Wei," she said, but she did not move.

"Chen Wei, tell your wife to stand aside," Zheng said. The aunties gathered at the edge of the house looked amused. They pinched at one another's sides, and some chuckled under their breath.

Chen Wei shook his head, but he was unable to affect his detached pose while looking his cousin in the eye, so he found a point in the distance and focused.

Zheng scanned the faces ringing the yard. The children were watching him. The aunties were watching him. The uncles were watching him.

He made a fist. "Don't make me use this," Zheng said to Li Yan. She closed her eyes and presented her chin.

Chen Wei dropped his knife. He drew up his shoulders and moved between his wife and Zheng.

Though Chen Wei wasn't steady on his feet, his palm fell on Zheng's cheek with all the delicacy of a lover's touch. He patted his cousin's rough face. The aunties all got very quiet. There wasn't much they hadn't seen before, and when Chen Wei drew his hand away, they each tensed imperceptibly. Chen Wei turned his slight shoulders to the side, coiling, and brought the back of his hand across Zheng's face with such force that Zheng, twice his size, staggered back a step.

Chen Wei's hand hovered in the dead air between them.

"Ha," Zheng said. "Ha!" A wide smile split his face. "Good one," he said.

If there were terrestrial sounds in the world at that moment, a swallow crying for its mate or a breeze pushing through the grass, they were absorbed into the wake of silence radiating from his voice. For a moment it seemed to Li Yan that the rotation of the earth had locked, that the natural world was pinned like a butterfly to a cardboard frame. She felt the silence enveloping her, the two men, the family, the village, and extending outward like a shadow until it seemed that the entire world was somehow flattened against itself, dark. It was this oppressive airlessness, the locus of suffocation within her own body, that caused Li Yan, desperate to set the world once again in motion, to speak.

"You idiot," she said to her husband. She may as well have clubbed

The Dog

him with a length of pipe. His chin dropped to his chest. He sighed.

It would take years for him to leave her, but after he had moved out and their daughter had left for America, and Li Yan was left alone to pass from the subway to the tailor's shop and home again, where she sat in silence with a cup of tea and tried to rest, to drop the hulking weariness that had sunk itself in her chest, she returned to the yard again and again. Of course she wished that she'd held her tongue. But in her old age, she reasoned it out: standing there in Zheng's barren yard, before his family, the words had risen up out of an unavoidable instinct.

"Give him a break, he's drunk," Zheng said. "We did worse than that when we were kids, that's for sure."

Chen Wei nodded.

"Well, send her to the market," Zheng said.

"Go to the market," Chen Wei whispered.

"Right!" Zheng said. "You're going to cook for us, right? You saved a dog's life. We'll celebrate life, right? Go to the market, and we'll get the fire going while you're gone. Come on, don't look so ashamed. It's time to make up." He took the couple's hands in his and joined them. Their fingers mashed together. "See? No problem," Zheng said.

Li Yan was lucky to find anyone still selling in the market. Most of the vendors had already gone home, but she found a woman with two buckets of limp carp.

"I want both," she said.

"You're from Tianjin, right?" the woman said.

Li Yan didn't have time to banter. She was sure Zheng would kill the dog while she was gone. "Beijing. How much for both buckets?"

"Beijing! I could tell from your clothes. Why do you want both buckets? Hungry?"

"I'm cooking for my husband's family. How much?"

"Who's your husband? I've never seen you before. Wedding feast?"

"Please tell me how much."

"No need to be rude. What's the rush? If you're cooking, they'll wait for you. They can't eat air."

"I'll give you twenty kuai for them."

"Twenty kuai," the woman said, as though divining a greater truth from the words. "One hundred."

"One hundred," Li Yan said. She looked around the empty market.

"They're worth twice that much right now. Don't try to put one over on me just because I'm a simple country girl." Her teeth made an eerie whistling sound when she spoke.

"Your house isn't worth one hundred kuai," Li Yan said.

"Good thing it's not for sale," the woman said. "One hundred kuai."

Li Yan didn't know what else to do. She held out the money. She'd stuffed her wallet that morning in case of emergency, but this was half a week's salary.

"Who's your husband?" the woman said as Li Yan reached for the buckets.

"Chen Wei," she said.

The woman said, "I remember a Chen Wei who moved to Beijing." But she didn't say any more.

Li Yan started to leave.

"Where are you going with my buckets?" the woman said.

"I gave you one hundred kuai."

"But you didn't bring any newspaper. I'll need a deposit for the buckets. Fifty kuai."

Li Yan didn't see the point of arguing. She gave the woman her last note. If Chen Wei didn't have enough for tickets home, they'd borrow from Zheng.

"May your family choke on it," the woman said, but Li Yan was already sloshing down the dirt road to Zheng's house.

The sun had disappeared behind the hills by the time she got there, and her legs were soaked with smelly water. At the gate, she set the buckets down. The fire pit was piled with sticks, dark, just as when she'd left. Through the window she saw the men playing cards at the table. She crept around the side of the house and walked along the wall. The cage was open, and the dog was lying in the far corner of the wall. She patted the stone wall and said, "Come here." The dog caught the scent of fish on her and trotted halfway across the yard, but stalled, unsure of her motives. She looked at it staring dumbly back at her, its tongue drooping from the side of its mouth. It looked happy. Animals have no memory, Li Yan thought.

She left the dog there. Back around front she lifted the buckets and walked to the door.

"Hey, the chef's back," Zheng said.

The room was packed solid with bodies. Chen Wei didn't look up from his cards when she entered. The children rushed over to see what she'd brought. "Rice fish," one said.

"What'd you expect from a Beijinger?" Zheng said. "They eat like this every day."

Li Yan slopped the buckets over to the iron stove. The aunties had a strong fire burning, and the stove radiated an intense heat. Sweat dripped from her face and sizzled on the iron surface. She hadn't cooked over a wood flame since she was little. In Beijing they had gas. But she'd make do. She plunked the buckets down and the aunts crowded around, doling out judgments about the size and color of the fish. Li Yan wrestled the largest wok onto the fire and the aunts swung into motion, chopping scallions, growling orders at one another, pouring oil and vinegar into the wok. The men's voices were loud and drunk. Each man seemed to be locked in a separate and discursive argument over the rules of English poker, which only Chen Wei knew how to play, but no one was paying attention to him. Wriggling across the floor, under the table, snaking around feet and chair legs, the children did their best to contribute to the chaos.

Li Yan closed her eyes. Her ill-fated cooking stories had gained her a reputation in English class, and the American teacher had nicknamed her "Chef." She knew that women in the neighborhood talked about her behind her back because her husband was skinny.

She would have to be extremely careful with the fish. The aunties would take care of the side dishes, but they wouldn't help with the main dish. She'd brought this on herself, and as she added ingredients to the wok — pepper, sesame oil, coriander, salt — the aunts maintained a loose ring of motion around her without ever coming too close.

Once the oil was popping, she reached into a bucket and pulled out a wriggling carp, wiped it with a cotton rag, and dropped it into the wok. The fish curled tightly, its bony mouth gaping.

"Smells like a five-star restaurant in here," Zheng called from the table. She couldn't tell whether he was trying to make amends or whether it was a joke at her expense. Concentrate, she thought. Concentrate and keep your mouth shut.

Li Yan ladled hot oil over the fish and pressed it flat against the wok. There was room for another one, and she quickly plunged her hand into the bucket. All together, she had ten fish — with side dishes, more than enough for the family — but by the time she would finish cooking the last one, the first fish would be cold. So she dropped yet another in the wok, three altogether. The aunt who had been looking after Li Yan's daughter peered into the wok and placed her hand on Li Yan's shoulder. Li Yan tucked a strand of hair behind her ear. She knew what she was doing. The men were so drunk they'd barely taste the meal. It was just a matter of presentation.

The aunties had completed a platter of scallion cakes and set them out before the men. There was a great clatter of porcelain and wood, and the cakes were gone. When Li Yan took the first three fish out of the wok, an aunt dropped an armload of spinach in and added soy sauce. "Just one minute," she said, holding Li Yan's wrist. They waited there by the wok until the spinach was transferred to the bare scallion cake platter. Again the platter was laid before the men and scored clean. Then came tomato soup with egg flower. Then sauced cucumber.

"Enough of the small fry," Zheng said, and the men all laughed. "Bring the main course!"

Li Yan was nearly done with the fish, but cooking three at a time was depleting the oil at such a rate that she had to add cold oil as she cooked, which killed the boil. She lost track of how many handfuls of scallions she'd added. The fish curled and she smashed them down. They came out of the wok dripping with oil, and more went in. Finally, the last fish looked ready. The aunties had prepared a plate for each fish, a mixed batch of stoneware and porcelain that Li Yan thought hardly worthy of the meal. Each fish was laid on a bed of bok choi and cabbage, which Li Yan would have said wasn't the proper presentation if she'd had time or space to argue. No matter, she thought, these peasants don't know any better.

The aunts took up plates and stood around the table.

"The fish should honor the head of the family," Li Yan said, laying a plate before Zheng with the glazed eyes facing him.

"No, no," he said, "to our honored guest," and he slid the plate to Chen Wei's place. "Now we'll see how they eat in Beijing."

The aunts laid plates before each of the men, fish heads pointing at Chen Wei.

"Go ahead, let us know what kind of cook your wife is," Zheng said. The men leaned in as Chen Wei held his chopsticks aloft. He felt their eyes on him. He felt the presence of his wife behind him.

"Dig in," Zheng said. "Join the Celebrate Life Movement."

Chen Wei lowered his chopsticks to the skin and pressed. Oil seeped out from the scales, but the skin didn't break. He pressed harder and more oil escaped, pooling on the cabbage leaves.

"Maybe you need a fork to eat Beijing cuisine?" Zheng said. The men laughed and threw back glasses of bijiu. "Do you want your butcher knife back?"

Chen Wei jabbed at the fish, desperately trying to puncture the skin. It wouldn't give. The fish was raw on top. He couldn't turn it over — that was bad luck for the fisherman who'd caught it, even if it had been raised in a rice field. He tried to get at the meat from the side, and succeeded in creating an incision in its belly, but the meat he pulled out dripped with oil and visceral fluid.

"Eat up. Looks tasty," Zheng said, smacking his lips. This time the men didn't laugh. The room was quiet as Chen Wei brought the meat to his mouth. He chewed slowly, his eyes set on a distant point. His mandible rose and fell. He swallowed and laid his chopsticks on the table. Wood crackled in the bowels of the stove.

"You want a drink, I bet," Zheng said, filling a glass. Chen Wei turned to him and forced a smile.

"Hey, don't give me the evil eye. She's the one who cooked it," Zheng said.

Li Yan laid her hand on Chen Wei's shoulder, and as if she had touched the first in a row of dominoes, he lunged forward with such violence that all the men reared back in response. He stood and calmly collected their plates into a pile at the center of the table. The men all looked at their laps. Chen Wei began to stack the plates in two towers, placing his own eviscerated meal at the top of one.

Li Yan backed away.

"No, you're going to help me," Chen Wei said.

He gathered up one tower and thrust it on her. Oil bled over her arms and clothes, but she stood firm.

"Come on," he said, his own arms loaded with plates. His voice sounded rough to her, as though his old country accent were again taking hold. He charged out the back door and into the walled yard, the plates balanced on one hand. Li Yan followed him, the family spilling out behind her.

"Hey, waiters," Zheng called. "Get back here with my dinner!"

"Hey, Chen Wei," he said. A laugh caught in his throat. "Hey." Zheng steadied himself in the doorway.

The dog emerged from the shadow of the wall, its nose high on the breeze.

It was obvious to everyone that Chen Wei meant to extract a measure of revenge from his wife. Sweat rolled over his brow and his jaw was working furiously at something. Everyone waited for him to make a move, and he stood in the yard for an embarrassingly long time, the plates clacking wetly against his chest while the dog arched its back playfully, just out of reach. Finally, Chen Wei turned to his wife and shouted, "You've cooked for a pack of dogs, so let the head of the family have the first bite." And with that, he hurled the plates at the dog. As the dog tore at the bounty before it, Li Yan tightened her grip on her stack of plates and turned to face her husband's family, as if to issue a challenge. But after a moment nothing had come to her. As she looked across the valley at the dark hills and the immense black sky, she had the strange feeling that she had made a great discovery, that she had entered uncharted waters. But she didn't yet know what to do with this knowledge, so for the time being she stood quietly, the plates clutched to her chest, as if she expected someone to wrest them from her.

YIYUN LI

After a Life
FROM ZOETROPE

MR. AND MRS. SU are finishing breakfast when the telephone rings. Neither moves to pick it up at first. Not many people know their number; fewer use it. Their son, Jian, a sophomore in college now, calls them once a month to report his well-being. He spends most of his holidays and school breaks with his friends' families, not offering even the most superficial excuses. Mr. and Mrs. Su do not have the heart to complain and remind Jian of their wish to see him more often. Their two-bedroom flat, small and cramped as it is, is filled with Beibei's screaming when she is not napping, and a foul smell when she dirties the cloth sheets beneath her. Jian grew up sleeping in a cot in the foyer and hiding from his friends the existence of an elder sister born with severe mental retardation and cerebral palsy. Mr. and Mrs. Su sensed their son's elation when he finally moved into his college dorm. They have held to the secret wish that after Beibei dies — she was not destined for longevity, after all — they will reclaim their lost son, though neither says anything to the other, both ashamed by the mere thought of the wish.

The ringing stops for a short moment and starts again. Mr. Su walks to the telephone and puts a hand on the receiver. "Do you want to take it?" he asks his wife.

"So early it must be Mr. Fong," Mrs. Su says.

"Mr. Fong is a man of courtesy. He wouldn't disturb other people's breakfast," Mr. Su says. Still, he picks up the receiver, and his expression relaxes. "Ah, yes, Mrs. Fong. My wife, she is right here," he says, and signals to Mrs. Su.

Mrs. Su does not take the call immediately. She goes into Beibei's bedroom and checks on her, though it is not yet time for her to wake up. Mrs. Su strokes the hair, light brown and baby-soft, on Beibei's forehead. Beibei is thirty-eight going on thirty-nine; she is big, requiring both her parents to turn her over and clean her; and afterward, she screams for hours; but for Mrs. Su, it takes only a wisp of hair to forget all the imperfections.

When she returns to the living room, her husband is still holding the receiver for her, one hand covering the mouthpiece. "She's in a bad mood," he whispers.

Mrs. Su sighs and takes the receiver. "Yes, Mrs. Fong, how are you today?"

"As bad as it can be. My legs are killing me. Listen, my husband just left. He said he was meeting your husband for breakfast and then they were going to the stock brokerage. Tell me it was a lie."

Mrs. Su watches her husband go into Beibei's bedroom. He sits with Beibei often; she does, too, though never at the same time as he. "My husband is putting on his jacket so he must be going out to meet Mr. Fong now," Mrs. Su says. "Do you want me to check with him?"

"Ask him," Mrs. Fong says.

Mrs. Su walks to Beibei's room and stops at the door. Her husband is sitting on the chair by the bed, his eyes closed for a quick rest. It's eight o'clock, early still, but for an aging man, morning, like everything else, means less than it used to. Mrs. Su goes back to the telephone and says, "Mrs. Fong? Yes, my husband is meeting your husband for breakfast."

"Are you sure? Do me a favor. Follow him and see if he's lying to you. You can never trust men."

Mrs. Su hesitates, and says, "But I'm busy."

"What are you busy with? Listen, my legs are hurting me. I would've gone after him myself otherwise."

"I don't think it looks good for husbands to be followed," Mrs. Su says.

"If your husband goes out every morning and comes home with another woman's scent, why should you care about what looks good or bad?"

It is not her husband who is having an affair, Mrs. Su retorts in her mind, but she doesn't want to point out the illogic. Her husband is indeed often used as a cover for Mr. Fong's affair, and Mrs.

Su feels guilty toward Mrs. Fong. "Mrs. Fong, I would help on another day, but today is bad."

"Whatever you say."

"I'm sorry," Mrs. Su says.

Mrs. Fong complains for another minute, of the untrustworthiness of husbands and friends in general, and hangs up. Mrs. Su knocks on the open door of Beibei's room and her husband jerks awake, quickly wiping the corner of his mouth. "Mrs. Fong wanted to know if you were meeting Mr. Fong," she says.

"Tell her yes."

"I did."

Mr. Su met Mr. Fong a year ago at the stock brokerage. Mr. Fong, at sixty-six, four years senior to Mr. Su, took a seat by him, and conversation started between the two men. He was there out of curiosity, Mr. Fong said. He asked Mr. Su if indeed the stock system would work for the country; and if so, how Marxist political economics could be adapted for this new, clearly capitalistic situation. Mr. Fong's question, obsolete and naïve as it was, moved Mr. Su. With almost everyone in the country going crazy about money, and money alone, it was rare to meet someone who was nostalgic about the old but also earnest in his effort to understand the new.

"You are on the wrong floor to ask the question," Mr. Su replied. "Those who would make a difference are in the VIP lounges upstairs."

The stock brokerage, like most of the brokerage firms in Beijing, rented space from a bankrupt state-run factory; this one had manufactured color TVs, and was profitable until losing a price war to a monopolizing corporation. The laid-off workers were among those who frequented the exchange floor, opening accounts with their limited means and hoping for good luck. Others on the floor were retirees, men and women of Mr. Su's age who dreamt of making their money grow, instead of letting it die in banks.

"What are these people doing here if they don't matter to the economy?" Mr. Fong asked.

"Thousands of sand grains make a tower," Mr. Su said. "Together their investments help a lot of factories run."

"But will they make money from the stock market?"

Mr. Su shook his head. He lowered his voice and said, "Most of them don't. Look at that woman there in the first row, the one with the hairnet. She buys and sells according to what the newspapers and television say. She'll never earn money that way. And there, the old man — eighty-two he is, too late to understand this market."

"And you, are you making money?" Mr. Fong asked.

"I'm the worst of all," Mr. Su said with a smile. "I don't even have money to get started." A retired mathematics instructor, Mr. Su had been observing the market for some time. With an imaginary fund, he had practiced trading, dutifully writing down all the transactions in a notebook; he read books on trading and developed his own theories. His prospects of earning money from the market were not at all bleak, he concluded after a year. His pension, however, was small. With a son in college, a wife, and a daughter totally dependent on him, he had not the courage to risk a penny on his hobby.

Very quickly, Mr. Fong and Mr. Su became close friends. They sat at teahouses and restaurants, exchanging opinions about the world. They were eager to back up each other's views; and at the first sign of disagreement, they changed topics. It surprised Mr. Su that he would make a friend at his age. He had been a quiet and lonely man all his life, and most people he knew were mere acquaintances. But perhaps this was what made old age a second childhood — friendship came easily out of companionship, with less practicality, less snobbishness.

After a month or so, at dinner, Mr. Fong confessed to Mr. Su that he was in a painful situation. Mr. Su poured a cup of rice wine for Mr. Fong, waiting for him to continue.

"I fell in love with a woman I met at a dance," Mr. Fong said.

Mr. Su nodded. Mr. Fong had once told him about attending classes to learn ballroom dancing, and had discussed the advantages: good exercise, a great chance to meet people when they were in a pleasant mood, and an aesthetic experience. Mr. Su had thought of teasing Mr. Fong for his surrendering to Western influences; but seeing Mr. Fong's sincerity, Mr. Su had given up the idea.

"The problem is, she is a younger woman," Mr. Fong said.

"How much younger?" Mr. Su asked.

"In her early forties."

"Age should not be a barrier to happiness," Mr. Su said.

"But it's not quite possible."

"Why, is she married?"

"Divorced," Mr. Fong said. "But think about it. She's my daughter's age."

Mr. Su looked at Mr. Fong. A soldier all his life, Mr. Fong was in good shape; except for his balding head, he looked younger than his age. "Put on a wig and people will think you are fifty," Mr. Su said. "Quite a decent bridegroom, no?"

"Old Su, don't make fun of me," Mr. Fong said, not concealing a smile, which vanished right away. "It's a futile love, I know."

"Chairman Mao said one can achieve anything as long as he dares to imagine it."

Mr. Fong shook his head sullenly and sipped his wine. Mr. Su regarded his friend, distressed by love. He downed a cup of wine and felt he was back in his teenaged years, consulting his best friend about girls, being consulted. "You know something?" he said. "My wife and I are first cousins. Everybody opposed the marriage, but we got married anyway. You just do it."

"That's quite a courageous thing," Mr. Fong said. "No wonder I've always had the feeling that you're not an ordinary person. You have to introduce me to your wife. Why don't I come to visit you tomorrow at your home? I need to pay respect to her."

Mr. Su felt a pang of panic. He had not invited a guest to his flat for decades. "Please don't trouble yourself," he said finally. "A wife is just the same old woman after a lifelong marriage, no?" It was a bad joke, and he regretted it right away.

Mr. Fong sighed. "You've got it right, Old Su. But the thing is, a wife is a wife, and you can't ditch her like a worn shirt after a life."

It was the first time Mr. Fong mentioned a wife. Mr. Su had thought Mr. Fong a widower, the way he talked only about his children and their families. "You mean, your wife's well and —" Mr. Su thought carefully and said, "She still lives with you?"

"She's in prison," Mr. Fong said and sighed again. He went on to tell the story of his wife. She had been the party secretary of an import-export branch of the agriculture department, and naturally there had been money coming from subdivisions and companies that needed her approval on paperwork. The usual cash-for-signature transactions, Mr. Fong explained, but someone told on her. She received a within-the-party disciplinary reprimand and was retired. "Fair enough, no? She's never harmed a soul in her life," Mr.

Fong said. But unfortunately, right at the time of her retirement, the president issued an order that for corrupt officials who had taken more than 170,000 yuan, the government would seek heavy punishments. "A hundred and seventy thousand is nothing compared to what he's taken!" Mr. Fong hit the table with a fist. In a lower voice, he said, "Believe me, Old Su, only the smaller fish pay for the government's facelift. The big ones — they just become bigger and fatter."

Mr. Su nodded: 170,000 yuan was more than he could imagine, but Mr. Fong must be right that hers was not a horrific crime. "So she had a case with that number?"

"Right over the limit, and she got a sentence of seven years."

"Seven years!" Mr. Su said. "How awful and unfair."

Mr. Fong shook his head. "In a word, Old Su, how can I abandon her now?"

"No," Mr. Su said. "That's not right."

They were silent for a moment, and both drank wine as they pondered the dilemma. After a while, Mr. Fong said, "I've been thinking: before my wife comes home, we — the woman I love and I — maybe we can have a temporary family. No contract, no obligation. Better than those, you know what they call, one night of something?"

"One-night stands?" Mr. Su blurted out, and then was embarrassed to have shown familiarity with such improper, modern vocabularies. He had learned the term from tabloids the women brought to the brokerage.

"Yes. I thought ours could be better than that. A dew marriage before the sunrise."

"What will happen when your wife comes back?" Mr. Su asked.

"Seven years is a long time," Mr. Fong said. "Who knows what will become of me in seven years? I may be resting with Marx and Engels in heaven then."

"Don't say that, Mr. Fong," Mr. Su said, saddened by their inevitable parting.

"You're a good friend, Old Su. Thank you for listening to me. All the people we used to be friends with — they left us right after my wife's sentence, as if our bad luck would contaminate them. Some of them used to come to our door and beg to entertain us!" Mr. Fong said, and then, out of the blue, he offered to loan Mr. Su ten thousand yuan to begin investing.

"Definitely not!" Mr. Su said. "I'm your friend, but not because of your money."

"Ah, how can you think of it that way?" Mr. Fong said. "Let's look at it like this: it's a good experiment for an old Marxist like me. If you make a profit, great; if not, good for my belief, no?"

Mr. Su thought Mr. Fong was drunk; but a few days afterward, Mr. Fong mentioned the loan once more, and Mr. Su did not reject the offer.

Mrs. Fong calls again two hours later. "I have a great idea," she says when Mrs. Su picks up the phone. "I'll hire a private detective to find out whom my husband is seeing."

"Private detective?"

"Why? You think I can't find the woman? Let me be honest with you — I don't trust that husband of yours either. I think he lies to you about my husband's whereabouts."

Mrs. Su panics. She didn't know there were private detectives available. It all sounds foreign and dangerous. She wonders if they could do some harm to her husband, his being Mr. Fong's accomplice in the affair. "Are you sure you'll find a reliable person?" she says.

"People will do anything if you have the money. Wait till I get the solid evidence," Mrs. Fong says. "The reason I'm calling you is this: if your husband, like you said, is spending every day away from home, why aren't you suspicious? Don't you think it possible that they are both having affairs and are covering up for each other?"

"No, it's impossible."

"How can you be so sure? I'll hire a private detective for both of us if you like."

"Ah, please no," Mrs. Su says.

"You don't have to pay."

"I trust my husband," Mrs. Su says, her legs weakened by a second fear: a private detective could find out about Beibei.

"Fine," Mrs. Fong says. "If you say so, I'll spare you the truth."

Mrs. Su has never met Mrs. Fong, who was recently released from prison because of health problems after serving a year of her sentence. A few days into her parole, she called the Sus' number — it being the only unfamiliar one in Mr. Fong's list of contacts — and grilled Mrs. Su about her relationship with Mr. Fong. Mrs. Su tried her best to convince Mrs. Fong that she had nothing to do with Mr.

Fong, nor was there a younger suspect in her household. Their only child was a son, Mrs. Su lied.

Since then, Mrs. Fong has made Mrs. Su a confidante, calling her several times a day. Life must be hard for Mrs. Fong now, with a criminal record, all her old friends turning their backs on her, and a husband in love with a younger woman. Mrs. Su was not particularly sympathetic with Mrs. Fong when she first learned of the sentence — 170,000 yuan was an astronomical sum to her — but now she does not have the heart to refuse Mrs. Fong's friendship.

Her husband is surely having a secret affair, Mrs. Fong confesses to Mrs. Su over the phone. He has developed some alarming and annoying habits — flossing his teeth after every meal, doing sit-ups at night, tucking his shirts more carefully, rubbing hair-growing ointment on his head. "As if he has another forty years to live," Mrs. Fong says. He goes out and meets Mr. Su every day, but what good reason is there for two men to see each other so often?

The stock market, Mrs. Su explains unconvincingly. Mrs. Fong's calls exhaust Mrs. Su, but sometimes, after a quiet morning, she feels anxious for the phone to ring.

Mrs. Su has lived most of her married life within the apartment walls, caring for her children and waiting for them to leave in one way or another. Beyond everyday greetings, she does not talk much with the neighbors when she goes out for groceries. When Mr. and Mrs. Su first moved in, the neighbors questioned her about all the noises from the apartment. Mrs. Su refused to satisfy their curiosity, and in turn they were enraged by the denial of their right to know the Sus' secret. Once, when Jian was four or five, a few women trapped him in the building entrance and pressed him for answers; later Mrs. Su found him on the stairs in tears, his lips tightly shut.

Mrs. Su walks to Beibei's door, which is closed so that Mrs. Fong would not hear her. She listens for a moment to Beibei's screaming before she enters the room. Beibei is agitated today, the noises she makes shriller and more impatient. Mrs. Su sits by the bed and strokes Beibei's eyebrows; it fails to soothe her. Mrs. Su tries to feed her a few spoonfuls of porridge, but she sputters it all onto Mrs. Su's face.

Mrs. Su gets up for a towel to clean them both. She looks around the bedroom and wonders if a private detective, despite the curtains closed day and night, might see Beibei through a crack in the wall. Mrs. Su studies Beibei and imagines how she looks to a stranger: a mountain of flesh that has never seen the sunshine, white like porcelain. Age has left no mark on Beibei's body and face; she is still a newborn, soft and tender, wrapped up in an oversized pink robe.

Beibei screeches, and the flesh on her cheeks trembles. Mrs. Su cups Beibei's plump hand in her own and sings in a whisper, "The little mouse climbs onto the counter. The little mouse drinks the cooking oil. The little mouse gets too full to move. Meow, meow, the cat is coming, and the little mouse gets caught."

Beibei was born against the warnings of all the relatives, who had not agreed with the marriage between the cousins in the first place. At her birth, the doctors said that she would probably die before ten; it would be a miracle if she lived to twenty. They suggested the couple give up the newborn as a specimen for the medical college. Mr. and Mrs. Su never brought Beibei back to the hospital after they were released.

Being in love, the couple was undaunted by the calamity. They moved to a different district, away from their families and old neighbors, he changing his job, she giving up work altogether to care for Beibei. They did not invite guests to their home; after a while, they stopped having friends. They applauded when Beibei started making sounds to express her needs for comfort and company; they watched her grow up into a bigger version of herself. It was a hard life, but their love for each other, and for their daughter, had made it the perfect life — the life Mrs. Su had dreamt of since she had fallen in love at twelve, when her cousin, a year older and already a lanky young man, had handed her a book of poems as a present.

The young cousin has become the stooping husband. The perfect life has turned out less so. The year Beibei reached twenty — a fortune worth celebrating, by all means — Mr. Su proposed a second baby. Why? Mrs. Su asked, and he talked about a healthier marriage, a more complete family. She understood his reasoning, and she knew, even when Jian was growing in her belly, that they would get a good baby and that it would do nothing to save them from what had been destroyed. They had built a world around Beibei, but her husband decided to trade it for a more common family. Mrs. Su found this hard to accept, but then, wasn't there an old saying about men always being interested in change, and women in preservation? A woman accepted anything from life and made it the best; a man bargained for the better but also the worse.

Mrs. Su sighs and looks at Beibei's shapeless features. She wishes she could sneak her into the next world. Beibei screams louder, white foam dripping from the corner of her mouth. It amazes and saddens Mrs. Su that Beibei's life is so tenacious that it has outlived the love that once made it.

With one finger, Mr. Su types in his password — a combination of Beibei's and Jian's birthdays — at a terminal booth. He is still clumsy in his operations on the computer; however, people on the floor, most of them aging and slow, are patient with one another. The software dutifully produces graphs and numbers, but Mr. Su cannot concentrate today. After a while, he quits to make room for another investor. He goes back to the seating area and looks for a good chair to take a rest. The brokerage, in the recent years of a downward economy, has slackened in maintenance, and a lot of chairs are missing orange plastic seats. Mr. Su finally sits down by a group of old housewives. The women, in their late fifties or early sixties, are the happiest and chattiest people on the floor. The only reason for which they come every day is companionship. They talk about their children and grandchildren, unbearable in-laws; soap operas and tabloid stories they analyze at length.

Mr. Su watches the numbers rolling on the big screen. The PA broadcasts a financial radio station, but its commentary is drowned by the women's stories. Most of the time, Mr. Su finds the women annoyingly noisy, but today he feels tenderness, almost endearment, toward them. His wife, quiet and pensive, will never become one of these chatty old hens; and for a moment he wishes that she would — cheered by the most mundane matters, mindlessly happy. Mr. Su sighs. Despite all his research, his investments perform no better than the old women's.

Things go wrong because people miscalculate. They buy stocks on good logic, but fail to anticipate life's own preference for improbabilities; husband and wife promise each other a lifelong love that turns out shorter than a life.

At thirteen Mr. Su fell in love with his wife, and she loved him back. Against both families' wills, they married; and against every

After a Life

warning, they decided to have a baby. Mr. Su, younger and more arrogant then, calculated that the odds for a problematic baby were very low, so low that fate was almost on their side. But then Beibei was born. His wife hid herself and the baby from the world.

He suggested another baby to give them a second chance, to save his wife from the unnecessary shame and pain with which she had insisted on living. Secretly he wished also to challenge fate again. The odds of another tragedy were low, very low, he tried to convince his wife; they could have a normal family. The new baby proved this calculation right — Jian was born healthy, and he grew up into a very handsome and bright boy, as if his parents were awarded doubly for what had been taken away the first time. Yet who would've predicted that such a success would turn Mr. Su's wife away from him? What had survived Beibei's birth did not survive Jian's, as if his wife could share misfortune with him but not happiness.

A finger taps Mr. Su's shoulder. He opens his eyes and realizes that he had fallen asleep. "I'm sorry," he says to the woman.

"You were snoring," she says with a reproachful smile.

Mr. Su apologizes again. The woman nods and turns back to the conversation with her companions. He looks at the clock on the screen. It's too early for lunch still, but he retrieves from his bag a package of instant noodles and a mug anyway. At a lunch stand, he soaks the noodles with boiling water, and they soften and swell. He sips the soup and thinks of going home and talking to his wife, asking her a few questions he has never gathered enough courage to ask; but then he shakes his head and decides that things unsaid had better remain so.

Mr. Su leaves the brokerage promptly at five o'clock. Outside the building, he sees Mr. Fong, sitting on the curb and looking up at him, like a sad, deserted child.

"Mr. Fong," Mr. Su says. "Are you all right? Why didn't you come in and find me?"

Mr. Fong suggests they go for a drink, then holds out a hand and lets Mr. Su pull him to his feet. They find a small roadside diner, and Mr. Fong orders a few cold plates and a bottle of strong yam wine. "Don't you sometimes wish a marriage wouldn't last as long as our lives?" he says over his drink.

"Is there anything wrong?" Mr. Su asks.

"Nothing's right with the wife since her release," Mr. Fong says.
"Are you going to divorce her?"
Mr. Fong downs the cup of wine. "I wish I could," he says and starts to sob. "I wish I didn't love her at all so I could just pack up and leave."

By late afternoon Mrs. Su is convinced that Beibei is having problems. Her eyes, usually clear and empty, glisten strangely and dart in their sockets, as if she is conscious of some pain. Mrs. Su tries in vain to calm her; and when all other methods have failed, she opens a bottle of sleeping pills. She puts two pills into a small porcelain mortar, and then, after a moment of hesitation, adds two more. Over the years she has fed the pill powders to Beibei so that the family can have occasional nights of undisturbed sleep.

Beibei stops screaming for a short period, and then starts again. Mrs. Su strokes Beibei's forehead and waits for the medicine to drown her limited consciousness. When the telephone first rings, Mrs. Su does not move. When it rings for the fifth time, she checks Beibei's eyes, half-closed in drowsiness, and then shuts the bedroom door before picking up the receiver.

"Why didn't you answer the phone? Are you tired of me, too?" Mrs. Fong says.

Mrs. Su offers excuses, but Mrs. Fong, uninterested in any of them, cuts her off. "I know who the woman is now."

"How much did it cost you to find out?"

"Zero. Listen, the husband — shameless old man — he confessed himself."

Mrs. Su feels relieved. "So the worst is over, Mrs. Fong."

"Over? Not at all. Guess what he said to me this afternoon? He asked me if we could all three of us live together in peace. He said it as if he was thinking on my behalf. 'We have plenty of rooms. It doesn't hurt to give her a room and a bed. She is a good woman, she'll take good care of us both.' Take care of his *thing*, for sure."

Mrs. Su blushes. "Does she want to live with you?"

"Guess what? She's been laid off. Ha-ha, not a surprise, right? I'm sure she wants to move in. Free meals. Free bed. Free man. What comes better? Maybe she's even set her eyes on an inheritance. Imagine what the husband suggested: he said I should think of her as a daughter. He said she lost her father at five and did not have a man good to her until she met him. So I said, 'Is she looking for a husband or a stepfather?' She's honey-mouthing him, you see? But the blind man! He begged me to feel for her pain. Why didn't he ask her to feel for mine?"

Something hits the front door with a heavy thump, and then the door swings open. Mrs. Su turns and sees an old man leaning against the jamb, supported by her husband.

"Mr. Fong's drunk," her husband whispers to her.

"Are you there?" Mrs. Fong says.

"Ah, yes, Mrs. Fong, something's come up and I have to go."

"Not yet. I haven't finished the story."

Mrs. Su watches the two men stumble into the bathroom. After a moment, she hears the sounds of vomiting and the running of tap water, her husband's low comforting words, Mr. Fong's weeping.

"So I said, 'Over my dead body,' and he cried and begged and said all these ridiculous things about opening one's mind. Many households have two women and one man living in peace now, he said. It's the marriage revolution, he said. Revolution? I said. It's retrogression. You think yourself a good Marxist, I said, but Marx didn't teach you bigamy. Chairman Mao didn't tell you to have a concubine."

Mr. Su helps Mr. Fong lie down on the couch, and Mr. Fong closes his eyes. Mrs. Su watches the old man's tear-smeared face twitch in pain. Soon Mrs. Fong's angry words blend with Mr. Fong's snoring.

With Mr. Fong fast asleep, Mr. Su stands up and walks into Beibei's room. A moment later, he comes out and looks at Mrs. Su with a sad and calm expression that makes her heart tremble. She lets go of the receiver with Mrs. Fong's blabbering and rushes to the room. There she finds Beibei resting undisturbed, the signs of pain gone from her face, porcelain-white with a bluish hue. Mrs. Su kneels by the bed and holds Beibei's hand, still plump and soft, in her own. Her husband comes close and strokes her hair, gray and thin now, but his gentle touch is the same one from a lifetime ago, when they were children playing in their grandparents' garden, where the pomegranate blossoms, fire-hued and in the shapes of bells, kept the bees busy and happy.

ALEKSANDAR HEMON

The Conductor

FROM THE NEW YORKER

IN THE 1989 "Anthology of Contemporary Bosnian Poetry," Muhamed D. was represented with four poems. My copy of the anthology disappeared during the war, and I can't recall the titles of the poems, but I do remember the subjects: one of them had all the minarets of Sarajevo lighting up simultaneously at sunset on a Ramadan day; another showed the deaf Beethoven conducting his Ninth Symphony, unaware of the audience's ovations until the contralto touched his shoulder and turned him around. I was in my midtwenties when the book came out, and compulsively writing poetry every day. I bought the anthology to see where I would fit into the pleiad of Bosnian poets. I found Muhamed D.'s poems silly and fake; his use of Beethoven struck me as pretentious and his mysticism alien to my own rock-and-roll affectations. But, in one of the few reviews the anthology received, the critic raved, in syntax tortured on the rack of platitudes, about the range of Muhamed D.'s poetic skills and the courage he had shown by shedding the primitive Bosnian tradition for more modern forms. "Not only is Muhamed D. the greatest living Bosnian poet," the reviewer said, "he is the only one who is truly alive."

I had not managed to get any of my poetry published — nor would I ever — but I considered myself to be a far better, more soulful poet than Muhamed D. I had written about a thousand poems in less than two years, and occasionally I shored those fragments into a book manuscript that I sent to various contests. I can confess — now that I've long since stopped writing poetry — that I never really understood what I wrote. I didn't know what my poems

The Conductor

were about, but I believed in them. I liked their titles ("Peter Pan and the Lesbians," "Love and Obstacles," etc.), and I felt that they captured a realm of human innocence and experience that was unknowable, even by me. I delayed showing them to anyone else; I was waiting for readers to evolve, I suppose, to the point where they could grasp the vast spaces of my ego.

I met Muhamed D. for the first time in 1991, at a café called Dom Pisaca — Writers' Home — which was adjacent to the offices of the Writers' Association of Bosnia-Herzegovina. He was short and stocky, suddenly balding in his midforties, his expression frozen in an ugly permanent frown. I shook his hand limply, barely concealing my contempt. He spoke with the clear, provincial inflections of Travnik, his hometown, and was misclad in a dun shirt, brown pants, and an inflammable-green tie. I was a cool-dressed city boy, all denim and T-shirts, born and bred in the purest concrete, skipping vowels and slurring my consonants in a way that cannot even be imitated by anyone who has not grown up inhaling Sarajevo smog. He offered me a seat at his table and I joined him, along with several of the other anthology veterans, all of whom wore the suffering faces of the sublime, as though they were forever imprisoned in the lofty dominion of poetry.

For some demented reason, Muhamed D. introduced me as an orchestra conductor. I tried to object, but the other poets started howling the "Ode to Joy" while making conducting gestures, and I was instantly nicknamed Dirigent — Conductor — thereby being safely and permanently marked as a nonpoet. I stopped trying to correct the mistake as soon as I realized that it didn't matter: my role was simply to be an audience for their drunken, anthological greatness.

Muhamed D. sat at the head of "the Table," governing confidently as they babbled, ranted, sang heartbreaking songs, and went about their bohemian business, guzzling ambrosial beer. I occupied the corner chair, witnessing and waiting, dreaming up putdowns that I would never utter, building up my arrogance while craving their acceptance. Later that night, Muhamed D. demanded that I explain musical notation. "How do you read those dots and flags?" he asked. "And what do you really do with the stick?" I had no idea, but I tried to come up with some reasonable answer, if only to expose his ignorance. He just shook his head in disappointment.

Almost every night I spent at the Table, there was a moment when I failed to enlighten the poets as to how music was written, thereby confirming their initial assumption that I was a lousy conductor, albeit a funny guy. I wondered how Muhamed D. could write a poem about Beethoven while being entirely oblivious of the way the damn notation system worked.

But the poets liked me, and I hoped that some of the pretty literature students who frequently served as their muses would like me, too. I particularly fancied three of them: Aida, Selma, and Ljilja, all of whom pouted their moist lips while pronouncing soft consonants and emitted an energy that caused instant erections. I kept trying to get at least one of them away from the Table, so that I could impress her with a recitation of "Peter Pan and the Lesbians." Not infrequently, I got sufficiently inebriated to find myself loudly singing a *sevdalinka*, sending significant glances toward the three muses, and emulating conducting moves for their amusement, while a brain-freezing vision of laying all three of them at once twinkled on my horizon. But it never happened: I couldn't sing, my conducting was ludicrous, I didn't recite any of my poems, I wasn't even published, and instead I had to listen to Muhamed D. singing his *sevdalinka* in a trembling voice that opened up the worlds of permanent dusk, where sorrow reigned and the mere sight of a woman's neck caused maddening bouts of desire. The eyes of the literature muses would fill with tears, and he could pick whichever volunteer he chose to entertain him for the rest of the night.

I'd totter home alone, composing a poem that would show them all that Muhamed D. had nothing on me, a poem that would make Aida, Selma, and Ljilja regret never having let me touch them. I celebrated and sang myself on empty Sarajevo streets, and by the time I had unlocked the door and sneaked into my bed without waking up my poetry-free parents I would have created a masterpiece, so formidable and memorable that I wouldn't bother to write it down. The next morning, I would wake up with my skin oozing a sticky alcoholic sweat, the sappy masterpiece gone forever. Then I would embark upon a furious series of unrhymed, anarchic poems, ridiculing Muhamed D. and the Table and the muses in impenetrably coded words, while envisioning the devoted scholar who, after decades of exploring my notes and papers, would finally decipher the lines and recognize how tragically unappreciated I was. After writing all day, I'd head off to the Writers' Home and start the whole process again.

One night, Muhamed D. recited a new poem called "Sarajevo," about two boys ("wisely chewing gum, / swallowing peppermint words") walking the streets with a soccer ball ("They throw the ball through the snow, across Mis Irbina Street / as if lobbing a hand grenade across the Lethe"). They accidentally drop the ball into the Miljacka River, and the ball floats downstream until it is caught in a whirlpool, from which they try to retrieve it, using a device I used once upon a time on my own lost ball: the boys string a crate on a rope that stretches from bank to bank, then manipulate the ends of the rope until the ball is caught. Muhamed D. watches them from a bridge:

> Whichever way I go, now, I'll reach the other shore.
> Old, I no longer know what they know:
> how to regain what is always lost. On the river surface
> snowflake after snowflake perishes.

He began his recitation in a susurrous voice, then rode a tide of iambic throttles and weighted caesuras up to thunderous orgasmic heights, from which he returned to a whisper and then ceased altogether, his head bowed, his eyes closed. He seemed to have fallen asleep. The Table was silent, the muses entranced. So I said, "Fuck! That's old. What are you now — a hundred?" Uncomfortable with the silence, doubtless as jealous as I was, the rest of the Table burst out laughing, slapping their knees. I sensed the solidarity in mocking Muhamed, and for the first time I thought I would be remembered for something other than conducting — I would be remembered for having made Muhamed old. He smiled at me benevolently, already forgiving. But that very night everybody at the Table started calling him Dedo — Old Man.

This took place just before the war, in the relatively rosy times when we were euphoric with the imminence of disaster — we drank and laughed and experimented with poetic forms into the late hours. We tried to keep the war away from the Table, but now and then a budding Serbian patriot would start ranting about the suppression of his people's culture, whereupon Dedo, with his newly acquired elder status, would indeed suppress him, with a sequence of carefully arranged insults and curses. Inevitably, the nationalist would declare Dedo an Islamo-fascist and storm off, never to return, while we, the fools, laughed uproariously. We knew — but we didn't want to know — what was going to happen, the sky descending upon our heads like the shadow of a falling piano in a cartoon.

Around that time, I found a way to come to the United States. In the weeks before I left, I roamed the city, haunting the territories of my past: here was the place where I had once stumbled and broken both of my index fingers; I was sitting on this bench when I first wedged my hand into Amela's tight brassiere; there was the kiosk where I had bought my first pack of cigarettes (Chesterfields); from that library I had checked out a copy of *Hamlet*, never to read it or return it; on this bridge Dedo had stood, watching boys recover a ball, and one of those boys may have been me.

Finally, I selected, reluctantly, some of my poems to show to Dedo. I met him at the Table early one afternoon, before everyone else arrived. I gave him the poems, and he read them, while I smoked and watched slush splatter against the windows, then slide slowly down. "You should stick to conducting," he said eventually, and lit a cigarette. His eyebrows looked like hirsute little comets. The clarity of his gaze was what hurt me. These poems were told in the voice of postmodern Old Testament prophets; they were the cries of tormented individuals whose very souls were being depleted by the plague of relentless modernity. Was it possible, my poems asked, to maintain the reality of a person's self in this cruelly unreal world? The very inadequacy of poetry was a testimony to the disintegration of humanity, etc. But, of course, I explained none of that. I stared at Dedo with watery eyes, pleading for compassion, while he berated my sloppy prosody and my cold self-centeredness, which was exactly the opposite of soul. "A poet is one with everything," he said. "He is everywhere, so he is never alone." Everywhere, my ass — the tears dried in my eyes, and with an air of triumphant rationalism I tore my poetry out of his hands and left him in the dust of his neoromantic ontology. But outside — outside I dumped those prophetic poems, the founding documents of my life, into a gaping garbage container. I never went back to the Table, I never wrote poetry again, and a few days later I left Sarajevo for good.

My story is boring: I was not in Sarajevo when the war began; I felt helplessness and guilt as I watched the destruction of my hometown on TV; I lived in America. Dedo, of course, stayed for the siege — if you are the greatest living Bosnian poet, if you write a poem called "Sarajevo," then it is your duty to stay. I contemplated going back to Sarajevo early in the war, but realized that I was not, and never would be, needed there. So I struggled to make a living, while Dedo struggled to stay alive. For a long time, I didn't hear anything about him and, to tell the truth, I didn't really investigate — I had many other people to worry about, starting with myself. But then news of him began to reach me: he had signed a petition; he had written an open letter to the Pope; in front of an audience of annoyed Western diplomats he had recited Herbert's "Report from the Besieged City" ("Too old to carry arms and fight like the others — / they graciously gave me the inferior role of chronicler"). Once, I heard that he had been killed; a hasty paper even published an obituary. But it turned out that he'd only been wounded — he had come back from the other side of the Lethe with a bullet in his thigh — and he wrote a poem about it. The paper that had published the obituary published the poem, too. Predictably, it was called "Resurrection." In it, he walks the city as a ghost, but nobody remembers him. He says to the people he meets:

> Can't you recall me? I am the one
> Who carried upstairs your bloodied cannisters,
> Who slipped his slimy hand under the widow's skirt.
> Who wailed the songs of sorrow
> Who kept himself alive when you were willing to die.

Then he meets himself after the siege, "older than old," and he tells himself, alluding to Dante, "I did not know death hath undone so much." It was a soul-rending poem and I found myself hating him for it: he had written it practically on his deathbed with no apparent effort, as his thigh wound throbbed with pus. I tried to translate it, but neither my Bosnian nor my English was good enough.

And he kept writing like a maniac, as though his resurrected life were to be given over entirely to poetry. Poems, mimeographed on coarse paper, bound in frail booklets, were sent to me by long-unheard-from friends, carrying the smells (and microorganisms) of the many hands that had touched them on their way out of besieged Sarajevo. In the poems, there were, of course, images of death and destruction: a boy rolls the body of a sniper-shot man down the street, much like Sisyphus; a surgeon puts his wife's face back together after it has been blown apart by shrapnel, but a piece of her cheek is missing, exactly the spot where he liked to plant his good-night kiss; clusters of amputated limbs burn in a hospital oven, as the poet faces "the toy hell." But there were also poems that were different, and I cannot quite define the difference: a boy kicks a soccer ball up to the nape of his neck and balances it there; a young woman inhales cigarette smoke and holds it in as she smiles, everything stopping at that moment, "no tracing bullets lighting up the sky, / no pain in my riven thigh"; a foreign conductor hangs on a rope, like a deft spider, over his orchestra as it plays the "Eroica" in a burned-out building. I must confess that I believed for a moment that I was the conductor, that I remained part of Dedo's world, that something of me had stayed in Sarajevo.

Still, living displaces false sentiments. I had to go on with my American life, busying myself with local survival, getting jobs, getting into graduate school, getting laid. Every once in a while, I unleashed the power of Dedo's words upon a sensitive American woman. The first one was Cheryl, the idle wife of a Barrington lawyer, whom I met at a Bosnian benefit dinner she was kind enough to organize. At least one Bosnian was required to benefit from her benefit dinner, so she'd tracked me down through a friend, an expert in disability studies, with whom I'd read a paper at a regional M.L.A. conference. Cheryl was generous beyond the dinner; before she went back to Barrington, I took her to my tiny studio — a monument to the struggles of immigrant life, with its sagging mattress, rotting shower curtain, and insomniac drummer next door. I recited Dedo's poems to her, pretending they were my own. She particularly liked the one about a lull in the shelling, during which a man goes for a walk with his rooster on a leash, "a soul fastened to a dying animal." Then I brushed the permed tresses from her forehead so that I could kiss it and slowly undressed her. Cheryl writhed in my embrace, kissed me with clammy passion, hoisted her hips, and moaned with pleasure, as though the intensity of her orgasm would directly succor the Bosnian resistance. I could not help thinking, in the end, that she was fucking Dedo, for it was his words that had seduced her. But I took what was given and then rolled off into the darkness of my actual life.

After the charitable Cheryl, I was somewhat ashamed, and for a

The Conductor

while I couldn't stand to look at Dedo's poetry. I finished graduate school; I sold my stories; I was an author now. And somewhere along the way the war ended. On my book tour, I traveled around the country, reading to minuscule audiences, explaining Bosnia to a mixture of international-relations and South Slavic–languages students, simplifying the incomprehensible, and fretting all the time that an enraged reader would stand up and expose me as a fraud, as someone who had no talent — and therefore no right — to talk about the suffering of others. It never happened: I looked and conducted myself like a Bosnian, and everyone was content to believe that I was in constant, uninterrupted communication with the tormented soul of my homeland.

At one of those readings, I met Bill T., a professor of Slavic languages. He seemed to speak all of them, Bosnian included, and he was translating Dedo's latest book. With his red face, long, curly beard, and squat, sinewy body, Bill looked like a Viking. His ferocity was frightening to me, so I immediately flattered him by saying how immeasurably important it was to have Dedo's poetry translated into English. We went out drinking, and he drank like a true Viking, too, while detailing the saga of his adventures in Slavic lands: living with shepherds in the mountains of Macedonia; teaching English in Siberia; interviewing Solidarnosc veterans; recording Slovenian carnival songs. He had also spent some years, just for the hell of it, in Guatemala, Honduras, and Morocco. The man had been everywhere, had done everything, and the drunker I got the greater he was, and the more of nothing I had to say.

This was in Iowa City, I believe. I woke up the next morning on Bill T.'s sofa. My pants were laid out on the coffee table. Along the walls there were dusty stacks of books. In the light fixture above me I could see the silhouettes of dead flies. A ruddy-faced boy with a gossamer mustache sat on the floor next to the sofa and watched me with enormous eyes.

"What are you doing here?" the boy asked calmly.

"I don't really know," I said, and sat up, exposing my naked thighs. "Where is Bill?"

"He stepped out."

"Where is your mom?"

"She's busy at the moment."

"What is your name?"

"Ethan."

"Nice to meet you, Ethan."

"Likewise," Ethan said. Then he grabbed my pants and threw them at me.

It was while I was slouching down the linden-lined street, people nodding at me from sunny porches and healthy-looking squirrels racing up and down trees — it was then that the story Bill had told me about Dedo the night before fully hit me and I had to sit down on the curb to deal with it.

Dedo had come to Iowa, Bill said, to be in the International Writing Program for twelve weeks. Bill had arranged it all and volunteered to put Dedo up in the room above his garage. Dedo had arrived with a small duffel bag, emaciated and exhausted, with the English he'd picked up while translating Yeats and a gallon of Johnnie Walker he'd picked up in a duty-free shop. The first week, he locked himself in above the garage and drank without pause. Every day, Bill knocked on the door, imploring him to come out, to meet the dean and the faculty, to mingle. Dedo refused to open the door and eventually stopped responding altogether. Finally, Bill broke down the door, and the room was an unreal mess: the bed was inexplicably wet; there were monstrous, bloody footprints everywhere, because Dedo had apparently broken the Johnnie Walker bottle, then walked all over it. A box of cookies had been torn open and the cookies crushed. In the trash can, there were dozens of Podravka liver-pâté cans, cleaned out and then filled up with cigarette butts. Dedo was sleeping on the floor in the corner farthest from the window, facing the wall.

Bill and his wife subjected Dedo to repeated cold showers; they cleaned him up and aired out the room; they practically force-fed him. For another week, he wouldn't stick his nose out of the room. And then, Bill said, he began writing. He did not sleep for a week, delivering poems first thing in the morning, demanding translations by the afternoon. "American poets used to be like that," Bill said wistfully. "Now all they do is teach and complain and fuck their students on the sly."

Bill cancelled his classes and set out to translate Dedo's poems. It was like entering the eye of a storm every day. In one poem, Bill said, a bee lands on a sniper's hand, and he waits for it to sting him. In another one, Dedo sees an orange for the first time since the siege began, and he is not sure what is inside it — he wonders if oranges have changed during his time away from the world; when he finally peels it, the smell inhales him. In another, Dedo is running down Sniper Alley when a woman tells him that his shoe is untied, and with perfect clarity of purpose, with the ultimate respect for death, he stoops to tie it, and the shooting ceases, for even the killers appreciate an orderly world. "I could not believe," Bill said, "that such things could come out of that pandemonium."

At the end of the third week, Dedo gave a reading. With a mug of Johnnie Walker at hand, he barked and hissed his verses at the audience, waving a shaky finger. After Dedo had read, Bill came out and read the translations slowly and serenely in his deep Viking voice. But the audience was confused by Dedo's hostility. They clapped politely. Afterward, faculty and students came up to Dedo to ask him about Bosnia and invite him to luncheons. He visibly loathed them. He livened up only when he realized that he had a chance to lay one of the graduate students who was willing to open her mind to other cultures. He was gone the next week, straight back to the siege, sick of America after less than a month.

In the years after the war, only the occasional rumor reached me: Dedo had survived a massive heart attack; he'd made a deal with his physician that he would stop drinking but go on smoking; he'd released a book based on conversations with his young niece during the siege. And then — this made the news all over Bosnia — he'd married an American lawyer, who was in Bosnia to collect war-crimes evidence. The newspapers cooed over the international romance: Dedo had wooed her by singing and writing poetry; she had taken him to mass-grave sites. A photograph from their wedding showed her to be a foot taller than he, a handsome woman in her forties with a long face and short hair. He consequently produced a volume of poems entitled "The Anatomy of My Love," which featured many parts of his wife's remarkably healthy body. There were poems about her instep and her heel, her armpit and her breasts, the nape of her neck and the size of her eyes, the knobs on her knees and the ridges on her spine. Her name was Rachel. I heard that they'd come to the United States; in pursuit of her body, Dedo had ended up in Madison, Wisconsin.

I do not want to give the impression that I thought about him a lot or even often. The way you never forget a song from your childhood, the way you hear it in your mind's ear every once in a while — that's how I remembered him. He was well outside my life, a past horizon visible only when the sky of the present was particularly clear.

As it was on the cloudless morning of September 11, 2001, when I was on a plane to D.C. The flight attendant was virginally blond. The man sitting next to me had a ring of biblical proportions on his pinkie. The woman on my right was immensely pregnant, squeezed into a tight red dress. I, of course, had no idea what was going on — the plane simply landed in Detroit and we disembarked. The Twin Towers were going down simultaneously on every screen at the unreal airport; maintenance personnel wept, leaning on their brooms; teenaged girls screamed into their cell phones; forlorn pilots sat at closed gates. I wandered around the airport, recalling the lines of one of Dedo's poems: "I will be alive, when everybody's dead. / But there will be no joy in that, for all those undone / by death need to pass through me, to get to hell."

While America settled into its mold of patriotic vulgarity, I began to despair, for everything reminded me of Bosnia in 1991. The war on terror took me to the verge of writing poetry again, but I knew better. Nevertheless, I kept having imaginary arguments with Dedo, alternately explaining to him why I *had to* write and why I *should not* write poetry, while he tried either to talk me out of it or to convince me that it was my duty. Then, last winter, I was invited to read in Madison and hesitantly accepted. Dedo was the reason for both the hesitation and the acceptance, for I was told that he would be the other reader.

So there I was, entering the large university auditorium. I recognized Dedo in the crowd by his conspicuous shortness, his bald dome reflecting the stage lights. He was changed: he'd lost weight; everything on him, from his limbs to his clothes, seemed older and more worn; he wiped his hands on his corduroy pants, nervously glancing up at the people around him. He was clearly dying to smoke, and I could tell that he was not drunk enough to enjoy the spotlight. He was so familiar to me, so related to everything I used to know: the view from my window, the bell of the dawn streetcar, the smell of smog in February.

"Dedo," I said. *"Šta ima?"*

The Conductor

He turned to me in a snap, as if I had just woken him up, and he did not smile. He didn't recognize me, of course. It was a painful moment, as the past was rendered both imaginary and false, as though I had never lived or loved. Even so, I introduced myself, told him how we used to drink together at the Writers' Home, how he used to sing beautifully, how often I had remembered those times. He still couldn't recall me. I proceeded with flattery: I had read everything he'd ever written; I admired him and, as a fellow Bosnian, I was so proud of him — I had no doubt that a Nobel Prize was around the corner. He liked all that, and nodded along, but I still did not exist in his memory. I told him, finally, that he used to think I was a conductor. *"Dirigent!"* he exclaimed, smiling at last, and here I emerged into the light. He embraced me, awkwardly pressing his cheek against my chest. Before I could tell him that I had never conducted and still was not conducting, we were called up to the stage. He had a rotten-fruit smell, as if his flesh had fermented; he went up the stairs with a stoop. Onstage, I poured him a glass of ice water and, instead of a thanks, he said, "You know, I wrote a poem about you."

I do not like reading in front of an audience, because I am conscious of my accent and I keep imagining some American listener collecting my mispronunciations, giggling at my muddled sentences. I read carefully, slowly, avoiding dialogue, and I always read the same passage. Often, I do it like a robot — I just read without even thinking about it, my lips moving but my mind elsewhere. So it was this time: I felt Dedo's gaze on my back; I thought about his mistaken memories of me conducting a nonexistent orchestra; I wondered about the poem he had written about me. It could not have been the poem with the spider-conductor, for he surely knew that I was not in Sarajevo during the siege. Who was I in his poem? Did I force the musicians to go beyond themselves, to produce sublime beauty on their mistuned instruments? What were they playing? A Beethoven symphony? *The Rite of Spring*? "Death and Transfiguration"? I sure as hell was not conducting the Madison audience well. They applauded feebly, having all checked out after the first paragraph or so. "Super," Dedo said when I crawled back into my seat, and I could not tell whether he was being generous or whether he just had no idea how bad it really was.

Dedo was barely visible behind the lectern, bending the microphone downward like a horribly wilted flower. He announced that he was going to read a few poems that had been translated into English by his "angel wife." He started from a deep register, then his voice rose steadily until it boomed. His vowels were flat, no diphthongs audible; his consonants were hard, maximally consonanty; "the"s were "duh"s, no "r"s rolled. His accent was atrocious, and I was happy to discover that his English was far worse than mine. But the bastard scorched through his verses, unfettered by self-consciousness. He flung his arms like a real conductor; he pointed his finger at the audience and he stomped his foot, leaning toward and away from the microphone, as two young black women in the first row followed the rhythm of his sway. Then he read as if to seduce them, whispering, slowly:

> Nobody is old anymore — either dead or young.
> Your wrinkles straighten up, the feet no longer flat.
> Cowering behind garbage containers, flying away
> from the snipers, everybody is a gorgeous body
> stepping over the dead ones, knowing:
> We are never as beautiful as now.

Later on, I bought him a series of drinks at a bar full of Badgers pennants and kids in college-sweatshirt uniforms, blaring TVs showing helmeted morons colliding head-on. We huddled in the corner, close to the toilets, and drank bourbon upon bourbon. We exchanged gossip about various people from Sarajevo: Sem was in D.C.; Goran was in Toronto; someone I knew but he could not remember was in New Zealand; someone I had never known was in South Africa. At a certain point he fell silent. I was the only one talking, and all the suppressed misery of living in America surged from me. Oh, how many times I had wished death to entire college football teams. It was impossible to meet a friend without making a fucking appointment weeks in advance, and there were no coffee gardens where you could sit and watch people walk by. I was sick of being asked where I was from and I hated Bush and his Jesus freaks. With every particle of my being I detested the word *carbs* and the systematic extermination of joy from American life, etc.

I don't know if he heard me at all. His head hung low and he could have been asleep, until he looked up and noticed a young woman with long blond hair passing on her way to the bathroom.

He kept his gaze on her backpack, then on the bathroom door, as if waiting for her.

"Cute," I said.

"She is crying," Dedo said.

We went to another bar, drank more, and left after midnight. Drunk out of my mind, I slipped and sat in a snow pile. We laughed, choking, at the round stain that made it look as if I had soiled my pants. The air was scented with burned burgers and patchouli. My butt was cold. Dedo was drunk, too, but he walked better than I did, skillfully avoiding tumbles. I do not know why I agreed to go home with him to meet his wife. We wobbled down quiet streets, where the trees were lined up as if dancing a quadrille. He made me sing, and so I sang: *Put putuje Latif-aga / Sa jaranom Sulejmanom.* We passed a house as big as a castle, a Volvo stickered with someone else's thought, Christmas lights and plastic angels eerily aglow. "How the fuck did we get here?" I asked him. "Everywhere is here," he said. Suddenly he pulled a cell phone out of his pocket, as if by magic — he belonged to a time before cell phones. He was calling home to tell Rachel that we were coming, he said, so that she could get some food ready for us. Rachel did not answer, and he kept redialing.

We stumbled up the porch, past a dwarf figure and a snow-covered rocking chair. Before Dedo could find his keys, Rachel opened the door. She was a burly woman, with austere hair and eventful earrings, her chin tucked into her underchin. She glared at us, and I have to say I was scared. As Dedo crossed the threshold, he professed his love to her in an accent so horrible that I thought for an instant he was kidding. The house smelled of chemical lavender; a drawing of a large-eyed mule hung on the wall. She kept saying nothing, her cheeks puckering with obvious fury. I was willing now to give my life for friendship — I might have abandoned him in Sarajevo, but here we would face Rachel together.

"This is my friend, Dirigent," he said, propping himself up on his toes to land a hapless kiss on her taut lips. "He is conductor." I made ridiculous conducting moves, as if to prove that I could still do it. She didn't even look at me; her eyes were pinned on Dedo.

"You're drunk," she said. "Again."

"Because I love you," he said.

I nodded.

"Excuse us," she said, and pulled him deeper into the house, while I stood in the hallway deliberating over whether or not to take off my shoes. A little ball of dust moved down the hall, away from the door, like a scared dog. I recalled Dedo's poem about the shoes he had bought the day before the siege began, and which he would never wear, "for they grow dirty on the streets filthy with death." Every day he polished those new shoes with what could have been his last breath, "hoping for blisters."

He emerged from the house depths and said, *"Daj pomozi"* — "Help me."

"Get the hell out, you drunken pig," Rachel snarled in his wake. "And take your stupid friend with you."

I decided not to take my shoes off and, stupidly, said, "It's O.K."

"It is not O.K.!" Rachel shouted. "It has never been O.K. It will never be O.K."

"You must be nice to him!" Dedo screamed at her. "You must respect."

"It's O.K.," I said.

"Not O.K. Never O.K. This is my friend." Dedo stabbed himself with his stubby finger. "Do you know me? Do you know who am I? I am biggest Bosnian poet alive."

"He is the greatest," I said.

"You're a fucking midget, is what you are!" She leaned into him, and I could see his pointed-finger hand unfolding and swinging for a slap.

"Come on, midget!" Rachel bellowed. "Hit me. Hit me. Let's have Officer Johnson for coffee and cookies again."

Detergent-like snow had already covered our footprints. We stood outside on the street, Dedo fixated on the closed door, as though his gaze could burn through it, cursing in the most beautiful Bosnian and listing all her sins against him: her bastard son, her puritanism, her president, her decaf coffee. Panting, he bent over and grabbed a handful of snow, shaped it into a frail snowball, and threw it at the house. It disintegrated into a little blizzard and sprinkled the dwarf's face. He was about to make another wretched snowball when I spotted a pair of headlights creeping down the street. It looked like a police car, and I did not want to risk coffee and cookies with Officer Johnson, so I started running.

The Conductor

Dedo caught up to me around the corner, and we staggered down an alley, which was deserted except for a sofa with a stuffed giraffe leaning on it. There were weak tire-mark gullies and fresh traces of what appeared to be a three-legged rat. We saw a woman in the kitchen window of one of the houses. She was circling around something we could not see, a glass full of red wine in her hand. The snow was ankle deep; we watched her, mesmerized: a long, shiny braid stretched down her back. The three-legged rat must have vanished, for the prints just stopped in the middle of the alley. We, too, could go neither forward nor back, so we sat down right there. I felt the intense pleasure of giving up, the expansive freedom of utter defeat. *Whichever way I go, now, I'll reach the other shore.* Dedo was humming a Bosnian song I didn't recognize, snowflakes melting on his lips. It was clear to me that we could freeze to death in a Madison back alley — it would be a famous way to die. I wanted to ask Dedo about the poem he had written about me, but he said, "This is like Sarajevo in '93." Perhaps because of what he'd said, or perhaps because I thought I saw Officer Johnson's car passing the alley, I got up and helped Dedo to his feet.

We caught a cab with an Arab driver, who hated us. He was listening to a light jazz station. Dedo tried to tell him, incoherently and unintelligibly, that he was a fellow Muslim. Madison was deserted. It was only a question of time before someone vomited.

"You are my brother," Dedo said, and squeezed my hand. "I wrote a poem about you."

I tried to kiss his cheek, as the cabbie glared at us in the rearview mirror, but managed only to leave some saliva on his forehead.

"I wrote a good poem about you," Dedo said again, and I asked him to recite it for me.

Dedo dropped his chin to his chest. He seemed to have passed out, so I shook him and, like a talking doll, he said, "He whips butterflies with his baton." But then we arrived at my hotel. Dedo kept reciting as I paid for the cab, and I didn't catch a word.

I dragged him to the elevator, his knees buckling, the snow thawing on his coat, releasing a closet-and-naphthalene smell. I could not tell whether he was still reciting or simply mumbling and cursing. I dropped him to the floor in the elevator and he fell asleep. He sat there in a pile while I was unlocking the door to my room, and the elevator closed its doors and took him away. The thought of him being discovered in the elevator, drooling and gibbering, gave me momentary pleasure. But I pressed the call button, and the elevator carrying Dedo came obediently back. *We are never as beautiful as now.*

The crushing sadness of hotel rooms, the gelid lights and clean notepads, the blank walls and particles of someone else's erased life: I rolled him into this as if into Hell. I hoisted him up onto the bed, took off his shoes and his socks. His toes were frostbitten, his heels brandished a pair of blisters. I peeled off his coat and pants and he was shivering, his skin goose-bumped, his navel hidden in a tuft of hair. I wrapped the bedcovers around him and threw a blanket on top. Then I lay down next to him, smelling his sweat and infected gums. He grunted and murmured, until his face calmed, the eyelids smoothing out into slumber, the brows unfurrowing. A deep sigh, as when dusk falls, settled in his body. He was a beautiful human being.

And then on Tuesday, last Tuesday, he died.

MARY GAITSKILL

Today I'm Yours

FROM ZOETROPE

I'VE DREAMT OF DANI only once that I can remember, but it was a deep delicious dream, like a maze of diaphanous silk, or a room of hidden chambers, each chamber nested inside the previous one — except that according to the inverse law of the dream, each inner chamber was bigger, not smaller, than the last.

In the dream, I was alone on the streets of Las Vegas, surrounded by speeding traffic and huge, streaming lights advertising monstrous casinos. There were thousands of people pouring in and out of the monstrous advertised mouths, but I didn't know any of them. I went to my hotel. The walls of its lobby were made of artificial forest, with animals and birds moving inside them. I went to my room; its walls seemed to shift and flux. Dani came out of the bathroom wearing a leopard-print mini-dress and black high-heeled shoes. The room stirred as if surprised; though she sometimes wore lipstick, Dani never wore a dress or high heels. She wore pants and clunky boys' shoes; she liked her lovers to wear dresses. But in the fluxing chamber of my dream, she walked toward me with a leopard-print dress purring on her haunches. Her slender little body was like a cold-blooded eel with electricity inside it; her movements too had the blithe, whipping ease of an eel traveling in deep water. But her flashing eyes were human. She came toward me as though she were going to kiss me; instead she walked past me, opened a door in the wall, and disappeared. I looked out the window and saw that I could see cities and countries; I could see into private rooms in other countries; I could see things that had happened hundreds of years ago. But I couldn't see Dani, even though she was inside my room.

A week later I was walking down the street in Manhattan, and there she was. It was during the first autumn of the Iraq War. On the newsstand a magazine cover read: "Why We Haven't Been Hit Again: Ten Reasons to Feel Safe — and Scared." In the middle of town a building fell down and crushed people to death, and before sadness there was relief that it was merely more decay, and not terrorism. A bus stop advertisement for bras read: "Who Needs Inner Beauty?" and someone had written across it in black marker: "You do asshole."

I was carrying wine and fuchsia flowers, the flowers nervously waving their wobbling fingers over the top of my bag. It was a humid afternoon, and the air was heavy with the burnt tang of fresh-laid asphalt and hot salted nuts. I walked past a wall layered with many seasons of damp movie posters; the suggestion of a circus seeped up under the face of an actress until a whole half-tiger leapt roaring through the hoop of her eye. Loud, clashing music poured out car windows and ran together in a muddy pool of sound with a single bell-like instrument sparkling in and around the murk. I looked up, my mind suddenly tingling with a half-remembered song, and there she was, looking at me. A smiling beggar wandered between us, jiggling the coins in his cup, and I remembered that when we first met she had put her finger on my sternum, lightly run it down to my navel, and turned away. "Hello, Ella," she said.

She was on her way home from her job as an editor of a small press distinguished mainly by its embroilment in several lawsuits. I was preparing for a dinner party my husband was giving for some pleasant, foolish people who had once been well regarded in bohemian literary circles. She knew I was married, but still, when I said the word *husband* she let contempt touch her eyes and lips. We clasped hands, and I kissed her cool, porous cheek. Dani used contempt like a clever accessory, worn lightly enough to beguile and unsettle the eye before blending into otherwise ordinary clothing. I've never seen her without it, though sometimes it fails to catch the light and flash.

During the last ten years we've met several times like this. When we first met, nothing was like this. That was fifteen years ago. I had

Today I'm Yours

just published a book that was like a little box with monsters inside it. I had spent five dreary years writing it in a tiny apartment with a sink and a stove against one wall and a mattress against the other, building the box and its inhabitants out of words that ran, stumbled, posed, and pirouetted across cheap notepaper as if a swarm of hornets were after them. I neglected my family. I forgot how to talk to people except to have sex. I paced the room while feverish tinny songs poured from a transistor radio with a broken antenna, and fantasized about the social identity that might be mine if the book were to succeed.

I did not realize I had made monsters, nor how strong they were, until the book was published and they lifted the roof off my apartment, scaled the wall, and roamed the streets in clothes I never would've worn myself. Everywhere I went it seemed my monsters had preceded me; and by the time I appeared, people saw me through their aura. This could've worked for me socially; monsters were and always will be fashionable. But in my mind, my monsters and I were separate. Painful and complicated situations arose, and I lacked the skill to handle them with finesse. I left the monsters behind and moved to California, where I rented a cottage in a canyon heavily grown with trees. I purchased a rug with large, bright polka dots on it and a red couch on which I sat for hours hypnotized by the prize of my new social identity. It was an appealing thing, and I longed to put it on — but when I did, I couldn't quite make it fit. Hesitant to go out in something so ill-fitting, and uncertain how to alter it, I stayed home with the cat, who accepted my private identity as she always had.

Back in New York several new acquaintances became concerned. They gave me the names of people I might introduce myself to in San Francisco, and one day I took the bus across the Golden Gate Bridge to meet one of them. The warm, dim, creaking old coach traveled low on its haunches, half-full of adults heavily wrapped in their bodies and minds, plus light-limbed, yawping teens, bounding and darting even as they sat in their seats. On the highway, the bus accelerated, and with a high whining sound we sprouted crude wings and flew across luminous bay on humming bridge, between radiant, declaiming sky and enrapt, answering sea, flecked with flying brightness and lightly spangled with little tossing boats. We barreled along a winding avenue thickly built with motels (the stick-legged ball of a smiling sheep leaping over the words COMFORT INN still exists somewhere in my brain) and squat chunks of fast-food stores. The distant ocean flashed and brimmed at intersections. We turned right, climbed a hill; at the top, fog boiled through the air on wings of mystery and delight. Down the hill, lit slabs of business rose up into the coming night. Floods of quick, smart people surged along with the hobbled and toiling; the felled sat beached and stunned against buildings in heaps of rags. Turn and turn again. Out the window I saw a strip club with a poster on its wall featuring one half-naked girl walking another on a leash. The leashed girl looked up and raised a paw in a patently ironic expression of submission and desire. I was meeting Dani in a neighborhood of bars and old burlesque clubs, a place of cockeyed streets lined with doors like jack-o'-lantern mouths of teeth. The fog lolled in the sky, sluggish as a fat white woman on rumpled sheets. I was in a place where people dressed up as monsters; and after going to so much trouble to make them, I'd left mine behind. Feeling small and naked, I walked under big neon signs: a naked woman, an apple, a snake. It was not frightening. It was a relief to feel small and naked again.

I entered the appointed spot, a dive with a slanted, vertiginous floor. It took a moment to figure out who she was, but I believe she saw my nakedness at once. So did the man sitting with her, a middle-aged academic with a red shelflike brow. "Your stories are interesting for their subject matter," he peevishly remarked to me. "But they aren't formally aggressive enough for me." He went on to describe his formal needs; Dani listened with droll courtesy, then turned to me with an amused grin. She put her cold finger on my sternum and ran it lightly down to my navel, then turned back with mock solemnity as her companion lowered his drained glass and held forth again. He left minutes later, banging a table cockeyed as his curled arm and flipper hand worried the torn sleeve of his jacket.

"I'm sorry about that," she said. "I just ran into him. He's lonely and he talks too much when he's drunk."

She was twenty-five. I was thirty-three. She was already editor-in-chief of a venerable avant-garde press, a veritable circus of caged monsters and their stylish keepers. She spoke with a combination of real confidence and its flimsy counterfeit. Monsterless, I barely knew how to speak at all, and what I could say was timid and unctuous. It didn't matter. She wore a heavy silver necklace over her white T-shirt, under which her small breasts gave off dark, glandular warmth. Behind the bar a mountain of green, blue, and gold bottles glimmered before a murky mirror lake. On the television above the bar, a rock star in an elaborate video drew a door in the air with a piece of chalk, smiled, and stepped through it. Jukebox music rose up, making a forest of sound through which young girls traveled on their way to the bathroom. Above us the fog traveled too, laughing and quick. The bathroom door creaked loud and long; slim thighs went past, along with a swinging little wrist loaded with shining jewelry. We were hungry for this, all of this, and for each of us *this* took form in the other. We ate each other with our eyes and, completely apart from our inconsequential words, our voices said, *How delicious.* We impulsively kissed, and separated quickly, laughing like people who had accidentally brushed against each other on the sidewalk. Then with a nervous toss of her head, she glided in close again. Soft heat came off her face, and then there was the dark, sucking heat of her mouth. She said, "I'd take you to dinner, but my girlfriend is expecting me."

She drove me to the bus stop in front of a doughnut place and stood waiting with me. She lived with her girlfriend, she said, but they had an understanding. Gum wrappers and plastic bags stirred in the cold, light-echoing wake of night traffic. Behind the glass of the doughnut place a dark woman with rhythmic arms labored over golden dough. On the street a hunched man with a sour face strutted back and forth displaying the masking-tape words on the back of his jacket: COPS ARE TOPS — I'M A BOTTOM, plus an arrow pointing at his butt. Really, I said, an understanding? Yes, said Dani, though it had been difficult to maintain. How had they arrived at it? I asked. How had they talked about it? They had not talked about it, she said. She thought it was more powerful for not being talked about. Bottom scowled as we kissed again. Golden doughnuts continued to fry. The bus arrived; I crossed its black rubber threshold, sat in the back, and almost immediately went to sleep.

Asleep on the bus, I dreamt that while watching a magic show I was plucked blank and tingling from the audience and led by a white-gloved assistant up onto the stage, where I was suddenly drenched with color and identity: I was the girl to be sawed in half. My heart pounded. I woke on the winding avenue thickly built with motels, their signs now hot and raptly glowing in the velvet dark.

Naturally it was nonsense about the understanding. That was just a door Dani had drawn in the air with her finger. But when we tried it, it opened, and so in we went.

We met almost every week for five months. Our time alone was as light and pleasantly shocking as her casual touch to my sternum, but with its meaning now thoroughly unfolded. We attended film screenings, dinner parties, the dull receptions that follow literary panels — and somehow we always found an unused room, an inviting stair, a hallway that would magically rearrange its molecules to become a sweet little seraglio, and modestly revert as soon as we left it, smoothing our clothes and hair. We would have dinner somewhere, and then she would drive me back home to Marin. We drove without talking, the tape deck playing and the landscape making dark, curved shapes all about us, shapes that would part to reveal the stars, then the ocean, then clusters of fleeing light. I remember a tape she played a lot, a song that went: "Let your love come through / Love come through to you." It was a lush and longing song, and after it, the silence between songs seemed dense and deep. During this silence Dani asked, "What are you thinking?" And so we began to talk.

We talked much like we made love — false and sincere, bold and fearful, vulnerable and shielded. I knew that her mother had had several facelifts, a tummy tuck, and liposuction. I knew that after an especially grueling set of operations, she had declared triumphantly to her daughter, "You have inherited an excellent set of healing genes!" She knew that my father had screamed to my mother, "I'm done with you, you phony! I'm going to find me a black lady with big flat feet and a hole up her butt!" I knew that one Thanksgiving her mother had burst into tears, run into the kitchen, and stuffed the turkey into the garbage, shouting, "And I wish I could do this to every one of you!" When Dani tried to comfort her, she turned away, shouting, "No! No!" Dani told this story not with self-pity but with laughter and love in her voice. When I showed her a picture of my parents taken at an ancient local studio known for its funereal tinting and suffocating airbrush technique, she said, entirely without irony, "They look great! They look so real!"

"She means we look like hell," stated my father when I told him what my friend had said.

"She meant you don't look like you've had a facelift," I answered.

"I would if I could afford it."

I repeated that to Dani, with laughter and love in my voice. We love our parents, our stories said to each other. We are people who can love. At thirty-three, I used my parents to explain me — to make me something more real than the outline of a woman drawn in the polluted air of a bar by the most casual of fingers. The thought makes me sad and a little ashamed, and yet our confidences were not entirely false. Standing on the street more than ten years later, we still felt the silken warmth of our stories breathing between us, a live tissue of affectionate trust that appears to give us shelter each time we meet.

The light changed, but instead of crossing the street toward my destination I went the other way with Dani, as if she had led me, even though she hadn't. I asked about her latest girlfriend, a poet as fashionable as Dani's orange hip-hugging jeans. "Yasmin is in LA for the month," she said, and paused while we recognized an actress striding toward us on starved stick legs, a little black poodle with a beautiful red tongue peering haplessly from the tensile cave of her bosom. "She's teaching a workshop," finished Dani. "And how is David?"

A grainy smell of gas rose off a torpid snake of traffic and snakily wound through the scent of damp bark and leaves. A taxi driver with his arm out the window beat out a song on his section of snake. Already it had formed, our invisible shelter, its walls hung with living pictures.

"So," said Dani lightly, "are we going somewhere?"

Down the hall and to the right, past the picture of Dani in her office talking on the telephone to her father; he is in San Francisco and wants to see *Tosca* with her. Dani is wearing black-and-white-checked stretch pants and bright red lipstick, her glossy hair flush against her wide cheekbones. "O.K., Daddy," she says, and her voice is softer and more seductive than it ever is with me.

We walk down the street in San Francisco, holding hands; a creamy-skinned young girl with a rosy smile rides up on a lavender bike, and says, "Dani!" She and Dani talk, the girl's long bare leg bracing tense and beautiful against the curb. Dani promises to call soon; the girl rides away in a wake of lavender and rosy eagerness. I ask, "Who's that?" and Dani smiles. "Oh," she answers, drawing it out, "just some girl."

In my bedroom we lounge on a summer afternoon. The air is thick with heat and vegetable smells: cat piss, armpit, rug mold, fruit, cunt; in the world around us fibrous green and fungal life unfurls to offer its inmost odor to the sun. We are naked, my blue comforter rolled back like a parted wave; the cat walks in and out with her tail up. I am showing Dani a picture of my father holding me in one arm and bending his head to kiss my infant foot. My mother is a blur of breast in the background; and my breast — just scored by Dani's teeth and tongue — poignantly echoes hers. Dani had called and asked me to meet her, and I'd said no because I had a cold. An hour later she showed up with a plastic bag of oranges and echinacea tea, and I was surprised and touched to realize she thought I might be lying.

I should not have been surprised: Dani's confidence lay almost entirely in her social identity, a smart, well-secured area beyond which lay hidden a verdant, private world longing for and afraid of form — hidden even from her. When she broke up with her girlfriend (a pretty blonde with pink, allergic eyes whom I was fated to run into at parties for the next dozen years), Dani said this woman, with whom she'd lived for two years, had not ever known her. "I feel like people accept the first thing I show them," she said, "and that's all I ever am to them." A month later, she broke up with me.

I said, "Do you have time to get a drink?"
"With your bag?"
"Why not?" I said. "It's easily checked."
"Umm."
A freckled girl walked by in a red raincoat, smiling to herself, and there was that same papered-over circus poster on another wall, this time showing a ghostly tiger leaping from a shouting model's open mouth.
"I dreamt about you last week," I said.
"Yes?" Her sidelong glance was piercing in the eye, but watchful in the heart; her dark hair was rough-textured, and layered in a ragged way that gave a casual carnality to her lips and jaw.

"I dreamt we were in Las Vegas again, and you were wearing high heels and a dress."

"Really!" She laughed, a hot, dry little sound, and — how ridiculous — on yet another wall a circus elephant dourly paraded across an advertisement for a rock concert against cancer, apparently holding another elephant by the tail. "So," she said, "where do you want to go?"

Back to that first dive with its passing girls, its flavor of fog and forest of music; or the sweet sad cave next to a vacant lot strung with darkish colored bulbs; or that odorous cavern glittering with earrings and rhinestone studs and sweat on the tossing hair of some dancer under a dirt-swarming light; that velvety cubbyhole like an emerald jewelry box with a false back, a secret compartment that, when we found it, revealed a place where we belonged together.

"Café Loup?" I said. "It's quiet."

Six months or so after the first time we broke up, we met again at the book fair in Las Vegas. I was there because my new book was coming soon; Dani was there as an editor. During the day the book fair was a bland caravan parked inside a pallid amphitheater tented with beige, a series of stalls and tables draped with colorless cloth and laden methodically with books. At night it was a giant Ferris wheel whirring ecstatically and predictably, each club, restaurant, and gaming room its own tossing car, blurred with lights and screaming faces while the sober carnie worked the machine. In this tossing blur I kept glimpsing Dani; walking down a hallway to an obligatory event, I glanced into a passing room and saw her crossing it with the feral stride particular to her — her hips never swaying, but projecting intently, rather coldly forward. I thought I saw her slender back and butt impatiently squeeze between a pair of outsized hams and heads in order to get to the bar, but more hams and heads crowded in and buried her before I could be sure. I was at a party for an author who has since become an actor when I saw her politely listening to someone I couldn't see, eyes flashing through the politeness as if in response to the flattered speaker — a fool who would not recognize the instinctive flashing of an eel in deep water. It was a few minutes later that she came up behind me while I was scooping a finger full of thick vanilla icing off the author's cake. Later that night, in front of a display of white tigers trapped behind the glass wall of a hotel lobby, I leaned against her and whispered, "Let's pretend we don't know each other." She embraced me from behind and roughly rubbed her head on mine. A brilliantly colored bird flew behind the glass; one tiger snarled at another that had come too close.

In my room we ordered a bottle of Scotch. An hour or so later, in a torrent of furious drunkenness, we used each other on the floor. I remember pungently but only dimly the terse movement of her lean arm and its maniacal shadow, my soft splayed leg, the gentle edifice of her chin, her underlip, the soft visual snarl as she turned her face sharply to the side. Amazement briefly lit my drunkenness as she gathered me in her arms and carried me to the bed. "I love you," I said, and sleep came batlike down upon us.

The next day we ordered breakfast from a huge menu in a fake-leather book, and I apologized for that intimacy — we were not after all supposed to know each other. "Oh, that's all right," she said. "People who don't know you are always saying that." For the rest of the book fair we were together every night, holding hands and kissing at strip shows, casinos, and women's boxing matches. Then we went back to San Francisco and broke up again.

During that breakup conversation I reminded her of what she'd said about no one really knowing her. "Don't you see why that is?" I said. "You've gone out of your way to create a perfect, seductive surface, and people want to believe in perfection. If they think they see it, they don't want to look further."

"Do *you* want to?"

If I said yes, I meant it, in a way. But in another way, I didn't. I loved to see myself reflected in her shiny surface. I loved to appear in public as that reflection — even if the reflection was that of a stupidly smiling woman in a sequined costume, waiting to be sawed in half.

Café Loup is an elegant establishment with a low ceiling, dim lighting, and a melancholy feeling of aquarium depth that subtly obscured the diners seated at the white-draped tables in the back — the elderly gentleman with his gallant fallen face and his pressed shirt, his companion's lowered white head and dark linen dress, her pale arm quivering slightly as she sawed the leg off a small bird.

I checked my bag at the door and we chose a table, even though the polished bar was almost empty. Dani ordered a martini with no olive; I had red wine. The waiter, a middle-aged man with a heavy face, silently approved of the elegant manner with which Dani placed her order. Silently, with upturned eyes, she accepted his approval. Then she turned to me and said, "So, how long has it been?"

Months passed; I moved from Marin to San Francisco. I saw Dani for dinner every now and then, or went with her to the movies. We were only friends, but still her face froze when, over pomegranate cocktails with lime, I told her I couldn't meet her later because I had to meet my boyfriend. Seeing her expression, I became so flustered I nearly stammered. She turned her head and became absorbed in the view — the chartreuse shrubbery tossing below, the blue and hazy sky above, as blissful as a watercolor, with a purple blur spreading poisonously across its middle.

After that our invisible shelter became less substantial, more like a series of tents gently billowing and hollowing in the night air. When I saw her at a poetry reading/performance that I attended with my boyfriend, it was almost not there at all. While he wandered through the room with an affable air I sought out Dani, half-afraid to find her. When I did she saw my fear and, rushing to press her advantage, she tried and failed to contemptuously curl her lip. Perhaps to steady her quavering mouth, she took my extended hand. "Hello," she said softly. *Hello,* said the heat of her hand.

It was around then that she took up with another writer, a preposterous person who once took offense at something I said or didn't say and, to my relief, refused to speak to me ever after. Suddenly there were long distances between one tent and the next, and I found myself walking under the stars, alone on dark, wet grass.

Dani sipped her martini and nibbled at a dish of nuts. She talked about Yasmin, with whom she had lived for the last three years — longer than with anyone else. Her posture was erect and alert, her small shoulders perfectly squared. But her hair was rough by then, not glossy. She was swollen under the eyes, and there were deep creases on either side of her mouth and between her brows; her lips were bare and dry. Her once insouciant slenderness had become gaunt and somehow stripped, like a car or motorcycle might be stripped to reveal the crude elegance of its engine.

"I don't want to be unfaithful anymore," she said. "I want to stay with Yasmin. I want to take care of her."

I teased her for being like a man; her abrupt smile was like a blush of pleasure. "I guess I am," she said.

In San Francisco I wandered into a maze that was sometimes peopled and sometimes empty, sometimes brightly lit and sometimes so dark I had to grope my way along it with my hands, heart pounding with fear that I would never find my way out. I quickly became lost and thought almost everyone I met was lost too. Sometimes it seemed to me an empty life, but that wasn't really true. It wasn't empty, it was more that the people and events in it were difficult to put together in any way that felt whole.

Before she met Yasmin, Dani said, she did not court or date or screw any girls for over a year. She was thirty-five then and she felt very old. She did not want to be the older lesbian going after young girls, did not have the heart for it. But she was very lonely, more lonely than she had ever been. She felt she didn't belong anywhere. She thought she would die. I didn't ask her why she didn't call me because I already knew. Instead I glanced down at my watch, saw that I needed to go, and ordered another drink.

At the end of the show, the magician goes home. And so does the girl who was sawed in half. She changes out of her costume into her jeans and sneakers and leaves out the back door, crushing a cigarette under her foot. It is a low form of performance, and a tawdry metaphor for any kind of affair. And yet the shows are wonderful. Even for jaded performers, they have a sheen of glamour, no matter if the sheen is threadbare and collecting dust. And in that sheen there may be hidden, in the sparkle of some stray rhinestone or store-bought glitter, the true magic that will, as the synthetic curtain opens, reveal a glimpse of something more real than one's strange and unreal life.

The curtain opened again at a boring book event in LA; I walked in and there was Dani, lying eel-like on a leather love seat, nodding at someone I couldn't see. She must've felt my gaze because she turned, saw me, and said, "Of all people — !" loud enough for me to hear her across the room. I knocked down a lamp as we stumbled into her room, a funky little box that my fun house memory has given three walls instead of four. To steady me, she took my hair in her fist. "We really *don't* know each other now," she said. The next day I woke alone in my room, where a lustily roaring hotel shower brightly stippled my bruised flesh. The curtain reopened that evening; silently she offered me her smartly clad arm, and silently I accepted.

Halfway through her second martini Dani asked, "Does David take care of you?"

"Yes," I said. "We take care of each other."

"Good," she said. "I'm glad."

In the back of the restaurant the elderly couple slowly rose from their seats, the man taking the woman's arm at the elbow. We paused to watch them. Ceiling fans with large wooden blades solemnly turned over our heads.

Each scene covers and is covered and shows through the others, fractured, shifting, and shaded, like bits of color in a kaleidoscope. I moved to Houston to teach; she moved to New York to work for a former jazz singer who wanted to write a memoir. She traveled often to LA to visit a woman she was courting there; I traveled often to New York to visit no one in particular. We were nothing to each other, really. I rarely thought of her; and although she said otherwise, I doubt she thought of me except when she saw me. Yet from time to time, in a little pit with a shimmering curtain, we would discover a room with a false back, and through the trapdoor we would willingly tumble, into a place where we were not a mere addendum to another, more genuine life — a place where we were the life, in this fervid red rectangle or this blue one.

Slowly the elderly couple moved past our table, the man still holding the woman's arm, the woman's small silver handbag dangling a little rakishly from her gentle, wrinkled hand. Dani watched them, her eyes softening even in profile.

Her strength, her social identity, had been stripped from her as time had stripped her youth. But her private world had moved forward to fill the empty space. I thought, *This is why I always trusted her;* because my private identity was my strength, I could sense hers even when I couldn't see it, and I knew it could be trusted.

Time and again, the curtain parted: Served by stylish hostesses, we sat in ornate chairs drinking martinis and eating caviar on toast. A lurid dream of music surged around us, mixed with the globule voices of strangers bent double, triple with personality. We held hands and kissed across the table; Dani said, "If we have sex again, I don't want us to be drunk." Drunk already, I took a ring out of my pocket, a flat amethyst I had bought that day. I had not bought it for her, but I gave it to her. "I love you," I said. "We can't be together, and maybe we'll never even have sex again. But I love you." Rosy young heterosexuals burst into laughter, gobbling olives and peanuts and beautiful colored drinks in shimmering glasses. We sat side by side in a modest music hall, my arm around her low back, feeling the knobs of her fiery spine. We were there because Dani knew the singer in the band, a sexy blonde no longer in her first youth. She sang "Today I'm Yours," and the music made shapes for her words: a flower; a rainy street in spring; an open hand; a wet, thumping heart. Each shape was crude and colored maybe a little too vividly with feeling. But we wanted those shapes and that feeling. My father was dead, and the writer Dani had once left me for was dead too. We were not young anymore. "Today I'm Yours." It is a crude and romantic song. Yet human feeling is crude and romantic. Sometimes, it is more vivid than anyone could color it. In some faraway, badly smudged mirror, Dani's striking arm flashes again and again; her face is in an almost featureless trance, and my red twisted mouth is the only thing I can see of myself.

"Here," she said, handing the taxi driver a bill. "Wait until she gets in the door, O.K.?" The cab bucked forward, and her hard, dear face disappeared in a rush of starless darkness and cold city lights. I woke sprawled half-naked in a room with all the lights on, the phone in one hand, my address book in the other, open to the page with Dani's number on it.

"I'm sorry about something," she said. "I've always wanted to tell you." We were waiting for the check. Playfully laughing waitpeople

Today I'm Yours

lingered at the warmly lit kitchen door; for them the evening was about to begin. "I wish I'd been a better friend to you," she said. "In San Francisco, I mean. I knew you were lonely. But I couldn't. I was too young and I just couldn't."

"It's all right," I said. "It would've been difficult." I looked down at the table; it was gleaming and hard, and there was a shining drop of water or alcohol graying the tip of Dani's spotless napkin. Soon my husband and I would be making chicken for five people. There would be little bowls of snacks and flowers and drinks. But how private the knobs of Dani's spine were when she was next to me and my arm was around her low back. How good it was to sit across from her and see the changes in her face. How heartless and ridiculous we had been with each other, how obscene. How strange if ten years from this moment, David and Yasmin were gone and instead Dani and I were living together. The image of this, our shared life, winked like a piece of glitter with a whole atomic globe whirring inside it, then vanished like the speck it was. The check came. We counted out the money. I paid the tab; Dani left a generous tip.

    We came out onto the street and saw it had rained. The pavement was steamy and darkly patched, and traffic moved with a soft shadowy hiss. The sky was pale, but gold light rimmed a rumpled horizon of old brick apartments, restaurants, and shops that had changed their names a dozen times in ten years. Dani said she'd walk me home. We passed the wall layered with movie posters, and I half saw that the circus tiger leaping through the rubbed-away eye of an actress had itself been rubbed away by the rain, leaving the image of a pale blue eye staring through rippling black stripes. I remembered the song "Today I'm Yours," and I asked Dani if she knew what the blond singer was doing now. "I don't," she said. "We lost touch somehow." We walked in silence for a while. Another piece of glitter winked; in it I saw my parents, smiling at each other, kissing and embracing. Like an afterimage, I saw Dani's parents embracing too. That night David and I would make food for people; we would talk and there would be music. We would smile, kiss, embrace — before we lost touch, or each turned into something else, another person or a spirit or ashes or bones in the dirt with a stone on it.

    Forgetting to look at the light I stepped off the curb into traffic. A panting car swerved and braked as Dani yanked me back against her. The driver, remarkably dressed as a clown without the red nose, shook his clown-gloved fist out the window and honked his rubber horn as he sped past. We laughed, our arms around each other, our lips and teeth nearly touching. Turning her head, she kissed my cheek. We let go. She said, "It's great to see you"; she said it as she always had. Then she walked away to be with Yasmin, and I walked away to be with David, hurrying now because I was late.

NATHAN ENGLANDER

How We Avenged the Blums

FROM THE ATLANTIC MONTHLY

IF YOU HEAD OUT TO GREENHEATH, LONG ISLAND, today, you'll find that the schoolyard where Zvi Blum was attacked is more or less as it was. The bell at the public school still rings through the weekend, and the bushes behind the lot where we played hockey still stand. The only difference is that the sharp screws and jagged edges of the jungle gym are gone, the playground stripped of all adventure, sissified and padded and covered with a snow of shredded tires.

It was onto this lot that Zvi Blum, the littlest of the three Blum boys, stepped. During the week we played in the parking lot of our yeshiva, where slap shots sent gravel flying, but on Shabbos afternoons we ventured onto the fine, uncracked asphalt at the public school. The first to arrive for our game, Zvi wore his helmet with the metal face protector snapped in place. He had on his gloves and held a stick in his hand.

Zvi worked up a sweat playing a fantasy game while he waited for the rest of us to arrive. After a fake around an imagined opponent, he found himself at a real and sudden halt. The boy we feared most stood before him. It was Greenheath's local Anti-Semite, with a row of friends beyond. The Anti-Semite had until then abided by a certain understanding. We stepped gingerly in his presence, looking beaten, which seemed to satisfy his need to beat us for real.

The Anti-Semite took hold of Zvi's facemask as if little Blum were a six-pack of beer.

Zvi looked past the bully and the jungle gym, through the chain-link fence and up Crocus Avenue, hoping we'd appear, a dozen or more boys, wearing helmets, wielding sticks. How nice if, like an army, we'd arrived.

The Anti-Semite let go of Zvi's mask.

"You Jewish?" he asked.

"I don't know," Zvi said.

"You don't know if you're Jewish?"

"No," Zvi said. He scratched at the asphalt with his stick.

The bully turned to his friends, taking a poll of suspicious glances.

"Your mother never told you?" the Anti-Semite asked.

Zvi shifted his weight and kept on with his scratching. "It never came up," he said.

Zvi remembered a distinct extended pause while the Anti-Semite considered. Zvi thought — he may have been wishing — that he saw the first of us coming down the road.

He was out cold when we got there, beaten unconscious with his helmet on, his stick and gloves missing. We were no experts at forensics, but we knew immediately that he'd been worsted. And because he was suspended by his underwear from one of the bolts on the swing set, we also knew that a wedgie had been administered along the way.

We thought he was dead.

We had no dimes even to make a telephone call, money being forbidden on the Sabbath. We did nothing for way too long. Then Beryl started crying, and Harry ran to the Vilmsteins, who debated, while they fetched the *mukzeh* keys, which of them should drive in an emergency.

Some whispered that our nemesis was half-Jewish. His house was nestled in the dead end behind our school. And the ire of the Anti-Semite and his family was said to have been awakened when, after he had attended kindergarten with us at our yeshiva for some months, and had been welcomed as a little son of Israel, the rabbis discovered that only his father was Jewish. The boy, deemed gentile, was ejected from the class and led home by his shamefaced mother. Rabbi Federbush latched the back gate behind them as the boy licked at the finger paint, nontoxic and still wet on his hands.

We all knew the story, and I wondered what it was like for that boy, growing up — growing large — on the other side of the fence. His mother sometimes looked our way as she came and went from the house. She didn't reveal anything that we were mature enough to read — only kept on, often with a hand pressed to the small of her back.

After Zvi's beating, the police were called. My parents wouldn't have done it, and let that fact be known. "What good will come?" my father said. Zvi's parents had already determined that their son had suffered nothing beyond bruising: his bones were unbroken and his brain unconcussed.

"Call the police on every anti-Semite," my mother said, "and they'll need a separate force." The Blums thought differently. Mrs. Blum's parents had been born in America. She had grown up in Connecticut and attended public school. She felt no distrust for the uniform, believed the authorities were there to protect her.

The police cruiser rolled slowly down the hill with the Blums in procession behind it. They marched, the parents and three sons, little Zvi with his gauze-wrapped head held high.

The police spoke to the Anti-Semite's mother, who propped the screen door open with a foot. After her son had been called to the door for questioning, Mrs. Blum and Zvi were waved up. They approached, but did not touch, the three brick steps.

It was word against word. An accusing mother and son, a pair disputing, and no witnesses to be had. The police didn't make an arrest, and the Blums did not press charges. The retribution exacted from the Anti-Semite that day came in the form of a motherly chiding.

The boy's mother looked at the police, at the Blums, and at the three steps between them. She took her boy by the collar and, pulling him down to a manageable height, slapped him across the face.

"Whether it's niggers or kids with horns," she said, "I don't want you beating on those that are small."

We'd long imagined that Greenheath was like any other town, except for its concentration of girls in ankle-length denim skirts and white-canvas Keds, and boys in sloppy oxford shirts, with their yarmulkes hanging down as if sewn to the side of their heads. There was the fathers' weekday ritual. When they disembarked from the cars of the Long Island Railroad in the evenings, hands reached into pockets and yarmulkes were slipped back in place. The beating reminded us that these differences were not so small.

Our parents were born and raised in Brooklyn. In Greenheath, they built us a Jewish Shangri-la, providing us with everything but the one crucial thing Brooklyn had offered. It wasn't stickball or kick-the-can — acceptable losses, though nostalgia ran high. No, it was a *quality* that we were missing, a toughness. As a group of boys thirteen and fourteen, we grew healthy, we grew polite, but our parents thought us soft.

Frightened as we were, we thought so too, which is why we turned to Ace Cohen. He was the biggest Jew in town, and our senior by half a dozen years. He was the toughest Jew we knew, the only one who smoked pot, who had ever been arrested, and who owned both a broken motorcycle and an arcade version of Asteroids. He left the coin panel open and would play endlessly on a single quarter, fishing it out when he was finished. In our admiration we never considered that at nineteen or twenty we might want to move out of our parents' basements, or go to college. We thought only that he lived the good life — no cares, no job, his own Asteroids, and a mini-fridge by his bed where he kept his Ring Dings ice-cold.

"Not my beef, little Jewboys," is what he told us, when we begged him to beat up the Anti-Semite on our behalf. "Violence breeds violence," he said, slapping at buttons. "Older and wiser — trust me when I tell you to let it go."

"We called the police," Zvi said. "We went to his house with my parents and them."

"Unfortunate," Ace said, looking down at little Zvi. "Unfortunate, my buddy, for you."

"It's a delicate thing being Jewish," Ace said. "It's a condition that aggravates the more mind you pay it. Let it go, I tell you. If you insist on fighting, then at least fight him yourselves."

"It would be easier if you did," we told him.

"And I bet, big as your Anti-Semite is, that he, too, in direct proportion, also has bigger friends. Escalation," Ace said. "Escalation built in. You don't want this to get so bad that you really need me."

"But what if we did?" we said.

Ace didn't answer. Frustrated and defeated, we left him — Ace Cohen, blowing the outlines of asteroids apart.

They were all heroes to us, every single one of Russia's oppressed. We'd seen *Gulag* on cable television, and learned that for escapes across vast snowy tundras, two prisoners would invite a third to join, so that they could eat him along the way. We were moved by this as boys, and fantasized about sacrifice, wondering which of our classmates we'd devour.

Our parents were active in the fight for the refuseniks' freedom in the 1980s, and every Russian Jew was a refusenik whether he wanted to be or not. We children donated our reversible-vested three-piece suits to help clothe Jewish unfortunates of all nations. And when occasion demanded, we were taken from our classes and put on buses to march for the release of our Soviet brethren.

We got our own refusenik in Greenheath right after Zvi's assault. Boris was the janitor at a Royal Hills yeshiva. He was refilling the towel dispenser in the faculty lounge when he heard of our troubles. Boris was Russian and Jewish, and he'd served in Brezhnev's army and the Israeli one to boot. He made his sympathies known to the teachers from Greenheath, voicing his outrage over our plight. That very Friday a space was made in the Chevy Nova in which they carpooled while listening to *mishna* on tape.

Boris came to town for a Shabbos, and then another, and had he slept twenty-four hours a day and eaten while he slept, he still couldn't have managed to be hosted by a fraction of the families that wanted to house and feed him and then feed him more.

The parents were thrilled to have their own refusenik — a menial laborer yet, a young man who for a living pushed a broom. They hadn't been so excited since the mothers went on an AMIT tour of the Holy Land and saw Jews driving buses and a man wearing *tzitzit* delivering mail. Boris was Greenheath's own Sharansky, and our parents gave great weight to his dire take on our situation. His sometimes fractured English added its own gravity to the proceedings. "When hooligan gets angry," he would say, "when drinking too much, the Anti-Semite will charge."

The first, informal self-defense class was given the day Boris was at Larry Lipshitz's playing Intellivision Hockey and teaching Larry to smoke. It ended with Larry on the basement floor, the wind knocked out of him and a sort of wheeze coming from his throat. "How much?" he said to Boris. "How much what?" was Boris's answer. He displayed a rare tentativeness that Larry might have noticed if he hadn't been trying to breathe. "For the lesson," Larry said. And here was the wonder of America, the land of opportunity. In Russia if you punched someone in the stomach, you did it for free. A monthly rate was set, and Larry spread the word.

That was also the day that Barry Pearlman was descended upon by our nemesis as he left Vardit's Pizza and Falafel. His food was taken. The vegetarian egg rolls (a staple of all places kosher, no matter the cuisine) were bitten into. A large pizza and a tahini platter were spread over the street. Barry was beaten, and then, as soon as he was able, he raced back into the store. Vardit, the owner, wiped the sauce from little Pearlman. She remade his order in full, charging only the pizza to his account. The Pearlmans didn't want trouble. The police were not called.

Barry Pearlman was the second to sign up. Then came the Kleins and cockeyed Shlomo, whose mother sent him because of the current climate, though really she wanted him to learn to defend himself from us.

Our rabbis at school needed to approve of the militant group we were forming. They remembered how Israel was founded with the aid of NILI and the Haganah and the undergrounds of yore. They didn't much approve of a Jewish state without a messiah, but they gave us permission to present our proposal to Rabbi Federbush, the founder of our community and the dean of our yeshiva.

His approval was granted, but only grudgingly. The old man is not to be blamed. Karate he knew nothing of; the closest sport he was familiar with was wrestling, and this from rabbinic lore — a Greco-Roman version. His main point of protest, therefore, was that we'd be wrestling the uncircumcised publicly and in the nude. When the proposal was rephrased, and he was told that we were being trained to battle the descendants of Amalek, who attacked the Israelites in the desert; that we were gearing up to face the modern-day spawn of Haman (cursed be his name); when told it was to fight the Anti-Semite, he nodded his head, understanding. "Cossacks," he said, and agreed.

It wasn't exactly a pure martial art but an amalgam of Israeli Krav Maga, Russian hand-to-hand combat, and Boris's own messy form of endless attack. He showed us how to fold a piece of paper so it could be used to take out an eye or open a throat, and he told us always to travel with a circuit tester clipped to our breast pocket like a pen. When possible, Boris advised us, have a new gun waiting at each destination. He claimed to have learned this during a stint in the Finger of God, searching out Nazis in Argentina and then —

acting as a military tribunal of one — finding them guilty and putting a bullet between their eyes.

We were taught to punch and kick, to stomp and bite, while the mainstay of all suburban martial-arts classes — when you can avoid confrontation, you do it — was removed. Boris told us to hold our ground. "Worst cases," he said, "raise hand like in defeat, and kick for ball."

After a few weeks of lessons, we began to understand the power we had. Boris had paired Larry Lipshitz, that wisp of a boy, with Aaron, the middle Blum. They went at it in Larry's back yard, circling and jabbing with a paltry amount of rage. Boris stood off to the side, his arms resting on his paunch — a belly that on him was the picture of good health, as if it were the place from which all his strength emanated, a single muscle providing power to all the other parts.

Boris spat in the grass and stepped forward. "You are fighting," he said. "Fight." He put his foot to Aaron's behind and catapulted him into his opponent. "Friends later. Now win." Larry Lipshitz let out a yawp befitting a larger man and then, with speed and with grace, he landed the first solid roundhouse kick we'd seen delivered. It was no sparring partner's hit but a shoulder fake and all-his-might strike, the ball of Lipshitz's bare foot connecting with Aaron's kidney. Larry didn't offer a hand. He stepped back like a champion and raised his fists high. Aaron hobbled to the nearest tree and displayed for us the first fruits of our training. He dropped his pants, took aim, and, I tell you, it was nothing less than water to wine for us when Aaron Blum peed blood.

It's curious that the story most often used to inspire Jewish battle-readiness is that of Masada, an episode involving the last holdouts of an ascetic Israelite sect, who committed suicide in a mountain fortress. The battle was fought valiantly, though without the enemy present. Jews bravely doing harm to themselves. The only Roman casualties died of frustration in their encampment below — eight months in the desert spent building a ramp to storm fortress walls for a slaughter, and the deed already done when they arrived.

When Israeli army recruits complete basic training they climb up that mountain and scream out into the echo, "A second time Masada won't fall." Boris made us do the same over the edge of

Greenheath Pond, a body of water whose circulation had slowed, a thick green soup that sent back no sound.

Mostly the harassment was aimed at the Blum boys and their house. I don't know if this was because of their proximity to the Anti-Semite's house, the call to the police, or the Anti-Semite's public slap in the face. I sometimes can't help thinking that the Blum boys were chosen as targets because they looked to the bully as they looked to me: enticingly victimlike and small. Over time an M-80 was used to blow up the Blum mailbox, and four tires were slashed on a sensible Blum car. A shaving-cream swastika was painted on their walkway, but it washed away in the rain before anyone could document that it had ever existed.

When we ran into the Anti-Semite, insults were inevitably hurled, and punches thrown. Larry took a thrashing without managing his now legendary kick. Shaken, he demanded his money's worth of Boris, and made very clear that he now feared for his life. Boris shrugged it off. "Not so easy," he assured him. "Shot and lived. Stabbed and lived. Not so easy to get dead."

My father witnessed the abuse. He came upon the three Blum boys crawling around and picking up pennies for the right to cross the street — the bully and his friends enforcing. My father scattered the boys, all but the three Blums, who stood there red in the face, hot pennies in their hands.

The most severe attack was the shotgun blast that shattered the Blums' bay window. We marked it as the start of dark days, though the shells were packed only with rock salt.

We stepped up our training and also our level of subterfuge. We memorized *katas* and combinations. We learned to march in lockstep; to run, leap, and roll in silence.

Lying on our backs in a row with feet raised, heads raised, and abdomens flexed, we listened to Boris lecture while he ran over us, stepping from stomach to stomach, as if crossing a river on stones. Peace, Boris insisted, was maintained through fear. "Do you know which countries have no anti-Semite?" he asked. We didn't have an answer. "The country with no Jew."

The struggle would not end on its own. The bully would not mature, see the error of his ways, or learn to love the other. He would hate until he was dead. He would fight until he was dead. And unless we killed him, or beat him until he thought we had killed him, we'd have no truce, no peace, no quiet. In case we didn't understand the limitations of even the best-case scenario, Boris explained it to us again. "The man hits. In future he will hit wife, hit son, hit dog. We want only that he won't hit Jew. Let him go hit someone else."

Despite all the bumps pushed back into foreheads and the braces freed from upper lips, I'm convinced our parents thought our training was worth the effort. Our mothers brought frozen steaks to press against black eyes and stood close as our fathers tilted our chins and hid smiles. "Quite a shiner," they would say, and they could hardly stand to give up staring when the steaks covered our wounds.

Along with the training injuries we had other setbacks. One was a tactical error when, post–shotgun blast, we went as a group to egg the Anti-Semite's house. Shlomo thought he heard a noise, and yelled "Anti-Semite!" in warning. We screamed back, dropped our eggs, and fled in response. This all took place more than a block away from the house. We hadn't even gotten our target in sight.

We weren't cohesive. We knew how to move as a group but not as a gang.

We needed practice.

After two thousand years of being chased, we didn't have any hunt in us.

We sought help from Chung-Shik through Yitzy — an Israeli with an unfortunate heritage. Yitzy's parents had brought him to America with the last name Penis, which even among kind children doesn't play well. We teased Yitzy Penis ruthlessly, and as a result he formed a real friendship with his gentile neighbor Chung-Shik, the only Asian boy in town. Both showed up happily, Yitzy delighted at being asked to bring his pal along.

And so we proposed it, our plan.

"Can we practice on you?" we asked.

"Practice what?" Chung-Shik said amiably, Yitzy practically aglow at his side.

When no one else answered, Harry spoke.

"A reverse pogrom," he said.

"A what?"

"We just want to menace you," Harry said. "Chase you around a bit as a group. You know, because you're different. To get a feel for it."

Chung-Shik looked to his friend. You could see we were losing him, and Yitzy had already lost his smile.

That's when Zvi pleaded, almost a cry of desperation, "Come on, you're the only different kid we know."

Yitzy held Chung-Shik's stare, the Asian boy looking back, not scared as much as disappointed.

"Chase me instead," Yitzy said, sort of pantomiming that he could be Chung-Shik and Chung-Shik could be him, switch off the yarmulke and all.

We abandoned the idea right then. It wouldn't be the same.

Our failed offensive got back to Boris — the reverse pogrom that wasn't, and the continuing rise in Blum-related trouble and chases-home-from-school. The rock salt still stung us all.

We met in the rec room of the shul. Boris had swiped a filmstrip and accompanying audiocassette from the yeshiva he worked at in Royal Hills. He advanced the strip in the projector, a single frame every time the tape went beep. We knew the film well. We knew when the image would shift from the pile of shoes to the pile of hair, from the pile of bodies to the pile of teeth to the pile of combs. The film was a sacred teaching tool brought out only on Yom Hashoah, the Holocaust memorial day.

Each year the most memorable part was the taped dramatization, the soundman's wooden blocks *clop-clopping*, the sound of those boots coming up the stairs. First they dragged off symbolic father and mother. And then, *clop, clop, clop*, those boots marched away.

The lights still dimmed, we would form two lines — one boys, one girls. We marched back to class this way singing "Ani Ma'amin" and holding in our heads the picture they'd painted for us: six million Jews marching into the gas chambers, two by two; a double line three million strong and singing in one voice, "I believe in the coming of the Messiah."

Boris did not split us into two quiet lines. He did not start us on a moving round of that song, or the equally rousing "We Are Leaving

Mother Russia," with its coda, "When they come for us, we'll be gone." After the film, he turned the lights back on and said to us, yelled at us, "Like sheep to the slaughter. Six million Jews is twelve million fists." And then he segued from fists and Jewish fighting to the story of brave Trumpeldor, who, Boris claimed, lost an arm in the battle of Tel Hai and then continued fighting with the one.

Galvanized, we went straight to the Anti-Semite's house. Zvi Blum, beaten, bothered, dug a hunk of paving stone out of the walkway to avenge his family's bay window. He tossed that rock with all his might; limited athlete that he was, it hooked left and hit the wall of the house with a great bang. We fled. Still imperfect, still in retreat, we ran with euphoria, hooting and hollering, victorious.

A newfound energy emerged at the start of the next class, which was also the start of a new session. We lined up to pay Boris what was now a quarterly fee. He took three months' worth of cash in one hand, patted us each on the back with the other, and said, "Not yet leaders, but you've turned into men." Boris even said this to the Conservative boy, though it was Elliot's first lesson. He then addressed us regarding our successful mission. "Anti-Semite will come back harder," he said, declaring that only a strong offense would see this conflict to its end. Pyrotechnics were in order.

We ventured out to the turnpike that marked the border of our town. In the alley behind ShopRite, we worked on demolitions following recipes from Boris's training along with the instructions on some pages torn from an Abbie Hoffman book. We made smoke bombs that didn't smoke and firebombs that never burned. And though we suspected that the recipes themselves were faulty, Boris shook his head as if we'd never learn.

We stuck with our bomb making, working feverishly, with Boris timing each attempt and at intervals yelling, "Too late, already dead." Then Elliot stood up with a concoction of his own, a bottle with a rag stuffed in the top, and announced, "This is how you build a bomb."

To prove it he lit the rag, arced back, and threw the bottle. We watched it soar, easily traceable by its fiery tail. We heard it hit and the sound of glass and then nothing. "So what," Aaron said. "That's not a bomb. By definition it has to go *boom!*" We went back to work until Boris said, "Lesson over," and a yellow light began to chip at the darkness in the sky, a warm yellow light and smoke. "Not a bomb," Elliot said, looking proud and terrified in equal measure. His bottle, we discovered, had hit the Te-Amo Cigar & Smoke Shop. It had ignited the garbage in the rear of the store. The drive-through window was engulfed in flames. "Simplest sometimes best," Boris said. And "Class dismissed." We started to panic, and he said, "Fire could be from anything." Right then, his pocket full of our money, and already in full possession of our hearts and heads, Boris walked off. He walked toward the burning store, so close to the flames that we covered our eyes. True to his teachings, Boris didn't turn and run. He didn't stop, either. We know for sure that he went back to Royal Hills and worked another day. All our parents ever said was "green card," and we heard that Boris continued west to Denver and built a new life.

Mr. Blum was still at the office. The three boys Blum were each manning a window and staring out into the dark. They had, on their own and in broad daylight, gone down that hill with toilet paper and shaving cream. They'd draped the trees and marked the sidewalks, unleashing on their target the suburban version of tar and feathers. Then they'd run up to their house and taken their posts, holding them through nightfall. When their mother pulled the car into the garage after her own long day at work, she saw only what the boys hadn't done. She made her way back down the driveway to the curb, where the garbage pails stood empty, one of them tipped by the wind. Basic responsibilities stand even in times of trouble. She had not borne three sons so that she'd have to drag garbage pails inside.

No one knows the quality of the Anti-Semite's night vision. The only claim that could be made in his defense is that until the lapse the Blum boys had been the sole draggers of the garbage pails on every other trash day in memory. In the Blum boys' defense — and they would forever feel they needed one — three watched windows leaves one side of the house unguarded. All that said, the sound of metal pails being dragged up a gravel driveway brought the Anti-Semite racing out of the dark — and masked his approach for Mrs. Blum.

Mrs. Blum, of course, had not been in our class. She had no notion of self-defense and was wholly unfamiliar with weaponry.

When this brute materialized before her, his arm already in motion, she did not assume a defensive posture. She did not raise her fists or prepare to lunge. What she did was turn at the last instant to get a look at the tiny leather wand sticking out from his swinging hand. She had never seen a blackjack before. When the single blow met with the muscles of her back, it sent a shock through her system so great that she saw a thousand pinpricks in her eyes and felt her legs give way completely. Connecticut or no, Mrs. Blum was a Jew. "*Shanda!*" she said to the boy, who was already loping off.

Oh, those poor Blums. As we had found Zvi, Zvi discovered his own mother — not hanging from a bolt but curled in the grass. Inside the house, an ice pack in place and refusing both hospital and house call, Mrs. Blum told her sons what she'd seen.

"*Shanda!*" she said again. "*Busha!*"

The boys agreed. A shame and an embarrassment.

When their mother lifted the receiver to call the police, Aaron pressed his finger down into the cradle of the phone. Mrs. Blum looked at her son and then replaced the receiver as Aaron slid his finger away. "Not this time," he said. And this time she didn't.

When my mother told my father what had happened, he didn't want to believe it. "Nobody ever wants to believe what happens to the Jews," she said, "not even us." My father simply shook his head. "Since when," my mother said, "do anti-Semites have limits? They will cross all lines. Greenheath no better." Then she, too, took to shaking her head. I was sorry I'd told her, sorry to witness her telling him. We'd known our parents would respond with hands to mouth and *oy-vey-iz-mir*s, but none of us expected to see such obvious disillusionment with the world they'd built. I turned away.

Though we'd been abandoned, Boris's wisdom still held sway. We were going to see to it that the Anti-Semite never hit back again. "Anti-Semite school," Harry Blum called it, mustering a Boris-like tone. A boy who attacks a woman half his size, who had already attacked her son, would, if able, do the same thing again. We decided we would use Zvi as our siren — set him out in the middle of the lot at the public school, so that the Anti-Semite might be drawn by the irresistible call of the vulnerable Jew. The rest of us would stay hidden in those bushes and then fall on our enemy as one. But looking from face to face, taking in skinny Lipshitz and fat Beryl, the three Blums full of anger and without any reach — we realized that we couldn't defeat the Anti-Semite, even as a group.

Boris was right. It was true what he'd said about us. We were ready, we were raring, and we were useless without a leader. We went off like that, leaderless, to Ace Cohen's house.

Tears, mind you. We saw tears in Ace Cohen's eyes. He stopped playing his Asteroids and did not get back into bed. Little Mrs. Blum attacked — it was too much to bear. Such aggression, he agreed, needed to be avenged. "So you'll join us," we said, assuming the matter had been decided. But he wouldn't. He still didn't want any part of us. A singular matter, the blow to Mrs. Blum. And likewise a singular matter, he felt, was the act of revenge.

One punch is what he offered. "You've got me, my Heebie-Jeebies. But only for one swing." We pressed him for more. We begged of him leadership. He showed us his empty hands. "One punch," he said. "Take it or leave it."

Certain things went according to plan. When the Anti-Semite arrived, he showed up alone. That he passed on a Saturday, and in a mood to confront Zvi, we took as a sign of the righteousness of our scheme.

We had already been hiding in those bushes all morning. Sore and stiff, we were sure that the creaking of our joints would give us away, that the sound of our breathing, as all our hearts raced, would reveal the trap we'd laid.

And Zvi — what can be said about that brave Blum, out there alone on the asphalt between the jungle gym and the bushes, cooking under the hot sun? Zvi was poised in his three-piece suit, a red yarmulke like a bull's-eye on top of his head.

The Anti-Semite immediately began to badger Zvi. Zvi, empowered, enraged, and under the impression that we would immediately charge, spewed his own epithets back. The moment was glorious. Little Zvi in his suit, addressing — apparently — the brass belt buckle on that mountain of a bully, raised an accusing finger. "You shouldn't have," Zvi said. His words came out tough; they came out beautiful — so well that they reached us in the bushes, and clearly moved the Anti-Semite to the point of imminent violence.

The situation would have been perfect if not for one unfortunate complication: the small matter of Ace Cohen's resistance. Ace Cohen was unwilling to budge. We begged him to charge with us, to rescue Zvi. "Second thoughts," he said. "A fine line between retaliation and aggression. Sorry. I'll need to see some torment for myself." We implored him, but we didn't charge alone. We all stayed put until push came to shove, until the Anti-Semite started beating Zvi Blum in earnest, until Zvi — his clip-on tie separated from his neck — hit, with a thud, the ground.

Then we sprang out of the bushes, on Ace's heels. We had the Anti-Semite surrounded, and Zvi pulled free with relative ease.

Ace Cohen, three inches taller and fifty pounds heavier, faced the bully down.

"Keep away" is all Ace said. Then, without form or chi power, his feet in no particular stance, Ace swung his fist so wide and so slowly that we couldn't believe anyone might fail to get out of the way. But maybe the punch just looked slow, because the bully took it. He caught it right on the chin. He took it without rocking back — an exceptional feat even before we knew that his jaw was broken. He remained stock-still for a second or two. Not a bit of him moved except for that bottom jaw, which had unhinged like a snake's and made a solid quarter turn to the side. Then he dropped.

Ace pushed his way through the circle we'd formed. It closed right back up around the Anti-Semite, bloodied and now writhing before us.

As I watched him, I knew I'd always feel that to be broken was better than to break — my failing. I also knew that the deep rumble rolling through us was only nerves, a sensitivity to imagined repercussion, as if a sound were built in to revenge.

What we really shared in that instant was simple. Anyone who stood with us that day will tell you the same. With the Anti-Semite at our feet, confusion came over us all. We stood there looking at that crushed boy. And none of us knew when to run.

ROBERT COOVER

Grandmother's Nose

FROM DAEDALUS

She had only just begun to think about the world around her. Until this summer, she and the world had been much the same thing, a sweet seamless blur of life in life. But now it had broken away from her and become, not herself, but the place her self resided in, a sometimes strange and ominous other that must for one's own sake be studied, be read like a book, like the books she'd begun to read at the same time the world receded. Or maybe it was her reading that had made the world step back. Things that had once been alive and talked to her because part of her — doll, house, cloud, well — were silent now, and apart, and things that lived still on their own — flower, butterfly, mother, grandmother — she now knew also died, another kind of distance.

This dying saddened her, though she understood it but dimly (it had little to do with her, only with the inconstant world she lived in), and it caused her to feel sorry for these ill-fated things. She used to think it was funny when her mother chopped the head off a chicken and it ran crazily around the garden; now she didn't. She no longer squashed ants and beetles underfoot or pulled the wings off flies and butterflies, and she watched old things precious to her, like her mother, with some anxiety, frightened by the possibility of their sudden absence. Since dying was a bad thing, she associated it with being bad, and so was good, at least as good as she could be: she wanted to keep her mother with her. If her mother asked her to do something, she did it. Which was why she was here.

She also associated dying with silence, for that was what it seemed to come to. So she chattered and sang the day through to chase the silence away. A futile endeavor, she knew (she somehow had this knowledge, perhaps it was something her grandmother taught her or showed her in a book), but she kept it up, doing her small part to hold back the end of things, cheerfully conversing with any creature who would stop to talk with her. This brought smiles to most faces (she was their little heroine), though her mother sometimes scolded her: Don't speak with strangers, she would say. Well, the whole world was somewhat strange to her, even her mother sometimes; it was talk to it or let the fearful stillness reign.

Though the world was less easy to live in than before, it was more intriguing. She looked at things more closely than she had when looking at the world was like looking in at herself, her eyes, then liquid mirrors in a liquid world, now more like windows, she poised behind them, staring out, big with purpose. To be at one with things was once enough, sameness then a comfort like a fragrant kitchen or a warm bath. Now it was difference that gave her pleasure: feathers (she had no feathers), petals, wrinkles, shells, brook water's murmuring trickle over stones, not one alike, her mother's teeth (she hadn't even seen them there in her mouth before), the way a door is made, and steps, and shoes. She thought about words like *dog, log,* and *fog,* and how unalike these things were that sounded so like cousins, and she peered intensely at everything, seeking out the mystery in the busyness of ants, the odd veiny shape of leaves, the way fire burned, the skins of things.

And now it was her grandmother's nose. It was a hideous thing to see, but for that reason alone aroused her curiosity. It was much longer and darker than she remembered, creased and hairy and swollen with her illness. She knew she ought not stare at it — poor Grandma! — but fascination gripped her. Such a nose! It was as if some creature had got inside her grandmother's face and was trying to get out. She wished to touch the nose to see if it were hot or cold (Grandma lay so still! it was frightening); she touched her own instead. Yes, dying, she thought (though her own nose reassured her), must be a horrid thing.

The rest of Grandma had been affected, too. Though she was mostly covered up under nightcap, gown, and heaped-up bedclothes as though perhaps to hide the shame of her disease, it was clear from what could be glimpsed that the dark hairy swelling had spread to other parts, and she longed — not without a little shudder of dread — to see them, to know better what dying was like. But what could not be hidden was the nose: a dark bristly outcropping poking out of the downy bedding like the toe of a dirty black boot from a cloud bank, or from snow. Plain, as her grandmother liked to say, as the nose on your face. Only a soft snort betrayed the life still in it. Grandma also liked to say that the nose was invented for old people to hang their spectacles on (Grandma's spectacles were on the table beside her bed, perched on a closed book), but the truth was, eyes were probably invented to show the nose where to go. The nose sat in the very middle of one's face for all to see, no matter how old one was, and it led the way, first to go wherever the rest went, pointing the direction. When she'd complained that she'd forgotten the way to Grandma's house, her mother had said: Oh, just follow your nose. And she had done that, and here she was. Nose to nose with Grandma.

Her grandmother opened one rheumy eye under the frill of her nightcap and stared gloomily at her as though not quite recognizing her. She backed away. She really didn't know what to do. It was very quiet. Perhaps she should sing a song. I've brought you some biscuits and butter, Grandma, she said at last, her voice a timid whisper. Her grandmother closed her eye again and from under her nose let loose a deep growly burp. A nose was also for smelling things. And Grandma did not smell very nice. On the way I also picked some herbs for tea. Shall I put some on? Tea might do you good.

No, just set those things on the table, little girl, her grandmother said without opening her lidded eye, and come get into bed with me. Her voice was hoarse and raw. Maybe it was a bad cold she was dying of.

I'd rather not, Grandma. She didn't want to hurt her grandmother's feelings, but she did not want to get close to her either, not the way she looked and smelled. She seemed to be scratching herself under the bedding. It's . . . not time for bed.

Her grandmother opened her near eye again and studied her a moment before emitting a mournful grunt and closing it again. All right then, she mumbled. Forget it. Do as you damn well please. Oh dear, she'd hurt her feelings anyway. Her grandmother burped sourly again and a big red tongue flopped out below her swollen nose and dangled like a dry rag on a line, or her own cap hanging there.

I'm sorry, Grandma. It's just that it scares me the way you look now.

However I look, she groaned, it can't be half so bad as how I feel. Her grandmother gaped her mouth hugely and ran her long dry tongue around the edges. It must have been — *fooshh!* — something I ate.

She felt an urge to remark on her grandmother's big toothy mouth, which was quite shocking to see when it opened all the way (so unlike her mother's mouth), but thought better of it. It would just make her grandmother even sadder. She'd said too much already, and once she started to ask questions, the list could get pretty long, not even counting the parts she couldn't see. Her big ears, for example, not quite hidden by the nightcap. She remembered a story her grandmother told her about a little boy who was born with donkey ears. And all the rest was donkey, too. It was a sad story that ended happily when the donkey boy got into bed with a princess. She began to regret not having crawled into bed with her poor grandmother when she begged it of her. If she asked again, she would do it. Hold her breath and do it. Isn't there some way I can help, Grandma?

The only thing you're good for, child, would just make things worse. Her grandmother lapped at her nose with her long tongue, making an ominous scratchy sound. Woof. I'm really not feeling well.

I'm sorry . . .

And so you should be. It's your fault, you know.

Oh! Was it something I brought you that made you sick?

No, she snapped crossly, but you led me to it.

Did I? I didn't mean to.

Bah. Innocence. I eat up innocence. Grandma gnashed her teeth and another rumble rolled up from deep inside and escaped her. When I'm able to eat anything at all . . . foo . . . She opened her eye and squinted it at her. What big eyes you have, young lady. What are you staring at?

Your . . . your nose, Grandma.

What's the matter with it? Her grandmother reached one hand out from under the bedding to touch it. Her hand was black and hairy like her nose and her fingernails had curled to ugly claws.

Oh, it's a very *nice* nose, but . . . it's so . . . Are you dying, Grandma? she blurted out at last.

There was a grumpy pause, filled only with a snort or two. Then her grandmother sighed morosely and grunted. Looks like it. Worse luck. Not what I had in mind at all. She turned her head to scowl at her with both dark eyes, the frill of the nightcap down over her thick brows giving her a clownish cross-eyed look. She had to smile, she couldn't stop herself. Hey, smarty-pants, what's funny? You're going to die, too, you know, you're not getting out of this.

I suppose so. But not now.

Her grandmother glared at her for a moment, quite ferociously, then turned her head away and closed her eyes once more. No, she said. Not now. And she lapped scratchily at her nose again. In a story she'd read in a book, there was a woman whose nose got turned into a long blood sausage because of a bad wish, and the way her grandmother tongued her black nose made her think of it. Did her grandmother wish for something she shouldn't have?

I sort of know what dying is, Grandma. I had a bird with a broken wing and it died and turned cold and didn't do anything after that. And living, well, that's like every day. Mostly I like it. But what's the point if you just have to die and not be and forget everything?

How should I know what the damn point is? her grandmother growled. She lay there in the heaped bedding, nose high, her red tongue dangling once more below it. She didn't move. It was very quiet. Was she already dead? Or just thinking? Appetite, her grandmother said finally, breaking the silence. And the end of appetite. That's it.

That was more like the Grandma she knew. She had lots of stories about being hungry or about eating too much or the wrong things. Like the one about the little girl whose father ate her brother. He liked the dish so much he sucked every bone (now every time she ate a chicken wing, she thought of that father). The little girl gathered all the bones he threw under the table and put them together and her brother became a boy again. Grandma often told stories about naughty boys and cruel fathers, but the little boy in this story was nice and the father was quite nice, too, even if he did sometimes eat children.

Her grandmother popped her eye open suddenly and barked in her deep raspy voice: Don't look too closely! It scared her and made her jump back. She'd been leaning in, trying to see the color of the skin under the black hairs. It was a color something like that of old driftwood. Look too closely at anything, her grandmother said, letting the dark lid fall over her eye once more and tilting her nose toward the ceiling, and what you'll see is nothing. And then you'll see it everywhere, you won't be able to see anything else. She gaped her jaws and burped grandly. Big mistake, she growled.

The thing about her grandmother's nose, so different from her own, or from anyone's she knew, she thought as she put the kettle on for tea, was that it seemed to say so much more to her than her grandmother did. Her nose was big and rough, but at the same time it looked so naked and sad and kind of embarrassing. She couldn't figure out exactly *what* she thought about it. Grandma's talk was blunt and plain and meant just what it said, no more. The nose was more mysterious and seemed to be saying several things to her at once. It was like reading a story about putting a brother back together with his licked bones and discovering later it was really about squashing bad ladies, one meaning hidden under another one, like bugs under a stone.

With a pestle she ground some of the herbs she'd brought in a mortar, then climbed up on a chair to get a cup down from the cupboard. Her grandmother's nose was both funny and frightening at the same time, and hinted at worlds beyond her imagination. Worlds, maybe, she didn't really want to live in. If you die, Grandma, she said, crawling down from the chair, I'll save all your bones.

To chew on, I hope, her grandmother snapped, sinking deeper into the bedding. Which reminds me, she added, somewhat more lugubriously. One thing your grandmother said, as I now recall, was: Don't bite off more than you can chew.

Yes. But *you're* my grandmother.

That's right. Well — *wuurpp!* — don't forget it. Now go away. Leave me alone. Before I bite your head off just to shut you up.

This dying was surely a hard thing that her grandmother was going through, one had to expect a little bad temper. Even her grandmother's nose seemed grayer than it had been before, her tongue more raglike in its lifeless dangle, her stomach rumblings more dangerously eruptive. It was as though she had some wild angry beast inside her. It made her shudder. Dying was definitely not something to look forward to. The kettle was boiling so she scraped the mortar grindings into the cup and filled it full of hot water, set the cup on the table beside the bed. Here, Grandma. This will make you feel better. Her grandmother only snarled peevishly.

Later, when she got home, her mother asked her how Grandma was feeling. Not very well, she said. A wolf had eaten her and got into bed in Grandma's nightclothes and he asked me to get in bed with him. Did you do that? No, I sort of wanted to. But then some men came in and chopped the wolf's head off and cut his tummy open to get Grandma out again. I didn't stay, but I think Grandma was pretty upset. Her mother smiled, showing her teeth, and told her it was time for bed.

Was that what really happened? Maybe, maybe not, she wasn't sure. But it was a way of remembering it, even if it was perhaps not the best way to remember poor Grandma (that nose!), though Grandma was dying or was already dead, so it didn't really matter.

She crawled into her bed, a place not so friendly as once it was, but first she touched her bedstead, the book beside it (Grandma had given it to her), her pillow, doll, felt the floorboards under her feet, convincing herself of the reality of all that, because some things today had caused her doubt. No sooner had her feet left the floor, however, than there was nothing left of that sensation except her memory of it, and that, she knew, would soon be gone, and the memory of her grandmother, too, and some day the memory of her, and she knew then that her grandmother's warning about the way she looked at things had come too late.

DAVID BEZMOZGIS

A New Gravestone for an Old Grave

FROM ZOETROPE

SHORTLY BEFORE VICTOR SHULMAN was to leave on his vacation, his father called him at the office to say that Sander Rabinsky had died. From the tone of his father's voice, and from the simple fact that his father had felt compelled to call him at work, Victor understood he was expected to recognize the name Sander Rabinsky and also to grasp the significance of the man's passing. Not wanting to disappoint his father he held the phone and said nothing. In recent years many of his father's friends had started to take ill and die. For the most part, these were friends from his father's youth, men whom Victor could not remember, having not seen them in the twenty-five years since the Shulmans left Riga and settled in Los Angeles. For Victor they existed, if at all, in the forty-year-old photos in which they, along with his own father, appeared bare-chested and vigorous on the Baltic shore. Simka, Yashka, Vadik, Salik: athletes, womanizers, and Jewish professionals, now interred in cemeteries in Calgary, New Jersey, and Ramat Gan. Victor assumed that Sander Rabinsky was of the same company, although that didn't quite explain why his death merited a special phone call.

Sander Rabinsky was dead, which was of course sad, Leon Shulman explained, but there was more to it. Sander had been Leon's last remaining connection in Riga and the one Leon had entrusted with overseeing the erection of a new monument to his own father, Wolf Shulman. Of late, Leon and Sander had been in constant contact. Sander had been acting on Leon's behalf with the stonecutter and functioning as liaison with the Jewish cemetery. Leon had already wired one thousand dollars to Sander's bank and Sander had assured him that a new stone would be installed in a matter of weeks. But now, with Sander's death, Leon was at a loss. With nobody there to supervise the job, he had no way of ensuring that it would be properly done.

— Believe me, I know how these things work. If nobody is standing over them, those thieves will just take the money and do nothing.

— The cemetery guy and the stonecutter?

— There are no bigger thieves.

Little more than a year before, Leon Shulman had been forced to retire from the pharmaceutical company where he had worked for twenty-three years. The diabetes that had precipitated his own father's death had progressed to the point where it rendered Leon Shulman clinically blind. Leon was a very competent chemist, enjoyed his job, and was well liked by his coworkers, but he could hardly argue when his supervisor took him aside and began enumerating the dangers posed by a blind man in a laboratory. Since then, as his vision continued to deteriorate, Leon imposed a strict regimen upon himself. His friends were dying and he was blind: another man might have surrendered to depression, but Leon informed anyone willing to listen that he had no intention of going down that road. It wasn't that he had any illusions about mortality; he was a sick man, but sick wasn't dead. So he woke each morning at a specific hour, performed a routine of calisthenics recalled from his days in the Russian army, dressed himself, made his own breakfast, listened to the news, and then immersed himself in unfinished business. At the top of the list of unfinished business was a new gravestone for his father's grave.

On occasion, particularly when the Shulmans observed the anniversary of their arrival in Los Angeles, Leon Shulman would recount the story of his father's death. Certainly Wolf Shulman had been ill. He'd been ill for years. But the week the Shulmans were scheduled to depart he had been no worse than he'd been in five years. Just that morning Leon had seen him, and the old man had made oatmeal. So there was no way Leon could have anticipated what happened. But still, the thought that he was in a black marketeer's kitchen haggling over the price of a Kiev camera — albeit a very expensive model, with excellent optics, based on the Hasselblad — while his father was dying was something for which Leon could not forgive himself. And then the frantic preparations for the funeral, and the fact that Leon had already spent all of their money on things like the camera so that they'd have something to sell in the bazaars of Vienna and Rome, made the whole cursed experience that much more unbearable. Lacking time and money, Leon grieved that he had abandoned his father, a man whom he had loved and respected, in a grave marked by a stone the size of a shoebox.

This, Victor understood, was the reason for the phone call to the office. And later that evening, after submitting himself to the indignities of rush hour on the 405 and the 101, Victor sat in the kitchen of his parents' Encino condominium and listened as his father explained how easy it would be for him to adjust his travel plans to include an extended weekend in Riga. Leon had already called a travel agent, a friend, who could — even on such short notice — arrange for a ticket from London to Riga. It was, after all, a direct flight. A matter of only a few hours. The same travel agent had also taken the liberty — just in case — of reserving a room for Victor at a very nice hotel in Jurmala, two minutes from the beach, near bars, restaurants, and the Dzintari station, where he could find a local train that would get him into Riga in a half hour.

— Ask your mother, Jurmala in July, the beach, if the weather is good, nothing is better.

— Pa, we live in Los Angeles, if I go it won't be because of the beach.

— I didn't say because of the beach. Of course it's not because of the beach. But you'll see. The sand is like flour. The water is calm. Before you were one year old I took you into that water. And anyway, you shouldn't worry. I'll pay for everything.

— That's right, that's my biggest worry.

When Victor was a sophomore in college he realized that he would need to make money. This was the same year he spent a semester abroad at Oxford — though living for three months among fledgling aristocrats had nothing to do with his decision. For Victor, having grown up in Los Angeles, the lives and privileges of rich people — English or otherwise — were no great revelation. What led to his decision were the first irrefutable signs of his father's declining health. Victor began driving his father to the offices of world-class specialists, experts in the pancreas, not one of whom had been able to arrest — never mind reverse — the advancement of Leon's blindness. It was then that Victor started the calculations that ultimately led him to law school and a position as a litigation associate at a Century City law firm. At nineteen, Victor recognized — not unlike an expectant father — the loom of impending responsibilities. He was the only son of aging parents with a predisposition to chronic illness. His father's mother had died of a stroke before her sixtieth birthday. His mother's sister had suffered with rheumatoid arthritis before experiencing the "women's troubles" that eventually led to her death. And diabetes stretched so far back in his lineage that his ancestors were dying of the disease long before they had a name for it. More than once Victor had joked to friends that, when confronted with forms inquiring after family medical history, he simply checked the first four boxes without looking. Still, the only reason Victor felt he could permit himself that joke was that he was thirty years old, earned one hundred and seventy thousand dollars a year, and knew that although he could not spare his parents the misery of illness he could at least spare them the misery of illness compounded by the insult of poverty.

After dinner, Victor's mother, instead of saying good-bye at the doors of the elevator, insisted on walking him down to his car. Victor had not committed to going to Riga, and she wanted him to understand — if he did not already — the effect his refusal would have on his father. Both Victor and his mother knew that Leon could be obsessive about the smallest things, and, considering his condition, this was in some ways a blessing. Sitting at home alone, his obsessions kept his mind occupied. He could fashion his plans and make his phone calls. At the university library where Victor's mother worked, her coworkers all recognized Leon's voice; he no longer needed to ask for her by name.

— Of course you don't know this, but he calls me five or six times a day. Over the last month all the time to consult about the preparations for the gravestone. You know how he is, he says he wants my advice. Should he send Sander all the money at once or half and half? Do I think he should make up a contract for Sander to sign or would Sander be offended? And then when they started talking about what kind of stone, what shape, what size. Finally, when it came time to compose an epitaph, he says to me: You studied literature. There, at least, I think he actually listened to what I said.

Standing in the street beside his car, Victor explained again why the trip would be much more complicated than his father imagined. He had only two weeks for vacation. And it wasn't the kind of vacation where he would be in one place all the time. He would be visiting the only close friend he had retained from his time at Oxford. The previous year this friend had gotten married, and Victor had been unable to attend the wedding. His friend wanted Victor to meet his wife and spend some time with them. They had been planning this trip for months. Not only had his friend coordinated his vacation to coincide with Victor's, but so had his new wife. They were to travel through Scotland, Ireland, and Wales. All the reservations had been made. So it wasn't that Victor didn't want to help put his father's mind at ease, but that there were other people involved and he could not change his plans without inconveniencing them.

— If you tell them why, they'll understand. People have emergencies.

— I know people have emergencies. But the grave has been there for twenty-five years. All of a sudden it's an emergency?

— For your father it's an emergency.

— If he waits six months, I promise I'll book a ticket and go.

In his mother's deliberate pause, Victor heard what neither of them dared speak out loud. Leon was careful about his diet, monitored his blood sugar, and took his insulin injections. There was nothing to say that he could not continue this way for twenty years. Nevertheless, Victor felt that it was irresponsible, even ominous, to project into the future — if only six months — and presume that his father would still be there.

Meeting his mother's eyes, Victor knew that the decision had been made. And when his mother spoke it was no longer to convince him but rather to assure him that he was doing the right thing.

— I understand it will be unpleasant to disappoint your friends. But it's only three days. And, after all, this is your grandfather's and not some stranger's grave.

Late on a Saturday night, Victor's flight made its approach to the Riga airport. On the descent Victor looked out his window at the flat, green Latvian landscape. His neighbor for the three-hour trip from Heathrow was a garrulous, ruddy-faced Latvian in his seventies — a San Diego resident since 1947. Following the collapse of Communism, the man had returned to Latvia every summer for the fishing. When Victor informed him that he was undertaking his first trip to Latvia since his family's emigration in 1978, the man invited him to his cabin. Though the man was sincere and friendly, Victor couldn't help but suspect that he was an unregenerate Nazi. To hear his parents tell it, innocent Latvians hadn't retreated with the Germans. Whether this were true or not, Victor was not exactly proud of the ease with which his mind slipped into clannish paranoia. But to maintain the necessary objectivity wasn't easy, particularly when buckled into an airplane full of blond heads.

In fact, after Los Angeles, and even London, Latvia struck him as remarkable in its blondness. At the customs desk, a pretty blond agent checked his passport. Tall blond baggage handlers handled the baggage. And it was a blond policewoman in a knee-length gray skirt who directed Victor up to the second floor, where he could find a taxi. He had returned to the city of his birth, but no place had ever seemed less familiar. He marveled even at the sky. His flight had landed after ten and he had spent close to an hour in the terminal, but when he stepped outside he emerged into daylight. The pavement, highway, and outlying buildings were illuminated by some bright, sunless source.

At the curb, a thin Russian hopped off the fender of a Volkswagen and reached for Victor's suitcase. He wore a New York Yankees T-shirt and Fila track pants and had the distinction of being not-blond. Identifying Victor immediately as a foreigner, he asked, American? Victor responded in Russian, speaking in a terser, gruffer register than he normally used — a register he hoped would disguise the extent of his foreignness, make him appear less dupable, less likely to be quoted an exorbitant fare. And so when the cabdriver said, Fifteen lats — equivalent to twenty-plus American dollars — a price Victor still suspected was inflated, he growled his disapproval and, to his satisfaction, succeeded in having the fare reduced by one lat.

On the road to Jurmala, Victor rode in silence. He focused on the passing scenery. At that hour, nearly midnight, there were few other cars on the four-lane highway. The view was unspectacular.

He registered certain banal observations. The road was smooth and clean. The passing cars were German, Swedish, Japanese — and clean. The few gas stations they passed appeared to be newly constructed. Victor kept expecting to feel something, be somehow inspired. He thought: I was born here, and I'm evaluating the infrastructure.

The cabdriver spoke over his shoulder and asked which hotel and Victor pronounced the name without turning his head.

— Villa Majori? Not bad. You know who owns it?
— No.
— The former mayor of Jurmala.

Victor gathered that the driver expected him to be impressed.

— He was mayor for six months. Now he has a hotel. The property alone is worth two hundred and fifty thousand lats.
— So he's a crook.
— Of course he's a crook.
— Did you vote for him?
— Did *I* vote for him? What difference does that make? Certain people decided he would be mayor, then later they decided he would no longer be mayor. It's not like that in America?
— In America he'd have two hotels.

The driver laughed, inspiring in Victor a self-congratulatory and yet fraternal feeling.

— The mayor: a crook and a bastard, but I hear the hotel is good and that the girls he hires are very attractive.

Minutes later, Victor discovered that the hotel was indeed modern, tidy, and staffed — even at that late hour — by a pretty clerk. The hotel consisted of three floors, giving the impression that, before being converted to suit the needs of the former mayor, it had been someone's home. Victor found his room on the second floor and stood looking out the window at the flux of people on Jomas Street. The street was closed to all but pedestrian traffic and was flanked on either side by bars, restaurants, and hotels. Through his closed window he could hear the undifferentiated din of voices and music from rival bars. Had he wanted to sleep, the noise would have been infuriating, but though he'd hardly slept in two days, he felt exceedingly, even pathologically, alert. So, as he watched the sky darken literally before his eyes — a change as fluid as time-lapse photography of dusk — Victor decided to call home.

As it was Saturday afternoon in Los Angeles, his mother picked up the phone. When she realized it was Victor, she deliberately kept her voice neutral so as not to attract Leon's attention.
— You're there?
— I'm there.
— In the hotel?
— In the hotel.
— On Jomas?
— I can see it from my window.
— How does it look?
— How did it look before?
— People were strolling all day. Everyone dressed up. All year long girls thought only about getting a new dress for the summer.

Victor heard Leon's voice, rising above his mother's, and the inevitable squabbling over possession of the phone.
— You see, if I tell him who it is, he won't let me talk.
— What do you need to talk about? You can talk when he gets home. Has he spoken to Sander's son?

Sander Rabinsky had a son in Riga whom Victor was supposed to have contacted upon his arrival. Sander's son was named Ilya and happened, as Leon enthusiastically pointed out, also to be a lawyer. It had been Ilya who had informed Leon of Sander's death. After not hearing from Sander for several days, Leon had called repeatedly, left messages, and kept calling until finally Ilya had answered the phone.
— Did you call him?
— It's midnight.
— Call him first thing.
— I will.
— Good. So how is it over there?
— Exactly like Los Angeles. Maybe better. The women are beautiful and there are no fat people.
— Latvians: they look good in uniforms and are wonderful at taking orders. God punished them with the Russians. The devil take them both. Don't forget to call Sander's son.

Victor slept only a few hours and awoke at first light. He lingered in bed, trying to will himself back to sleep, but after an hour of this futility he rose, showered, dressed, and ventured outside. He found Jomas Street deserted but for a handful of elderly city workers armed with straw brooms, engaged in the removal of evidence of the previous night's revelry. It was five o'clock, and Victor walked the length of the street, past the shuttered bars, small grocery stores, and souvenir shops. The only place not closed at that hour was an Internet café attended by a teenager slumped behind the counter. Victor wrote a too lengthy e-mail to his friend in England. He had little new to say, having parted from him and his wife less than a day before, but to kill time he reassured them that they should begin their trip without him and that he would join them as soon as he resolved the business with his grandfather's gravestone. At the very least, Victor joked, he would connect with them by the time they reached Dublin, where his friend's wife had promised to set him up with a former roommate. Victor knew little about the girl other than her name, Nathalie, and that in a picture from his friend's wedding she appeared as a slender, attractive, dark-haired girl in a bridesmaid's dress.

By eight o'clock Victor had eaten his complimentary breakfast in the hotel's dining room and decided, even though it was still possibly too early, to call Sander's son. He dialed from his room, and a woman answered. Leon had told him that Ilya was married with a young son of his own. Speaking to the woman, Victor tried to explain who he was. He mentioned Sander's name, the gravestone, and his father's name. Victor sensed a hint of displeasure in the way the woman replied, Yes, I know who you are, but he tried to dismiss it as cultural — Russians not generally inclined to American-grade enthusiasm — and he was relieved when he heard no trace of the same tone in Ilya's voice.

Ilya said, I spoke with your father. He said you would be coming.

Victor offered his condolences over Sander's death and then accepted Ilya's invitation to stop at his apartment before proceeding to the cemetery.

As the travel agent had indicated, Victor found Dzintari station a few minutes' walk from his hotel. This route — Dzintari to Riga — was identical to the route he would have taken twenty-five years earlier in the summers when his parents rented a small cottage by the seashore. Somewhere, not far from his hotel, the cottage probably still existed, although Victor didn't expect that he could find it.

For the trip, Victor assumed a window seat and watched as the train sped past the grassy banks of a river and then the russet stands of skinny pines. Since it was a Sunday morning, and as he was heading away from the beach and toward the city, there were few other people in his car. At the far end two young men with closely cropped hair shared a quart of malt liquor, and several benches across from Victor a grandmother was holding the hand of a serious little boy dressed in shorts, red socks, and brown leather sandals no self-respecting American child would have consented to wear. Now and again, Victor caught the boy's eyes as they examined him. The boy's interest appeared to be drawn particularly by the plastic bag Victor held in his lap: a large Robinsons-May bag in which he carried a bottle of tequila for Ilya and a small rubber LA Lakers basketball for Ilya's son.

From the train station Victor followed Ilya's directions and walked through the center of the city. Ilya lived on Bruninieku Street, formerly called Red Army Street, in the apartment Sander had occupied for more than fifty years. It was there, on Red Army Street, that Sander and Leon had become acquainted. They had been classmates in the Number 22 Middle School. Leon had lived around the corner and spent many afternoons playing soccer in the very courtyard where Victor now found himself. The courtyard and the building were older than the fifty years, closer to eighty or ninety, and the dim stairwell leading to the second floor suggested the handiwork of some pre–World War II electrician. Victor climbed stone steps, sooty and tread-worn to concavity, and squinted to read graffiti of indeterminate provenance. Some was in Latvian and seemed nationalistic in nature, some was in Russian, and if he read carefully he could make out what it meant: Igor was here; Nadja likes cock; Pushkin, Mayakovsky, Visotsky.

Victor found the number of Ilya's apartment stenciled above the peephole and rang the buzzer. Through the door he heard a child's high and excited cry of Papa, and then Ilya opened the door. He was slightly shorter than Victor but was of the same type — a type which in America could pass for Italian or Greek but which in Latvia wasn't likely to pass for anything other than itself. Ilya wore a pair of house slippers, track pants, and a short-sleeved collared shirt. Standing at Ilya's side was a little blond girl, no older than five. The little girl seemed excited to see Victor.

— Papa, look, the man is here.

Ilya gently put a hand on her shoulder and edged her out of the doorway.

— All right, Brigusha, let the man inside.

Victor followed Ilya into the living room, where Ilya's wife was arranging cups, wafers, and a small teapot on the coffee table. The mystery of genes and chromosomes accounted for the nearly identical resemblance between mother and daughter and, but for a fullness at the mouth, the complete absence of the father in the little girl's face.

As Victor, Ilya, and the little girl entered the room, Ilya's wife straightened up, looked at Victor, and appeared no happier at seeing him than she'd been at hearing his voice over the telephone. Ilya motioned for Victor to sit on the sofa and then performed the introductions.

— This is my wife, Salma, and Brigitta, our little girl.

Victor smiled awkwardly. He felt that he had made the mistake of taking his seat too soon. The upholstery claimed him in a way that made it difficult for him to lean forward or to rise. Undertaking the introductions while seated seemed wrong to the point of rudeness. As it was, he already felt less than welcome. He wanted to be on his feet, not only to shake hands, but also to offer the gifts — though the prospect of rising immediately after sitting down and then that of presenting the inappropriate basketball to Ilya's daughter momentarily paralyzed him. He was tempted to explain the misunderstanding about the basketball, but knew that to do so would be a betrayal of his father, portraying him as confused and inattentive, self-involved, possibly senile.

Doing his best to mask the exertion, Victor rose from the sofa and offered his hand to Salma and then, playfully, to the little girl. Because he knew that Salma didn't like him, Victor watched her face for some sign of détente, but as Brigitta's small hand gripped the tips of his fingers, Salma's smile merely devolved from token to weary. Her expression made Victor feel like a fraud even though, apart from trying to be social, he was quite sure he hadn't done anything fraudulent. Under different circumstances, Victor consoled himself, he wouldn't tolerate such a woman.

Turning his attention from her, Victor reached into his bag and retrieved first the bottle of tequila and then the ball. To his relief, the little girl took the ball with genuine pleasure and bounced it on the stone floor with both hands. Ilya, inspecting the bottle, looked up and watched as Brigitta chased the ball into the kitchen.

— Before she punctured it, she had a beach ball like that. She could bounce the thing all day. Brigusha, say thank you.

Victor, uncertain if he'd been commended or not, said that he hoped the gift was all right.

— You couldn't get her anything better. Right, Salma?

Salma, for the first time, looked — though not quite happy — at least somewhat less austere.

— It's very nice. Thank you.

She then picked up the empty Robinsons-May bag that Victor had left on the floor.

— Do you need the bag back?

— No.

— It's a good bag.

She called after her daughter.

— Brigusha, come here. Look at what a nice big bag the man left for you.

Carrying the ball, Brigitta returned to admire the bag.

— See what a big, fancy bag. You could keep all your toys in here. Come show the man how you can say thank you.

Brigitta looked up at Victor, down at her feet, and then pressed her face into Salma's hip. Ilya said, Now you're shy? Maybe later you can show the man how you say thank you. She can say it in four languages. Russian, Latvian, German, and English.

Placing the tequila on the table, Ilya asked his wife to bring glasses.

— Come, we'll sit. I should have put a bottle down to begin with. What kind of alcohol is this?

Victor resumed his place on the sofa.

— Mexican. They make it from a plant that grows in the desert. It's very popular in America.

Salma returned with two glasses, and Ilya poured. He proclaimed: To new friendship.

After Salma made the tea and distributed the wafers, she took Brigitta into a bedroom. From what Victor could see, that bedroom, plus another, along with the kitchen, a bathroom, and the living room, constituted the apartment. The ceilings were high, maybe twelve feet, and the floors and walls were in good repair. Also, the furniture, polished and solid, seemed to be many decades old and might have, for all Victor knew, qualified as antique.

A New Gravestone for an Old Grave

Ilya said, You like the apartment?
— It would be hard to find one as good in Los Angeles.
— This apartment is the only home I've ever had. Now it's my inheritance. After the war my grandparents returned from the evacuation and moved here. My father grew up here, married here, and when I was born this is where he brought me from the hospital. As a boy I slept on this sofa, my parents in the smaller room, my grandparents in the larger. When my grandparents died, my parents took their room and I was given the smaller one. Now it's my turn to take the big bedroom and move Brigitta into the little one. You could say I've been waiting my entire life to move into the big room. Though, if you follow the pattern, you can see where I go from there.
— So don't move into the big room. Then maybe you'll live forever.
— Well, we haven't moved yet. Brigitta still calls it Grandfather's room. She likes to go and see his white coat hanging on the hook.
— She's a good girl.
— Do you have children?
— No.
— Married?
— No.
— It's a different life in America.
— Probably not that different. At my age most Americans have children. Some are even married.
The mood had become a little too confessional for Victor's liking, and he took it as a good sign when Ilya grinned.
— One day I'd like to visit America. Salma's English is very good. Until recently she even worked for an American software company. Owned by Russians from San Francisco, Jews, who left here, like you, in the 1970s. They returned to take advantage of the smart programmers and the cheap labor. But the company went bankrupt after the problems with the American stock market.
— Unfortunately, it's a familiar story.
— Capitalism, as my father would have said. Though he wasn't much of a Communist. But when everyone was leaving he wasn't interested. He liked it here. He was a doctor; he wanted to remain a doctor. He had no regrets. Not long ago, after your father contacted him, he said to me: You see. What if I'd left? I'd be collecting

welfare in Brooklyn, and who would help blind Leon Shulman with his father's gravestone? He had a real sense of humor.

Wolf Shulman was buried in the "new" Jewish cemetery on Shmerle Street. An older cemetery, from before the war, could be found in the Moskovsky district, a traditionally poor, working-class neighborhood behind the train station. Before the Nazi occupation the neighborhood had been predominantly Jewish, and during the Nazi occupation it had served as the ghetto. Ilya said there wasn't much to see there but, if Victor liked, Ilya would show him around. The municipal courthouse, where Ilya worked as a prosecutor, was only a few minutes away by foot.

From Ilya's apartment Victor caught a bus that let out at the base of Shmerle Street — a winding tributary off the main road — which rose to the cemetery and beyond. A concrete wall painted a pale orange encircled the cemetery. Victor followed the wall to the gates, where three old Russian women minded a wooden flower stall. Business appeared less than brisk, but as Victor neared the entrance he saw a young couple select a bouquet of yellow carnations and so he did the same. He then passed through the gates and located the small stone building that served as the cemetery manager's office. Inside, the office was one single room, with dusty casement windows, a desk for the cemetery manager, and a lectern upon which rested a thick, leather-bound book. Upon entering, Victor found a short, heavyset man wearing faded jeans, a pink sweater, and a black yarmulke, examining a slip of paper which had been handed to him by the young couple with the yellow carnations.

Victor heard the man ask, *Ber*kovitz or *Per*kovitz? and the young woman reply, Berkovitz. Shura Efimovna Berkovitz.

— *Ber*kovitz, *Ber*kovitz, the man repeated, shuffled to the lectern, and opened the large book. Year of death? he inquired, and, given the year, flipped pages and ran his finger down a column of handwritten names.

Once he found the name, the manager wrote down the section and row and pointed the young couple in the appropriate direction. For his service, and for the upkeep of the cemetery, he drew their attention to a container for donations. In a practiced appeal that included Victor, the man said: We have more dead than living. And the dead don't donate.

A New Gravestone for an Old Grave

When the young couple left to seek Shura Berkovitz's grave, Victor introduced himself to the manager. For the second time that day he was surprised to be so effortlessly recognized. Using the same words Salma had used earlier that morning, though without the rancor, the manager said: Yes, I know who you are. Flipping more pages in the book, he looked for Wolf Shulman.

— Remind me, what year did he die?

— Nineteen seventy-eight.

— There. Shulman, Wolf Lazarovich, the manager said, and copied the information.

— And is everything ready for the new gravestone?

— The grave is there. It's always ready. When the stonecutter brings the new stone, he'll also remove the old one. Very easy. Tiktak.

— Is he here today?

Ilya had told Victor that sometimes, particularly on Sundays, the stonecutter could be found at the cemetery. He added that Victor would be well advised to speak to him as soon as possible because the stonecutter could be a difficult man to track down. Sander had expended no small amount of energy dealing with him.

The cemetery manager said, I'll call him at his shop, and dialed the number. Within seconds he was speaking to the stonecutter. He spoke partly in Yiddish and partly in Russian. After a very brief exchange, he hung up. Victor, trying to suppress his irritation, explained that he had wished to speak to the stonecutter himself.

— He said he can see you tomorrow morning. He's very busy right now, but he'll be able to speak to you then. He keeps an office at the Jewish Community Center. He'll be waiting for you at ten-thirty.

— I understand. But, you see, I'm only here for a short time and I want to be sure there are no miscommunications.

— You shouldn't worry. I know of the matter. He knows of the matter. There will be no miscommunications. You'll see him tomorrow, and everything will be just as you wish.

Victor paused, assumed an expression he often employed with obdurate lawyers and clients, an expression intended to imply sincere deliberation, and then said, Nevertheless.

The cemetery manager raised his palms in a sign of surrender. He scribbled a number on a piece of paper.

— Here is the number. Please. I wouldn't want you to think I am interfering. I was only trying to help you. The stonecutter is one of those men who, when he is busy, doesn't like to be disturbed.

Victor took the number and dialed. After a short while he heard a man's terse hello. Before Victor could finish introducing himself the man barked, Tomorrow, ten-thirty, and hung up. Victor replaced the phone and turned reluctantly to face the cemetery manager's obsequious grin.

The cemetery at Shmerle had been hewn from a forest, but enough trees were spared so as to retain a sense of the arboreal. Different types of trees — birch, elm, maple, ash — provided texture and shade and resembled in their randomness the different species of gravestones — marble, granite, limestone — which sprouted from the ground as naturally as the trees. Though arranged in sections and rows, the gravestones did not follow any other order, and so large dwarfed small, traditional opposed modern, and dark contrasted light. The only commonality among them was that each stone featured a photograph of the deceased and that in each photograph the deceased possessed the same grudging expression. Soldiers, grandmothers, engineers, mathematicians: all stared into eternity with a face that declared not *I was alive*, but rather *This was my life*. After walking some distance, Victor found his grandmother and grandfather wearing this same face.

Until he saw his grandmother's grave, Victor had at some level forgotten about it. That he carried only one bouquet reminded him of the extent to which he had forgotten. His grandmother had died when he was still an infant and so he had no memory of her at all. Somewhere there was a picture of the two of them together: a baby in the arms of a stout, prematurely old woman. Her gravestone confirmed what little he knew of her: Etel Solomonovna Shulman, beloved wife, mother, and grandmother. Died before her sixtieth birthday. This information, beneath her photo, was etched into a thick, rectangular slab of black granite. And this slab, almost a meter high, towered over its partner, a limestone monument one-third the size, already weather-worn and tilting slightly backward. Seeing the two gravestones side by side, Victor could understand his father's anguish. What was left for Wolf Shulman seemed a slight against a man whose solemn face — due to the backward tilting of the stone — appealed vaguely heavenward with an expression that could also be interpreted as: *Is this all I deserve?*

After taking some pains to divide his bouquet into two equal halves, Victor paused and contemplated his grandparents' graves. They evoked in him a peculiar timbre of grief — grief not over what he had lost but over what he had never had. A baser, more selfish form of grief. The kind that permitted him only to mumble a self-conscious good-bye before turning back up the path. He then retraced his steps through the cemetery, stopping at times to appraise certain gravestones, look at pictures, and read names and dates. There were other members of his family buried here, and he discovered the grave of a great-uncle as well as some other graves with the last name Shulman — although he couldn't be sure if they were definitively his relations. The only other name he recognized appeared in a section occupied by more recent graves. On a reddish marble stone he read the name RABINSKY and saw a picture of a woman who must have been Ilya's mother. The picture, like all such pictures, was not of the best quality, but Victor could discern enough to draw the obvious conclusion. And beside this grave was another, still lacking a stone; but pressed into the soft earth was a small plastic sign on which was stenciled the name S. RABINSKY.

It was only noon when Victor left the cemetery, and though he felt the sluggishness of two days without sleep he decided to take a tour of the city. He caught a bus back into the vicinity of Ilya's apartment and then walked to the heart of medieval Riga. The city had been established in the twelfth century and had, throughout its history, been the subject of every Baltic power. Germanic knights, Poles, and Swedes had tramped through its cobblestone streets. In the twentieth century alone — but for a brief spell of interwar independence — it had belonged to the tsar, the kaiser, Stalin, Hitler, and then Stalin once more. The heart of Old Riga had been destroyed by the Germans in the first days of World War II, rebuilt unfaithfully by the Soviets, but corrected to some extent by the new Latvian government. And so Victor was able to observe the storied Blackheads House, pass through winding alleyways, and visit the Domsky Cathedral, home to a world-famous organ.

Later, by leaving the old city, he found many examples of art nouveau buildings, with their elaborate stucco figures and faces. However, not particularly interested in architecture, Victor saw just enough to get a sense of the place. And after he'd acquired this sense, he took a seat at an outdoor café and ate his lunch in view of pedestrians, vendors, drunks, policemen, and bus drivers. In its constituent parts, the city displayed itself, and seemed, with its imported cars and Western fashions, none the worse for fifty years of Soviet rule.

On the ride back to Jurmala, Victor allowed himself to drift off. It was the deepest sleep he had experienced since leaving Los Angeles, and when his cab reached the hotel, a tremendous effort was required to rouse himself. He wanted nothing other than to sleep until morning, but at the front desk there were messages waiting for him from his father and from Ilya. So, as tired as he was, Victor began by calling Ilya and recounting the episode at the cemetery manager's office. The incident, according to Ilya, was consistent with the man's character.

— But you have to consider how many others are practicing his trade. The man has no competition and so, unfortunately, he's become arrogant.

Ilya wished Victor luck and then invited him to come to the courthouse after his meeting with the stonecutter. He framed the invitation in collegial terms. As a fellow jurist, Ilya imagined that Victor possessed some professional curiosity. This way, Ilya said, you will be able to see the fabulous workings of the Latvian legal system.

Victor then placed his call home. This time Leon answered, after hardly a single ring, as though he had been sitting, primed, by the telephone. Whatever reservations Victor harbored about the cemetery manager and stonecutter, he knew better than to reveal them to his father. To Leon's detailed questions, he responded honestly but without elaboration. Yes, he had seen Sander's son. Yes, he had been received cordially. Yes, he had given the *child* the present and the *child* had been pleased. Yes, he had been to the cemetery, seen his grandparents' graves, and left flowers. And yes, he had also spoken with the cemetery manager and with the stonecutter — the latter of whom he had not seen personally but would the very next morning.

After the conversations with his father and with Ilya, Victor discovered — to his frustration — that he had lost his overwhelming need for sleep. The prospect of another sleepless night was unbearable and so Victor drew the blinds, climbed into bed, and resolved to nurture even the slightest vestige of fatigue. But once again his body refused to cooperate. He slept only fitfully, waking up disoriented, sometimes because of voices in the street, other times because of some malformed thought. At one point he found himself bolt upright, unsure whether or not he had indeed requested a wake-up call. He then spent what felt like an eternity torn over whether or not to call the front desk and confirm yes or no. Later, he lost the better part of an hour recreating the scene at the cemetery manager's office and formulating alternate scenarios in which he didn't come off looking like an idiot. Eventually, in despair, he turned on the television and watched an American action movie, dubbed in Latvian with Russian subtitles.

At five in the morning, Victor was back among the sweepers on Jomas Street. The sky was cloudless and approaching full daylight. Victor made a circuit of Jomas, covering its entire length, and then turned north and walked the few blocks to the beach, which, like the streets, was largely deserted. Narrow and white, it stretched from east to west, seemingly to infinity. The tide was still high and sandpipers skittered neurotically at the fringes of the waves. A short distance away, balancing against each other and advancing gingerly out into the Baltic, were two middle-aged women in bathing suits. They had already progressed about fifty yards, but the water was not yet to their waists. The sight triggered Victor's first memory of his Soviet childhood: stepping out into a dark blue sea, conscious of danger, but feeling as though he could go a great distance before he had anything to fear.

To find the Jewish Community Center, Victor crossed a large municipal park and looked for the spire of a Russian Orthodox church. As he was extremely early, he trolled past the community center, made sure he was in the right place, and then sat and waited in the park until he thought it was reasonable to go and look for the stonecutter.

The community center, contrary to Victor's expectations, was a substantial building — four stories tall and designed in the art nouveau style. From a fairly dark and dreary-looking lobby a broad stone stairway led to the upper floors, all of which benefited from an abundance of natural light. Not knowing whom to ask or where to look, Victor climbed the staircase and roamed the hallways hoping to stumble upon something that would announce itself as the stonecutter's office. He wandered for what seemed like a long time, finding an adult choir practicing Hebrew songs in a rehearsal room; a grand theater, with crumbling plaster and a seating capacity of hundreds; the locked doors of the Latvian Jewish Museum; and a tribute dedicated to a handful of Latvians who had protected Jews during the war.

He found these things but no explicit sign of the stonecutter, and little in the way of assistance until a young Latvian woman emerged from an office and cheerily informed Victor that the stonecutter did indeed use a room in the building, but he kept no regular hours and she hadn't seen him that morning. However, keen to help, she led Victor down one floor and pointed out the stonecutter's door. She even knocked, waited, and then apologized profusely, as if she were personally responsible for the stonecutter's absence. There was a phone in her office, she said, if Victor wanted to call the stonecutter, and also magazines, if he wished to occupy himself while waiting.

Seeing no other recourse, Victor followed the woman to her office and made the pointless phone call. The stonecutter was admittedly only fifteen minutes late, and the fact that he did not pick up the phone could actually be construed as a good sign — the man was on his way — so there was, in essence, no logical reason for despair. And yet, each unanswered ring reinforced Victor's suspicion that the stonecutter would not show up.

Victor put down the phone. Beside him, the woman looked on with a doleful expression, and he dreaded that, at any moment, she would repeat her offer of the telephone and the magazines. He couldn't recall if he'd seen a pay phone down in the lobby, but he was quite sure that he had seen one in the park. Calling from the park would require that he go somewhere and make change and then walk the two blocks between the community center and the park every time he wanted to make a phone call — thereby introducing a risk of missing the stonecutter should the man make a brief appearance at his office — but all this still seemed preferable to remaining, for even one second longer, the object of this woman's sympathy. Once again, Victor walked up and down the staircase. He listened to the choir and then descended to the lobby, where he found a handful of elderly Jews convened at a table, speaking Yiddish, chewing sandwiches, and playing cards. Victor stood for a few moments, debating whether or not to go outside, until a man brushed past him, hunched, bent under the weight of some psychological burden. He wore an ancient raincoat and a beaten fedora, and he carried a briefcase. The man made his way for the doors of the public toilet, and Victor heard him muttering to himself, If only to go and shit like a human being. Victor decided to go outside.

Sitting in the park — having run the same coin through a pay phone yet once more — Victor thought it funny that there had been a time when the purpose of his vacation had absolutely nothing to do with Latvia. That at some point he had conceived of a relaxing trip with friends, touring the U.K. And when the excursion to Riga had been introduced (or, rather, imposed), he had treated it as only a minor deviation. A filial duty quickly and easily dispatched. But now, amid his exhaustion and anxiety, it seemed inconceivable that he would ever reunite with his friends and see Ireland, Scotland, and Wales. His fate was to be perpetually trapped in Latvia, pursuing a stonecutter, thinking obsessively about gravestones. Victor laughed out loud. It was possible that people at neighboring benches turned and stared. He didn't bother to check one way or the other. He had made his phone calls, he had knocked on the stonecutter's door, he had sat and waited. It was now time to walk to the courthouse and continue the farce.

Unlike most of the buildings Victor had seen in Riga, the courthouse was new and therefore outfitted with most of the contemporary trappings. The courtroom doors locked automatically when a session was in order, the faint whir of air conditioning was omnipresent, and the furniture — though constructed from Latvian pine — had a vague Ikea-like quality. At the very back of the courtroom, to the right of the door, the accused sat on a bench inside a little gated prisoner's dock. Along the wall, just ahead of him, two policemen in green uniforms sat on their benches. They were both young men, barely in their twenties, but already possessing the dull, indolent posture common to all court officers. Victor had his place across the aisle from the policemen. Behind him were a young woman and a teenaged boy and ahead was an old woman, presumably the defendant's family. When Victor entered the courtroom, there was no sight of the bailiff, judge, or — more to the point — Ilya. Only the defense attorney, a tall, thin woman with tired, houndlike features, was present. Ilya did not appear until the bailiff emerged from the back door and called the session to order.

All were made to rise while the judge mounted his podium. He was dressed in a burgundy robe and wore a chain of ornamental, golden medallions — evidently some folkloric symbol of Latvian authority. After the judge assumed his position, there followed the routine sequence of statements and exchanges — all of them in Latvian.

Victor understood hardly anything that happened over the next hour. He had no idea what the man had done to warrant his confinement, and he couldn't determine the purpose of the proceedings. He assumed they were preliminary, since, at one point, the defendant made a plea of not guilty. However, beyond that, the sense of things was impenetrable. And so Victor paid attention only long enough to register that Ilya, in his suit and tie, seemed to be a good lawyer. He was organized, spoke succinctly, and carried himself with an aloofness that bordered on menace. All of which probably didn't bode well for the man in handcuffs who sat in the prisoner's dock, looking not so much like a criminal but rather like a weary commuter waiting for the train. Victor assumed the same attitude of forbearance from the woman and the teenaged boy as he heard not a sound behind him. The only person showing any sign of distress was the old woman in the front row. She had been in tears from the outset of the proceedings, and, as time wore on, her breathing became shallower and more labored. Despite the air conditioning, perspiration gathered in the folds of her neck. She drank water from a plastic, bear-shaped bottle — a kind manufactured to contain honey — and alternately wiped her eyes with a handkerchief and attempted to cool herself with a paper fan. But it was all to little effect as, ultimately, her breathing seized up and Victor was convinced that she was on the verge of a heart attack. It was only at this point that the judge turned his attention to her and considered a pause in the proceedings, but when she managed to collect herself things resumed as before.

The hearing was the last of the day for Ilya, and so, at its conclusion, he suggested they have lunch. They stopped at a small cafeteria where Victor bought half a dozen meat and cabbage buns and two bottles of Latvian beer. They then walked back toward the municipal park where Victor had spent much of his morning. On the way, Ilya explained what had transpired in the courtroom.

It was, as Victor had surmised, an arraignment. The man had already spent six months in custody waiting for the date. He would probably wait another several months before his next appearance. His crime was serious, though not uncommon. He was charged with attempting to murder his boss. The man was a mechanic and had worked in an auto shop. He had been on the job for three months — the standard probationary period during which a new employee is paid poorly, if at all. After three months, the boss is legally bound either to keep him on full-time or let him go. Generally, to avoid the higher taxes associated with a full-time employee, a boss will let the person go and find another — there being no shortage of desperate people. In this case, the man claimed that his boss had promised to keep him. But when he came to work after his probationary period, he found someone else at his post. His boss told him to go to hell, and so the man stabbed him in the neck with a screwdriver.

The boss probably had it coming, but Ilya had no choice but to prosecute. If he didn't, then every boss would be walking around with a screwdriver in his neck.

— So what will he get for stabbing his boss in the neck?

— Hard to say. Ten years? Or nothing. He'll say it was self-defense. The boss attacked him. He supports a wife, a younger brother. Nobody really wants to put him in jail. But who knows? Maybe things will turn out badly and he'll be put away for a long time.

— Which will probably be the end of the old woman.

Ilya considered this and then confessed that he had his doubts about the old woman. It struck him as peculiar that while the rest of the family sat in the back, she had taken her place in the front. Obviously, the old woman was supposed to be the defendant's mother, but this wasn't something anyone had bothered to verify. So she could just as well have been any old woman off the street. Which meant that there was nothing to say that the family hadn't scraped three lats together and paid her to come to the courthouse and act hysterical. Such things were not without precedent. Though, for an arraignment, Ilya believed it a waste of money. But one couldn't blame the old woman. She probably received sixty lats a month pension. Equivalent to one hundred dollars. And, Ilya said, he didn't need to describe to Victor what it was like to live on one hundred dollars a month.

They entered the park, and Ilya sought out a vacant bench in the shade. It was now early afternoon and much quieter than when Victor had been there in the morning. There were a few young mothers with children and strollers. Now and again, a businessman strode past speaking into a cell phone. A few tourists stopped to buy ice cream and study their maps. Victor sipped his beer and wondered if he should admit to Ilya that he had absolutely no idea what it meant to live on one hundred dollars a month in Riga. Judging from Ilya's tone, he gathered that one hundred dollars a month was a pathetic sum. It certainly didn't sound like a lot of money, but then again, Latvia wasn't Los Angeles and, had Ilya phrased things differently, Victor could just as easily have been convinced that, in Latvian terms, one hundred dollars was a fortune. And though Victor subscribed to a sober view of the world and of the forces that ruled it — forces for which the financial welfare of old ladies was generally not a top priority — he was in a strange country and therefore prone to a higher level of credulity; liable, practically, to believe the opposite of everything he believed.

Ilya said, Do you want to know how much money I make? and then answered his own question before Victor had a chance to object.

— Two hundred lats a month. This is considered a good salary. Just enough so that I will think twice before taking a bribe. My father made the same as a dermatologist with forty years' experience. Salma, when she worked for the Americans, made two hundred and fifty. For a time, with three salaries, a total of six hundred and fifty lats a month, we were relatively well off.

Ilya then proceeded to quote a litany of expenses, most of which, he said, were common to everyone in the city. Rent, food, transportation, miscellaneous items for children and the elderly. The figure he quoted for rent alone exhausted the total of the old woman's pension. There was, Ilya said, really no such thing as disposable income. This was why, to cite an extreme example, most of Riga's prostitutes had abandoned the city for points west. And as for the young mothers in the park, the businessmen, the pretty girls in summer dresses — in short, the reason Victor saw no squalor — well, it was Europe, after all. Not Africa. One good suit, one designer blouse — though secondhand from Germany — represented the difference between self-respect and despondency.

Ilya recited all of this information with detachment, as though he were addressing something merely statistical, academic, impersonal. His voice contained no resentment, which was why, when he asked Victor how much money he made, Victor felt less than his normal reticence to respond. However, he chopped fifty thousand off the number, which, given the context, still sounded obscenely excessive.

— But, Victor qualified, I work for a large firm. We do most of our business with corporations. Someone doing your job would make less. And then you still have to adjust for the higher cost of living . . .

He realized that his was not a very persuasive argument. It was, even in terms of Los Angeles, not a very persuasive argument. He made a lot of money. Probably more than he deserved. But then again, he knew of others who earned even more and deserved even less.

Ilya leaned back on the bench and regarded, as though with intense botanical interest, the leaves and branches of the shade tree.

— I have some money saved up. Enough to send Salma and Brigitta to America. As I say, Salma is an accomplished programmer and her English is very good. And Brigitta is young and will easily learn the language. I am the only impediment. But I have my job here and am prepared to wait until they are ready for me.

Ilya then turned his attention from the tree and focused on Victor. As Ilya prepared to speak, Victor noted an inchoate defensiveness in the set of his features, as though Ilya, like a teenaged suitor, was poised for imminent rejection; prepared, at any moment, to dismiss the proposition with a never-mind. Which was precisely what he said, but not before he said: I'm not asking for money. And not before Victor replied: I do not practice that kind of law.

— But perhaps someone in your firm?

— We deal only with corporations. Trade issues. Never individual immigration cases.

Which — other than the exceptions made for the sons and mistresses of wealthy clients — was the truth. Immigration cases were frustrating and time-consuming, entailing a morass of paperwork and almost always ending in recriminations. Given the choice, he would have preferred it if Ilya actually had asked for money.

— And what about other means?
— What other means?
— Marriage.

— But you are already married.
— We could divorce. Temporarily, of course. I have heard it done.
— And then what?
— Salma could marry an American.
— Just like that?
— How else?
— And where would she find this American?

Which, Victor immediately understood, was a stupid question.

— Never mind, Ilya said. I see that it is asking too much.

Victor considered explaining, so far as he knew, the problems inherent in this option, to try to exonerate himself, to impress upon Ilya the impracticality; beyond that, he considered lying, consenting to fill out forms, marry the man's wife, adopt his daughter, do whatever, since it was pitifully clear that between him and the stonecutter remained — even if only tenuously — Ilya. But he couldn't quite bring himself to do that. Instead, he sat beside Ilya and resigned himself to a punitive silence.

After some time, as if having reached a conclusion, Ilya repeated, Never mind, and ended the silence. I realize that this isn't why you came here, he said, with each word distancing himself from the man who had, only moments before, offered Victor his wife and child.

— Fortunately, your problem is easier to solve. I will call the stonecutter for you.

Ilya rose and went to the phone booth, though Victor was sure that he hadn't said anything to him about his most recent frustrations. And when Victor approached the phone booth, Ilya was already dialing a number. Then he was speaking in Latvian, exhibiting the same bloodless composure he had evinced in the courtroom. The conversation did not last very long, and Ilya did most of the talking. Once again, as at the cemetery manager's office, Victor felt himself excluded from considerations related to his own life. His input wasn't requested except to establish the departure time of his flight the next day.

When the conversation was over, Ilya exited the phone booth and announced, If you like, he can see us now.

— That was the stonecutter?
— Yes.
— Is he at the community center?

— No.
— So, where is he?
— At his shop. In the Moskovsky district. It's possible to walk, although I would recommend a cab. A cab would get us there in ten minutes. We can get one easily on Brivibas Street.

Ilya half turned in the direction of the street, ready to hail the cab, as if Victor's consent were foregone and incidental. Angered by Ilya's presumptuousness, and momentarily unsure of what he wanted, Victor said:

— What if I don't want to go?
— You don't want to go?
— I don't understand the rush.
— I thought you left tomorrow.
— In the afternoon. I could see him in the morning.
— But he can see you now.
— I waited for him for two hours today. Where was he then?

Ilya regarded Victor as one might a child or a dog, as some thing ruled by impulse and deficient in reason.

— I couldn't say. Though I imagine if we went you could ask him yourself.

The flatness of Ilya's tone discouraged Victor from asking anything further. Which was fine, since Victor no longer had anything to ask. He now recognized that he was in a situation that provided for only a binary choice. He could go with Ilya and see things through to their conclusion — whatever that might be — or he could refuse and claim the transitory pleasure of refusal. Those were his choices. There was nothing else. Calling the stonecutter and repeating his mistake at the cemetery was out of the question. And though he had misgivings about the likelihood of things turning out right, he had also an almost inexorable curiosity to meet the man. It seemed ridiculous — and likely a symptom of his delirium — but he had begun to doubt the very fact of the stonecutter's existence. And he entertained the thought, in some subrational recess, that meeting the stonecutter might be like meeting God or the president or the Wizard of Oz — equal parts disappointment and reward — but at least the truth would be revealed.

Victor followed Ilya out to Brivibas Street, where, as predicted, they had no trouble finding a cab. Ilya rode up front and directed the driver while Victor sat in the back seat. The driver navigated along streets now familiar to Victor. They passed through the medieval city, looped behind the central markets and the train station, and followed a route that brought them to the courthouse and the limit of Victor's knowledge. They then continued south, into what could have been generically described as the bad part of town. The change was abrupt, as though the result of a civic consensus: no tourists expected beyond this point. The streets were gray and dingy. Old buildings deteriorated unchecked. Not infrequently, Victor saw listing, wooden hovels — seemingly anomalous in an urban setting — beside concrete apartment houses. People moved about the streets, tending to their everyday affairs, but there were also shadowy figures loitering in doorways. In America, the place would have qualified as a slum, depressing and interesting only in a sordid way. But Nazis had commanded here and perpetrated horrific crimes, the knowledge of which invested the place with a sense of historical gravity; the slum felt like more than just a slum. And, assuming he didn't get mugged or clubbed to death, Victor thought it fitting that he should come here to get to the bottom of things.

After traveling for several more minutes, Ilya pointed to a dark green cottage and instructed the driver to stop. Victor then paid the driver and joined Ilya at the cottage's entrance. They stood there for a short while, but Ilya offered nothing in the way of explanation, not even a word to assure Victor that the dilapidated structure — bearing nothing to identify it as the stonecutter's shop or as a place of business of any kind — was where they needed to be. Victor had expected to find heavy machinery and stacked rock, but there were only a peeling facade, drawn curtains, uncut grass, and a dirt path that turned ninety degrees at the front steps and wound around the side of the house. Taking this path, Ilya led Victor the length of the house and into a yard dominated by a Mitsubishi pickup truck with a sunken rear suspension. The truck had been backed into the yard so that its tailgate was only a few feet from the doors of a garage and from a large manual winch. The winch looked ancient, a relic from previous centuries, but Victor could see that it was still very much in use. By its heavy rope, it suspended a rough marble obelisk three feet in the air. The obelisk spun lazily, as though it had only recently been disturbed.

Ilya placed a hand on the obelisk, indicated the garage, and said: Well, here you have him.

A New Gravestone for an Old Grave

Victor stepped past a door and looked into the garage. Looking back at him was a man in his sixties. He wore scuffed work pants and a sleeveless undershirt, and he had the hands and arms befitting a man who spent his days working with stone. He sat on a low stool with his legs splayed out before him. In one hand he held an abrasive cloth, which he had been using to polish a granite tombstone propped against a nearby wall. He blinked sullenly and looked very much like someone who hadn't been happy to see anyone in years.

— Shimon, Ilya said, I brought you your client.

Shimon blinked again and showed no indication that he heard what Ilya had said.

Ilya gave the obelisk a firm shove, putting the weight in motion, and eliciting squeals of protest from the winch.

— Aren't you even going to say thank you, you old goat?

— Go to the devil, Shimon said, and take him with you.

— You shouldn't talk like that. He came all the way from America just to see you.

— All the worse for him.

Shimon glared from Victor to Ilya as though trying to determine which of them he despised more. For a moment, Victor wondered if maybe the old man had him confused with someone else. He'd not yet said one word to the stonecutter — barely looked at him, done nothing more than show up — and yet the man seemed to loathe him in a personal way. Victor found it unsettling, like the opprobrium of a cripple or a religious person. However, it didn't appear to bother Ilya, who responded to the stonecutter's hatred with a patrician smugness.

— Listen, if you don't want the business, we'll leave.

Shimon shrugged, hatred undiminished, but evidently not prepared to lose the business. Though, what business, Victor could not quite figure out. The money had been sent months ago and the work reportedly done.

Shimon lifted his face to Victor and said: Well, did you come from America to stand here like a mute? What is it you want from me?

It could only be, Victor thought, that the man had confused him with someone else. Either that or he suffered from a mental illness.

— I spoke to you yesterday. We had an appointment for this morning. I waited for you for hours. We were supposed to discuss the gravestone for my grandfather's grave. Work which I was told you had finished. Work for which you have already been paid. So, how exactly do you mean what do I want?

— Who told you it was finished?

— His father promised my father it would be finished. Money was wired. Are you saying it's not finished?

— Ask your friend the parasite if it's finished.

Shimon jerked his head toward Ilya, the parasite, who had allowed a shadow to fall over his smugness.

— You see how he talks. You see what it's like to deal with him. My father literally spent weeks trying to have a reasonable conversation with him. And though I saw the trouble he was having, my father refused to let me intervene. Now, you've seen the Latvian legal system. You have seen where I work. It's nothing to be proud of. But, for what it's worth, it gives me access to certain people. And, if absolutely necessary, I can complicate someone's life.

Ilya frowned in the stonecutter's direction.

— Not that it's something I enjoy. What's to enjoy? Old men like him pass through the court every day. You'd have to be a sick person to enjoy making someone's miserable life even more miserable. Right?

Ilya smiled philosophically at Victor, his eyes seeking confirmation, as though the question had not been rhetorical.

Just to be clear, he repeated it.

— Right?

— Right.

— But what choice do I have with someone like him?

From the roof of his skull, Victor felt the spreading of a vaporous warmth. It filled him, like helium but not exactly, making him very light and very heavy all at once. It took him a second to identify this sensation as a powerful swell of fatigue. His legs were like pillars, rooted to the ground, and yet he believed he might tip over. Out of the corner of his eye, he thought he saw a lumbering, retarded man. The man was Shimon's son. He helped his father load and unload the heavy rocks. Victor turned to get a better look, but when he did he saw only Shimon sitting by himself in the garage.

Victor turned back to Ilya and said, What does any of this have to do with my grandfather's gravestone? Ilya wavered before him, for a second blurry and then immaculately sharp.

— Let me explain it to you, Ilya said.

— Three weeks ago my father got on a bus to go and see this man. This man who could not be relied upon to keep an appointment or return a phone call. On a hot day, after working for eight hours, at five o'clock, when the buses are full, my father had to ride across town. Before he got here he had a heart attack. They had to stop the bus. We only received a phone call when he was already in the hospital. I, my daughter, my wife, none of us even had a chance to say good-bye. This is what it has to do with your grandfather's gravestone. My father, who from the goodness of his heart agreed to help. My father, whom your father only pestered. Calling all the time. And then wanting to negotiate payment in installments. As if my father was a thief. And later sent him a *contract* —

Ilya spat out *contract* as if a more offensive word did not exist in the Russian language.

— This is what it has to do with anything. That my father killed himself over this gravestone. This gravestone which nobody would ever even visit. And what did my father get in return? Never a thank-you. Only a hundred lats for his trouble. A hundred lats that won't even buy a stone a fifth as big for his memory. Now you tell me if that's fair.

Through the murk of fatigue, Victor heard the things Ilya said, but his brain processed only the rudiments: my father, your father, my father, your father. If there were an argument here, Victor didn't see how anyone could hope to win it. There was nothing to win. There was Sander, an old man suffering a heart attack on a cramped city bus: Ilya's father, but an abstraction to Victor. And there was Leon, an abstraction to Ilya, but as real to Victor as if he were standing before him. There he was, stumbling around the apartment, feeling the walls. There he was, every morning, in his tracksuit, doing deep knee bends and other ludicrous Soviet calisthenics. There he was, injecting himself with insulin and fretting about one thing or another at the kitchen table. His father.

— I thought I would give you a chance. If you would help, Ilya said. And even now, I give you a chance. You can buy yourself another gravestone. God knows you have the money. Give this old bastard the business he doesn't deserve. And I'll send you a photo to prove it gets done.

In a daze, Victor didn't quite remember refusing the arrangement. Because he was already picturing his cab ride and the blur of pine trees on the way to Jurmala. And he was already in his hotel room, lying in bed, asleep and having a dream in which Nathalie, the Irish bridesmaid, appeared to him either on the beach in Jurmala or on the beach in Los Angeles — maybe both — and in which she professed her undying love, had sex with him, became his wife, and then — with the confounding logic of dreams — transformed into Salma, who, stranger still, did nothing to undermine the benign quality of the dream but rather, in some illicit way, only enhanced the sense of pleasure. And then he awoke and dialed and had a conversation with his father. A conversation in which his father asked him how everything went. If he met the stonecutter. If he saw the gravestone. If everything looked as it should. And Victor answered his father, saying yes about the stonecutter, yes about the gravestone. Yes about everything. He answered him and said that everything was perfect, just the way he imagined it.

KATHERINE BELL

The Casual Car Pool

FROM PLOUGHSHARES

HE HAD JUMPED A RADIO TOWER and a cliff in Norway, but never a bridge. He chose a Wednesday morning when the fog was expected to burn off early and called in sick to work. At dawn, he climbed the tower. The riskiest part, he thought, would be landing in the water, where his friends would be waiting with a boat.

While he fell he counted to three and pushed it to four, though he'd promised he wouldn't, and his canopy opened without any trouble, exactly as it should. But a freak wind came and lofted him — he didn't remember this, but it must have happened — and now his chute was snared in the steel ropes of the bridge, and he was dangling like a hurt insect a hundred feet above the morning traffic. His right arm had snapped inside its Gore-Tex sleeve, and though he wanted to tuck it close to his body, he couldn't. He couldn't reach his radio, either. He looked down at the cars on the top deck. They glittered in the sun as they streamed toward the city, the very edge of the continent. It was stupid to have jumped so close to rush hour.

Now, because of him, more than eighty thousand people would be late to work. Across the city, deadlines would be missed, meetings canceled, stores understaffed. The host of the nine o'clock show on KQED would not arrive in time; at every major hospital, surgeries would be postponed. The driver of the Nissan Altima stalled near the end of the Yerba Buena tunnel would be late, and so would the woman beside him. The girl in the back seat did not have a job. School had already started, but that was behind her, before the bridge. She had never planned to go.

*

Ian tapped the steering wheel and stared hopefully at the tunnel's bright mouth. Usually, when you came out from under the manmade island, the traffic sped up until it hit land and clogged again. The pattern was roughly the same every day. If you hit the 880 loop at the right time, you could slip straight into the car pool lane and not stop until the toll plaza. That's why it was worth it to pull off the freeway in Oakland to pick up passengers — you saved the two-dollar toll and at least twenty minutes. It always struck Ian as odd, the idea of ferrying strangers across the bridge. He couldn't help feeling responsible for their safety and comfort. He limited the mess in the car to the floor behind his own seat and drove more cautiously than he did when he was alone. Until Oakland, he listened to the symphonies and concertos that bored his wife, and sometimes the outdated pop music that embarrassed her, but after Oakland he turned the volume down and switched to news, the least political of the stations, with weather and traffic repeated every fifteen minutes.

He stole a look at his front-seat passenger, her dark head bent over a stack of papers. She'd unhitched her seat belt when they reached the bridge, which meant she'd lived in the Bay Area long enough to remember the earthquake in '89, to prefer the risk of a car accident to the risk of being trapped under rubble.

The girl in the back had never put hers on. She couldn't sit still, kept shifting her limbs about, running her nails back and forth along the beige velour edge of her seat, leaning her head against the window and clouding up the glass. She'd rather be on the train, hurtling under the Bay, unstoppable. But the train was expensive, the car pool was free, and though her parents had money, plenty of it, she didn't have any of her own. Their money came weighed down with rules and obligations that Julia, a month and a half before her sixteenth birthday, did not want or need.

The first couple of times she'd ridden the car pool into the city, she'd felt a little thrill of danger as she waited in the parking lot under the overpass for the first car to drive up. Her mother would kill her if she knew. It was like hitchhiking, only more organized. The drivers were usually men in luxury cars, who could afford parking in the city, who draped their suit jackets over one back-seat window, obscuring the view, but Julia wasn't naïve — she knew that they could be rapists or murderers, too. Even this guy, who looked so ordinary, so suburban, so *nice*, could stop the car at any minute and put a knife to her throat. The fact that two random passengers rode in each car helped; it meant that there was a chance they could work together to overpower the driver if he turned on them, although the woman in the front could be his accomplice — they could have planned it so that she'd wait in line behind Julia, and maybe she'd be the one to pull the knife. Except they were stuck in traffic inside a tunnel, trapped in the middle of five lanes, where you couldn't pull over to go to the bathroom or change a blown tire, let alone to commit a crime. Julia listened to the weather report for the third time. It hadn't changed — outside the tunnel the sky remained an immaculate blue, and the temperature was still sixty-four degrees. Nothing interesting was going to happen.

"It's bad today," the driver said.

Hannah looked up from the papers in her lap. "What is?" she said.

"The traffic. We've hardly moved in ten minutes."

When she'd moved to Oakland for Kate and started commuting across the Bay, something she'd always said she'd never do, Hannah had been relieved to discover that the casual car pool was not casual at all, but a complex and predictable system that operated under its own code of etiquette. You had to get into the first car that arrived, no picking and choosing, although women could skip pickup trucks and two-seater convertibles in which they'd have to ride alone with a man. The first person in line always took the back seat, unless he was unusually tall. Worse-than-usual traffic and worse-than-usual weather were the only acceptable topics of conversation, after *Good morning* and before *Thank you, have a good day*, and passengers were expected never to speak unless the driver spoke first. No one ever explained the rules, but they were so clear and universally accepted that you figured them out yourself the first day you took the car pool. Hannah had witnessed someone break the code only once, a middle-aged white woman driving a Volvo station wagon with a FREE TIBET sticker on its rear bumper. There'd been a news item on NPR about a black kid beaten to death by the police, and she'd started apologizing to the suited, briefcased black man in the front seat. In back, Hannah had cringed, but she hadn't said anything. Later, she wished she had.

She looked at the blue-lit clock on the dashboard. Seven thirty-eight. She'd been running late all morning, in a foul mood, snapping at Kate for hitting the snooze button one more time than Hannah could tolerate and for buying the wrong kind of coffee, but on her way out she'd discovered in yesterday's unchecked mail the thick manila envelope that might change everything. She should have taken the envelope back into the apartment as a peace offering, should have wanted to open it with Kate — it was addressed to both of them — but instead, she brought it with her, leaving the rest of the mail for Kate to find when she finally left for work.

Reading in cars made Hannah feel sick to her stomach, especially in traffic. It helped to train her eyes on the horizon or on anything far enough away that it didn't appear to move, but today she couldn't resist the packet in her lap. Luckily the driver shifted gears and changed lanes smoothly and only when necessary. As soon as he'd merged safely onto the freeway Hannah slid her nail under the envelope's seal and drew out a stack of papers, each two sheets, stapled, letterheaded *The Bay Area Cryogenic Center,* containing a brief description — not only physical but biographical, medical, and genealogical — of a man Hannah would never meet, who had agreed, in advance and for reasons of his own, to become the father of her child.

Only it wasn't going to be her child, not only hers, but hers and Kate's. Which meant that this preview, this flipping through profiles in a stranger's car, felt like a small betrayal.

Ian squinted at the headlights reflected in his rearview mirror, trying to determine if the car behind him remained at a reasonable distance, or if it had crept closer, the way he'd eased off his own brake to shorten the gap between his car and the one in front. He knew it was pointless, this edging forward, but he could not help feeling anxious to get out of the tunnel. If he was going to sit in traffic, he wanted a view: the silver lip of the city, the roll of fog cushioning the Golden Gate. He thought about how the prisoners on Alcatraz used to hear the boisterous city at night, the sounds of glass and laughter. Nothing was very far away. He checked his mirror again, and this time saw not the river of lights but the girl, the one in back, with her arm bent at an awkward angle, shoulders bare, T-shirt noosed around her neck. He glanced at the car in front, then at the woman beside him. She was oblivious, still completely absorbed in whatever she was reading.

"Is it warm back there?" Ian asked. "I can turn the air on if you want." Ian never turned the air on. He liked to feel the climate change as he drove to work. Most days, the temperature dropped ten degrees between home and Oakland, and another ten as he crossed the Bay.

"It's fine," Julia said. She was an expert at changing her clothes without revealing anything more than her shoulders and a couple of inches of belly, parts that other girls showed off all the time. She'd spent a long time choosing the T-shirt she changed into: fading black, emblazoned with the name of a band she'd never heard play, slightly ripped along one seam. She envied people who lived casually, who did not need to try as hard as she did to pick out the right T-shirt, or to think of the right things to say. She snapped a studded leather bracelet around a wrist, extracted a hook of silver from a tiny Ziploc bag, and threaded it through the nearly imperceptible hole in her nose. Watching in the rearview mirror, Ian thought she looked as though she were dressing for work, or for a performance, and in a sense she was. If she made it off the bridge alive, if she did not die of boredom first, Julia would take the streetcar to the Castro, where she would sit on the gum-splotched sidewalk outside the Ben and Jerry's next to Isaac, a fourteen-year-old runaway Mormon from the shore of the Great Salt Lake. She would put a coffee cup in front of her, a few coins in the bottom for seed, and stare into Sweetie's eyes while she waited for change. Sweetie, Isaac's half-grown pit bull, was good for protection but discouraged donations, while Julia, with her wispy blond hair and new-to-the-streets fragility, elicited sympathy and dollar bills from the older women and straight men who were immune to Isaac's charms. It made no sense that passersby rewarded cleanliness among panhandlers, but they did. Julia bought Diet Cokes with the money she earned, and cookie-dough ice cream cones for both of them, but at the end of the day she turned what was left of her takings over to Isaac before boarding the F Market to the Embarcadero and then the bus back across the bridge.

Later, lying awake in the pink room she'd slept in since she was small, she thought about Isaac. They didn't allow dogs at the shelters, so he either camped in the park with the other street kids, or he let someone buy him a sandwich and take him somewhere where afterward. If he was lucky, he might be able to sleep for a few hours. Julia wished she could bring him home with her, but she couldn't; her parents, though they donated to several charities and dropped loose coins into Styrofoam cups more often than not, would never open their guest room to a runaway kid and his dog, no matter how sweet and desperate they looked, no matter how much Julia pleaded.

She'd met Isaac in the summer, when she started riding the car pool into the city to escape the boredom that hung over the East Bay like smog. Julia had no friends. She used to have a friend, her best and only friend, Serena. Serena was the kind of girl who liked to keep only one friend at a time, and for almost two years she adored Julia. Her attention was bright and uncomfortable and hard to resist. They spent nearly all their time together. Whenever Julia spoke to anyone else, or mentioned another girl's name, or, worse, a boy's, unless it was in a mean way, Serena acted possessive and jealous, like a boyfriend. Then, in the spring of their freshman year, she replaced Julia. She found a new best friend who'd just moved to Oakland from Florida, who needed her more than Julia did and who would do whatever she asked. Almost overnight, and with no explanation, Serena stopped talking to Julia entirely. It was too late in the school year to make new friends. Everyone was organized already, into twos and threes and bigger groups; it didn't matter. No one, not even the outcasts, would make room for Julia.

She wanted to get a summer job, but her mother wouldn't let her. She said she wanted Julia to enjoy herself, to do whatever she pleased, within reason. In the future there would be jobs and SAT prep classes and trips to Europe. This might be the last summer she could be completely free.

"You used to have such fun at the pool with Serena," her mother said.

"I hate Serena," Julia said.

Her mother threatened to send her away to camp. Julia hated camp. She hated even the idea of camp. She refused to go. She went to the pool once by herself and felt so conspicuous and so alone that she never went back. After her parents left for work, Julia lay on the sofa in her underwear and a tank top, drinking cold milk with Hershey's syrup and watching TV reruns from before she was born. By July she was so lonely she wanted to die. One day she went for a walk and noticed several people standing in a parking lot. A fancy car pulled up, and two people got in. Julia walked over to a woman in a cranberry suit who reminded her of her father's secretary.

"Where are you going?" Julia had asked.

A space opened up, and they fell out into the light. Ian switched off his headlights. Now he could see that the traffic extended all the way to the city, a two-mile ribbon of wasted time.

Hannah was thinking in control statements: *If (these conditions are true) then this will be the outcome. Else if. Else if. Else.* She'd worked as a programmer for a couple of years before she'd begun to think in code. Now, she found that it calmed her; it helped her to make decisions. *If* (the father is a mechanical engineer, six foot one). *Else if* (a Russian lawyer, in perfect health). *Else if* (a musician, with light brown hair like Kate's and a slight risk of cancer on his mother's side). *Else if. Else.*

There was a reason to reject every profile. A disappointing academic record, an alcoholic grandparent, acne scars left over from adolescence, dishonesty or arrogance discernable in the way he answered the question "Why did you decide to do this?"

Of course, on terms like this she'd reject Kate. She'd reject herself. In their immediate families, she could count three alcoholics, two early heart attacks, three types of cancer, a paranoid schizophrenic, a case of multiple sclerosis, and one probable suicide. Kate sunburned easily (why was that a question on the profile; did anyone reject a donor for that?) and was frequently depressed. Hannah had an unimpressive college GPA and a late-blooming career.

She read the next profile. A twenty-three-year-old computer scientist, five eleven, a hundred and eighty-two pounds, brown hair and eyes. No health problems, either mental or physical, no evidence of male pattern baldness. He was half-Armenian, half-Greek. Under cause of death for three of four grandparents he'd written "civil war."

She knew things about these men she'd never bothered to ask Kate — their blood types, the occupations of their aunts and uncles — but she didn't know if they were charming or considerate, if they could be trusted. She knew the particulars of their appearance, their eye color and so on, but she couldn't tell if they were handsome or ugly or strange. Hannah had been a bartender for most of her twenties. She wished she could watch the possible fathers from the other side of a long slick bar. She would listen to their voices and assess their looks. She'd notice their liquors of choice, how much they tipped, whether or not they carried drinks to their companions before they came back for their own.

Hannah looked at the driver. She could decipher almost as much about him as she knew about the possible fathers. He appeared to be in his late thirties, average in height and weight, his dark hair cut short to control the curl. He looked as though he worked out, though not every day. He wore a narrow wedding band (which meant, she thought, that he'd married while still young and relatively poor) and the sort of business-casual attire — wide-wale corduroy pants and a carefully ironed, untucked white shirt — that suggested a media job of some kind.

"Jesus," he said. "What's that?" Now that she was paying attention, Hannah noticed his voice. Beneath evidence of education and moving about, she could hear the trace of an accent.

She squinted up through the windshield. "A helicopter," she said.

"No, look at the bridge."

Hannah looked. A butterfly: enormous, implausible, trussed in the steel cabling of the bridge.

"I don't know," she said. At such an angle, in the early glare, she could not be sure of the scale of the thing. Perhaps it was only a kite. Except that a helicopter fluttered mechanically near the suspension tower. Up ahead, in the right lane, several police cars, a fire engine with its ladder raised, and two ambulances waited, and in the Bay, beside the bridge, were two coast guard boats.

"Maybe it's a suicide." Suicides usually preferred the more romantic and accessible Golden Gate, so many they'd had to install phones with direct lines to counselors, but Ian liked the Bay Bridge better. It looked like a piece of the city, a cord tying it to the rest of the continent, while the Golden Gate was purely decorative.

"It's turquoise," Hannah said. "I think it has wings. It must be a hang glider."

"A hang glider could never make it this far."

"Someone with a parachute?"

"They're probably just filming a movie," the girl in the back seat said. She didn't care what was happening ahead on the bridge. If a person wanted to fly, he should stay away from bridges. If he wanted to kill himself, he should do it privately, not at rush hour.

"I don't think so," Hannah said. She often saw camera crews filming chase scenes or commercials on hilly picturesque streets in the city, but this looked like a real accident, not a made-for-TV disaster.

For his thirty-eighth birthday, Ian's wife had given him a skydiving lesson. A calculated risk in the form of a gift certificate. Miranda had driven him to Napa and sat on a blanket in a yellow field, reading a book, while he climbed into the hold of the little plane and flew up into the cloudless sky. The fall had not been as terrifying as he'd hoped. He just closed his eyes and jumped, that was all. He was tethered to the instructor the whole time. Later, during lunch, as he poured the last of an expensive bottle of chardonnay, he asked Miranda if she'd been watching as he plunged toward her, and she said yes, of course she'd watched. He knew she wasn't telling the truth.

He fiddled with the radio dial, against car pool etiquette, to see whether he could find out anything about the person (he was sure, now, it was a person) caught above the bridge. But there was nothing; not even the traffic reports included the backup on the Bay Bridge. Ian wondered if he'd imagined the traffic, his two passengers, the parachutist. The morning had begun ordinarily enough. He'd eaten his usual breakfast: two slices of rye toast and a glass of grapefruit juice. He'd had a pleasant conversation with Miranda before leaving the house. He'd backed the car out of the driveway and into the street, without hitting the awkwardly placed mailbox or scraping the paint on the untrimmed hedge. As he veered onto the freeway, he thought: *If I wanted to, I could leave today and never go back.* This was a shock. It wasn't the first time he'd had such a thought — everyone entertained such ideas, no matter how content, how responsible, how in love they might be. But it was the first time Ian had thought this in quite this way, purposefully, as if it were possible. As if it were true.

He forced himself to look out, rather than down. White sails flecked the water. The city shone. He was used to seeing the Bay from above; he'd been skydiving for years. But stilled, the view was smaller, painful in detail. The tiny whitecaps looked like accents:

grave, acute. He was in pain, slipping in and out of consciousness. His right arm was useless; with his left he clung to a steel rope as thick as his waist, although if he let go he would not fall. His rig was caught in the suspension wires like a bird in netting. In his most alert moments, he felt more embarrassed than scared.

Julia leaned her head against the cool window and stared at the sliver of visible city. She wished Isaac would send up a balloon or raise a flag to signal her. In the closet in the front hallway of her house, behind the coats, there was a white cloth safety-pinned to a wire hanger. Julia, at nine or ten, had insisted on it. Across the fabric, a square ripped from a linen tablecloth, she had colored in the letters *O* and *K* in dark blue Magic Marker. If there were another fire, she would hang the sign from a window, so the firemen would know she and her family had survived.

She'd been only six the last time, but she remembered everything: the too bright sky, her mother's panicked, resolute voice. Before the fire came close, they packed a bag, just one for the two of them, and went to stay with one of her mother's friends in a small mint-colored bungalow far down on the flats. Julia's father was in Europe, on a business trip. Julia called for her cat, but Samson was off hunting or curled somewhere napping, and he didn't come. She sobbed for three days, inconsolable, until her father, who'd flown back from Europe as soon as he could, took her as close as possible to the ruined house. They stood among charred eucalyptus, calling and whistling for Samson. Of course he never came.

Her parents built a new house with the insurance money. A bigger, better house made of wide redwood planks, with walls of windows facing the Bay. Julia was allowed to help design her new bedroom. She wanted a window seat with a secret compartment. She wanted everything painted pink. Their neighbors on one side built a monstrous Tudor mansion, while the family on the other side chose an Italian villa with trellises and a red tile roof. All of the new houses, too big for their lots, looked as if they might fall off the scorched hill at any moment. For years, there were hardly any trees.

She did not know exactly what happened to Isaac at night — he'd never tell her, no matter how many times she asked — but she knew it was bad. She came to believe that he needed her, that her attention kept him safe. Whenever she climbed onto the F, he said he'd see her soon, and because he'd promised, he would. It was as though she'd imagined him, and she had to see him to make him real. It was harder now that school had started. In the first week and a half she'd skipped two days, and she hadn't been caught yet.

"What are you reading?" Ian asked his front-seat passenger.

Hannah resisted the urge to turn the papers upside down. She didn't want to get into a complicated discussion. "Applications," she said. It was true, in a way.

"What do you do?"

"Tech stuff, nothing very interesting." *If,* she thought, *we sit here forever on this bridge. Else if. Else.*

The girl in the back seat put headphones on. Hannah could hear the hiss and static of her music. She pulled down the sun visor and looked in the little mirror. The girl nodded in time with the rhythm. She looked even younger, Hannah thought, in black.

The possible fathers made her anxious. She tried to imagine the twin-helixed thread of a stranger's DNA wrapped two-ply with her own.

"Do you have children?" she asked, surprising herself.

Ian shifted and closed the gap between his car and the one in front. "A daughter," he said. "Natalie. She just turned six."

They'd flown to Beijing to get her when she was eleven months old. For weeks before he saw her, Ian had carried her picture everywhere with him, a tiny, wisp-haired girl, unsmiling in a red smocked dress and white shoes. Those weeks before they finalized the paperwork, when she was still an ocean away, had been torture. And then the plane ride, the longest he'd ever endured, longer even than the journey home, Natalie on Miranda's lap with the stiff posture and stern mouth of a judge. In the hotel room in Beijing those first numb, amazed nights, Natalie had whimpered and refused to eat, and they'd had no idea how to calm her. Ian held the baby so awkwardly his shoulders had ached for days.

"You're lucky," Hannah said.

Ian nodded. "You don't have kids?"

"Not yet."

He had no idea how difficult it could be. She could not believe she'd ever thought it was easy herself, that she had worried about getting pregnant by accident. When she was younger and slept with boys, it seemed as though all it took was a single mistake, but now that she wanted it to happen, the process was fraught with complications. She and Kate had made a list of possible fathers, men whose appearance and intelligence they approved of, whom they could trust not to panic or steal the baby away. They asked Kate's cousin, their gay friends Salvatore, Danny, and Tim, and Hannah's college roommate, the one she'd dated for a short time in her final effort at straightness. All of them said they'd think about it, then all of them said no.

An unknown donor was simpler logistically and safer legally, but still, Hannah worried. Several of their friends used the sperm bank in Berkeley. What if one chose the same donor as Hannah and Kate? In California, only twelve children could have the same unknown father, but the number of babies wasn't restricted in the rest of the country, and she'd read that England had started importing American sperm. She couldn't stop thinking about all those half brothers and half sisters, possibly hundreds of them, meeting accidentally as adults. What if two of them fell in love?

If only they could make a test-tube baby from two eggs, fusing one of her X chromosomes with one of Kate's. It had to be possible scientifically, although she'd never heard of a successful case. There were social and ethical implications, of course, but Hannah would gladly settle for girls.

He couldn't help it: he looked down. A river, glistering. He was confused, until the river broke into rectangles. Cars and SUVs and buses. He counted three white tops of buses, and counting roused him. Who was down there? People he knew, certainly. Coworkers, maybe an ex-girlfriend, people he knew but didn't know: security guards and bank tellers. Somehow, by jumping, he had stopped the morning. He thought: *I could shake this tower and break this bridge.* His shoulder hurt. He would not fall. He thought: *All of us are going to die.*

"That poor man, I can't imagine what he's going through. If it is a man." Hannah had always been afraid of heights. "It might be a woman," she said.

"Less likely," Ian said.

He watched a firefighter climb up the nearest tower. He hoped the rescue effort wouldn't take much longer. He was almost out of gas. His habit of letting the needle drop into the red zone drove Miranda crazy. She worried about exactly this type of situation: Ian stranded on the bridge. Irresponsibly, he'd let his cell phone run out of batteries. He considered turning the ignition off, risking a rear-end collision if the traffic behind him started suddenly, but decided against it. He could hear someone singing, far away, behind him, a sweet faint voice, but he couldn't make out the song.

Julia tried to distract herself with music, but it didn't work. Two leather-clad men zoomed past on Harleys, in between lanes of stopped cars. She wished for a motorcycle, or even an ordinary bicycle. Once, not very long ago, a man had ridden his bicycle across the bridge, eastbound. Julia had seen it on the news. When the police tried to stop him, he pulled a gun, and they shot him. Julia wanted to get out of the car. She was thirsty, and she had to pee, a combination of sensations so irritatingly contradictory they must have been used for torture in China, or somewhere. She had to get out of the car. She could hitch a ride with the next motorcyclist to pass, or she could walk. She'd be perfectly safe. The traffic was hardly moving. The cops were busy with whatever was stuck up on the bridge like a kitten in a tree, and anyway, they'd be unlikely to shoot at a girl.

"Did you know," Ian said, "this bridge is actually three bridges?"

No one said anything.

"In the middle of the western span," he continued, "just up ahead, there's a block of concrete thrust into the floor of the Bay. More concrete than the Empire State Building."

"How do you know?" Julia asked.

Ian shrugged at his rearview mirror. "I read it somewhere. I don't remember where."

Over the guardrail Hannah could see Treasure Island: a hopeful name for a gray plate of landfill striped with military housing.

She pointed. "Imagine living there," she said. "Marooned in the middle of the Bay. You couldn't go *anywhere* without crossing the bridge."

Julia wrapped the cord around her headphones and zipped them into the front pocket of her backpack. The coating on the door handle had begun to peel. She worried it with her nails, etching flakes of rubber away like sunburned skin and flicking them onto the floor. She kicked a child's toy she hadn't noticed before and leaned to pick it up. An action figure, a lithe plastic girl wearing a silver costume, her ponytail frozen in midswing, arms upheld in a karate pose. Julia's door was locked; all four of the Altima's doors locked automatically when the car reached five miles per hour. She pressed the button to unlock it, but nothing happened. The child lock must have been turned on. What if the driver *were* a kidnapper or a rapist? She'd be trapped. Julia did not panic. Instead she tried to pry open the lock using the karate girl's slender hand. The driver looked back over his shoulder at her, but he didn't say anything. He looked like the kind of man who never said anything until it was too late. She tried again, but she couldn't lift the lock.

"Excuse me." Julia leaned forward. "Could you unlock the doors, please?"

"I don't think that's a good idea," Ian said.

"I'd just feel safer, that's all," the girl said.

"Safer?" Ian said.

"Yeah, I mean, I'm in a stranger's car. Anything could happen."

"Very little could happen." Ian gestured vaguely at the surrounding traffic, the water only slightly touched by wind. "We're stuck."

Julia sighed loudly and switched tactics. "Please?" she said. "It's not like there's anywhere I could go."

Ian didn't feel like arguing. He looked at the woman in the front seat. She was doing her best to ignore the conversation. He clicked the locks.

"Thanks," Julia said. She opened the door and stepped out onto the bridge, calmly, as if onto a curb.

The girl slammed the door harder than necessary. Ian's first reaction was irritation. Why did she have to slam the door every time? But this was the first time, the only time, and she wasn't his daughter grown tall and sullen. She was someone else's kid. What was she doing in the car pool, anyway? He'd never let Natalie ride with strangers, not at sixteen, not at twenty-two. This girl was lucky she'd ended up riding with him. Not that he'd kept her safe — he hadn't even managed to keep her in the car.

"Damn it," he said. "What does she think she's doing?" He'd been responsible for her, and he'd failed.

"You can't just let her go," Hannah said.

"What else am I supposed to do?" Ian glared at her. "You could have said something before."

Hannah looked up at the man on the bridge. At any moment he

might fall. She pictured him plummeting to earth, breaking every bone in his body when he hit the surface of the Bay. The girl was already several car lengths away, darting between cars and SUVs and minivans, her red backpack bobbing. Hannah was quick in a crisis. She opened her door and half fell onto the tarmac. She hadn't expected the wind on the bridge.

For a second she forgot why she was there. The whole bridge vibrated, tens of thousands of engines idling at once. She looked up, felt dizzy, looked back down. People shouted at her through car windows, but she couldn't understand them. The girl up ahead, running. Hannah chased her between the stalled cars. It felt as if she was running on a conveyor belt; she was sure the bridge beneath her moved. The air fumed with exhaust. She was out of shape, and her chest began to hurt almost immediately. She didn't know the girl's name.

"Hey!" Hannah yelled. "Slow down!"

Julia didn't hear, and neither slowed nor turned. Nobody paid attention to her. No one ever noticed Julia when she didn't want to be noticed.

A *News 24* helicopter had joined the police helicopter near the tower. They floated, as noisy as bees, the beginning of a swarm. Alone again, Ian waited for the woman to catch the girl. His phone was dead; he couldn't call 911. Should he abandon his car and follow them? He was tempted to lock the doors and put on some Bach, the partitas or a cello concerto, something soothing. Let them chase each other to the city. He didn't mind waiting for the man on the bridge to be rescued. He reached over and picked up one of the résumés the woman had left on the passenger seat. It looked more like a police report than a CV, the word RESTRICTED stamped in red across the top. The first page listed the applicant's vital statistics: height, weight, age, etc. There was a full medical history. He turned to the last page and read: "My children are the most important thing in my life, I want to give someone else the chance to start a family. Also, I think my genes are worth passing on."

It wasn't a résumé.

Ian gave up before Miranda did, even though she was the one who endured the painful tests and treatments, the weeks confined to their bed. She refused to believe that her body had failed her this first, important time, but after three years of worry and disappointments, he'd had enough. He wanted a child, but he was willing to live without the thrill of combining his genetic code with hers.

Hannah couldn't keep up with the girl. She slowed her pace enough to look up at the man still clinging to the steel ropes that held them all up. For the first time she wondered if he was already dead, if the helicopters, the emergency crews, the traffic jam, if all of it were a wasted effort. Why should the girl wait on the bridge with everybody else? Why shouldn't she walk across the Bay if that's what she wanted to do? She'd be safe enough, as long as she kept to the white line between lanes, as long as she watched out for motorcycles. She would reach the Embarcadero in fifteen or twenty minutes. Hannah let her go.

Julia stopped when she reached the flashing lights. She couldn't help it. She stopped and looked up at the glittering bridge. There was a person up there. For a moment she forgot about Isaac. She forgot about Serena, about school and her parents and the coins she'd have earned if she hadn't been stuck on the bridge. All she could see was a slip of turquoise, like a tatter of fabric caught in barbed wire, but she knew there was a person up there.

Hannah made her way back to the car, peering through windshields. Everyone looked sad and separate. How would she recognize the car? She could not remember what make it was, or what color. She did not notice that she'd passed it until she'd nearly reached the tunnel's opening. She considered climbing up onto the island; she had no idea what she'd find there — an enclave of houses, more military buildings, a bird sanctuary? But then she heard her name behind her, at least she thought she heard it over the din of cars and radios and helicopters.

The woman stopped, and he called again: "Hannah, Kate." He didn't know which of the two names on the envelope was hers. She didn't look like a Hannah — too small and dark — but he wasn't convinced she was a Kate, either. She must have been one or the other, though, because she turned and started toward him. As she moved closer, away from the tunnel's grip, she appeared to float above the tarmac. He wasn't sure what caused the effect; perhaps simply the strangeness of watching someone walk where he'd never seen anybody walk before.

"What happened?" he asked.

"I couldn't catch up with her."

Ian went to the passenger side of the car first and held the door open for her. He wasn't sure what brought on the gallant gesture — once he'd prided himself on opening the passenger door before his own not just on dates but all the time, no matter what his intentions toward his passenger were (he even did it for men, and for Miranda after he married her), but when he bought the Altima, with its electronic key that locked and unlocked all four doors remotely, such courtesy began to seem excessive.

He turned the key in the ignition. "So are you Hannah or Kate?"

"Hannah," she said. "How did you — ?"

He nodded at the manila envelope. He'd put it on the dashboard; its reflection glowed faintly in the windshield. "After a while I wasn't sure you were coming back. I checked for an address in case you didn't."

He wanted to ask about the contents of the envelope, but she seemed so enclosed, staring through her side window at Angel Island to the north.

"I wonder what was so urgent," she said. She missed the girl in the back seat. With only two passengers, the car no longer qualified as a high-occupancy vehicle. Officially, it didn't matter, because the car pool lane ended at the toll plaza. But inside the car, the rules disappeared.

"Everything's urgent when you're a kid." Except for his daughter, who was more patient and reasonable than most adults he knew. It unnerved him. He looked sideways at Hannah. "See what you have to look forward to?"

Hannah picked up the envelope. "Did you open this?" she asked.

"I shouldn't have. My curiosity got the better of me." Ian watched her face change. "I'm sorry," he said.

"It's private," Hannah said, although it wasn't. She'd already dealt with the unnaturally buoyant staff of the cryogenic center, already endured a lesson on optimal sperm insertion from a midwife who'd once been on a blind date with Kate. And then there were the possible fathers themselves.

"I really am sorry," Ian said. Hannah ignored him, but he was nervous now, and when he was nervous he could never stop talking. "It's quite a process, isn't it? My wife and I tried everything: bed rest, hormone shots, in vitro, acupuncture, awful-smelling herbs. Nothing worked."

"Really?" Hannah couldn't keep the surprise out of her voice.

"We ended up adopting."

"That's great," Hannah said. "I mean, it's great that it worked out. Your daughter's very lucky."

"We're all lucky. Natalie's a great kid."

Hannah shook out the profiles. "So did you see anyone you liked?" she asked.

Ian's smile flickered. "I liked the Armenian."

"I was curious about him, too."

"Couldn't you just ask someone you know?"

"We tried that. Everyone said no." Hannah looked over at the driver as she said this. Sitting there beside her, tapping one hand on his corduroy thigh, he seemed as plausible as any of the possible fathers. In programming, you had to take into account every parameter, every circumstance, every possible factor. Hannah thought she'd done that, but she hadn't. Here was proof of her mistake: another option. If she wanted it to, it could happen. She felt absolutely certain of that. She'd never have to see him again. But there was Kate, who by now would be at work in downtown Oakland, beside the garlanded lake. Kate, who would not yet have heard about the man with the parachute.

Someone knocked on Ian's window. A cop. He put his gloved hand on the rim of the door, leaned, and peered in, then motioned to Ian to open the window.

The girl from the back seat was standing next to him, her cheeks flushed from running, her small chin pointed and defiant. She was still holding the silver-clad karate girl.

"This your daughter?" the cop asked.

"No," Ian said.

"Yes," Hannah said at exactly the same time. She did not know why she felt such a compulsion to lie for the girl.

"Which is it?"

"He's my stepfather," the girl explained. "We don't get along."

Inexplicably, Ian felt hurt and tempted to defend himself.

"I caught her wandering on the bridge," the cop said.

"Thank you, officer," Hannah said. "We were worried."

Ian gave the girl the most punishing look he could muster. "Get in the car."

The cop opened the back door like a valet. "Please watch your daughter more carefully in the future. We have enough to deal with as it is."

"Oh, we will," Ian said.

Julia slipped in behind him and slouched in her seat.

"You're lucky we covered for you," Ian said. "You could have been in serious trouble."

"Thanks," Julia said.

"What happened?" Hannah asked.

"I stopped to look, and that guy saw me," Julia said. "I didn't want him to call my parents."

"So you lied," Ian said.

"I guess."

"Could you see any more from up there?" Hannah asked.

"Not really," Julia said.

The jumper watched his rescuer draw closer, sidestepping along the suspension cable, a high-wire acrobat above an audience of thousands. The man appeared to shout, but the jumper couldn't hear him above the din of the helicopter treading air above him. For the first time since smashing into the bridge, he blistered with panic. He watched as the man lowered himself onto the spun-steel cable and cut the lines to his canopy.

He did not fall. He did not plunge three hundred rushing feet and hit the water, and he did not arch into the cool sea-level air. His rescuers (suddenly there were two; he did not know where the second had come from) tended to the wound on his neck, splinted his arm, and wrapped him in a silver blanket. A basket fastened to a cord appeared, and they lifted him into it. He shut his eyes and let them haul him up to safety.

ANN BEATTIE with Harry Mathews

Mr. Nobody at All

FROM MCSWEENEY'S

New York City

Monica Kreider
   I'm really happy to be here today, even though I'm brokenhearted. I'm happy because seeing all of you and realizing again what wonderful, devoted friends Geoff had just makes me so, so happy that he had all of you in his life, especially during his difficult last years. He would want us to be together this way, and he wouldn't be surprised that it was Kathy who arranged such a beautiful occasion, and I know I speak for all of us when I say that our hearts are full of joy for having known Geoff, not just with sadness at his passing. He'd be so happy to see us gathered here and, looking around the room, I wonder if he might be looking out at us from some strange vantage point we wouldn't expect, like even his spirit maybe attaching itself to that beautiful Corot over there, over Kathy's table, because it's not impossible that he might just for a second *be* that little cow — the little eyes of that little cow — looking at us from a place we'd least expect, seeing all of us gathered here in this beautiful room. I don't know about reincarnation, but I've thought of the spirit existing as a sort of snowflake — some little, very unique thing — and on its way to melting we might see it for a split second before it disappeared, and even if it wasn't distinguishable from other snowflakes, we would be looking at something and it would be registering as part of a pattern, and we all, really, live by patterns, so it would be reassuring, but then, of

course, like beauty itself, it would be sure to turn into something else, and someone might just look out the window and say, "A snowstorm!"

Geoff really loved to ski, and go snowboarding, even though he also really loved to go windsurfing. I thought about what I could say that would offer a perspective on Geoff that might be a little different from what other people would say, and I remembered a trip he took me on to Vail, when I was fifteen or sixteen. I was so upset, because I had my skis but my luggage had gotten lost, and he said, "We can always buy toothpaste at the drugstore, or whatever you need." *Whatever you need:* that was Geoff. I thought to myself, Why does that particular remark stick in your mind? And then I thought, Well, probably everybody knows this about Geoff, his generosity and just how nice he was, you know, levelheaded, but there I was, a silly teenager, and I just thought I'd die without the exact right shade of lipstick, and I didn't know how to tell him how complicated it would be — that it wouldn't just be a matter of buying Crest, or something. And right that minute, thinking that, I realized that he would get on the phone and have the company send me the lipstick, if that's what it took, he'd do anything he could, but that really, I could do without lipstick, because I had a stepfather as nice as Geoff. I mean, to this day I hardly wear any makeup. It just liberated me, what he said, because he pointed out that things could be replaced. Well, I'm here today to say that things might be replaceable, but Geoff will never be. You already know that. But what you might not know is that we ended up in a grocery store, not a drugstore, and he bought coffee and other things we'd need, cigarettes — because this was a little before it was so clear you'd die if you smoked them . . . Anyway, there was Geoff, throwing things into the shopping cart, putting in toothpaste he swept from the shelf, just making an avalanche of toothpaste tubes in their boxes into the cart. If he had an idea, he went all out. I can remember him so clearly, keeping a straight face even though I was giggling, when the checkout girl rang up tube after tube of toothpaste, and I couldn't imagine what she must be thinking. He must have brought the bags into the house, because he treated me like a princess, and I doubt I carried more than one little bag in, because I had my big, bulging purse to carry anyway, with everything inside that I couldn't live without, like my planner, and my diary, and my little zipped makeup kit, which I fortunately did have, and, I don't know, we probably had dinner and everything, but I just remember the coffee and the cigarettes and all the fun we had, and how he made me understand that you shouldn't sweat the little stuff, in part because you could always get all the little stuff you wanted again, because little stuff is always available. We probably didn't have to buy toothpaste for five years! But it was back then that I realized that I shouldn't worry, that things would work out, and for all I know, the luggage probably arrived that night after I'd gone to bed, because the airlines were always losing everything in those days, and then they'd send someone out to your house, which is probably what they did.

I think we all feel that Geoff protected us and took care of us, and he'd be so pleased to know that today we're all gathered together in Kathy's beautiful library to take care of him, and his memory, before it becomes a melting snowflake.

Duncan Rand

Wow. That was really honest, Monica. You set a high standard for being yourself. No. Just kidding. No, what I want to say is that I really didn't prepare remarks like Monica, but everybody goes about things differently, which is something Geoffrey taught me. I mean, like Monica, I just sort of happened in his life, the way it just snows: you look out the window and, like Monica says, there it is. That's the way it was, being a stepbrother to Geoff. You know, when his father married my mother, there was this huge age difference between us, like twenty years or something. I mean, he could have ignored me because I was just an ignorant kid, but he came around and he was always very nice to me. They thought I had an allergy to chocolate, and I never did. Everybody knows now that an allergy to chocolate does not cause acne, but that was the thing back then, and if there was anything my mother was intent on, it was keeping me off chocolate. When Monica said that about the toothpaste, I thought back to how Geoff would have his pockets stuffed with really nice chocolate bars for me. I'd have eaten Hershey's all the time if Geoff hadn't introduced me to imported chocolates, but he'd have his pockets stuffed, so you wonder what they thought, hanging up his coat, when the pockets were about five pounds each. I guess that was why he hung it up himself, even though Nana was there to do it, God rest her soul.

So he was obviously a generous man, and I wouldn't have had much chocolate if not for him. I used to fantasize that he'd take me away with him, and that we'd eat chocolate all day, but of course he'd sort of been thrown out of the family at that point, and I'm not even sure how he got together the money to visit so much, because let's face it: they could have been a lot more supportive of Geoff, and when he got to be a success, what did they do but pretend that they'd always believed in him — this might be difficult for you to hear, maybe, Monica — but as I recall, Geoff didn't have it so easy, and C.C. could have been quite a bit more generous. Witness his investing in that friend of a friend who started that software company that took off like a rocket. But I think the bottom line was that C.C. understood business, but he had no real sympathy for the arts, even though he knew Geoff could draw anything, whether it was scaffolding that looked like you were right in front of scaffolding and could see the whole mess rising sky-high, or a little pat of butter, and believe me, it is not that easy to have people understand what that little square is that they're looking at, because a pat of butter — that could be anything.

No, he was really good at what he did, and of course I thought of him as something between a big brother and somebody who might have saved my life, if he'd ever asked me to leave with him, but at the same time, I knew he wasn't going to take me, as a little boy, out of the house and take him to Cambridge, Mass., and move him into a painting studio, because what would I have done? How helpful is some self-absorbed little brat eating chocolate to making a painting? Not very. I'll be honest and say I always thought of him as my way out, as a kid. And today I thank him for setting an example and showing me that you could use your talent to express yourself and not have to go into business. Present company excepted, of course. Now I have a song I'd like to play on the dulcimer that always brought tears to Geoffrey's eyes.

Harmony

I knew Geoffrey in a very different way from the way I might know him now, because of the radical change my life has undergone. I feel that if he and I had stayed in touch better, he would have come to understand my decision. As others have mentioned, he was extremely considerate, and I think there was a time in my life when things would not even have been as clear as they were —

and they were pretty foggy — if Geoffrey hadn't set an example by the way he lived, surrounded by the paintings he invested so much love and energy in. In the same way he always had an understanding of form, and color, I understood, as a young person who was unable to give voice to what I felt internally, that there was a world of exteriors and a world of interiors, and that I was not the same person on the inside as on the outside. But today isn't about me, or about the masks we all wear until we find the courage to strip them away, if we ever do. It's about Geoffrey, who might have been Geoff to us, but who was Geoffrey Chestnut, *the* Geoffrey Chestnut, to the rest of the world. When I look at the dazzling interplay of light in his paintings, I remember the person who was himself composed of lights and darks, but whose shining eyes came straight from his soul. There's a danger at a memorial service of saying things that you wouldn't dare say to the person's face if he still stood before you, but today I am not saying anything I didn't say to Geoffrey Chestnut when he was alive and gave me the money to continue on my personal road to self-actualization. "Thank you more than I can say — more than *both* of me can say," I said to him. You all know what a gracious man he was. We were sitting at the Harvest, in Cambridge, and so many people who came in greeted him. He was so warmly received, and he was not egotistical at all. A private person, yes. A person who other people, maybe people who felt envious of his talent, didn't understand, and therefore sometimes didn't like. But in this room, today, are people who knew far more than the public figure, the celebrated artistic figure, the man who dared to be himself and to bring beauty to so many. And in dying, he has not disappeared. No, we can still find him in his dazzling paintings: at once tentative, then sure. I had the pleasure of observing some works in progress, when the charcoal marks were all there was. He spent a lot of time, in life and in painting, preparing — always mapping out, trying to understand. We can find him in our memory of the complex human being who so loved Corot that he gave all the paintings of his first, early years in exchange for a Corot painting that hangs today in this room. There are those among us who thought it unwise for him to part with what we might as well be honest and call his "inventory." Those who spoke of donating the very paintings he relinquished to one of the fine museums of this beautiful city that he came to love as a second home. But nevertheless, he did what his conscience dictated, and one of those things was to exchange his early work for something he must have found far more meaningful. Nothing suggests that he bought it as an investment, since he invested in the stock market, and he invested — well, he once invested in my future. I look toward the Corot and I ask: What can this pastoral scene tell us? That he was a man who loved peace. Beauty. That he admired those who sought the light, as he also sought it. He offered me the example of being himself, a fearless, brilliant person who not only paid every check in the restaurants we ate in, but who hoped, in return, only for the other person's happiness. You will all understand what I mean when I say that that wintery night in Cambridge, after the wine, after the good discussions, after my dilemma had been set forth and he had quickly acted to solve it — even then, he would not let me leave the tip. He would not let me leave the tip.

Frederick Frowley
Tim, I think that was a very beautiful metaphor you left us with, and I want to thank you for coming all this way from San Francisco.
Geoffrey. My dear uncle Geoffrey: I raise an imaginary glass to your kindness, for when you were alive, you were like a long, refreshing drink to me. I salute you, though I was never in the military, because you dutifully applied yourself to your job, and in observing your days of dedication to your work, I learned that I must be the soldier of my own fortune. I embrace you, as well, because that is what we did when we met, though what others saw, no doubt, was only that our hands touched, in the firm clench of a handshake. From you, I learned that love comes not from predictable gestures, but from significantly insignificant moments. You may ask: How did I know, how did I know for certain, that the subtext I sensed could be understood from the book that was you? Well, I was a good reader. And though you are gone, the reading light still burns bright. So I offer a Thanksgiving, though this day is not that holiday. Nevertheless, Uncle, you provided a feast for your family. Once more I raise my glass, and end, in words as sincere as any toast: a reading of one of my favorite poems, and his. "The Coat," by William Butler Yeats. *Yeats,* excuse me. I always say that wrong. "The Coat," by William Butler Yeats:

>I made my song a coat
>Covered with embroideries

> Out of old mythologies
> From heel to throat;
> But the fools caught it,
> Wore it in the world's eyes
> As though they'd wrought it.
> Song, let them take it,
> For there's more enterprise
> In walking naked.

George Jenkins

"Jenks, we must put forth our best selves, though those selves may sometimes be lost to us at the very moments we need most to call on them."

"But, Geoffrey, Geoffrey. You have always been devoted. And kind. And fair."

"If so, then it has been luck. Luck that pulled the best from me, buried, though it must have been, as a tooth in a jawbone."

"And if this might be true: does it take away anything? Are you a lesser man for having luck, and for appreciating the lucky luck of luck?"

"Jenks, that is most generous of you, to point me in the right direction by seeming to ask a rhetorical question."

"There is no trickery in my heart. Knowing you has banished trickery from my heart."

"Then, if I vanish, in each heartbeat find my memory, as in my heart, I shall always find yours."

Oh, please. I was not expecting applause. It's very kind of you, but a meaningful improvisation was all I could offer, bereft as I am, and as overcome with so many truly and bravely remembered words. You are much too kind. Really, it is such a privilege to be invited here to sit among you and to summon both memories and the oddly lingering music that sets their tone. Thank you.

Really, I do thank you very much.

Esther Halsey

By strange coincidence, I, too, intend to read something I wrote about Geoffrey. I guess I'll go ahead — though, of course, what I have to say won't be in the same league as Mr. Jenkins.

Well, this is from my diary. June 1989. "G. came by my studio, bringing with him a girl who means to write an article about his

'Rapture' series. G. looking tired, still, after dreadful burst-appendix surgery two months ago. G. mentions my own recent work, and only then, silly goose that I am, do I realize the entire coffee and pound cake ceremony has been staged because the girl might write about my work, as well. He is such a good and loyal friend, and I'd thought him so silly, going on and on about the store-bought pound cake I offered the last time he came 'round. By what miracle did I bake a pound cake last night? First one in what — five years? Since Alison L. went back to London, in any case. So there we sat, the girl almost thirty, it turned out, graduate of B.U., her grandfather editor of publication. G. asked if I would make an exception and show work in progress. In the guise of commenting on my painting, he made two cogent points about recent art. Suddenly he and I had become a movement! Never knew a more thoughtful man."

I picked that entry almost at random, because any time he made a studio visit, he had some nice surprise for me, even if it wasn't a journalist. Once, he brought Tim, and we had such a good time, everyone eating chocolates some admirer had sent him and champagne he'd bought because he so admired his family and friends, and there we were, joking about whether our work would appreciate if we smeared our sticky fingers on the canvas.

What I remember most about Geoff is the way he remained reasonable about adversity and expected the best of everyone. I see him as the handsome young man he was — maybe a bit too driven, but what reservations can one have about another's life, if all's well with the art? I don't know how many people here today know he had a sort of breakdown, not long after I made that diary entry. Because the woman had betrayed him, you see. Her piece wasn't anything she'd told him it would be. It was all trivializing, as if he was some simpleton who came out of his cave for a bit of cake, a bit of cake and champagne she didn't deem good enough, though I remember how she devoured those Teuscher chocolates. When his high expectations of people weren't in sync with how things turned out, it really hurt him. The alcohol was an attempt to smooth that hurt, I think. He became a teetotaler and he pulled out of it, but for months and months it was as if he believed what that silly girl had said. Maybe I shouldn't say what he said to me at a time like this, but I haven't heard this Geoffrey remarked upon, yet I'm sure

I wasn't the only one who knew this aspect of him. He said: "An iceberg is tantalizing because most of it hides under the surface. She was tantalizing until I found out that what she dragged around underneath her was shit. She grew out of it like a weed that thrives in adversity. People like that don't need to be cursed by you and me. Their unhappiness will get rooted like an intractable weed, because its taproot goes down to shit."

He could be so hurt, you see. It wasn't about some silly journalist, it was about someone's power to fool him. And last night when I was thinking what I could possibly say that would be true to his dark side — even though one's dark side is never supposed to be acknowledged in this country, least of all at a memorial service — anyway, last night I thought that I might point out that he hated deception, and that he was also very wise about it, because his insightfulness was not by any means limited to painting.

Jane Vegas-Villasenor

I thought I was going to be able to do this, but I'm not sure. I don't want to stand here blubbering. He wouldn't want that. But I'm not sure that what I just heard was what he'd want to hear, either, if he was sitting here. Everyone will say it's because we've always been jealous of each other, having both lived with Jared at one point, and maybe I should take the high road and say nothing, but, Esther, I construe your remarks as passive-aggressive. I'm going to sit down and let other people, who seem not quite as affected by that as I was, have their say.

Caitlin Kreeberg

My mom asked me to say things because she couldn't be here today, because she had to teach. First, I have some things to say that I thought of myself. The first is that I really liked Mr. Chestnut, because he helped me with my math homework, as well as showing me some things about drawing. We were lucky to live in the same building where he had his studio. Another thing is that last Christmas he gave me one of my favorite things, which is a puffy. It's my favorite color, and when I curl up in it at night I'm never cold in bed. It was really a thoughtful present, because I'm always cold. Thank you, family, for asking us here. Mom's sorry she couldn't get out of teaching, and I have to tell her everything that happened.

David and Daniel Richardson

Hi, I'm David. And I'm Daniel. We're friends of Caitlin, and she already said he was our neighbor. What? I'm going to let my brother talk. He was really nice to us and he just thought it was funny that we called him Horse-Chestnuts-for-Brains. We liked him, and it was just a special name. Yeah, and my brother asked him if he'd still play basketball with us if he had kids of his own, and he said yes. He would have, too. He painted really good tiger faces on us for Halloween.

Craig Howell

Watch out, boys! This isn't the sort of room you can toss things around in. What have you got there? A toy car. O.K.

Well, I don't have written remarks, either. We met in the hospital, when we were both being evaluated for liver problems. Kathy had driven him there that day, and she was kind enough to give me a lift, too. For which I still thank you, Kathy. We've heard a lot about the family's generosity, but there's generosity, and there's generosity, and I live significantly *below* Houston.

I'll make it brief.

Like his young neighbors, I had no idea at first who Geoffrey was. But we ran into each other on the street about a week after he and Kathy had given me a lift, and we started talking, and I invited myself up to his loft to see the paintings he was talking about, which wasn't like me, because I'm a shy person, but he really did have a way of making people comfortable. And let me tell you: *Then I knew who he was.* I said to my wife: The guy whose wife gave me a lift home from Sinai, he's the one who painted the mural in the Page Building's lobby!

That was the last digression, I promise.

True artists are few and far between, and when you get to know the man behind the picture, you're lucky if you aren't disappointed. As it turned out, I was like him and jumped ship and didn't go through the treatment, but life's ironic, and in the last year things got better for me, for some reason, and right now I've got a pretty good prognosis, and Geoffrey's gone.

Excuse me. I have trouble speaking in front of people. This is the first memorial service I've been able to go to in years, but I guess that's the miracle of certain drugs that are much joked about. Anyway: he wanted me to have a notebook of his of sepia sketches he'd made in Rome, of Bernini sculptures. For a while I felt guilty, because I knew he'd given it to me impulsively to cheer me up when we were both feeling so lousy, and he was sorry for what I was going through. Then there I am on the bus, and I open the *Times*, and I see his face in the obits, and I say to myself, *Oh no, I still have his notebook.* I was going to keep it, because technically it was a gift, but I don't think that would be right. So, Kathy, I will be returning it to you, and the family can do whatever they think best. I stopped at Kinko's on the way and photocopied every page. I was standing there at the machine crying like a kid. But I don't need the originals. He had a lot more people to offer his kindness to than me, but in the short time we knew each other, it means a lot that we became friends.

Take care of yourselves, everybody. Take one day at a time.

Boz Cray

Well, I guess I was one of the lucky ones who wrote about art and didn't arouse Geoffrey's ire. When my Significant Other and I were running *Artforce* in the Village, in the seventies, I had the pleasure of reviewing one of Geoffrey's shows, and we came to be friends. He'd liked the way I'd written about his work's purity, and if I could write about his current, or I suppose I should say his tragically late work — if any publication existed that wasn't dominated by politics — I'd say that aside from its obvious *homage* to Ad Reinhardt, it retains Geoffrey's Zen-like purity that still suggests we might consider surface as interchangeable with *objet* qua *objet*. His suppressed brushstroke clearly rejects the semi-spiritualism inherent in Malevich's residual marks, as well as Stella's degeneration into the carnivalesque, a failure of nerve we needn't address here. After all, this was a man whose early work had the courage to say, in so many words, what you see is what you see, or what you get. Of course, early Stellas keep mysteriously showing up on the market, so Frank must have a really deep closet, not to hint at anything untoward. So every museum must have a Stella, but only the canny or lucky ones have one of the pinstripe works, let alone a protractor canvas. How anyone can tolerate the most recent debacles, those tangles of undisciplined aluminum, is beyond me, but then don't get me started on the loss of purity and purpose in our laughable art world. But

Frank's betrayal of all that used to be held dear is just going to make my blood pressure rise, so suffice it to say that Geoffrey would have undoubtedly shared my distress. He might even have seen fit to hide his pain by presenting the art world as comical or — for those in the know — as comics.

My former Significant Other, who is here today, will no doubt have astute remarks to make about the last paintings, but since she did not care to share with me what she intended to say, I can only hope that we are still enough in sync — even after that heartbreaking custody battle for *le pauvre* Napoleon, our former poodle. I think I must delegate to my former Significant Other to explain to us all, not just privately, to Kathy — because I am given to understand that some insight about the work was requested of my former Significant Other, and I do trust that this was not a discussion undertaken for any remuneration — Geoffrey's poetics of blackness.

Royce Talhadas

Yeah, thank you very much, Mrs. Whitehall, for fitting me in, because I've got to get back to work. My wife and I say a prayer every night for Mr. Chestnut, because when we opened the coffee shop, he led the way for all his friends to go there. There was a Starbucks two blocks away that opened almost when we did. I'd go by his apartment after work sometimes and just knock and say I was leaving something like blueberry muffins, or something that I knew he liked, because he'd told me he wasn't eating anymore. You don't know what that means, when somebody says it. It can mean they're on Sugar Busters, or something. But my wife said no, she didn't think he felt good, and she suggested to him that he have herbal tea instead of coffee, so bingo: every afternoon she was putting a bag of chamomile in a mug for him, and he was having that and maybe talking to somebody from the neighborhood who came in, but my wife said that, Look, you can't make a person eat, but you can make food look appetizing, so she'd peel the wrapper off a muffin and say no charge, just see if you don't want a bite of this, because you know, we made our own, we didn't get them delivered from Brooklyn, and he knew it. And even when I'd go over and knock on the door, and he wouldn't open the door, I'd say, Hey, just joking a little. I'd say, Hey, we all know some little furry friend will eat this if you don't, and it got so my wife would go and pick up the plate in the morning and maybe he was fooling us, but the food was *gone*. I'm not standing here telling you we was saints, but just that my wife figured out a way to get him to eat a little, and to my wife that was another goal accomplished. You know, he came by one day with a lady's coat that fit her perfect, and *that* was some mystery, but you know, she wears it proudly, and we asked Mrs. Whitehall, and she said it wasn't hers, so my wife's it is, I guess. He gave me a whole load of art books I'm going to educate myself with, and, assuming nobody minds, we're going to have him be our Frank Sinatra, so to speak. We don't care if the picture's not autographed, we put up the Polaroid we took near last Christmas of everybody who came in regularly. We just wanted to have them to remember things when we got old, but we're going to put up his picture, and hey, from what I hear today, might be any number of people who ask after him because he was so famous, like, "Is that Geoffrey Chestnut?" O.K. Thank you, and it was a pleasure to be here to meet his family, and I appreciate that Mrs. Whitehall remembered where he said he went every day for coffee, which was really chamomile tea. God bless. We'll remember you all in our prayers, him especially. O.K.: God bless. This is really not the bad city people think it is, when they don't know New York. I've never seen an apartment like this in my whole life. My wife and I miss him.

Tina Jackson Chestnut

That was a lovely luncheon, Kathy, and the taste of the Alsatian wine brought back so many memories. I guess memories have a particular smell, sometimes, and a particular taste . . . We won't easily forget Geoff's enthusiasms, will we? I used to say to him that jonquils had no odor, and he couldn't understand what I was talking about because that little grainy sort of smell that they do have, that slightly rusty smell, to Geoff that was a triumphant aroma. He just loved jonquils and tulips — especially parrot tulips — and so many other flowers, the hyacinth, of course, and the little crocus that came first, before anything else, just so many things that grew in the spring in my garden in Connecticut. I can well understand why everyone couldn't tromp out there in the snow, but if you had, I was going to give out drawings I'd made of where the flowers were planted, and have you stand looking out the windows with my flower drawings and the garden blueprint for reference, and I had also thought to serve Alsatian wine, so that was an extraspecial touch by you, Kathy. We thank you for such a lovely meal, and I also want to take this opportunity to ask you all to come to Litchfield in May, on whatever day is convenient, so we can walk the grounds and talk about some of the flowers he particularly liked. I gave him a bird book once, because we were both bad at identifying birds, and he said, "Tina, do you think I have time to learn about everything you have an enthusiasm for?" He had such a sense of humor, and he loved to tease. I mean, I'd given him a book about tulips that he absolutely adored and kept on his bedside table, so yes, I did think he had an inquiring mind, and until the end he had so much energy — excuse me; this isn't easy for any of us, of course — he had so much energy that I thought he'd like to learn the names of birds. I just didn't know what to give him, sometimes, to tell the truth, and he was so good at gift-giving. They were always so right. He made a mobile for me out of bottle caps and old crystals that is my favorite thing in my whole house. He made it when he had the flu and got stuck at our house because of an unexpected snowstorm. I suppose, Kathy, that I might also return the painted bottle-cap mobile with the crystals from my aunt's broken light fixture, but I somehow feel that he really would want me to keep it dangling just where it is. When the sun shines just so, it casts the most beautiful colors on the linoleum, and I think of him. I think of him embodied in the colors, but I also think of him because he loved color, lavish color, and I can't understand what happened in his last years, when he renounced color and made those paintings the critics hate — I suppose that's a factor, that critics hate something — but for me, those did not express the Geoffrey Chestnut I knew. I knew the man who gathered up all my bath towels and soaked them in purple Rit dye, and who laughed and laughed when I protested. The man who had my porch ceiling painted the color of the sky, as a surprise for me on my birthday. I have to admit, I've never seen such an intense shade of blue in the sky, but it really transformed the porch ceiling.

 He was my father-in-law, for the brief time I was married to Jared, but he was more like a father to me. Look at how devoted he remained, long after Jared's accident. He would come visit on the train, and he'd have a bag of groceries in his arms. He could only eat so many of my simple meals, I guess! Toward the end when he didn't come anymore, I'd stop at the florist's and buy him a bunch of spring flowers, if they had them: daffodils, or peonies. He loved peonies. One of his last paintings was of the peonies, which were such a beautiful shade of pink, all assorted, with some pale pink, and some the same pale pink but flecked with darker pink, and then I'd selected one pure white one, and I felt so proud of myself, because his face lit up. That was the best painting of his I ever saw. It wasn't an abstract painting at all, though it was black and white. So I just have to think that the colors seemed irrelevant to him, and it was the arrangement, the peony-ness of the peonies, because if you look very carefully, what was written about as "whorls" were really the flowers, and that's why every "whorl" has a line — has a stem — protruding. It's as if he tossed the flowers in the air and painted them in midfall, though I can assure you he was the perfect houseguest and never did that. When he left the next day, he left the painting behind, because it was still wet, but then Atticus came for it at the end of the week and I said, Oh, Atticus — he painted my peonies, you see. And Atticus wouldn't hear of it. It was as if I hadn't spoken. Do you remember that, Atticus? Standing there with that padded dolly, as if you expected to roll out a six-foot painting, and it was only a little canvas, about so big, wasn't it? The peonies had died and I'd tossed them out, so I'd lost my evidence. Like the frozen ice someone uses to commit the perfect murder. Whose story is that? You know, it melts, and then no one can find the weapon.

 I'm not going to get gloomy. I think we should rejoice for all the years he did see in Technicolor, and maybe we'll come to appreciate the black paintings he started the day he painted my peonies, as well. Those did eventually have to be wheeled out, didn't they, Atticus? It's perplexing to someone who isn't a painter why it's so important that paintings be of such size that they have to be wheeled out. Maybe men think something isn't quite real if it doesn't present a logistical problem.

 Does Atticus speak next? I take it that's no. Well, I'll let him give his version whenever we do hear from him.

Rensler Croft

 That which is composed is *put together.* How does a painter best *put things together?* By knowing their *components.* The dictionary offers, as a synonym of *component:* "ingredient, element, factor, constituent." Let me stress the word *constituent.* For Geoffrey, himself, stressed this word, in naming his most acclaimed series of paintings *The Constituents.* It is a four-syllable word. There are four paintings. Geoffrey was a methodical man, who thought carefully about what he was doing. Let me leave you with that thought: He thought carefully — so it was not talent alone; it was, I stress, his careful nature — Geoffrey was a painter who thought *carefully* about what he was doing.

Tomiko Watanabe

Let me say thank you to be invited. It is a great honor to speak after Mr. Croft, so I hope you forgive that today I so sad.

Mr. Chestnut used to look at work in his studio, my studio. One night we went to park bench, and he like squirrels. Some people say rats with long tails, squirrels, but Mr. Chestnut is the Mr. Chestnut all friends and family know as good man, and no one know you at all except friends and family. We took rye bread from the sandwich I did not eat — excuse me: had not eaten. So he already knew he wanted to feed, and we go to Washington Square. We talk about art other times than in studio when looking at his art, my art. So many times I think — excuse me: had thought — that there I was still in New York, which I thought I have to leave and go back to my mother, but instead I am blessed and can buy her an apartment. All because Mr. Chestnut speak to Mr. Greene, who put my studio on tour, and Marla Maples's friend come from magazine and say, Mr. Chestnut take some publicity, but you take other. This was like cutting piece of pie, him; then another piece, me. Because of him, everything changed. Changed? Yes. *Changed.* Because then when we sat on park bench there was more to talk about than bad luck, which is sometimes what they call cherry on top of real-talent sundae. That was private joke between us, because I like ice cream. And I don't know, all I can think is that he say he love ocher, because never I'm aware is popular color, but next I am on cover. Great honor. He say, said, to me on bench: "Stupid critics for paper are like the Graiae, who were the sister of Gorgons. There were three Graiae, gray women, and both men and one woman have only one eye to share. So many critics say things, but they are like Graiae, at paper, where all look, but there is only one eye between them. We laugh at this joke, which we know is mean, but is right. He show me doodles of Graiae. He says: Four-hundred-dollar Gucci glasses, five-hundred-dollar Oliver Peoples's glasses. They put them on and look with their one eye and still think squirrels are a big mystery: maybe they're small cats that like peanuts and make nests in trees. He doodle Graiae all the time.

Now he die, *has died,* and I go every day with bread and feed squirrels and so thankful for what he did always, because he was a good friend as well as one of very best contemporary artists, every bit as good as Cy Twombly, and my late friend very much respect Mr. Twombly.

I understand why paintings became black, because my ocher is step on way to black. Thank you for asking me to your beautiful home looks out on Madison Avenue.

Anne Cray

Geoffrey lived each day, with its many variables, as if he'd select what was important later, and love the day in retrospect. I suppose this is what artists leave as their legacy: their backward glance, as a gift we can take with us into our future.

Martin Trakis

In 1988, Geoff got a postcard. It was of two friends, on top of a rooftop in Italy, the woman in a chair, leaning back in a pink blouse knotted at her waist, the man rustling her hair, standing in what looked to be baggy shorts, or maybe bathing trunks, and both had expressions of such affection on their faces.

He didn't do any work that day. Did he love the woman? Was the man his best friend? Maybe somebody sitting here today knows the answer: Who would send postcards, rubber-stamped on the back with the date of their marriage, and no further comment?

No takers? O.K., then how about this: Another time, he judged a contest. Not for money, not for recognition. Just a small exhibit that would be mounted at a library in New York State. And afterward, the sponsor had the winners write the judges, and one day Geoff went to his mailbox and there were letters, tied together with ribbon, inside a manila envelope, like love letters, or something. But they weren't. They were letters of appreciation. He didn't work that day, either, because he was a modest man, and it never occurred to him that he'd hear from the winners. Some of them had bought expensive cards to thank him, and it was such a poor community, there wasn't money to waste on cards.

What I'm saying is that small things — even very, very happy things — affected him, and sometimes he let life in, instead of studying it, and transforming it, and counting on painting, if I may be honest, to keep life at a distance. Sometimes the postcard arrived, or the unexpected packet of letters, and that was it: no more painting by Geoffrey Chestnut that day.

So the question arises: How do artists let life in, but not so much that it keeps us from our task? There's a danger if someone else's good fortune suffices, as if it were our own good fortune — because we are not the ones who can afford to live vicariously, we are the ones whose imperative is to live in our own moments, so our work will get done.

Could I imagine that I would stand before you today and say that I have come up with the perfect answer? From everything you've heard, I seem to imply that one should retreat, retain insularity, tune out the world, however happy its moments, for the greater good of expressing ourselves in art. Well, I've been divorced three times, and if Geoff was here today, he'd tell me the same thing he told me time and time again: that you've got to be willing to live in the world, in order to truly escape it.

Tomorrow, as fate would have it, I will be marrying the love of my life, Jennifer Lee Jacobson, and if he'd been alive, Geoff would have been my best man. I suppose we might have expected a prank or two: tin cans tied to the bumper and some spray paint . . . As some of us know, he liked to take a bit of paint to a car, occasionally.

I put this boutonniere on my own collar this morning, Geoff, feeling your sure fingers pushing in the pin, remembering that you urged me — as you would have urged all artists — to go with the flow, because even the smallest tributary can surprise us by emptying into the sea.

Jane Wyman

When I was a kid in school, everybody teased me because I had the name of the president's ex-wife. There certainly must have been boys out there who were named Ronald Reagan, and I'm sure their lives were made miserable because that was the president's name, too. Maybe everybody is taunted in their childhood for some reason: because their hair is frizzy, or their nose is big, or they have big feet. It's not a time I'd want to return to. Neither is the tempestuous relationship I had with Jared anything I would want to return to — if that brings you any peace, Tina. It is obvious that he married the woman he loved, and that was you. But Geoffrey was a loyal person, and even when my relationship with Jared ended, Geoffrey still let me borrow money so that — and I really mean this, Kathy, it is money I still intend to repay — I could go into therapy. I didn't want to take the easy way out and call myself by the name of the man I did subsequently marry, which had nothing to do with his being famous and me not being famous, I assure you. It was all about this unresolved issue of having been made fun of because of my name which wouldn't be resolved by sidestepping it. Anyway, I paid him back about half the money. Well — maybe a third. I even tried to give him my firstborn son — that's a joke — and today, my husband remembers Geoffrey as the man who saved me, his wife, and I remember him as the man who let me borrow money to go into therapy.

Bless you, Geoffrey.

Loverne Green

I've had a lifelong fear of standing in front of people, and I was getting more and more nervous, waiting to speak, so I'm a little shook up. I guess most of you . . . Listen, what I write is not me. I'm going to put this away and speak from my heart.

Even though I've had my differences with some members of Mr. Chestnut's family, I know he would appreciate your including me, in that I worked for him for more than three-plus years. Mr. Chestnut always treated me like a lady. Even when I was mopping the floor, he'd say did I want a cup of coffee, did I find the work too difficult? There I was, doing the work I was paid to do, but lavishing extra love on his floors, and he knew it.

My godson is a minister, and he suggested a psalm I should read today, but I don't remember the Bible being part of Mr. Chestnut's days, so then why would I come in now and say something that might make me out to sound good, but it was never anything Mr. Chestnut and I talked about? We did talk about things that were happening in my life, because he used to joke and say he was on the way out and not much was happening in his life, though I know

Mr. Nobody at All

he valued you all and didn't mean nothing bad about you. I saw some of you come to take him to lunch, or do something nice for him, or whatever. I think he might be happier if I talked about how funny he thought that Lake Wobegon man was and how much we both liked the music and sometimes sang along. Mr. Chestnut was just regular. He listened to what happened with Guy Noir and he explained to me that *noir* was a foreign word. Sometimes I explained the lyrics of songs to him, though. He never minded if somebody contributed something, if they knew something to contribute. And if his wife kept her previous husband's name? He was a liberated man, as he always said. Why bear a grudge if a woman's always been who she's been and then you marry her? He asked would I make that decision, keeping my name, and I said yes I would, after being Mrs. Washington like a million other Mrs. Washingtons, and almost Mrs. Lester Royal, but let me tell you, I was one lucky woman to find out in time that Mr. Royal was already married in Paramus, New Jersey.

I guess everyone might want me to say something important that they wouldn't know otherwise, but I feel like except for listening to the radio and just being regular, Mr. Chestnut and I had a sort of understanding that wouldn't hold up well in trying to say more about it. The funniest thing ever happened was when the spray thing wouldn't work on his kitchen sink, and he was poking it with an ice pick and it must of sunk in extradeep, because before you knew it he was holding the hose over the sink, but it was spraying every which way, like a fire hydrant opened. Water all over both of us, me standing there with the mop — I guess that came in handy! — him screaming and trying to aim it down, but weren't no way to do that because it was spraying from all directions. He dropped the sprayer thing and tried to turn the water off, but doing so he got zapped in the face, and when he raised up his head, he was as soaking as a cat taken after with a fire hose. Times like that, we laughed like to die.

He would go downstairs and he was such a gentleman, he would stand out by the curb and hail me a cab so a cab would stop, and then I would come out from the doorway and get in and he always had the cab money in an envelope for me, which was different from the check he wrote me for my working. Well, the time he sprayed himself he toweled off real good, but he forgot and had the towel around his neck downstairs, and no cabs would stop because they knew it wasn't no scarf on him and cabdrivers take who they want and leave the others. We used to say that the Lake Wobegon man could do a really funny story about what was going on inside a cabdriver's mind, but probably it might have been nothing nobody would think was O.K. to have someone thinking over the radio. Anyway, probably the time we laughed longest and loudest was me having to remind him that he *could* turn the water off and that would end the spraying in all directions. He was so embarrassed and wet, he just looked at me and said, "I'm really losing it," and I said, "Well, next time I might best bring my bathing suit."

In closing, let me say that working for him was a real pleasure, and every Saturday around three, I get to thinking that I'll never have coffee with him again. I might have some differences with some of you, but to Mr. Chestnut you were family, right or wrong, and I abide with that as I know God abides with me.

Last, I want to say that I have never in my life spoken so long, but I do want to note that a woman moved into the building and tried to take me away from him on Saturdays, telling me she had a lot of money, just like Mr. Royal told me one time, and I said, No, I work for Mr. Chestnut, and she got so mad she stopped the elevator, which scared me to death, and she tried to talk to me about how she could pay this and that, you know that kind of person, and I said, You ought to be ashamed, trying to take away a loyal person who works for a person in your very own building, and to tell you the truth — this is me talking to you, now — to tell the truth, I did something I never *would* have done, if I hadn't seen how Mr. Chestnut acted all those years, talking on the telephone and telling people what for, when they needed to be told what for. I reached over that lady's shoulder and I hit the elevator alarm and *then* it wasn't so funny. When we got to the next floor, I got off of that elevator like a lady out for a stroll, which is what Mr. Chestnut always made me feel like I was.

You turn on your radio and hear that Wobegon man saying some famous person's cleaning lady had some remarks to make about what it was like to be employed by the famous, you'd best know you're going to hear one funny story about the day a spray hose went wild.

That is the truth about stories: tell the truth, and some will laugh, some won't.

Chad Winton Giles

Geoffrey was on the committee that looked at my work when I applied to Yale, and I will be forever grateful that he reacted as he did. You know what those occasions can be like: so dismissive, so cynical, so let's-get-this-over-with-so-we-can-go-for-latte. I mean, for all I know everyone was on the same page, but one person who shall remain nameless took me aside later and said it was Geoffrey whose enthusiasm put me over the top. As many of you may know, my wife is a designer of chessboards, and Geoffrey ran interference with several, let's just say, *prominent painters* whose names need not be mentioned, helping Gila and me acquire the rights to certain images from certain, let us say, *masterpieces* for our chess pieces. For a while, we were all under the impression that he was even going to pull off *Guernica*, but I guess that was a real, shall we say, "dream on" situation.

Gila is so sorry she could not be here, but she's in Paris. We spoke on the phone last night, and she said, "When I think of Geoffrey, I think of someone who really tried to find joy in things." And that is true: the time he took us around to see galleries on Newbury Street, the Swan Boats we rode on in Boston later that day; the merry-go-round outside Washington, and the completely un*believable* party he took us to after hours at the Corcoran — the merry-go-round at Glen Echo, oh . . . Let's just say I remember it well, and I do *not* mean to offer any homage to Maurice Chevalier; the bumper cars that everyone rode in oh-so-politely, in Vienna, until Geoffrey whirled in a circle and went crashing into every one he could hit, head-on. Joy? Yes — he found joy in so many things: fireworks, useless items from tourist shops, dressing up last year as Big Bird in bondage for Fantasy Fest in Key West.

Yet when an image of Geoffrey comes to mind, he isn't smiling, but frowning slightly, those blue eyes narrowed. What interrupted his living fully in the present, I think, was his not having left the past behind — though in marrying Kathy, he obviously opted for refinement and stability above the shall we say excesses of his youth. Perhaps it benefits us that he did not entirely choose to leave the past behind, because so many of his friends were part of that past, and we would have been cut off from him. Although, even there . . . he screened calls; he refused to communicate by e-mail with anyone except his agent. He didn't really make it that easy to get in touch with him. Ms. Green will be pleased to know that one Saturday when I made it through his screening process, he said that he had just had a cup of coffee with his cleaning lady, and that she understood him better than anyone else. He said, "I know she understands me by looking at the way she folds my laundry."

Gila and I remember him as a true friend, and as a true original. One time he and I went to Washington to see a show of Vuillard's paintings. Always the eager young man, even into middle age, let us just say in retrospect that I gave far too many opinions about Vuillard's interiors to my mentor that day, as if he couldn't form his own opinion about the paintings and the stunning achievement they represented. And to my surprise, he listened — he always listened politely, those few times he'd agree to meet or, more infrequently, when he'd pick up the phone. Anyway, he listened to my discourse and then, as if searching his own memory, he lit up, and he said, "Did you know that as a child, Vuillard had an imaginary playmate? The playmate's name was Mr. Nobody at All."

George Palin

I first met Geoffrey at the Vandelborg apartment at 140 Park standing in the mess another firm had made, before the Vandelborgs fired them — I'd been working all week flat out when I looked up, and there was this man with his portfolio. Anne Vandelborg had forgotten she'd said she'd meet with him. We called and called, and she was nowhere to be found (why she didn't have him go to the other apartment, I'll never know), and since coffee has been much mentioned today, I must add that he and I found ourselves having coffee — from a Mr. Coffee on the floor, I might add. We sat on stools and started talking, nowhere else to sit, and I soon realized I was talking to Geoffrey Chestnut, whose work I'd seen the year before at the de Menil. I mean, this I had not expected: Geoffrey Chestnut in the rubble of the Vandelborgs' apartment.

I told him how the layout of the rooms was going to change, and we walked around a bit and looked at things. Finally, much to my delight, he took out some transparencies of recent paintings Anne had been interested in, and just holding them up to the window light, I could tell that my advice to Anne was going to be that the paintings become the focal point of the library, rather than the massive granite-and-marble fireplace surround from Vermont her husband wanted to put in. Then, while we were expressing mutual admiration for each other's ideas, the doorman appears, and he's got a dog in his arms. It seems Anne had come and gone, asking the doorman to bring me — to this day, I don't know why — her little dog. So there was quite a bit of confusion, as you might imagine, but finally the doorman went away and there stood the dog — no one had the slightest explanation for her actions, but this was before I knew Anne a bit better, bless her unique heart — and we continued talking. It was my work he found so interesting, the rearrangement of the rooms, not his own work — when Geoffrey picks up the plans and the dog goes for his ankle. I saved Geoffrey Chestnut from a biting dog by throwing the Yellow Pages at it! And then before I knew it, there is this amazing painter, this *astonishing talent*, behind a closet door, telling me to get rid of the dog, as if I hadn't already nearly killed it dropping the phone book right behind its butt. So I started laughing. I mean, he'd run into the closet to get away from this terrified little dog, and I kept saying, "Oh, Geoffrey, come out, he'll never come at you again, he's cowering in the other room!" So slooooowly the door opens, and he peeks out, and I got hysterical all over again, so this time, so did he. I mean, it was such a New York moment. It ended with us taking the dog out for ice cream, and all was well — or at least as normal as things ever got at the Vandelborgs', where his paintings, on my recommendation, did indeed come to occupy the place of honor in the library. I can still remember the first time I met Jack Vandelborg, when Anne had signed off on all the rooms. In walks this very tall man in a plaid shirt and khaki pants, wearing a red down vest and *hiking boots*, and suddenly it's Jack, and he's bug-eyed, saying, "Where's my fireplace?" Really, it was my dear Anne's problem, not mine, so I said, "Oh, maybe she forgot." He said, "How could anyone forget a fireplace? We had to reinforce the floor so the marble could be brought in, the granite, the marble, so tell me, how could anyone . . ." Well, you get the idea. Then flip forward a year, two years, really, and there we both are, on the same evening, at the housewarming for Anne Vandelborg, because by then poor Jack had died in a climbing accident. Calla lilies and little devotional lights everywhere, just magic. Pure magic. Eventually Geoffrey comes up to me, and he says, "Did the dog die too?" and I didn't know, but we went looking. In the kitchen we asked one of the cooks if she'd seen the dog, and she said she thought she had, and it had probably curled up under the counter. But that wasn't where it was. Geoffrey was the one who finally saw its eyes staring out from the closet. The same closet the dog had backed him into! And I thought, this has really come full circle. So of course the two of us couldn't stop laughing, and nobody knew *what* we were laughing about, and meanwhile the dog just kept cowering. It was the housewarming, so we could hardly take it out for ice cream.

I only saw him twice after that. Once at the Katz opening at the Guggenheim, and last year when he almost smacked into me, coming up behind me so fast, in that way he had of walking like he was his own tornado, as Rem and I were about to go out through the revolving door at the Plaza. I said, "Hey, fella, what do you think you are? A tornado?" and he said, "I'm afraid of dogs, so I've got to get out of here!" Because the Plaza wouldn't be his sort of place, you know. Rem and I had gone there because that's always where the Japanese want to meet. I just stood there laughing. He was great at carrying off a funny line. Then he walked around me and entered the revolving door, and just like that, like we saw each other every day, he was gone.

Mala

I had the honor of representing Geoffrey for a number of years, when I had my gallery on Spring Street. He was a very talented painter, but there are many talented painters. He was sui generis as well. When I closed the gallery to study in India, he wished me well, and when I returned to New York a year later, he was the first person I called, although of course we were on entirely different paths spiritually. We had a vegan meal in the Village, and afterward he bought me a book about Tibet at the Strand — he'd gone there to see if anyone had sold the new Philip Roth galleys yet, so that will tell you that spiritually, we were not on the same path. Afterward, we went into a bar and I had tea — the bartender was extremely kind, because they don't take kindly to women only ordering tea and not spending a little money, but it was fine because I was a friend of Geoffrey's — and he had a drink, a beer, and he asked if I was still in touch with my former partner, who had also been the love of my life, though our paths had diverged. And that was how the plan got hatched to go to Connecticut to visit Franklin. We went to the garage and got the car and off we went, and halfway there, a snowstorm started. We thought it best to pull off the highway for a period, and we went to a tavern — no one knew us, so I didn't dare ask for tea. Bartenders are irrational in their hatred of women who sit at the bar and ask for tea. I think I had a bottle of mineral water, and he had a martini and he said, "Mala" — because I'd taken the name Mala — he said, "What do you think they'd write in my obit if we walked out of this bar and stood in the snow in this two-bit town until we froze? You could meld with the world of nature." Which was not exactly my prayer, but he had of course grasped the general concept, in the two days we'd been talking — and, about himself, he said, "Would they write that Geoffrey Chestnut froze to death mysteriously, in the shape of a snowman with olive eyes and a toothpick nose, along with an enlightened being holding a Perrier bottle, known as Mala? And then would they quote the bartender: 'Jeez — they froze? Who exactly *were* those guys?' They love that! The *Times* loves that! Casting doubt at the last possible second of your pathetic fucking fifteen minutes of fame. Forget the art reviews: let condescension raise its ugly head in the obit!"

Finally we got going again for Connecticut. We'd sat out the worst of the storm by a fireplace in the tavern, and I drove, though I'd renounced driving, because Geoffrey really wanted to see Franklin again and so did I, I have to be honest and say. We did get there, hours late, but you know what a mysterious person Geoffrey could be. Franklin was dealing privately in deco, then, and everything deco — including those unbelievable cocktail shakers — became an excuse. Orchids in the just-so vase, cocktails shaken in the stainless-steel cocktail shaker. Geoffrey had a martini, and before I knew it he was standing on Franklin's lawn, trying to balance the toothpick with the olives on his nose, like he was a seal doing a trick — and we had quite the time trying to get him inside. He kept saying that he was martyring himself for the *Times,* and if I wasn't enlightened enough to join him and become one with nature, in West Redding, Connecticut, nevertheless he'd come to freeze to death in Franklin's yard.

This might be a sad story — especially if he'd frozen! — but as things turned out, Franklin was always a big believer in distractions; he would just turn the tables, so to speak, so what did he do but start building an igloo, and eventually Geoffrey was lured into the fun. We ended up putting on the spotlight outside the house and working long after it was dark, and I took Franklin aside and I said to him, "What are we going to do if he wants to sleep in the igloo? We're back to the problem of his freezing to death." But Geoffrey had snapped out of it by then, and again we sat inside by a fireplace, and I drank some mineral water and he drank a martini, and then he brought up a certain painting by Corot. A Corot he'd heard was going to be coming up for sale, privately, and would Franklin be willing to involve himself? That was how it all began — the trade of Geoffrey's *Dance to the Music of Time* series for the Corot that hangs here today, which, in my considered opinion, is ever so slightly unexpected in some respects, but was most certainly painted by the estimable Corot.

I'll bet you didn't know the painting's history, Kathy. I hope I haven't upset you by saying how close I feared Geoffrey might come to freezing to death that day, the day I found out he'd had more of a plan than just seeing Franklin, that really our trip was because he had his eye on a painting.

If you stay in the moment, you do not need to ask which way the breeze will blow, for you will be one with it.

Atticus Kimball-Smith

Our beloved Geoffrey is gone, and so many mysteries have been left behind. I hope it is not a faux pas to remark on his separation from Kathy who, even at his bleakest, Geoffrey did not have an unkind word to say about. The loft left to someone most of us have not met until today — by which I mean no disrespect to someone so obviously valued by our dear, departed friend. The early paintings, the ones I had no control over, works whose importance will still be reevaluated years from now, traded to a gentleman from Monaco to hang in his yacht, in exchange for a single work from this man's collection. I never heard Geoffrey say an admiring word about Corot. In fact, time and again, in various museums, Geoffrey would frown that trademark frown and say of one Corot or another that he wondered whether it wasn't a fake.

There is a further mystery: why did Geoffrey cut himself off from friends and loved ones so precipitously, during the last years of his life? One suffers self-doubt, not entirely mitigated by the knowledge that so many were summarily dismissed.

And the inventory of black paintings: Did he paint them? There is no signature. Sleuthing has resulted in only the fact that there was not one single tube of black oil paint among his paints when he died.

The voluminous correspondence with Harry — a comic-strip "artist" from California: Could it be true that this counterculture person relied on Geoffrey for virtually all his ideas? Even so, why were Geoffrey's friends blanket-e-mailed, in the days preceding his death, with lists of his still unpublished story lines, unless he expected reparation to his estate for what *are* apparently *his ideas* in "Special Agent Dogface: Starfucker"? He never had a dog. Never had a cat. If he took an interest in cartoons, did any of us ever hear him speak of Krazy Kat or Charlie Brown?

Then comes the information that his car was missing; impounded, after being towed from an area he must have known very well, because it was smack in front of his building, by a fire hydrant. Add to this the information that, when found, it had been spray-painted with graffiti.

I know: everything I have mentioned is what I was not supposed to speak of, but I have searched my conscience and know that in spite of the expressions on your faces, in spite of the pain I reluctantly add to this already sad occasion, we can only begin to get at the mystery of Geoffrey if we confront his curious behavior.

Drink? Some have spoken of drink. Misplaced anger? How else to interpret the anecdote about his raging against the *Times*? Ambition so repugnant to him, he became a parody of himself? I defy anyone, except the few critics we've already heard from, whose opinions Geoffrey did not value — and that is an understatement — to say that there is beauty, or even significance, in the last works, if, please God, they can even be authenticated. And the loft, which at first his beloved wife, Kathy, thought would be just a painting studio, and which of course she assumed would revert to her . . . She remains his executrix and — along with me — stands prepared to inventory his work, and to disperse his paintings to appropriate museums and galleries — by which I mean real museums and galleries, not the Personal Gallery of Mala. I hope I do not overstep my bounds to say that it is extremely curious that Kathy is mentioned in his last will — which we are now preparing to formally contest — only as the person to whom he bequeaths a Corot that, in my opinion, has every possibility of being a fake. I direct your attention to the lack of volume in the cow's head, the uncharacteristic brushstrokes in the extreme foreground. Please: you can see what I mean when you inspect it after I have concluded my remarks, Mala.

If he had traded his youthful efforts for a Vuillard, that we could understand. If he had encountered a great bargain by an artist we did not know he revered — something undervalued, that his estate might benefit by owning . . . who could not accept a person being motivated, sad as that might ultimately be, by profit?

But the parts of this puzzle make no sense. I am confounded. At least, I am confounded when searching within the obvious parameters for an explanation. When I look beyond that which is obvious, however — and that is what all artists must do, and though no artist myself, I have learned much from artists such as Geoffrey Chestnut — I have the feeling that in facing some contradictions head-on I might possibly reencounter, in a more honest way, the Geoffrey I did know: a man who can be looked at, and then spoken about, honestly. He was a supremely childish person — and I mean "childish" in the sense of one who remains open to experience. I look beyond what I am sad to say seems to be self-contempt and see love for his friends, a love that is affecting because he was willing to let us see that it was complicated, and contradictory. Certain things will, of necessity, remain opaque. We knew his brightness, but he also let us see his dark side, even encouraged us — might I say taunted us? — to explore his last inexplicable adventure with a West Coast comic-book artist, and to put it together — or not — with the fine artist we knew. We are left not only with his dreams, so often transcribed as transcendent paintings, but with his nightmares, his comic-book-loving self, as his legacy. Mala, I will be concluding my remarks momentarily, so I would appreciate your attention. I was speaking of his legacy: beauty expressed as order, and disorder; a fine eye for perfection and an irascible spirit for mischief; a man conflicted by love and hate, which he is hardly the first to figure out are flip sides of the same coin.

Let us look proudly at a man who would not let us retain any simple sense of him. His death, after all, is *his death*, not merely our confusion of memories.

Kathy

Thank you for redeeming our beloved Geoffrey. Before we adjourn for tea, Geoffrey's young friends, David and Daniel, will be returning from the other room, where they've been playing quietly, to say a final thank-you to everyone who has come here today, some of them traveling considerable distances to be with us.

Harry Mathews

Mrs. Whitehall, may I say a few words? You agreed I could if the occasion arose, and the occasion has arisen. Atticus said that he mentioned things he wasn't supposed to, and I myself would never have spoken about them otherwise.

I wasn't a friend of Geoff's, but I was a confidant, and a fairly intimate one. You see, the name of the California comic-strip artist was Harry Matthews, which is my name, too. I live in Key West and write quality lit, and I don't or at least normally don't have anything to do with pornographic comic strips. But one day in my e-mail I found a message from Geoff praising my work on Krazy Kunt Komix and wondering if he could get involved in some way. Of course I realized he had the wrong Harry Mathews, and it didn't take long to check out the one he was after, who had two *t*'s in his name anyway. But I couldn't resist the chance of working with Geoff — I wasn't exactly a fan of his, but I knew he was a serious painter — especially since I felt I could give him what he wanted. So I e-mailed him back offering to supply scenarios for porn strips provided he would draw them. I even included my first story line as an attachment. It wasn't "Special Agent Dogface: Starfucker"; that came later. It was something like "Trinidadian Banana Tag Open: Mixed Doubles." He went for it.

He couldn't get enough of my stories. I had to drop everything to keep up. (I also had to create a new outlet for our stuff, but desktop publishing makes such things a lot easier.) I didn't mind.

Anyway, the more we collaborated, the more he confided in me, and soon we were telling each other all about our lives. Naturally I had to invent my own, which was fun. After a while I was able to ask him the kind of questions probably none of you ever did. For instance, why the interest in comic strips? Well, he said, he's always admired Philip Guston for giving up his gorgeous abstractions to make cartoonlike designs. O.K., but then why porn? He said he'd been drawn to pornography for years, (a) because he enjoyed it, and (b) because it was the only place he'd ever found where relationships were immediately satisfying and complete. I think incidentally that is at least an indirect answer to why Geoff cut himself off from his loved ones, as one of you has said.

What else? Oh, yes, the black paintings. I have to admit I encouraged him in this line. I told him that black on black was where painting was inevitably headed, just like life. But he should avoid doing Ad Reinhardt all over again. So forget brushstrokes, go the Yves Klein route, lay it on with a roller. Which is what he did. There was no way Atticus could find any *tubes* of black paint. He should have been looking for cans.

As for *why* black paint, his personal reasons I mean: Geoff wanted out, in every way. He was tired of being told who he was, what a wonderful man he was, and what his work meant — he hated the word *transcendent*. He wanted to lead another life all his own. His drinking — Esther Halsey thinks he became a teetotaler, that's what he wanted everyone to think. When he went out he made a point of never touching a drop. Then he'd go home and drink a couple of highball glasses of cheap vodka, straight, no ice. I even had a kind of drinking date with him once. We set a time by e-mail and agreed to knock back a few when the moment came. I drank Ketel One, though.

One last thing: those e-mails at the end. I confess I sent them myself. I found a hacker who got into AOL and retrieved Geoff's password and address book. I knew he was in a bad way — *he* knew he was killing himself with the booze. I thought it would be simpler for everybody if he was recognized as the sole author of our collaborations. That was what he was in point of fact. I would never have written a word if he hadn't inspired me to. So there's the situation, and I'm certainly never going to do anything to change it.

He told me about the Corot, too; but that was a sworn secret.

Thanks to all of you, and particular thanks to you, Mrs. Whitehall.

Kathy

Thank you so much, Mr. Mathews. I had thought we might hear again from the boys, but they seem to be fast asleep. Thank you for checking, Monica. I know we don't want to awaken them. Let me say just a few final words, then. Geoffrey's family does so appreciate your love and support . . . oh, what's that? Well! Daniel seems to be awake, and dressed as . . . what is that red on your hand, Daniel? What are you dressed as? As someone who looks just a little silly in the dress I wore to the opening at the Met! Is that lipstick on your face? Oh, you must remember the way Geoffrey painted your face to make you a tiger on Halloween. Monica, can you get that tube of lipstick?

Please, let's adjourn. Maybe Atticus was right, and Geoffrey's impish spirit has influenced Daniel.

Daniel Richardson

I can say both parts. I'm Daniel, and David's under the bed. But I can do both. We spray-painted Geoffrey's car with him to make it a Screw-Society-Mobile. We're going to be artists like him. We loved him very much. This is our first memorial service. We will remember him always.

Los Angeles

Dennis Bryll

I want to thank you, one and all, for coming to Pinnacle Modern Gallery. Atticus, of course, deserves a high-five for searching for so many tickets on Expedia, which can't have been easy with his carpal tunnel, and also for arranging the dinner afterward — I assume it will be a meal to remember — at Spago. Because of flu — that's what we call a hangover out here — I was unable to attend the remembrance session in New York. As you know, I was incarcerated when I began my correspondence with the deceased. I never imagined that my letter would find its way out, let alone into the hands of the intended recipient: Geoffrey Chestnut, a.k.a. Sleazeman Uppity. I have Atticus to thank for that, because I found out that when Geoffrey was in such a funk he didn't pull the mail out of his mailbox anymore, Atticus started opening it, and he must have thought, Hey, this is the real thing — I mean, with someone admiring Geoffrey as the great talent he was, not just wanting to exploit him. Nope — pure admiration on my part, which, from me, was as unusual as uncut H. Meaning, of course, that in the old days I distributed my stuff and it was thereafter cut, or otherwise half of LA would be dead, but what I'm saying is that my admiration for Geoffrey was as pure as uncut H. Listen, I don't want to talk about drugs, when a man who only took by prescription has passed, but my point is that somehow good luck got into the picture, in the person of Atticus Kimball-Smith, who gave my fan letter to Geoffrey, and sure enough, what happens next but the Sleazeman, himself, is e-mailing, asking do I want to give him story lines from jail. You know: collaborate. Hey — that can be a bad word, but he was talking about ideas for comix, not collaborate as in *the accused says you were a collaborator.*

O.K., I'm receiving signals from my friend there that I should pick up the beat. So let me say that when I knew I was going to be given the opportunity to speak today, I was shitting pickles, just like I was with the parole board. I mean, I've moved on with my life, working at a very deluxe resort on the ocean, tending bar. Come on by, all of you, and have a Maker's Mark on the house, or whatever you like, even though we don't have hors d'oeuvres of shrimp-wrapped Boston baked beans with a dusting of deadly nightshade, or whatever the hell. Get back to basics, and roasted mixed nuts, that's power to the people! Other night, Madonna was in with some Londoner who wasn't Guy Ritchie, because he's in all the time to watch the Lakers, but hey, I care? Geoffrey was alive, I'd have called him and he might have stopped by, always ready to get an idea from anybody pretty in a bustier, right? Right? There was the Material Girl, with these two cones pointed at my face, and no cross in the cleavage, you know what I mean? Took the Maker's Mark complimentary, and let me tell you — O.K.: no more stories!

What I want to say is that I knew Geoffrey as a regular guy, and I don't bring that up because I'm some ex-con, ex-druggie on an ego trip. I say that because late at night, we'd be hangin' at the bar and he'd tell me about the times at the Cedar in New York, and about his early life, not shittin' diapers or like that, but about scoring chicks and having a wild time and being righteous about paintin', and let me tell you, he was a force to be reckoned with. One time I got LaDonna to cover for me, and the two of us went upstairs where there was the empty banquet room and we stood on the balcony and pissed a waterfall on the French doors inside of which CAA suits and their trophies were sittin', and even if they'd looked up and seen us and known who they were lookin' at, they'd have been some surprised that the famous Geoffrey Chestnut and some ex-con were pissin' a waterfall, just to make things more romantic. O.K., I'm done with stories, and I want to say that Geoffrey took me out to his car one night, popped the trunk, and inside were some paintings wrapped in bubble wrap, his new prize possession among them. A Corot, which I never heard of, being the ignorant shit I am, but there we were in the driveway, looking at this painting with all this little stuff in it, flowers and so forth, a cow, and this frame you could have knocked out Muhammad Ali with, and this sandstorm comes up and we're both doing a full-body block, protecting the painting from getting the shit scratched out of it by this unbelievable Malibu windstorm, and meanwhile I'm gettin' an art history lesson. Took it into the bar and took down this opera poster and put it there to admire, and then I see that there's Ryan O'Neal and Farrah — no doubt knockin' a couple back while their sutures dissolved — so I send over Maker's, and the guy goes ballistic with LaDonna, who happens to be a lovely person from Cleveland whose screenplay is already in development. I think *whoa!* She's gonna get pissed at this jerk and pick up the painting and break it over his head, because she's got her black belt, but Farrah's totally nice, nothing like on *Letterman,* she's like, Everybody chill. Please take this back and bring the man what he wants. Anyway, Geoffrey really liked comin' by, and he'd overhear people talkin' about shit he used later, when he wrote Harry, because before I know it, Geoffrey's coming in with his new best bud and all they want is to overhear every conversation they can. Late at night, Geoffrey'd be like, Give me a glass of water between Maker's, otherwise my liver might turn to wax and ooze out my ears. No, forgive me, this is a respectful occasion, and I totally respect that. Geoffrey took me one time to the Temp Contemp, which sounds like the name of a drink some asshole would order to bust your nuts, am I right? Anyway, it's real, and he told me one hell of a lot about what was happening in art. So today I feel obliged to honor his memory by saying something about art and comix. What happened was, it's like those machines with the big claw, where you plug in your quarters and the machine's fixed not to grab what you're aiming for, it moves left and right and opens its claws and it's like another busted piece of shit from Cape Kennedy: it looks good, but it can't grab, or the camera's broken, or all the guys are dead or somethin'. It's like, certain pop artists wanted to be the claws, because they thought they'd goof on everyday stuff, paint their soup cans and their electric chairs. No more of these Great Masters too heavy for the claws to pick up, staying stuck in the machine to cheat the customer while the quarters kept making the house rich, right? Because that was the system. And the artists caught wise, and they thought, Hey, the game's rigged? We'll grip *somethin'* and make like it's the prize, so they dredged up ordinary stuff, like Roy Lichtenstein did — hey, I won five dollars off of Geoffrey, because he bet I couldn't put down two Maker's and say that dude's name! — anyway, they *wanted* crappy stuff, but then they pretended like they'd scored. Like you go to the store and all you can afford is soup, but if you say soup's great, you feel better. Because formerly the fix was in, and somebody else, some money guys, were steering the claws. The game was rigged? Then fuck the game! They'd dredge up the sparkly shit from the bottom and call it stardust. So Lichtenstein says, Let's put a bubble out of this bimbo's mouth and say "I WONDER IF BRAD WILL CALL," and suddenly they've used stupid shit to turn the tables and whatever shit they want is art. Geoffrey decided, I'll sit down at the machine. He knows what he might grab. So he gets the chance to move his claws over to the Corot . . . nyaaaaaaaak, more to the left, little to the right, left, farther, more, aaaaaaaah, ennnnhhhhhhhhhhhhhh . . . bingo! He's writing ideas to Harry, but part of him thinks, Hey, I'll give this creative dude some real ideas and change the game, but what's to lose by playin' it safe at the same time? I'll create this Dogface character and send it to Harry — but meanwhile stash a Corot masterpiece and take care of myself in my old age if everybody stops laughin' at funny stuff, when Social Security's belly-up.

Like all people smart enough to figure it out, Geoffrey knew how to play both sides against the middle. Standin' there in that sandstorm, I said, Man, what are you doin' with some scene of shitty little animals? And you know what? He gave me that smile I know you know. That smile that let you know that he knew that even when things were ridiculous, *most of all* when things were ridiculous, you could hedge your bets and save your ass.

Jane Vegas-Villasenor

What can I possibly have done to be in the position of speaking not once, but twice, after totally inappropriate remarks have been made about a kind, brilliant, talented, troubled man? We all knew of Geoffrey's emotional difficulties, but we have gathered here today to honor his memory, and holding forth with self-centered, pointless anecdotes about a very great painter who had his demons and who, late in life, decided to live ironically, or whatever poor Geoffrey thought he was doing . . . Let me gather my thoughts. Which will be more than some people have bothered to do.

Geoffrey Chestnut taught so many people that often something good comes out of adversity, if only we remain receptive to new possibilities. Many of you may have heard about the time he ran over a dog in Connecticut. Of course that was an awful thing, but it was late at night, it was raining, and the dog ran into the road and there was nothing to be done. He got out of the car and saw that the dog was dead. He picked it up and moved it to the side of the road. Then he parked and walked up a walkway where the dog had darted out, and as he approached the front door, feeling dreadful, of course, but doing the right thing, the light went out on the front stoop. Still, he knocked. And then the lamppost was turned off. He knocked again — you know Geoffrey, when he thought he must do the right thing — and someone hollered, "Go away." He was mystified, but still, he began talking, telling the person inside that he was terribly sorry, but did they have a dog, because he had hit a dog. All that was said, again, was, "Go away." "Was it your dog?" he asked, and no one responded. Then he heard what sounded like furniture being dragged across the floor. He was a little frightened, naturally, and shivering, standing there with the rain splashing around him. As he was about to leave, the light went on. The door was opened a crack, with the chain pulled across it. An old man peered out, but did not speak again. "Did I hit your dog?" Geoffrey asked, and the old man squinted harder and said, "Geoffrey Chestnut?" In answer to his own question, he opened the door, and whom did Geoffrey see standing in front of him but his former high school art teacher, who had recognized his talent many years before. Geoffrey recognized him immediately. But no: it had not been the man's dog, nor did he know whom the dog belonged to. It was his first night alone in the house, after his wife's funeral, and he had been frightened that the person knocking might be her ghost. Instead, it was his pupil from years before, and they were reunited, though it was otherwise a very sad night for both of them.

Such strange things happened to Geoffrey. He seemed fated to be in certain places at certain times, though initially it might have seemed that he merely had bad luck. Not if he could transform things, he didn't. Once a piece of his ceiling fell on his head and later he had such vivid dreams that he credits the incident with starting his *Falling Moments* series. He wrote me a letter one time and said that though he sometimes thought he'd lost his way — as an artist; he was talking about being an artist — he persevered because although the ceiling had already fallen in on him, and though he expected the rug might be yanked out from under him next, he'd learned that there was never a wrong place to be, if you were at peace with yourself. With making your art, he meant. If you were at peace with that.

Zarah Pinnacle

Excuse me. I intended to start things off by welcoming you to the gallery myself, but I had to take a call from Leonard, who's in Japan shooting a commercial. I'd hoped he could come today, but we all recognize the necessity of responding to an opportunity when it presents itself.

In the sixties, when I lived in Rome, our group was involved in performance art. We'd get in the Trevi Fountain and use the sculpture as a backdrop and restage gladiatorial battles naked, and then, instead of passing the hat, we'd pass a urinal painted Day-Glo green, dangling streamers — it's over there, with the orchid growing out of it. I think telling Geoffrey about those days and showing him one of our films was part of the reason why he decided to allow us the honor of showing his work at the gallery — though of course it was Atticus Kimball-Smith who pointed him in our direction. I heard Julian mentioned earlier, and, in fact, I was on the phone, speaking to Julian out in the Hamptons, when Geoffrey first called, with that strange Japanese koto music he was so addicted to playing very loudly in the background, identifying himself as Sleazeman Uppity, though it was lost on me, because I hadn't read a comic strip since Roy died. But I knew who it was — and not because I'd just hung up with Atticus, who'd assured me Geoffrey would call in five minutes. I knew from his voice: a sonorous, sensitive voice that reminded me of Anselm's quiet modulations. I told him I would be over the moon if he wanted to show at Pinnacle Modern. He and Atticus flew out, together, that weekend. When Geoffrey came in, he and Atticus and I settled in and looked at the Roman statesmen in the Trevi Fountain film, and we had such a relaxed, happy time that business as such was never discussed. Geoffrey told me about his interest in pornography, and in the comic strip. He told me about the black paintings. Of course, Atticus had sent me slides of those. I must say, the first time I looked at them on the light table, I thought a mistake had been made developing them! But Geoffrey was adamant about having a show as Sleazeman Uppity first, even if he was later to have a show as Geoffrey Chestnut, so I called Carrie. What to do? And she said — she's such a focused person; her ideas always come from a calm center — she said, Have the openings one right after the other, and every reviewer out here will jump all over it. Send out a press release saying Geoffrey Chestnut is Sleazeman Uppity! Which I did, and she was right. And then . . . but you all know this. You know how Geoffrey, who could take such wonderfully funny ideas into his head, sent an inflatable man, wrapped in an old fur coat, wearing a fedora, in the back seat of the limo we sent to the Peninsula and didn't attend his own opening! That certainly convinced Atticus that he had to accompany him to the second opening. And the rest is history, of course.

I had a dream last night that Geoffrey was walking on clouds, wearing that same fedora, and a tux, which mystified me even in the dream, because from the first minute I met Geoffrey, he wore the same sweatpants and T-shirt that he wore to bed everywhere else, too, including the Polo Lounge! And the clouds kept wafting upward as he walked until finally there was nothing more of Geoffrey than his head, and then suddenly the enveloping clouds blew away, and Geoffrey was walking into Swifty's Oscar party in heaven.

Sleazeman Uppity forever! I hereby proclaim this to be the Age of Geoffrey Chestnut! Long live Cristal!

Paul Newman

I offer my condolences to the friends and family of Geoffrey Chestnut. He contacted me not as the important painter I later found out he was, but as a potential donor to Newman's Own. It is not our policy to accept contributions, but even though we don't work that way, his check was magnanimous. I e-mailed him and thanked him for such generosity. Then things went a little wacky in technology-land: the wrong message came back to me, an attachment of several paintings for downloading, one of which was already in the collection of Eli Wallach, and another I'd seen recently when Gore Vidal moved back to Hollywood. I guess things were mixed up between us from the start, because when I wrote to compliment his paintings, he responded by snail mail, with a note accompanying his check saying that our Plantain Fiesta Dip — something we don't happen to manufacture, alas — was a favorite for late-night snacking. The next thing I knew, he'd pulled a prank on me. I got a call from CAA saying that his comic strip — I thought, What? Comic strip? — featured me, at a cocktail party, listening to a woman complimenting my performance in *Hud*, while I was completely preoccupied, devising a recipe for Plantain Fiesta Dip! Takes one to know one. I mean, one artist to know another, and to know what we're really thinking when we're being broadsided, no pun intended.

Joanne and I have decided to purchase *Black Painting #66*, which you see in the background. She and I are there today in spirit, fortunate to have had a correspondence with the witty, and very talented, Geoffrey Chestnut. Though his painting is magnificent, we're sure it's a poor second best to knowing him.

Our prayers are with you.

Atticus Kimball-Smith

Are those blue eyes, or are those blue eyes? Amazing. Absolutely amazing.

My plane was much delayed. My apologies, because I was to speak first. I'm glad I made it. Not so much because security was a nightmare, but because Kim Basinger was on the plane, and the pilot kept flirting with her. I don't know who was flying the plane.

Our beloved Geoffrey is gone, and we are gradually reconciling ourselves to his untimely death. Yet I do not think anyone can answer the question: Why did he cut himself off from his loved ones? I asked this question at the New York service, but since that time I have given increasing thought to the question, and although I am hardly happy with my answer, I do think I might have an answer.

Because we weren't much fun. He began to find more fun in going underground with his art, so to speak: sending ideas that he truly enjoyed working on out here, and keeping the happy secret that when they made a stir, *he* was making a stir, though he lived on another coast and though for a long time he never shared the secret that he was involved in them. He let some of us know that in doing the black paintings, he was doing his most important art, and what did we do but back off, keep quiet, give him — as we thought we were doing — space and time. Yet he didn't need any *more* space and time. *We were just in awe of him,* as we are of artists. And do you know what happens when you are in awe of someone? They don't feel free to have fun in your presence. He was angry. We had failed him, by being too respectful, by honoring the public Geoffrey, not the real down-deep-and-dirty Geoff. Hard as it is for us to hear, his friends at the end of his life were his cleaning woman and a couple who worked in a coffee shop across from his apartment. *A pornographer was his friend.* We were not his friends, because we didn't ask the right questions. Forget the "we." *I.* I didn't ask the right questions. I should have said, "What are you doing hanging out with Mala, who is, quite frankly, a barely functional lunatic?" I should have said, "If you really care, have two independent appraisers look at that so-called Corot." The cow's head isn't right, anyone can see.

But then I think: Maybe he wanted to leave us a legacy that would disappoint us. Maybe he thought we were too materialistic and naïve. Maybe he felt he reached a more significant portion of the population with the comic strip. In considering it, over time, I am coming to see it, ultimately, as political.

What else does "Special Agent Dogface: Starfucker" tell us, beyond the political? I am not here, today, to cast blame. I hope, instead, to offer enlightenment. In turning to my former Episcopal priest from boyhood for advice, *he* was the one who pointed out immediately what was transparent to anyone but me: S-A-D. Geoffrey was sad. I see that Mala is not here today, but had she been, I would still say the same thing: "Starfucking made him sad."

I will not end on a negative note. Instead, I will say that just as we can feel an inherently spiritual shimmer rise from the black paintings, which I now feel will surely be authenticated, since two young boys' home movies of Geoffrey at work may be much, much more important than they ever suspected, so can we carry away a humbling message from Geoffrey's comic strip about being free, having fun. Is that too slight? Too much a cliché? Think about it. Freedom. Fun.

Tom Smith

I met Geoff when he first went coastal — that's coastal, not postal — at his opening at Politik in Santa Monica, in '01, which was his first gallery out here, but as we see, he moved on to better things. I wanted to be his West Coast rep — that's no secret. I already had Schnabel, and I wanted to get Geoffrey out of Politik and, quite frankly, I was so aggressive, I'm still surprised we ended up friends. As you probably know, I got out of the business and went to work for Disney, but I like to think that if I'd lasted, he would have come around, and I would have chosen this very gallery to show his work. As it was, he was always kidding me and asking me to send him free passes to Disneyland, and I usually kidded him back and said I'd comp him the day he brought Michael Jackson from Neverland. Well, eventually he showed up with Michael Jackson. Let's leave aside Michael's problems, for a moment, and just concentrate on Geoff, standing there at the private entrance with this guy who's got a towel over his head, not a mask, a towel with eyes cut out, and he whips the thing off and smiles, and I realize, my God, it's Michael Jackson. Somehow, he's got Michael Jackson. We'll leave aside the fact that Geoff's a little old for Michael. Anyway, there we are, staring at each other. The limo driver's waiting in the lot, and Geoff waves the guy off. Geoff's holding his cell phone and grinning and saying that it's his free day at Disneyland, and I almost lost my voice, I choked up and couldn't speak for a couple of seconds, but I got myself together and I took them both through, and I'm thinking: *Michael Jackson.* White socks and black shoes, same as in the video. But don't get too excited. It turns out it's the world's best Michael Jackson *impersonator.* And do you know what Geoff says to me? He says, "I wouldn't sign with you, and you never got Michael Jackson, but you know what you *do* have? My everlasting respect, because for a minute there, I was sure you were gonna piss your pants." That's it. I guess I should have known, because so-called Michael Jackson was sans kids, and even sans chimpanzee. Anyway, that's what Geoff says, and the impersonator stands there looking very satisfied, grinning like mad because in his own way, he's a celebrity. Meanwhile, it's like we're bread bits. These Asian girls land like pigeons and start taking pictures. They're too stunned to speak: just flash-flash-flash-flash. *And they don't know.* The next thing I know, and the first time *ever* I figure out that Geoffrey Chestnut is involved with a certain very hip comic strip that gets e-mailed to the privileged few a day earlier than its official publication, is that my friend happens to be in Eisner's office when Eisner is laughing his head off about the new comic strip and this idiot who is very precisely drawn, let me tell you — suddenly Geoff turns into Dürer — anyway, this idiot, *me*, thinks Michael Jackson's just sauntered up to Disneyland, and later that day it's messengered over — not that I haven't heard, anyway — *framed*, to add insult to injury. It's signed, "Geoffrey Chestnut and Michael Jackson," and I just wonder what I could get for that on eBay!

He was quite the prankster. The impersonator went into the john and took off his wig and makeup, his nose putty, or whatever it was that made his nose look like a needlefish, and I'm such a great guy, I arranged for them to jump the line for Space Mountain, anyway. I got a Mickey Mouse and had him march them to the front of the line. Back in the park the Asians were still where they'd taken the pictures, looking around like Michael Jackson was sure to come back.

Geoff really, really liked a practical joke. I meet people out here, and they shake their heads about the lengths he'd go to. You've got to figure that the impersonator didn't come cheap. But nothing would stop him. I look at the black paintings, and I think: maybe months later, mailed from Bora Bora, is going to come a letter, saying that we should remove the top layer of paint, and underneath is going to be the real art. You could never stay ahead of Geoffrey.

Dianne Abagani

He won me in an auction benefiting amFAR, which meant I'd have him to the restaurant and give him a cooking lesson. Then later the same night, I was high bidder to have him give me a painting lesson. That's about as much agreement as people have, these days, going into marriage. They don't know where they'll work, where they'll live, whether they want kids or how many, but the guy thinks the girl can teach him to windsurf, and she thinks he'll give her free advice about the market. They maybe rehearse married life by upping the Prozac dosage and taking a dog home from the pound to see if it works out, and sometimes if they see a place they like, they rent with an option to buy. That was more or less my position. I ran my travel agency out of my spare bedroom, until Expedia, and then I figured what the hell and opened Le L.A.

The first dog I brought home didn't have any desires. I named it Madagascar, because I'd never been there, if you know what I mean. It wouldn't really play with toys, and it just nosed around its food. I think it had already made its decision to leave the world. But Geoff crated it up and pretended it was his, got it to New York, enrolled it in doggy boarding school, and the next thing you know, my dog's tossing plush mice in the air like a pig snorting truffles and running to my side the second I call him. This cost me over five thousand I didn't have at the time, so I thought I couldn't go there, but Geoff put it on my bill, and just so you know I have a clear conscience, I paid my bill for the dog training and for *Black Painting #59* before he died. He might have won a more prestigious chef if he'd bid more, but I do the low-carb thing with style, and once the salt's out of your diet, you don't so much crave fat. We taught Madagascar to bark at the word *carbs*. Geoff and I'd turn on *Oprah* and do fake voice-overs, like *carbs* were wrongly assessed on the food pyramid, *carbs* put you in strange glucose absorption situations, *carbs* made you fat, *carbs* were no good when they were simple *carbs*, and of course he got to associate all the *carb* talk with Oprah's face. She'd come on and he'd start barking, because Madagascar associated her with carbs.

So what did he do, dying on me? Going back to New York and cutting himself off from everybody? Do we take it personally, or how, exactly, do we understand why such a talented painter and such a great friend would decide to starve himself to death? I'm sure I'm not supposed to mention that, but Kathy saw the body.

O.K., please don't have attitude and sit up in your seats and stare at me. I'm supposed to talk about the spirit, and be a California asshole and wish everybody a nice day. Well, I don't feel like saying *whatever*. I think we have to figure this out, before we leave here today. How could he be having G-and-T's with me one week, and leaving L.A. and not taking my calls the next? Who was the Spanish woman who answered his phone in New York, with all that ridiculous "Mr. Chestnut is not available at present"? Suddenly he's a Kennedy and he's killed another girl, or something? Oh, *excuse me.* I know that some of you are personally acquainted with Maria Shriver. Well, she's not here, that I notice — big hair anywhere? no? — and I don't think Arnold's sent spies. We have a responsibility to try to understand what happened in Geoff's life, and we should have a serious discussion, even if it doesn't happen right this second — even if the *ahi on pepper crackers* and *Cakebread Cellars*

Mr. Nobody at All

has to be brought out first. We have a responsibility to try to figure out what happened, the same way Geoffrey obliged us to look long and hard to understand the depth and beauty, the variation and majesty, of the black paintings.

The Uncle Bobbies (Morgan, Lynn, David K., Alice, Fidelio, Jennica, Efram, George, and Dadee)
  We're here today to do a sendoff song for Mr. Chestnut.

> We really like to sing.
> He who sings is king.

Shut up, Fidelio! I'm doing the intro.
  So, like I say, we're here for the sendoff. Uncle, as you may know, draws some comix, himself, and he met Mr. Chestnut and helped him hang the last show, and they later had the pleasure of each other's company at a Jane Siberry performance.
  Jane Siberry is righteous! And Mr. Chestnut really liked her music, so this is a little bit inspired by our Canadian sister, Jane Siberry. We do it a cappella.
  If he who sings is king, then she who sings is queen.
  Shut up. Ready?
It's a pleasure to be here today, because we've had the honor of performing at the gallery a couple of times before, and to be honest with you, that's how we got one of our most important bookings. So thank y'all.

> He came to California, and he really loved the sun.
> We'd see him at the pier, before the day was done.
> The . . . day . . . was . . . done.
> Knew he loved to paint, knew he could cartoon.
> Never knew, though we knew him, that he would die so soon.
> Die . . . so . . . soon.
> But a gift that man did leave us
> It's around us everywhere
> Ev . . . ery . . . where.
> For he painted life's great mystery
> As the beauty of despair.
> O, he came to California, and he really loved the sun.
> Now we're here to praise him, each and every one.

Lewis Lanall

I teach fifth grade and I bring my students to the gallery all the time, and they particularly liked the black paintings, so Zarah asked if I could read some of their reactions and maybe add a word of my own, though Mr. Chestnut and I never met. Should I just read one or two of the students' reactions, then? That was very melodious singing. Really very haunting. I suppose all of us love the sun here, don't we? And perhaps we take it for granted. Very beautifully expressed. O.K., here goes. "Black is the absence of color, but it is as good as color? When I see Mr. Chestnut's painting, I think of the way the water looks late at night. Maybe in some of them he could show something by making the moon shine. He is a very good painter who makes me happy. I think his paintings are of the Pacific when there's no moon." That was very nice, I think. The students never met him, either, but I think he would have enjoyed meeting them. I'm very sorry that never happened. Since I didn't know him myself, I'm thinking that I should just read one more and keep my remarks short. O.K., here's this one, that's quite different. The students liked his paintings much more than any other show they'd seen here, by the way. O.K. — just an excerpt: "If Mr. Chestnut was a real nut found on a tree, maybe the paintings expressed the way he felt inside, being a nut that was all dark inside because it wasn't cracked. There is a person behind every painting, and he might have been saying he was the inside of his own nut person." The children don't pun, so I think it's best to envision what she wants us to see. She read that aloud in class and was very proud of what she'd come up with. It might not be conventional art criticism, but we can always learn from the unique perspective of children, I would say. I see the musicians are leaving. Well, thank you very much. Your music was most inspiring. Take care, now. O.K. Personally, I want to say that teaching art has been one of the great pleasures of my life. I appreciate being asked here today, but quite frankly I don't think I'll share with the fifth-graders the information about his contribution to the comic strip. Not that some of them aren't very advanced, because I'm always surprised at how fast they grow up and how much they know, but I think it might have to wait until they're in a higher grade — talking to them about artists expressing themselves very differently in different genres, I mean.

Thank you.

Kathy Whitehall

It's lovely to finally see the gallery where Geoffrey showed his paintings in Santa Monica. This is a lovely setting. Thank you for arranging this, Zarah. Being in an environment I know Geoffrey loved makes me feel closer to him. The family very much appreciates everyone gathering to share thoughts of our dearly departed.

Harry Matthews

Excuse me, are you taking volunteers? Can I just say a few words? I'll just stand here like Ricki Lake's called on me. O.K. I'm the other Harry Matthews, the one with two *t*'s. I got a report on the New York memorial service, and if the other Harry Mathews has decided to speak, so will I.

The last time I met up with Geoff was not long before he died, when I was in New York for a Barbie doll convention and we got together and had a few drinks and ended up doing some spray-painting of the Fourteenth Street subway of some Krazy Kunt characters with these neighbor kids of his. This waitress came out of the bar with us, and she was this little thing in a denim jacket, and Geoff said, Hey, don't you have something warmer? And somehow we all stopped for drinks after we took the kids home . . . There was some store open by Tower Records, and Geoff went in and bought her a coat, but then she got into this thing of she couldn't take it, she had savings if she really needed a coat. I mean, first she's all smiles, but there's this thing about New York women: the air hits them outside, and they turn on a dime. Suddenly she can't have the coat, she doesn't want the coat, and all at once she's ballistic about her savings, do we think she's just some loser waitress with no savings, is that what we think? Meanwhile, he's paid for the coat and the two of us don't know what to do to shut her up. Geoff just sort of raises his hand, and a cab stops, and what does he do? He shoves me in and jumps into the cab on top of me, and he says, "Take off! This woman's threatening to shoot us!" and the driver takes off like he's got a stick of dynamite up his ass. That did make it into the strip, by the way. Anyway, we get to his place, and he says to me, "Nice to have known you." *Nice to have known me?* What the fuck! It's one in the morning, we've been collaborating on our strip for some time now, and furthermore, he's confessed that there are two Harrys in his life and he's been working with both of us, which really puts me in a tailspin, then suddenly he's like a kid signing off on his imaginary playmate. He's all formality, there in the cab; he could be Charlton Heston walking away from Michael Moore. The meter's ticking, his hand is extended. I shake it. Nothing else to do. He gets out of the cab with the coat the waitress rejected slung over his shoulder. And back in California, I open my e-mail and what's there, like nothing happened, but more ideas for the strip.

But you know what? I loved him even if he knew this lunatic like Harry Mathews, off in Florida. Geoff apparently sent some e-mail to me that went haywire, early on — you'd have to know Geoff and his capacity for Skyy straight up and Googling at the same time, I guess — and I come to find out this Harry pretended to Geoff to be *me*. I mean, I still might talk to a lawyer. But anyway, what the hey, suddenly they're doing strips too. Apparently this Florida nut's got delusions of grandeur, like anybody can collaborate on comix. But it's spilled Lactaid, right? I'm not gonna cry over it. I still loved the guy. *Il miglior fabbro*, Geoff.

George Jenkins

May I briefly mention that at eight this evening, I will go onstage at the Geffen as Othello.

"Oh, Jenks, has the moment come then to conclude?"
"Geoff, there is no need to conclude. Let small minds conclude."
"Has the moment come, Jenks, when you understand I am at peace?"
"We accept that you are at peace, though we do not aspire, in this life, Geoff, to be protected from chaos. If we have not known chaos, how can we know peace? Just as the bird fashions its nest from twine and twigs and discarded remnants of man's discontents, so we must fashion an image of you — in a heavenly nest that nurtures the newly arrived Geoffrey Chestnut. And if, from time to time, a twig of sorrow may prick our flesh, still we will know you to be safely nestled in an eternal patchwork of security that protects you from the inevitable storms of earthly trials."

Thank you so much, Kathy. Really, it flatters me too greatly that you've risen from your seat. It is most gracious of you. I thank you more than I can say.

Contributors' Notes

*100 Other Distinguished
Stories of 2005*

Editorial Addresses

Contributors' Notes

ANN BEATTIE has written eight novels and eight story collections. In 2005 she won the Rea Award for the Short Story. Her most recent book is *Follies: New Stories*. She is the Edgar Allan Poe Professor of Literature and Creative Writing at the University of Virginia.

• I've burned out on memorial services in which you sit immobilized while people, in the guise of talking about the dearly departed, talk about themselves, so I thought it would be funny to do a send-up of memorial services. Once I had that idea — and I almost never write with any idea in mind at all — the characters clamored to rise out of their chairs to have their moment onstage. Of course, the art world comes in for kidding, too. I picked up one of my husband's books and began reading randomly. Vuillard had so little to do with the world I was writing about that it was perfect; and then I discovered that when he was a child "Mr. Nobody at All" was the nickname of Vuillard's imaginary friend. The title handed itself to me. I was amused — always a bad sign — and showed what I had to my friend Harry Mathews, working up my courage to get him to contribute. The real Harry Mathews (he's used to strange requests; we all know he was CIA) gave me his testimonial, I invented the other Harry Matthews (two *t*'s), and there it was. I asked Harry what else I could do, because my piece would never be complete, and he suggested a second service, in a different place. Yet again, saved by my friend, and by the asterisk. LA was too obvious a venue to resist, so I didn't.

KATHERINE BELL grew up in Cardiff, Wales, and New Jersey. "The Casual Car Pool" was her second story published in *Ploughshares*. She now lives in Somerville, Massachusetts, where she is completing her first novel.

• On a summer evening in the late nineties I was driving across the Bay Bridge when I noticed what looked like a hang glider caught up in the suspension wires. Two or three emergency vehicles were parked below, but traffic was moving normally. I was used to seeing the *MacGyver* crew filming all over the city, but this didn't look like a film set. I searched the Internet but couldn't find any mention of the stuck hang glider. A couple of years later, I moved to Oakland, took a job in San Francisco, and started commuting the other way across the bridge. Sometimes I drove, occasionally I took the bus, but most of the time I rode in the casual car pool. The system fascinated me. It's unofficial but extremely formal, and perhaps that's why it works so well. In more than twenty-five years, according to everyone I've asked, not a single crime has been committed in the car pool. But I always wondered, What if something unexpected happened? Years later, when I began writing a story about sperm donation, another complex social system that upends traditional notions of public and private and depends on happenstance, the casual car pool came immediately to mind.

The last element of the story was a formal challenge I set for myself. I loved the way Virginia Woolf and Katherine Mansfield handled point of view, and I wanted to see if I could manage shifting among several characters' consciousnesses from paragraph to paragraph, or even sentence to sentence, without ever zooming out. I ended up buying myself that freedom by limiting the story in another way — I didn't let my characters off the bridge or even, for most of the story, out of the car.

DAVID BEZMOZGIS is the author of *Natasha and Other Stories*. His work has appeared in various publications including *The New Yorker*, *Harper's Magazine*, *Threepenny Review*, and *The Walrus*. Bezmozgis is a John Simon Guggenheim Fellow. He lives in Toronto.

• In the summer of 2003 I traveled with my parents to Riga, Latvia, the city of my birth. We had left in 1979 and had not been back since. The trip was intended to serve a number of purposes: family vacation, historic homecoming, literary research.

We spent three weeks in the Baltics. For much of that time we lived in a small, modern hotel in the resort town of Jurmala. We shared the hotel with guests much like ourselves: former Soviet Jews, now citizens of Western countries — America, Germany, Israel, Canada. Having attained middle-class prosperity, we were able to return to Jurmala in style, stay at decent hotels and dine at restaurants. This was in stark contrast to most of the locals, including a number of my father's old friends. The gulf between us was striking, and it created a compromising and unpleasant undertone. We saw, reflected in each other, our alternate lives. Contemplating my alternate life, I felt grateful and fortunate but also guilty, trifling, naïve, and envious. I wouldn't have traded places, but I was nonetheless plagued by a feeling I considered both legitimate and trite. Having been spared certain hardships, I believed that I possessed only a partial understanding of the world.

The story was the product of that sensation.

It was also the product of having visited many cemeteries. With no living relatives in Latvia, we went to see the dead. Other tourists did the same. At our hotel I overheard a woman from California discussing the arrangements she had made to replace an old gravestone. I caught only a snippet of the conversation, few details, but the curious and pathetic idea of replacing an old gravestone with a new one seemed somehow to exemplify my experience of Latvia.

ROBERT COOVER is the author of many books, including *Pinocchio in Venice, The Adventures of Lucky Pierre: Directors' Cut,* and, most recently, *A Child Again*. He teaches experimental and electronic writing at Brown University.

• Stories often begin with an image, sometimes a perplexing and haunting one, or maybe a passing notion in a concert or a subway or a café, or a curious phrase that comes to mind just as one's falling asleep or walking in the woods — writers have thousands of these scribbled on the backs of receipts, stuffed in file drawers, clogging up unread computer files, and only occasionally does one float to the surface and begin to acquire the stuff of story. Thus, here, idle thoughts about a wolf who, having swallowed Grandmother, begins to change, adopting Grandmother's ways, and about a child who is aware that this is not her grandmother in the bed, and yet is somehow, in her innocence, at the same time not aware, took a sudden turning one day when the opening two paragraphs occurred to me, more or less whole, and changed the tenor of the piece. It did not then "write itself," nothing ever does, but, even though I didn't know the ending until it ended, it proceeded the way it had to proceed because the voice and central metaphor told me so.

NATHAN ENGLANDER was born in New York, in 1970. He is the author of *For the Relief of Unbearable Urges* and has recently completed his first novel. He finished writing "How We Avenged the Blums" while he was a Fellow at the Dorothy and Lewis B. Cullman Center for Scholars and Writers at the New York Public Library.

• "How We Avenged the Blums" is set in suburban Long Island, but it's an Israeli story for me. I grew up wearing a yarmulke. I was sometimes very aware of it in public, and was sometimes made to be aware of it by others — which is the whole point. While it's on your head you think, I am a Jew and connected to God. When I was living in Jerusalem, I took notice of the modern Israeli religious kids. It was like discovering a new species. They looked the same and dressed the same. They had the yarmulke on. But they carried themselves differently. They seemed to be missing some of the complicated elements of otherness that were central to my experience. I began to think about it on a national, secular level, as it related to larger ideas of Israeli identity and the way certain leaders tried to shape it. What does it mean if you choose to see yourself as weak in the region or strong in the neighborhood? And, back to the story, if the children of Greenheath defined themselves as victims in some way, what would they become when standing over a vanquished enemy?

MARY GAITSKILL is the author of the novels *Two Girls, Fat and Thin* and *Veronica*, as well as the story collections *Bad Behavior* and *Because They Wanted To*, which was nominated for the PEN/Faulkner Award in 1998. Her story "Secretary" was the basis for the feature film of the same name. Her stories and essays have appeared in *The New Yorker, Harper's Magazine, Esquire, The Best American Short Stories 1993,* and *The O. Henry Prize Stories 1998*. In 2002 she was awarded a Guggenheim fellowship for fiction; she is currently an associate professor of English at Syracuse University. Her novel *Veronica* was nominated for the National Book Award in 2005 and the National Book Critic's Circle Award.

- "Today I'm Yours" came to me in an embryonic state when I was listening to a sentimental song in a public place. I was with a friend and, as I listened to the music, feelings in the form of images swarmed across my mind. The song had nothing to do with families, but I thought of my family, of my mother and father when they were young, smiling and embracing. I imagined some shadow of that embracing in every embrace of mine, even the most trivial. The song seemed like some kind of secret passageway I had stumbled into, and through it I found this strange emotional place that eventually led to this story about secret chambers in which the inside is bigger, not smaller, than the outside.

ALEKSANDAR HEMON was born and raised in Sarajevo, where he lived until 1992, when he came to the United States. He is the author of *The Question of Bruno* (2000) and *Nowhere Man* (2002). He writes a biweekly column in Bosnian, cumbersomely called "Hemonwood," for the Sarajevo magazine *Dani*. He lives in Chicago, where he frequently teaches at Northwestern University's School of Continuing Studies. He is a Guggenheim, a MacArthur, and a decent fellow. That's pretty much it.

- In some ways, "The Conductor" is a result of an awkward coupling between Lawrence Weschler and the Chicago Symphony Orchestra. I had read Mr. Weschler's brilliant essay "Vermeer in Bosnia," in which he suggests that in his paintings Vermeer was inventing zones "filled with peace" in the Holland and Europe that were, much like Bosnia in the nineties, "replete with sieges and famines and massacres and mass rapes, unspeakable tortures and wholesale devastation." I started thinking about someone who would produce such zones filled with peace in the midst of Bosnian mayhem. Dedo was then hurried into existence by a vision I would have whenever I saw the conductor at a CSO performance return to the stage to a thundering applause and then pick the musicians to stand up and accept the ovation, until the whole orchestra finally stood up. I would always imagine the conductor ordering the whole orchestra to stand up except for one guy in the back (a tuba, a xylophone, a glockenspiel). "You," the conductor would say with the stick heartlessly pointing at the unfortunate musician, "you sit down."

YIYUN LI grew up in Beijing, China. She came to the United States to study immunology but then gave up this scientific pursuit to become a writer. Her stories and essays have appeared in *The New Yorker*, the *New York Times*, and many other publications. Her collection of stories, *A Thousand Years of Good Prayers*, won the Frank O'Connor International Short Story Award and the PEN/Hemingway Award. She lives in Oakland, California, with her husband and their two sons.

- When I grew up in Beijing, a couple who lived in an apartment close to ours were first cousins, and they had a daughter born with extreme birth defects whom they hid from the world. For many years we had heard this girl's screaming from their apartment, but nobody had ever seen her. The parents had two more children, the second born with some birth defects but the third healthy, a year older than I. It amazed me how some people did not lose hope when, for others, there was little hope left. For the same reason I was moved and saddened by the people in China, especially the older people (my father included) who sincerely hoped they could, by studying and understanding how the stock system worked in China, make money. For me, it is a similar situation where people stay hopeful when there is not much hope to start with (at least for the people who were at the ground floor of the stockbrokerage where they had little access to the world above them). But for the two couples in "After a Life," love existed despite misunderstanding. So does hope, I think, out of misunderstanding, or perhaps understanding, of one's fate.

JACK LIVINGS attended the Iowa Writers' Workshop and was a Wallace Stegner Fellow at Stanford. His work has appeared in *Tin House* and *The Paris Review*. He lives with his wife and daughter in New York, where he is completing a collection of short stories.

- In the mid-1990s I taught conversational English in Beijing. Three nights a week forty students, bleary-eyed from their day jobs, filed into a pea green classroom, where I tortured them with pronunciation drills and canned dialogues. One, a somber woman who had chosen the English name Carrie, used the weekly "free talk" period to relay harrowing reports about her culinary catastrophes. They all ended the same way: billowing smoke, a charred hunk of meat, a hungry family. One night she stood up and said, "As you know, the Beijing municipal government has outlawed dog racing."

In fact, I did not know, nor could I have conceived that anyone's relatives might summon her to slaughter and eat their expensive, now useless, dog. Years passed before I tried to write any of it down. By the time I was finished, I could recall only the first line she spoke and the last, which she delivered clearly and loudly over her classmates' applause: "In this way I believe I have saved a life."

THOMAS MCGUANE was born in Michigan and educated at Michigan State University, the Yale School of Drama, and Stanford, where he was a Stegner Fellow in writing. He has lived in rural Montana since 1968.

• I have lived on a ranch for the past thirty-five years and have had various ranch hands work for me; and the older, committed cowboys always seemed to me to be melancholy characters without much to look forward to. Additionally, I have judged ranch horses for Billings Livestock Sales, a firm that sells seven hundred horses a month, and I've seen old cowboys who have lost their jobs or their health bring their saddle horses in to be sold. Brooding about all this led to my writing "Cowboy."

KEVIN MOFFETT was born and raised in Daytona Beach, Florida. His collection of stories, *Permanent Visitors*, won the Iowa Short Fiction Prize and was published this year. His fiction has received the Nelson Algren Award and has appeared in *McSweeney's*, *Tin House*, *Oxford American*, the *Chicago Tribune*, and elsewhere. He writes a monthly column about zoos and amusement parks for *Funworld Magazine*.

• I started with this scrap, remembered: an artist friend wanted to learn how to give tattoos and, correctly figuring that no one would volunteer to be his sketchpad, began practicing on himself. He was easily distracted, and most of the tattoos were half-finished. He tattooed the word JAM on his thigh; he explained that he'd planned to tattoo the phrase JAM ON IT, but after repeating it to himself a few dozen times thought it started to sound silly. Dixon's story unfurled cartoonishly at first. And then, while he was sitting in the art store, looking for something to want, Andrea showed up, instantly familiar. She hijacked the story, and its prospects brightened.

Contributors' Notes

ALICE MUNRO was born in Wingham, Ontario, on July 10, 1931, and was educated in the Wingham public schools and the University of Western Ontario. In 1951 she married James Munro, then lived in Vancouver and Victoria for twenty years. She bore three daughters, divorced, married Gerry Fremlin, and has lived for the past thirty years in Clinton, Ontario, twenty miles from where she grew up. She has, she says, "been writing hopefully since I was around eighteen years old." "The View from Castle Rock" is the title story in her new collection, published in the fall of 2006.

- "The View from Castle Rock" is part invention, part historical reality. Members of my family, bearing the names of the characters in the story, did sail from the port of Leith to Quebec City, taking six weeks for the journey, in the summer of 1818. One of them, Walter, did keep a journal of the voyage, which I have quoted throughout. The characters have been formed partly from other information available to me — particularly in the case of Old James — and partly out of my own imagination. I've confessed to this in the presence of the dead at the end of the story. I do wish I knew what happened to my favorite character — Young James — but I don't.

EDITH PEARLMAN has published more than 250 works of short fiction and short nonfiction in national magazines, literary journals, anthologies, and online publications. Her work has been chosen for selection in *The Best American Short Stories, The O. Henry Prize Stories, Best Short Stories from the South*, and the Pushcart Prize collection. Her essays and travel writing have appeared in the *Atlantic Monthly, Smithsonian, Preservation, Yankee*, the *New York Times*, the *Boston Globe*, and Salon.com. She is the author of three collections of stories: *Vaquita* (1997), *Love Among the Greats* (2002), and *How to Fall* (2005).

- Every so often I speak to high school English classes. I enjoy their eager and predictable queries: Where do you get your ideas? Wouldn't you like to make a movie? But one morning a mischievous-looking boy popped an unexpected question: "If you were allowed to write only one more story, what would it be about?" "Death," I answered without thinking. I wasn't even sure the voice was mine.

So I had been assigned a subject, not for my final story (I trusted) but for my next one. All I needed was a protagonist, a situation, a setting, and a resolution. Damn that boy! I got to work. The austere Cornelia Fitch had been wandering around in my mind for a while; I became better acquainted with her. I stole the setting from a place I love. Aunt Shelley strutted into one of the drafts and made herself at home. Cornelia's final transformative journey is my own hopeful invention.

I frequently wonder what's become of that classroom imp.

BENJAMIN PERCY is the author of the short story collection *The Language of Elk*. His fiction has appeared in *The Paris Review*, the *Chicago Tribune*, *Amazing Stories*, *Swink*, the *Greensboro Review*, and many other publications. He was raised in the high desert of central Oregon and now lives with his wife, Lisa, in Milwaukee, Wisconsin, where he teaches writing at Marquette University.

• When I'm working on a novel, I need a break every three weeks or so. "Refresh, Refresh" came out of one of those breaks. During this time I was reading article after article, but never any short stories, about the war in Iraq. So I decided to write one. Like all of my work, it boiled out of me quickly, in a week of eight-hour days hunched over the keyboard. There are many facts underlying the fiction, over which I sprinkled a healthy serving of imagination. The setting is the setting of my youth. Hole in the Ground actually exists. My friends and I actually used to beat the shit out of one another and tear around on dirt bikes. As for the military base, the reservists who all at once shipped off and left behind their families, this comes from an article I read about a small town in Ohio. I cannot recall the particulars, but in one night something like fifteen fathers and husbands and sons died in an ambush. Their loss, the bleeding cavity that appeared overnight and undoubtedly still hasn't scarred over, informs this story. The original draft spanned nearly forty pages. The first published version clocks in at nineteen. For this, Philip Gourevitch and Nathaniel Rich at *The Paris Review* have earned my eternal gratitude, as they helped guide the scalpel that tore through the excess flesh and found the heart of this story.

PATRICK RYAN'S stories have appeared in *The Iowa Review*, *The Yale Review*, *Denver Quarterly*, and *One Story*, among other journals. His first book, *Send Me*, was published in early 2006. He is the recipient of a 2006 Literary Fellowship from the National Endowment for the Arts, as well as the 2004 Smart Family Foundation Prize for Fiction. A graduate of the M.F.A. Writing Program at Bowling Green State University in Ohio, Ryan was born in Washington, D.C., and lives in New York City.

• "So Much for Artemis" began as an idea for two separate stories: one about a boy who has a friend with the aging disease progeria, and another about that same boy watching his father lose both his job and, temporarily, his mental stability. When I realized that the boy, Frankie, would be the same age in both stories, I began to think about merging the two ideas. From that point on, one story line seemed to help the other along. The biggest challenge came with trying to figure out an ending that would merge the two worlds (Jennifer's and Roy's). For some reason, I didn't want them to confront each other in the penultimate scene. I went through several drafts that had flat, murky endings. Finally — and thankfully — Hannah Tinti at *One Story* convinced me that the confrontation was worth exploring. That led to my going back to the middle of the story and adding the short scene in which Jennifer and her mother pull up alongside Frankie's house and observe what his father has done to the lawn — providing Jennifer with the ammunition she later uses against Roy, in the backyard.

While the events in the story are fictitious, the character of Jennifer is based on a girl I knew when I was a child. She was a very brave little kid — and very smart. She was constantly correcting me, even though we were both five years old. I was crazy about her. Years later, when I first started toying with the idea of creating a character based on her, anything I put down felt nostalgic. I like nostalgia in measure, but it didn't feel right for this character — and certainly not right for a character interacting with her. Because of that, while it went through many different drafts, "Artemis" always had a third-person narrator, which to my mind helped the events feel somewhat immediate — as opposed to feeling as if they existed in Frankie's memory.

MARK SLOUKA is the author of the novel *God's Fool* (2002); a collection of stories, *Lost Lake* (1998); and *War of the Worlds* (1995), a humanist critique of the digital revolution. His novel *The Visible World* and a collection of essays are both forthcoming in early 2007. His fiction and essays have appeared in *Harper's Magazine, Story, Epoch, Agni, The Georgia Review,* and *The Best American Essays 1999, 2000,* and *2004.* A recipient of National Endowment for the Arts and Guggenheim fellowships, as well as a contributing editor at *Harper's,* he is currently a professor of English and the chairman of the Creative Writing Program at the University of Chicago.

• If a story is something large seen through a small window, a shard that suggests not only the pot but the potter's thoughts on the morning he made it, then the coyotes in "Dominion" are the small thing, the shard; the big thing is death. The story grew from an autobiographical seed: My family and I have a cabin on a pond. There are coyotes there. I find the remains of their kills in the woods; once, bizarrely, they nosed their way into my writing shack and left blood and rabbit hair all over my papers. Sometimes at night they go off in the pasture just above us. The sound is primal, gorgeous, terrifying. That sound is the window; beyond it is the territory of my private obsessions — with time, with death — the place where the actual story begins.

MAXINE SWANN'S short story "Flower Children" won the Cohen Award and was included in *The Best American Short Stories, The O. Henry Prize Stories,* and the Pushcart collection. Her novel *Serious Girls* was published in 2003. "Secret" will appear in her novel in stories, *Flower Children*, scheduled for publication in March 2007. She has lived in Paris and Pakistan and currently lives in Buenos Aires.

• I wrote "Secret" when I was staying in a little pink house near the Uruguayan seaside, also inhabited by nonlethal scorpions. The idea was to write about how the eruption of a new person in your world can change everything — the light, the air, not only the thoughts you have but the way you think, the very laws of your universe. In this case, the "bad boys," however unintentionally, change the sisters' entire world. The figures of the two sisters, heads tilted, conscientious, at once brave and shy, came to me vividly from reading the poet Louise Glück's book *The Seven Ages*. Also very much in my mind was the thrilling and perilous nature of adolescence, when everything for a moment is held in the balance, fates not yet sealed, and, consequently, the staggering blow of adolescent suicide. From the beginning, when I began writing, I saw that pink light — a mixture of the seaside light I was seeing, the fantasy light of the girls' new world, the last light of childhood, and, further even, the lingering light of the hippie era coming to a close.

DONNA TARTT's first novel, *The Secret History*, has been translated into more than twenty languages; her second novel, *The Little Friend*, was also a worldwide bestseller and the winner of the WHSmith Literary Award in Britain.

• "The Ambush" turned out to be quite different from the story I'd set out to write. For years, I'd had in my mind the image of a dying Vietnam soldier whose death lives on, in backyard ritual, as sort of a neighborhood passion play among children. Originally I wanted to tell the story from the point of view of the dying soldier who, lying in the rice paddy, undergoes some strange transcendental realization of how his death will be falsely glorified, as a ritual event for his son to endure again and again in backyard games — Ambrose Bierce's "Incident at Owl Creek Bridge" was strongly in my mind, and also the Chekhov story "The Bishop." But when I sat down to write the story, I found myself drawn wholly to the children's point of view — which makes sense, I suppose, since after all the children are the custodians and preservers of the story.

TOBIAS WOLFF's books include the memoirs *This Boy's Life* and *In Pharaoh's Army: Memories of the Lost War;* the short novel *The Barracks Thief;* three collections of short stories, *In the Garden of the North American Martyrs, Back in the World,* and *The Night in Question;* and, most recently, the novel *Old School.* He has also edited several anthologies, among them *The Best*

Contributors' Notes

American Short Stories 1994, A Doctor's Visit: The Short Stories of Anton Chekhov, and *The Vintage Book of Contemporary American Short Stories.* His work is translated widely and has received numerous awards, including the PEN/Faulkner Award, the Los Angeles Times Book Prize, both the PEN/Malamud and the Rea awards for Excellence in the Short Story, and the Academy Award in Literature from the American Academy of Arts and Letters. He is the Ward W. and Priscilla B. Woods Professor of English at Stanford.

• "Awaiting Orders" is simply my attempt to tell a human story. "Issues" — gay marriage, abortion, evolution, capital punishment, gays in the military — have the effect of making us imagine demons on one side and angels on the other. This is a crude and degrading habit of mind, and stories are one cure for it. They have been for me, anyway.

In writing this story I found myself remembering the loneliness of life in the army, the feeling of a hot summer night, of pulling solitary duty in an orderly room and dying for someone, anyone, to talk to; of sexual longing, and the longing for love, and how those hungers can frustrate each other. This much was drawn from memory. The rest came from my attempts to imagine the life of another man.

PAUL YOON was born in New York City and attended Phillips Exeter Academy and Wesleyan University. He currently lives in Boston. His work has appeared in *One Story, Small Spiral Notebook, Clackamas Literary Review, Redivider, Chelsea,* and *Post Road.* "Once the Shore" was his first published story.

• In the 1970s, my father, a physician, was doing his residency at a hospital in New York City. He would shower after work and visit my mother. This was before they were married. And when my mother opened the door every evening, the first thing she noticed was his wet hair. She found this amusing. I found it romantic. This image, or scene, was how the story started. Sometime later, I remembered the tragedy involving the *Ehime Maru,* a Japanese fishing boat that was struck by an American submarine, the USS *Greeneville,* as it surfaced. Again, it was the image of this collision that stayed with me. Once I had these two moments fixed in my mind, the story became a matter of finding some sort of bridge to connect them. Although "Once the Shore" takes place in South Korea, it is in memory of everyone who was on the *Ehime Maru.* I am grateful to my family, Laura van den Berg, Ethan Rutherford, Hannah Tinti, and *One Story* for their faith and support.

100 Other Distinguished Stories of 2005

Selected by Katrina Kenison

ABU-JABER, DIANA
  Clean Room. *The Southern Review*, Vol. 41, No. 4.
ADAMS, MICHELE
  Infinite Speed. *The Fiddlehead*, No. 223.
ADONZIO, KIM
  Ever After. *Fairy Tale Review*, Blue volume.
ADRIAN, CHRIS
  The Stepfather. *McSweeney's*, No. 18.
AKPAN, UWEM
  An Ex-Mas Feast. *The New Yorker*, June 13 and 20.
ALI, MOHAMMED NASEEHU
  Malla Sile. *The New Yorker*, April 11.
ALLISON, DOROTHY
  Seven Times Seven. *Tin House*, No. 25.
ALMOND, STEVE
  Nobody Here but Us Chickens. *Tin House*, No. 25.
ALTSCHUL, ANDREW FOSTER
  The Rules. *One Story*, No. 62.
ARVIN, NICK
  Along the Highways. *The New Yorker*, May 8.

BARTHELME, DONALD
  The School. *Gulf Coast*, Vol. 17, No. 2.
BAXTER, CHARLES
  Poor Devil. *The Atlantic Monthly*, June.
BEATTIE, ANN
  Coping Stones. *The New Yorker*, September 12.
BENEDICT, PINKNEY
  Mudman. *Tin House*, Vol. 6, No. 3.
BERRY, WENDELL
  Mike. *The Sewanee Review*, Vol. CXIII, No. 1.
BEZMOZGIS, DAVID
  The Russian River. *The New Yorker*, May 30.
BRAVERMAN, KATE
  Cocktail Hour. *The Mississippi Review*, Vol. 37, Nos. 1 and 2.
BRINKMAN, KIARA
  Counting Underwater. *McSweeney's*, No. 15.
BUDNITZ, JUDY
  Nadia. *One Story*, No. 50.

Other Distinguished Stories of 2005

BUSCH, FREDERICK
 The Bottom of the Glass.
 Ploughshares, Vol. 31, Nos. 2 and 3.
BYNUM, SARAH SHUN-LIEN
 The Voyage Over. *The Literary Review*. Vol. 48, No. 3.

CANTY, KEVIN
 They Were Expendable. *Tin House*, Vol. 6, No. 3.
CARLSON, RON
 In the Old Firehouse. *Ploughshares*, Vol. 31, No. 3.
CHAPMAN, MAILE
 Compulsion Vigil. *The Literary Review*, Vol. 48, No. 3.
CLARK, BROCK
 The Ghosts We Love. *The Virginia Quarterly Review*, Vol. 81, No. 3.
COAKE, CHRISTOPHER
 Solos. *Five Points*, Vol. 9, No. 1.
COOVER, ROBERT
 Sir John Paper Returns to Honah-Lee. *Conjunctions*, No. 44.
CURTIS, REBECCA
 The Sno-Cone Cart. *McSweeney's*, No. 18.
 Summer, with Twins. *Harper's Magazine*, June.

D'AMBROSIO, CHARLES
 Blessing. *Zoetrope*, Vol. 9, No. 4.
 Up North. *The New Yorker*, February 14 and 21.
DALTON, QUINN
 The Music You Never Hear. *One Story*, No. 61.
DANTICAT, EDWIDGE
 Reading Lessons. *The New Yorker*, February 14 and 21.
DAUGHERTY, JANICE
 Going to Jackson. *The Ontario Review*, No. 63.
DAVIS, JENNIFER S.
 The Way We Were Meant to Grow. *Epoch*, Vol. 54, No. 1.

DELANEY, EDWARD J.
 Medicine. *The Alaska Quarterly Review*, Vol. 22, Nos. 1 and 2.
DE PONTES PEEBLES, FRANCES
 The Disappearance of Luísa Porto. *Zoetrope*, Vol. 9, No. 4.
DERMONT, AMBER
 Stella and the Winter Palace. *Tin House*, Vol. 6, No. 4.
DESAULNIERS, JANET
 We Were with Pehoe. *Other Voices*, Vol. 18, No. 43.
DORMAN, LESLIE
 Curvy. *Ploughshares*, Vol. 31, Nos. 2 and 3.
D'SOUZA, TONY
 Club des Amis. *The New Yorker*, September 5.
DURROW, HEIDI W.
 Light-skinned Girl. *The Alaska Quarterly Review*, Vol. 22, Nos. 1 and 2.
DYMOND, JUSTINE
 Cherubs. *The Massachusetts Review*, Vol. XLVI, No. 3.

EARLEY, TONY
 Yard Art. *Tin House*, Vol. 6, No. 4.
ENRIGHT, ANN
 Della. *The New Yorker*, March 14.
EUGENIDES, JEFFREY
 Early Music. *The New Yorker*, October 10.

GALGUT, DAVID
 Chicken. *Zoetrope*, Vol. 9, No. 2.
GATES, DAVID
 A Secret Station. *The New Yorker*, March 28.
GAY, WILLIAM
 The Wreck on the Highway. *Chattahoochee Review*, Vol. XXV, No. 3.
GOODMAN, ALLEGRA
 Long-Distance Client. *The New Yorker*, July 11 and 18.

GORDON, PETER
Celia. *Ploughshares*, Vol. 31,
Nos. 2 and 3.
GREHAN, ELLEN
The Tinker's Bairn. *The Ontario Review*, No. 63.

HAGY, ALYSON
Border. *Ploughshares*, Vol. 31, No. 1.
HEATHCOCK, ALAN
Peacekeeper. *The Virginia Quarterly Review*, Vol. 81, No. 4.
HEMON, ALEKSANDAR
Love and Obstacles. *The New Yorker*, November 28.
HOFFMAN, ALICE
Saint Helene. *Ploughshares*, Vol. 31, No. 4.

KING, LILY
Five Tuesdays in Winter. *Ploughshares*, Vol. 31, Nos. 2 and 3.
KRASIKOV, SANA
Companion. *The New Yorker*, October 3.

LAPCHAROENSAP, RATTAWUT
Sightseeing. *Glimmer Train*, No. 55.
LASDUN, JAMES
An Anxious Man. *The Paris Review*, No. 173.
LENNON, J. ROBERT
The Girl Who Disappeared. *Epoch*, Vol. 54, No. 2.
LI, YIYUN
The Proprietress. *Zoetrope*, Vol. 9, No. 3.

MATTISON, ALICE
Election Day. *The Michigan Quarterly Review*, Vol. XLIV, No. 3.
In the Dark, Who Pats the Air. *Shenandoah*, Vol. 55, No. 1.
Pastries at the Bus Stop. *Ms.*, Spring
MCFADYEN, ANNIE
Bleeders. *Tin House*, No. 25.
MCGUANE, THOMAS
Ice. *The New Yorker*, January 24 and 31.

MCMILLAN, JON
Born on Fire. *Five Points*, Vol. 9, No. 2.
MEANS, DAVID
Reading Chekhov. *Zoetrope*, Vol. 9, No. 3.
MILLER, ARTHUR
Beavers. *Harper's Magazine*, February.
MONTEMARANO, NICHOLAS
Poster Child. *The Agni Review*, No. 62.
MOORE, LORRIE
The Juniper Tree. *The New Yorker*, January 17.
MUNRO, ALICE
Wenlock Edge. *The New Yorker*, December 5.
MURPHY, YANNICK
In a Bear's Eye. *McSweeney's*, No. 18.

NEVAI, LUCIA
Emile. *Glimmer Train*, No. 56.
NICHOLSON, GEOFF
Some Language, Some Nudity. *Black Clock*, No. 3.
NOVAKOVICH, JOSEPH
A Purple Story. *Boulevard*, No. 61.

OATES, JOYCE CAROL
Smother. *The Virginia Quarterly Review*, Vol. 81, No. 4.
OTIS, MARY
Unstruck. *Tin House*, Vol. 6, No. 4.

PEARLMAN, EDITH
On Junius Bridge. *The Agni Review*, No. 61.

RAFFEL, DAWN
Our Heaven. *The Mississippi Review*, Vol. 33, Nos. 1 and 2.
REIFLER, NELLY
The Railway Nurse. *McSweeney's*, No. 18.

Other Distinguished Stories of 2005

ROBINSON, ROXANA
  A Perfect Stranger. *One Story,* No. 55.
ROCK, PETER
  The Sharpest Knife. *The Cincinnati Review,* Vol. 2, No. 1.
ROSENBAUM, BENJAMIN
  Orphans. *McSweeney's,* No. 15.
RYAN, CONALL
  Hostivar. *News from the Republic of Letters,* Nos. 14 and 15.

SCHUMAN, DAVID
  Stay. *The Missouri Review,* Vol. 28, No. 2.
SHEPARD, JIM
  Trample the Dead, Hurdle the Weak. *Harper's Magazine,* September.
SHIELDS, CAROL
  Segue. *The Virginia Quarterly Review.* Vol. 81, No. 1.
SILVER, MARISSA
  The God of War. *The New Yorker,* November 7.
SINGLETON, GEORGE
  Lickers. *The Kenyon Review,* Vol. XXVII, No. 3.
SMYTH, JESSAMYN
  A More Perfect Union. *American Letters and Commentary,* No. 17.

SWANN, MAXINE
  I May Look Dumb. *Open City,* No. 20.

TAIT, JOHN
  I Will Soon Be Married. *The Sun,* September.
TAYLOR, KATHERINE
  The Heiress from Horn Lake. *Ploughshares,* Vol. 31, No. 4.
THEROUX, PAUL
  The Best Year of My Life. *The New Yorker,* November 14.
TUCK, LILY
  Lucky. *The Kenyon Review,* Vol. XXVII, No. 4.
TUSSING, JUSTIN
  The Laser Age. *The New Yorker,* June 13 and 20.

UPDIKE, JOHN
  The Roads of Home. *The New Yorker,* February 7.

WALLACE, DANIEL
  One Small Man. *One Story,* No. 49.

Editorial Addresses of American and Canadian Magazines Publishing Short Stories

African American Review
St. Louis University
Humanities 317
3800 Lindell Boulevard
St. Louis, MO 63108-2007
$40, Joycelyn Moody

Agni Magazine
Boston University Writing Program
Boston University
236 Bay State Road
Boston, MA 02115
$17, Sven Birkerts

Alabama Literary Review
272 Smith Hall
Troy State University
Troy, AL 36082
$10, Donald Noble

Alaska Quarterly Review
University of Alaska, Anchorage
3211 Providence Drive
Anchorage, AK 99508
$10, Ronald Spatz

Alfred Hitchcock Mystery Magazine
1540 Broadway
New York, NY 10036
$34.97, Cathleen Jordan

Alligator Juniper
Prescott College
220 Grove Avenue
Prescott, AZ 86301
$7.50, Miles Waggener

American Letters and Commentary
850 Park Avenue, Suite 5B
New York, NY 10021
$8, Anna Rabinowitz

American Literary Review
University of North Texas
P.O. Box 311307
Denton, TX 76203-1307
$10, John Tait

Another Chicago Magazine
Left Field Press
3709 North Kenmore
Chicago, IL 60613
$8, Sharon Solwitz

Antioch Review
Antioch University
150 East South College Street
Yellow Springs, OH 45387
$35, Robert S. Fogerty

Apalachee Review
P.O. Box 10469
Tallahassee, FL 32302
$15, group

Addresses of American and Canadian Magazines

Argosy
P.O. Box 1421
Taylor, AZ 85939
coppervale@skyboot.com
$49.95, Lou Anders, James Owen

Arkansas Review
Department of English and Philosophy
P.O. Box 1890
Arkansas State University
State University, AR 72467
$20, Tom Williams

Ascent
English Department
Concordia College
901 Eighth Street
Moorhead, MN 56562
$12, W. Scott Olsen

Asimov's Science Fiction
475 Park Avenue South
11th Floor
New York, NY 10016
$43.90, Sheila Williams

At Length
submissions@atlength.com
$20, Jonathan Farmer

Atlantic Monthly
The Watergate
600 NH Avenue NW
Washington, DC 20037
$14.95, C. Michael Curtis

Backwards City Review
P.O. Box 41317
Greensboro, NC 27404
$10, Gerry Canavan

Baltimore Review
P.O. Box 36418
Towson, MD 21286
$15, Barbara Westwood Diehl

Bamboo Ridge
P.O. Box 6176
Honolulu, HI 96839-1781
$35, Eric Chock, Darrell H.Y. Lum

Bayou
Department of English
University of New Orleans
2000 Lakeshore Drive
New Orleans, LA 70148
$10, Joanna Leake

Bellevue Literary Review
Department of Medicine
New York University School of Medicine
550 First Avenue
New York, NY 10016
$12, Danielle Ofri

Bellingham Review
MS-9053
Western Washington University
Bellingham, WA 98225
$14, Brenda Miller

Bellowing Ark
P.O. Box 55564
Shoreline, WA 98155
$18, Robert Ward

Berkshire Review
P.O. Box 105
Richmond, MA 01254-0023
$8.95, Vivian Dorsel

The Best of Carve
P.O. Box 1573
Tallahassee, FL 32302
$15, Melvin Sterne

Black Warrior Review
P.O. Box 862936
Tuscaloosa, AL 35486-0027
$14, Laura Hendrix

Blackbird
Department of English
Virginia Commonwealth University
P.O. Box 843082
Richmond, VA 23284-3082
Anna Journey

Blood and Thunder
University of Oklahoma
Health Sciences Center
941 Stanton L. Young Boulevard

BSEB Room 100
Oklahoma City, OK 73190
$8, Stacie Herndon Elfrink

Blue Mesa Review
Department of English
University of New Mexico
Albuquerque, NM 87131
Julie Shigekuni

Bomb
New Art Publications
594 Broadway, 10th Floor
New York, NY 10012
$18, Betsy Sussler

Boston Review
Building E53-407 MIT
Cambridge, MA 02139
$17, Joshua Cohen, Deborah Chasman

Boulevard
PMB 325
6614 Clayton Road
Richmond Heights, MO 63117
$15, Richard Burgin

Brain, Child: The Magazine for Thinking Mothers
P.O. Box 714
Lexington, VA 24450-0714
$18, Jennifer Niesslein, Stephanie Wilkinson

Briar Cliff Review
3303 Rebecca Street
P.O. Box 2100
Sioux City, IA 51104-2100
$10, Tricia Currans-Sheehan

Bridges
P.O. Box 24839
Eugene, OR 97402
$15, Clare Kinberg

Callaloo
Department of English
Texas A&M University
4227 TAMU
College Station, TX 77843-4227
$40, Charles H. Rowell

Calyx
P.O. Box B
Corvallis, OR 97339
$19.50, Margarita Donnelly and collective

Capilano Review
Capilano College
2055 Purcell Way
North Vancouver
British Columbia V7J 3H5
$25, Sharon Thesen

Carolina Quarterly
Greenlaw Hall CB 3520
University of North Carolina
Chapel Hill, NC 27599-3520
$12, Amy Weldon

Chariton Review
Truman State University
Kirksville, MO 63501
$9, Jim Barnes

Chattahoochee Review
Georgia Perimeter College
2101 Womack Road
Dunwoody, GA 30338-4497
$16, Lawrence Hetrick

Chelsea
P.O. Box 773
Cooper Station
New York, NY 10276
$13, Alfredo de Palchi

Chicago Quarterly Review
517 Sherman Avenue
Evanston, IL 60202
$10, S. Afzal Haider, Jane Lawrence, Lisa McKenzie

Chicago Review
5801 South Kenwood
University of Chicago
Chicago, IL 60637
$18, Erik Steinhoff

Cimarron Review
205 Morrill Hall
Oklahoma State University
Stillwater, OK 74078-0135
$24, E. P. Walkiewicz

Addresses of American and Canadian Magazines

Cincinnati Review
Department of English
McMicken Hall, Room 369
P.O. Box 210069
Cincinnati, OH 45221
$12, *Brock Clarke*

Colorado Review
Department of English
Colorado State University
Fort Collins, CO 80523
$24, *Stephanie G'Schwind*

Columbia
2960 Broadway
415 Dodge Hall
Columbia University
New York, NY 10027-6902
$15, *S. K. Beringer*

Concho River Review
English Department
Angelo State University
San Angelo, TX 76909
$12, *Terence A. Dalrymple*

Confrontation
English Department
C. W. Post College of Long Island University
Greenvale, NY 11548
$10, *Martin Tucker*

Conjunctions
21 East 10th Street, Suite 3E
New York, NY 10003
$18, *Bradford Morrow*

Connecticut Review
English Department
Southern Connecticut State University
501 Crescent Street
New Haven, CT 06515
John Briggs

Crab Creek Review
P.O. Box 840
Vashon Island, WA 98070
$10, *editorial group*

Crab Orchard Review
Department of English
Southern Illinois University at Carbondale
Carbondale, IL 62901
$15, *Carolyn Alessio*

Crazyhorse
Department of English
College of Charleston
66 George Street
Charleston, SC 29424
$15, *Carol Ann Davis*

Crucible
Barton College
P.O. Box 5000
Wilson, NC 27893-7000
Terrence L. Grimes

CutBank
Department of English
University of Montana
Missoula, MT 59812
$12, *Elizabeth Conway*

Daedalus
136 Irving Street, Suite 100
Cambridge, MA 02138
$33, *James Miller*

Denver Quarterly
University of Denver
Denver, CO 80208
$20, *Bin Ramke*

Descant
P.O. Box 314
Station P
Toronto, Ontario M5S 2S8
$25, *Karen Mulhallen*

Descant
TCU
Box 297270
Fort Worth, TX 76129
$12, *Lynn Risser, David Kuhne*

Ecotone
Department of Creative Writing
University of North Carolina, Wilmington
601 South College Road

Wilmington, NC 28403
$18, David Gessner

Edgar Literary Magazine
P.O. Box 5776
San Leon, TX 77539
Sue Mayfield-Geiger

Epoch
251 Goldwin Smith Hall
Cornell University
Ithaca, NY 14853-3201
$11, Michael Koch

Esopus
532 LaGuardia Place, Suite 486
New York, NY 10012
$18, Tod Lippy

Esquire
250 West 55th Street
New York, NY 10019
$17.94, Adrienne Miller

Eureka Literary Magazine
Eureka College
300 East College Avenue
Eureka, IL 61530-1500
$15, Loren Logsdon

Event
Douglas College
P.O. Box 2503
New Westminster
British Columbia V3L 5B2
$22, Cathy Stonehouse

Fairy Tale Review
University of Alabama
English Department
Box 780224
Tuscaloosa, AL 35487
$12, Kate Bernheimer

Fantasy and Science Fiction
P.O. Box 3447
Hoboken, NJ 07030
$44.89, Gordon Van Gelder

Fiction International
Department of English and
Comparative Literature
San Diego State University
San Diego, CA 92182
$12, Harold Jaffe

Fiddlehead
UNB P.O. Box 4400
Fredericton
New Brunswick E3B 5A3
$20, Mark Anthony Jarman

Five Points
Georgia State University
Department of English
University Plaza
Atlanta, GA 30303-3083
$20, David Bottoms

Florida Review
Box 161346
University of Central Florida
Orlando, FL 32816-1346
$15, Jeanne Leiby

Flyway
206 Ross Hall
Department of English
Iowa State University
Ames, IA 50011
$18, Stephen Pett

Focus
Box 323
Spelman College
350 Spelman Lane
Atlanta, GA 30314
Ariele Elise LeGrand

Folio
Department of Literature
The American University
Washington, DC 20016
$12, Amina Hafiz

Frostproof Review
P.O. Box 3397
Lake Wales, FL 33859
$15, Kyle Minor

Fugue
Department of English

Brink Hall 200
University of Idaho
Moscow, ID 83844-1102
$14, Ben George, Jeff P. Jones

Furnace
Historic Bohemian House
3009 Tillman
Detroit, MI 48216
$20, Kelli B. Kavanaugh

Gargoyle
P.O. Box 6216
Arlington, VA 22206-0216
$20, Richard Peabody, Lucinda Ebersole

Georgia Review
University of Georgia
Athens, GA 30602
$24, T. R. Hummer

Gettysburg Review
Gettysburg College
Gettysburg, PA 17325-1491
$24, Peter Stitt

Gingko Tree Review
Drury University
900 North Benton Avenue
Springfield, MO 65802
$10, Randall Fuller

Glimmer Train Stories
1211 NW Glisan Street, Suite 207
Portland, OR 97209
$36, Susan Burmeister-Brown, Linda Swanson-Davies

Gobshite Quarterly
P.O. Box 11346
Portland, OR 97205
$16, R. V. Branham

Grain
Box 1154
Regina, Saskatchewan S4P 3B4
$26.95, Kent Bruyneel

Granta
1755 Broadway, 5th Floor
New York, NY 10019-3780
$39.95, Ian Jack

Green Mountains Review
Box A58
Johnson State College
Johnson, VT 05656
$15, Jack Pulaski

Greensboro Review
134 McIver Building
P.O. Box 26170
University of North Carolina
Greensboro, NC 27412
$10, Jim Clark

Gulf Coast
Department of English
University of Houston
4800 Calhoun Road
Houston, TX 77204-3012
$14, Mark Doty

Gulf Stream
English Department
Florida International University
Biscayne Bay Campus
3000 NE 151st Street
North Miami, FL 33181
$15, John Dufresne, Cindy Chinelly

Hanging Loose
231 Wyckoff Street
Brooklyn, NY 11217
$17.50, group

Harper's Magazine
666 Broadway
New York, NY 10012
$16, Lewis Lapham

Harpur Palate
Department of English
Binghamton University
P.O. Box 6000
Binghamton, NY 13902
$16, Letitia Moffitt, Doris Umbers

Harvard Review
Poetry Room
Harvard College Library

Cambridge, MA 02138
$16, Christina Thompson

Hawaii Review
Department of English
University of Hawaii
1733 Donaghho Road
Honolulu, HI 96822
$20, Jonathan Padua

Hayden's Ferry Review
Box 871502
Arizona State University
Tempe, AZ 85287-1502
$14, Christopher Becker, Eric Day

Hotel Amerika
Department of English
360 Ellis Hall
Ohio University
Athens, OH 45701
$18, David Lazar

Hudson Review
684 Park Avenue
New York, NY 10021
$24, Paula Deitz

Idaho Review
Boise State University
1910 University Drive
Boise, ID 83725
$9.95, Mitch Wieland

Image
Center for Religious Humanism
3307 Third Avenue West
Seattle, WA 98119
$36, Gregory Wolfe

Indiana Review
Ballantine Hall 465
1020 East Kirkwood Avenue
Bloomington, IN 47405-7103
$14, Esther Lee

Indy Men's Magazine
8500 Keystone Crossing, Suite 100
Indianapolis, IN 46240
Lou Harry

InkPot
Lit Pot Press, Inc.
3909 Reche Road, Suite 132
Fallbrook, CA 92028
$30, Beverly Jackson, Carol Peters

Inkwell
Manhattanville College
2900 Purchase Street
Purchase, NY 10577
$15, Diana Spindler

Iowa Review
Department of English
University of Iowa
308 EPB
Iowa City, IA 52242
$20, David Hamilton

Iris
University of Virginia Women's Center
P.O. Box 800588
Charlottesville, VA 22908
$9, Gina Welch

Iron Horse Literary Review
Department of English
Texas Tech University
Box 43091
Lubbock, TX 79409-3091
$12, Leslie Jill Patterson

Italian Americana
University of Rhode Island
Providence Campus
80 Washington Street
Providence, RI 02903
$20, Carol Bonomo Albright

Jabberwock Review
Department of English
Drawer E
Mississippi State University
Mississippi State, MS 39762
$12, Joy Murphy

Jewish Currents
22 East 17th Street
New York, NY 10003
$20, editorial board

Addresses of American and Canadian Magazines

The Journal
Department of English
Ohio State University
164 West Seventeenth Avenue
Columbus, OH 43210
$12, Kathy Fagan, Michelle Herman

Kalliope
Florida Community College
3939 Roosevelt Boulevard
Jacksonville, FL 32205
$12.50, Mary Sue Koeppel

Kenyon Review
Kenyon College
Gambier, OH 43022
$30, David H. Lynn

Lady Churchill's Rosebud Wristlet
Small Beer Press
176 Prospect Avenue
Northampton, MA 01060
$20, Kelly Link

Lake Effect
Penn State Erie
5091 Station Road
Erie, PA 16563-1501
$6, George Looney

Land-Grant College Review
P.O. Box 1164
New York, NY 10159
$18, Tara Wray

The Literary Review
Fairleigh Dickinson University
285 Madison Avenue
Madison, NJ 07940
$18, Rene Steinke

Louisiana Literature
LSU 10792
Southeastern Louisiana University
Hammond, LA 70402
$12, Jack B. Bedell

Louisville Review
Spalding University
851 South Fourth Street
Louisville, KY 40203
$14, Sena Jeter Naslund

Lynx Eye
ScribbleFest Literary Group
542 Mitchell Drive
Los Osos, CA 93402
$25, Pam McCully, Kathryn Morrison

Madison Review
University of Wisconsin
Department of English
H. C. White Hall
600 North Park Street
Madison, WI 53706
$12, Andrea Kurz, Sonya Larson

Manoa
English Department
University of Hawaii
Honolulu, HI 96822
$22, Frank Stewart

Massachusetts Review
South College
Box 37140
University of Massachusetts
Amherst, MA 01003
$22, David Lenson, Ellen Dore Watson

Matrix
1455 de Maisonneuve Boulevard West
Suite LB-514-8
Montreal, Quebec H3G IM8
$21, R.E.N. Allen

McSweeney's
826 Valencia Street
San Francisco, CA 94110
$36, Dave Eggers

Meridian
Department of English
P.O. Box 400145
University of Virginia
Charlottesville, VA 22904-4145
$10, Caitlin Johnson

Michigan Quarterly Review
3032 Rackham Building
915 East Washington Street

University of Michigan
Ann Arbor, MI 48109
$25, Laurence Goldstein

Mid-American Review
Department of English
Bowling Green State University
Bowling Green, OH 43403
$12, Michael Czyzniejewski

Midnight Mind
P.O. Box 146912
Chicago, IL 60614
$12, Brett Van Emst

Minnesota Review
Department of English
Carnegie Mellon University
Pittsburgh, PA 15213
$30, Jeffrey Williams

Mississippi Review
University of Southern Mississippi
Southern Station, Box 5144
Hattiesburg, MS 39406-5144
$15, Frederick Barthelme

Missouri Review
1507 Hillcrest Hall
University of Missouri
Columbia, MO 65211
$22, Speer Morgan

Ms.
433 South Beverly Drive
Beverly Hills, CA 90212
$45, Amy Bloom

n + 1
Park West Finance Station
P.O. Box 20688
New York, NY 10025
$16, Allison Lorentzen

Natural Bridge
Department of English
University of Missouri, St. Louis
8001 Natural Bridge Road
St. Louis, MO 63121-4499
$15, Jason Rizos

Nebraska Review
Writers Workshop
WFAB 212
University of Nebraska at Omaha
Omaha, NE 68182-0324
$15, James Reed

New England Review
Middlebury College
Middlebury, VT 05753
$25, Stephen Donadio

New Letters
University of Missouri
5100 Rockhill Road
Kansas City, MO 64110
$22, Robert Stewart

New Orleans Review
P.O. Box 195
Loyola University
New Orleans, LA 70118
$12, Christopher Chambers

New Orphic Review
706 Mill Street
Nelson, British Columbia V1L 4S5
$25, Ernest Hekkanen

New Quarterly
English Language Proficiency
Programme
Saint Jerome's University
200 University Avenue West
Waterloo, Ontario N2L 3G3
$36, Kim Jernigan

New Renaissance
26 Heath Road, Suite 11
Arlington, MA 02474
$13.50, Louise T. Reynolds

New York Stories
English Department
LaGuardia Community College
31-10 Thomson Avenue
Long Island City, NY 11101
$13.40, Daniel Caplice Lynch

The New Yorker
4 Times Square

Addresses of American and Canadian Magazines

New York, NY 10036
$46, Deborah Treisman

NFG
Sheppard Centre
P.O. Box 43112
Toronto, Ontario M2N 6N1
$20, Shar O'Brien

Night Train
85 Orchard Street
Somerville, MA 02144
$17.95, Rod Siino, Rusty Barnes

Nimrod International Journal
Arts and Humanities Council of Tulsa
600 South College Avenue
Tulsa, OK 74104
$17.50, Francine Ringold

Ninth Letter
Department of English
University of Illinois
608 South Wright Street
Urbana, IL 61801
$19.95, Jodee Rubins

Noon
1369 Madison Avenue
PMB 298
New York, NY 10128
$9, Diane Williams

North American Review
University of Northern Iowa
1222 West 27th Street
Cedar Falls, IA 50614
$22, Grant Tracey

North Carolina Literary Review
Department of English
2201 Bate Building
East Carolina University
Greenville, NC 27858-4353
$20, Margaret Bauer

North Dakota Quarterly
University of North Dakota
P.O. Box 8237
Grand Forks, ND 58202
$25, Robert Lewis

Northwest Review
369 PLC
University of Oregon
Eugene, OR 97403
$22, John Witte

Notre Dame Review
Department of English
356 O'Shag
University of Notre Dame
Notre Dame, IN 46556-5639
$15, John Matthias, William O'Rourke

Oasis
P.O. Box 626
Largo, FL 34649-0626
$20, Neal Storrs

Oklahoma Today
15 North Robinson, Suite 100
P.O. Box 53384
Oklahoma City, OK 73102
$16.95, Louisa McCune

One Story
425 Third Street, No. 2
Brooklyn, NY 11215
$21, Maribeth Batcha, Hannah Tinti

Ontario Review
9 Honey Brook Drive
Princeton, NJ 08540
$16, Raymond J. Smith

Open City
225 Lafayette Street, Suite 1114
New York, NY 10012
$32, Thomas Beller, Joanna Yas

Orchid
3096 Williamsburg
P.O. Box 131457
Ann Arbor, MI 48113-1457
$16, Keith Hood, Amy Sumerton

Other Voices
University of Illinois at Chicago
Department of English, M/C 162
601 South Morgan Street
Chicago, IL 60607-7120
$24, Gina Frangello

Oxalis
Stone Ridge Poetry Society
P.O. Box 3993
Kingston, NY 12401
$18, Shirley Powell

Oxford American
201 Donaghey Avenue, Main 107
Conway, AR 72035
$29.95, Marc Smirnoff

Oyster Boy Review
P.O. Box 77842
San Francisco, CA 94107
$20, Damon Sauve

Pangolin Papers
Turtle Press
P.O. Box 241
Norland, WA 98358
$20, Pat Britt

Paper Street
Paper Street Press
P.O. Box 14786
Pittsburgh, PA 15234
Dory Adams

Paris Review
62 White Street
New York, NY 10013
$34, Philip Gourevitch

Parting Gifts
3413 Wilshire Drive
Greensboro, NC 27408-2923
Robert Bixby

Passages North
English Department
Northern Michigan University
1401 Presque Isle Avenue
Marquette, MI 49007-5363
$10, Katie Hanson

Pearl
3030 East Second Street
Long Beach, CA 90803
$18, group

Penny Dreadful
P.O. Box 719
Radio City Station
New York, NY 10101-0719
$12

Phantasmagoria
English Department
Century Community and Technical College
3300 Century Avenue North
White Bear Lake, MN 55110
$15, Abigail Allen

Phoebe
George Mason University
MSN 2D6
4400 University Drive
Fairfax, VA 22030-4444
$12, Lisa Ampleman

Pindeldyboz
25–53 36th Street, 2nd Floor
Astoria, NY 11103
$12, Jeff Boison

Pleiades
Department of English and Philosophy
Central Missouri State University
P.O. Box 800
Warrensburg, MO 64093
$12, Susan Steinberg

Ploughshares
Emerson College
120 Boylston Street
Boston, MA 02116
$22, Don Lee

Poem Memoir Story
Department of English
University of Alabama at Birmingham
217 Humanities Building
900 South 13th Street
Birmingham, AL 35294-1260
$7, Linda Frost

Porcupine
P.O. Box 259

Cedarburg, WI 53012
$15.95, editorial group

Post Road
P.O. Box 400951
Cambridge, MA 02420
$18, Mary Cotton

Potomac Review
Montgomery College
51 Mannakee Street
Rockville, MD 20850
$20, Eli Flam

Prairie Fire
423-100 Arthur Street
Winnipeg, Manitoba R3B 1H3
$25, Andris Taskans

Prairie Schooner
201 Andrews Hall
University of Nebraska
Lincoln, NE 68588-0334
$26, Hilda Raz

Primavera
P.O. Box 37-7547
Chicago, IL 60637
Editorial group

Prism International
Department of Creative Writing
University of British Columbia
Buchanan E-462
Vancouver, British Columbia V6T 1W5
$22, Catharine Chen

Provincetown Arts
650 Commercial Street
Provincetown, MA 02657
$10, Christopher Busa

Puerto del Sol
MSCC 3E
New Mexico State University
P.O. Box 30001
Las Cruces, NM 88003
$10, Kevin McIlvoy

Quarterly West
2055 South Central Campus Drive

Department of English/LNCO 3500
University of Utah
Salt Lake City, Utah 84112
$14, David Hawkins, Nicole Walker

Red Rock Review
English Department, J2A
Community College of Southern Nevada
3200 East Cheyenne Avenue
North Las Vegas, NV 89030
$9.50, Richard Logsdon

Red Wheelbarrow
De Anza College
21250 Stevens Creek Boulevard
Cupertino, CA 95014-5702
$5, Randolph Splitter

Republic of Letters
120 Cushing Avenue
Boston, MA 02125-2033
$35, Keith Botsford

River City
Department of English
University of Memphis
Memphis, TN 38152
$12, Kristen Iverson

River Oak Review
River Oak Arts
P.O. Box 3127
Oak Park, IL 60303
$12, Mary Lee MacDonald

River Styx
Big River Association
634 North Grand Boulevard,
12th Floor
St. Louis, MO 63103-1002
$20, Richard Newman

Room of One's Own
P.O. Box 46160
Station D
Vancouver, British Columbia V6J 5G5
$25, Patricia Robitaille

Rosebud
P.O. Box 459

Cambridge, WI 53523
$18, Roderick Clark

Sacred Fire
10720 NW Lost Park Drive
Portland, OR 97229
$27.80, Jonathan Merritt

Salmagundi
Skidmore College
Saratoga Springs, NY 12866
$20, Robert Boyers

Salon.com
41 East 11th Street, 11th Floor
New York, NY 10003
Joan Walsh

Salt Hill
English Department
Syracuse University
Syracuse, NY 13244
$15, Ellen Litman

Santa Monica Review
1900 Pico Boulevard
Santa Monica, CA 90405
$12, Andrew Tonkovich

Sewanee Review
University of the South
Sewanee, TN 37375-4009
$24, George Core

Shenandoah
Mattingly House
2 Lee Avenue
Washington and Lee University
Lexington, VA 24450-0303
$22, R. T. Smith, Lynn Leech

Slow Trains Literary Journal
Samba Mountain Press
P.O. Box 4741
Englewood, CO 80155
$14.95, Susannah Indigo

Small Spiral Notebook
172 Fifth Avenue, Suite 104
Brooklyn, NY 11217
$12, Felicia Sullivan

So to Speak: A Feminist Journal of Language
4400 University Drive
George Mason University
Fairfax, VA 22030
$12, Nancy Pearson

Songs of Innocence
Pendragon Publications
P.O. Box 719
Radio City Station
New York, NY 10101-0719
$12, Michael M. Pendragon

Sonora Review
Department of English
University of Arizona
Tucson, AZ 85721
$12, Kristi Maxwell, Carol Test

South Dakota Review
University of South Dakota
P.O. Box 111 University Exchange
Vermilion, SD 57069
$15, Brian Bedard

Southeast Review
Department of English
Florida State University
Tallahassee, FL 32306
$10, Tony R. Morris

Southern Exposure
P.O. Box 531
Durham, NC 27702
$24, Chris Kromm

Southern Humanities Review
9088 Haley Center
Auburn University
Auburn, AL 36849
$15, Dan R. Latimer, Virginia M. Kouidis

Southern Review
43 Allen Hall
Louisiana State University
Baton Rouge, LA 70803
$25, Brett Lott

Addresses of American and Canadian Magazines

Southwest Review
Southern Methodist University
P.O. Box 4374
Dallas, TX 75275
$24, Willard Spiegelman

Spire
532 LaGuardia Place, Suite 298
New York, NY 10012
$18

StoryQuarterly
431 Sheridan Road
Kenilworth, IL 60043-1220
$12, M.M.M. Hayes

StorySouth
898 Chelsea Avenue
Bexley, OH 43209
Jason Sanford

Sun
107 North Roberson Street
Chapel Hill, NC 27516
$34, Sy Safransky

Swink
244 Fifth Avenue, No. 2722
New York, NY 10001
$16, Leelila Strogov

Sycamore Review
Department of English
500 Oval Drive
Purdue University
West Lafayette, IN 47907
$12, Sean M. Conrey

Talking River Review
Division of Literature and Languages
Lewis-Clark State College
500 Eighth Avenue
Lewiston, ID 83501
$14, editorial board

Tampa Review
University of Tampa
401 West Kennedy Boulevard
Tampa, FL 33606-1490
$15, Richard Mathews

Third Coast
Department of English
Western Michigan University
Kalamazoo, MI 49008-5092
$11, Glenn Deutsch

Threepenny Review
P.O. Box 9131
Berkeley, CA 94709
$16, Wendy Lesser

Timber Creek Review
8969 UNCG Station
Greensboro, NC 27413
$15, John Freiermuth

Tin House
P.O. Box 10500
Portland, OR 97296-0500
$39.80, Rob Spillman

Transition
69 Dunster Street
Harvard University
Cambridge, MA 02138
$28, Kwame Anthony Appiah, Henry Louis Gates, Jr., Michael Vazquez

TriQuarterly
629 Noyes Street
Evanston, IL 60208
$24, Susan Firestone Hahn

Vanderbilt Review
Vanderbilt University
Station B
Box 357016
Nashville, TN 37235-7016
$10, rotating

Virginia Quarterly Review
One West Range
P.O. Box 400223
Charlottesville, VA 22903
$18, Ted Genoways

War, Literature, and the Arts
Department of English and Fine Arts
2354 Fairchild Drive, Suite 6D45
USAF Academy, CO 80840-6242
$10, Donald Anderson

Wascana Review
English Department
University of Regina
Regina, Saskatchewan S4S 0A2
$10, Marcel DeCoste

Washington Square
Creative Writing Program
New York University
19 University Place, 2nd Floor
New York, NY 10003-4556
$6, James Pritchard

Watchword
P.O. Box 5755
Berkeley, CA 94705
Kasia Newman, Liz Lisle

Weber Studies
Weber State University
1214 University Circle
Ogden, UT 84408-1214
$20, Brad Roghaar

West Branch
Bucknell Hall
Bucknell University
Lewisburg, PA 17837
$10, Paula Clossen Buck

Western Humanities Review
University of Utah
255 South Central Campus Drive
Room 3500
Salt Lake City, UT 84112
$16, Barry Weller

Willow Springs
Eastern Washington University
705 West First Avenue
Spokane, WA 99201
$13, Samuel Ligon

Windsor Review
Department of English
University of Windsor
Windsor, Ontario N9B 3P4
$29.95, Alistair MacLeod

Writers' Forum
University of Colorado
P.O. Box 7150
Colorado Springs, CO 80933-7150
$8.95, Alexander Blackburn

Yale Review
P.O. Box 208243
New Haven, CT 06520-8243
$27, J. D. McClatchy

Zoetrope
The Sentinel Building
916 Kearney Street
San Francisco, CA 94133
$19.95, Michael Ray

Zyzzyva
P.O. Box 590069
San Francisco, CA 94109
$28, Howard Junker